Samuel Pepys, Richard Griffin Braybrooke

Diary and correspondence of Samuel Pepys from his MS. cypher in the Pepsyian Library, with a life and notes by Richard Lord Braybrooke

Vol.3

Samuel Pepys, Richard Griffin Braybrooke

Diary and correspondence of Samuel Pepys from his MS. cypher in the Pepsyian Library, with a life and notes by Richard Lord Braybrooke
Vol.3

ISBN/EAN: 9783337018474

Printed in Europe, USA, Canada, Australia, Japan

Cover: Foto ©Raphael Reischuk / pixelio.de

More available books at **www.hansebooks.com**

DIARY AND CORRESPONDENCE OF

SAMUEL PEPYS, ESQ., F.R.S.

Mens cujusque is est

DIARY

AND

CORRESPONDENCE

OF

SAMUEL PEPYS, ESQ., F.R.S.

FROM HIS MS. CYPHER IN THE PEPYSIAN LIBRARY,

WITH A LIFE AND NOTES BY

RICHARD LORD BRAYBROOKE.

DECIPHERED, WITH ADDITIONAL NOTES, BY

REV. MYNORS BRIGHT, M.A.,

PRESIDENT AND SENIOR FELLOW OF MAGDALENE COLLEGE, CAMBRIDGE.

VOL. III.

OCTOBER 15, 1662—OCTOBER 31, 1663.

NEW-YORK:

DODD, MEAD & COMPANY.

1885.

DIARY OF SAMUEL PEPYS.

OCT. 15TH, 1662.   Waked very early; and, when it was time, did call up Will, and we rose, and musique (with a bandore [1] for the base) did give me a levett; [2] and so we got ready; and while breakfast was providing, I went forth and showed Mr. Cooke King's College Chapel, Trinity College, and St. John's College Library; and that being done, to our inne again: where I met Dr. Fairbrother.   He told us how the room we were in was the room where Cromwell and his associated officers did begin to plot and act their mischiefs in these counties.   Took leave of all, and begun our journey about nine o'clock, and came to Ware about three o'clock in the afternoon, the ways being every where but bad; but finding our horses

---

[1] *Bandore.* A musical instrument, very similar in form to a guitar, but whether strung with wires or with catgut, like the lute, we are not told. (M. B.)

[2] *Levett.* "A blast on the trumpet, probably that by which soldiers are called in the morning." — JOHNSON. From "lever," French.

> "First he that led the Cavalcade
> Wore a Sow-gelder's Flagellet,
> On which he blew as strong a *Levet*
> As well-feed Lawyer on his breviate."
>
> *Hudibras,* II. ii. v. 609. (M. B.)

in good case, we even made shift to reach London, though both of us very weary. Found all things well, there happening nothing since our going to my discontent in the least degree; which do so please me, that I cannot but bless God for my journey, observing a whole course of successe from the beginning to the end of it.

16th. I rose in good temper, finding a good chimney-piece made in my upper dining-room chamber, and the dining-room wainscoate in a good forwardness. Then to the office. We sat till noon. This afternoon to the Treasury office, where Sir John Minnes and I did stay late paying some money to the men that are saved out of the Satisfaction that was lost the other day. The King gives them half-pay, which is more than is used in such cases, for they never used to have any thing, and yet the men were most outrageously discontented, and did rail and curse us till I was troubled to hear it, and wished myself unconcerned therein. Here late, and so home, and at the office set down my journey-journall to this houre, and so shut up my book, giving God thanks for my good successe therein, and so home, and to supper, and to bed. I hear Mr. Moore is in a way of recovery. Sir H. Bennet [1] made Secretary of State in Sir Edward Nicholas's stead; not known whether by consent or not.

---

[1] Created Baron of Arlington 1663, and Viscount Thetford and Earl of Arlington, 1672: he was also K.G., and Chamberlain to the King. Ob. 1685. His daughter and sole heir married the first Duke of Grafton.

17th. This morning Tom comes to me, and I advise him how to deale with his mistress's mother about his giving her a joynture, but I intend to speak with her shortly, and tell her my mind. Then to my Lord Sandwich by water, and told him how well things do go in the country with me, of which he was very glad, and seems to concern himself much for me. To Creed's chamber, and there sat a good while and drank chocolate. Here I am told how things go at Court; that the young men get uppermost, and the old serious lords are out of favour; that Sir H. Bennet, being brought into Sir Edward Nicholas's place, Sir Charles Barkeley[1] is made Privy Purse; a most vicious person, and one whom Mr. Pierce, the surgeon, did tell me that he offered his wife 300*l.* per annum to be his mistress. He also told me that none in Court hath more the King's eare now than Sir Charles Barkeley, and Sir H. Bennet, and my Lady Castlemaine, whose interest is now as great as ever: and that Mrs. Haslerigge, the great beauty, is now brought to bed, and lays it to the King or the Duke of York.[2] He tells me also that my Lord St. Albans is like to be Lord Treasurer: all which things do trouble me much.

19th (Lord's day). Put on my first new lace-band;

---

[1] Created Lord Berkeley of Rathdown, and Viscount Fitzharding (Irish honours) soon afterwards, and, in 1664, Baron Bottetourt, and Earl of Falmouth, in England. He was the second son of Sir Charles Berkeley, of Bruton.

[2] The child was owned by neither of the royal brothers.

and so neat it is, that I am resolved my great expence shall be lace-bands, and it will set off any thing else the more.   So walked to my brother's, where I met Mr. Cooke, and discoursing with him do find that he and Tom have promised a joynture of 50*l.* to his mistress, and say that I did give my consent that she should be joyntured in 30*l.* per ann. for Sturtlow, and the rest to be made up out of her portion.   At which I was stark mad, and very angry the business should be carried with so much folly and against my mind and all reason.   I took leave, and to see Mr. Moore, who recovers well; and his doctor coming to him, one Dr. Merrit,[1] we had some of his very good discourse of anatomy, and other things, very pleasant. I am sorry to hear that the newes of the selling of Dunkirke is taken so generally ill, as I find it is among the merchants; and other things, as removal of officers at Court, good for worse; and all things else made much worse in their report among people than they are.   And this night, I know not upon what ground, the gates of the City ordered to be kept shut, and double guards every where.   Indeed I do find every body's spirit very full of trouble; and the things of the Court and Council very ill taken; so as to be apt to appear in bad colours, if there should ever be a beginning of trouble, which God forbid !

20th.   In Sir J. Minnes's coach with him and Sir W. Batten to White Hall, where now the Duke is

---

[1] Christopher Merret, M.D., a native of Gloucestershire, author of several works on medicine and natural history. Ob. 1695.

come again to lodge : and to Mr. Coventry's little new chamber there. And by and by up to the Duke, who was making himself ready; and there young Killigrew did so commend "The Villaine," [1] a new play made by Tom Porter, and acted only on Saturday at the Duke's house, as if there never had been any such play come upon the stage. The same yesterday was told me by Captain Ferrers; and this morning afterwards by Dr. Clerke, who saw it. After I had done with the Duke, with Commissioner Pett to Mr. Lilly's, the great painter, who came forth to us; but believing that I came to bespeak a picture, he prevented us by telling us, that he should not be at leisure these three weeks; which methinks is a rare thing. And then to see in what pomp his table was laid for himself to go to dinner; and here, among other pictures, saw the so much desired by me picture of my Lady Castlemaine, which is a most blessed picture; and one that I must have a copy of. From thence I took my wife by coach to the Duke's house, and there was the house full of company : but whether it was in over-expecting or what, I know not, but I was never less pleased with a play in my life. Though there was good singing and dancing, yet no fancy in the play, but something that made it less contenting

---

[1] A Tragedy, by T. Porter. "The Villain, a tragedy which I have seen acted at the Duke's Theatre with great applause: the part of Malignii being incomparably played by Mr. Sandford."—*Langbaine*, p. 407. "This person [Sandford] acted strongly with his face; and, as King Charles said, was the best villain in the world."—*Tony Aston*, p. 11.

was my conscience that I ought not to have gone by my vowe, and, besides, my business commanded me elsewhere. But, however, as soon as I came home I did pay my crowne to the poor's box, according to my vowe, and so no harme as to that is done, but only business lost and money lost, and my old habit of pleasure wakened, which I will keep down the more hereafter, for I thank God these pleasures are not sweet to me now in the very enjoying of them. So by coach home, and after a little business at my office, and seeing Sir W. Pen, who continues ill, I went to bed. Dunkirke, I am confirmed, is absolutely sold ; for which I am very sorry.

21st. To the office, and there all the morning, and in the middle of our sitting my workmen setting about the putting up of my rails upon my leades, Sir J. Minnes did spy them and fell a-swearing, which I took no notice of, but was vexed, and am still to the very heart for it, for fear it should put him upon taking the closett and my chamber from me. But it is my very great folly to be so much troubled at these trifles, more than at the loss of 100*l.*, or things of greater concernment ; but I forget the lesson I use to preach to others of $\tau\grave{\alpha}\ \grave{\epsilon}\phi'\ \grave{\eta}\mu\hat{\iota}\nu\ \kappa\alpha\grave{\iota}\ \tau\grave{\alpha}\ o\grave{\upsilon}\kappa\ \grave{\epsilon}\phi'\ \grave{\eta}\mu\hat{\iota}\nu$. Thence by water with Mr. Smith, to Mr. Lechmore,[1] the Councellor at the Temple, about Field's business ; and he tells me plainly that there being a verdict against me, there is no help for it, but it must proceed

---

[1] Nicholas Lechmere, knighted and made a Baron of the Exchequer, 1689. Ob. 1701.

to judgement. It is 30*l.* damage to me for my joining with others in committing Field to prison, we being not Justices of the Peace in the City, though in Middlesex; this troubled me, but I hope the King will make it good to us. Thence to Mr. Smith, the scrivener, upon Ludgate Hill, to whom Mrs. Butler do committ her business concerning her daughter and my brother. He tells me her daughter's portion is but 400*l.*, at which I am more troubled than before; and they find fault that his house is too little.

22nd. To my Lord Sandwich's, who receives me now more and more kindly, now he sees that I am respected in the world; and is my most noble patron. To Mr. Smith's, and there by appointment met Mrs. Butler, with whom I plainly discoursed and she with me. I find she will give but 400*l.*, and no more, and is not willing to do that without a joynture, which she expects and I will not grant for that portion, and upon the whole I find that Cooke has made great brags on both sides, and so has abused us both. But however we did break off the business wholly, but with great love and kindness between her and me, and would have been glad we had known one another's minds sooner, without being misguided by this fellow to both our shames and trouble. For I find her a very discreet, sober woman, and her daughter, I understand and believe, is a good lady; and if portions did agree, though she finds fault with Tom's house, and his bad imperfection in his speech, I believe we should well agree in other matters.

Home, being first trimmed by Benier, who being acquainted with all the players, do tell me that Betterton is not married to Ianthe, as they say; but also that he is a very sober, serious man, and studious and humble, following of his studies, and is rich already with what he gets and saves. This night was buried, as I hear by the bells at Barking Church, my poor Morena,[1] whose sicknesse being desperate, did kill her poor father; and he being dead for sorrow, she could not recover, nor desire to live, but from that time do languish more and more, and so is now dead and buried.

24th. Dined with my wife upon a most excellent dish of tripes of my own directing, covered with mustard, as I have heretofore seen them done at my Lord Crew's, of which I made a very great meal, and sent for a glass of wine for myself, and so to see Sir W. Pen, who continues bed-rid in great pain, and hence to the Treasury to Sir J. Minnes paying off of tickets, and at night home. This noon came to see me and

---

[1] The only burial recorded in the parish Register of All Hallows, Barking, as having taken place on the 22nd October, 1662, is that of Elizabeth, daughter of John Dickens: and the circumstance of her father's interment being entered in the same book, just a week before, leaves no question that she was the person alluded to. The word being doubtful in the MS., Morena is here substituted for Morma, which has no intelligible signification, at the suggestion of Mr. J. S. Warden; see "Notes and Queries," vol. vii. p. 118. Morena, he tells us, is good Portuguese for a Brunette; and it was probably adopted by Pepys to indicate that Miss Dickens had a dark complexion. It is further possible that the same expression was applied to Catherine of Braganza, who, as is well known, was a beauty of a similar description, and the courtiers might naturally wish to pay Her Majesty a compliment in the language of her own country. See note, 27th Jan., 1661-62.

sat with me Mr. Pierce, the chyrurgeon, who tells me how ill things go at Court: that the King do show no countenance to any that belong to the Queene; nor, above all, to such English as she brought over with her, or hath here since, for fear they should tell her how he carries himself to Mrs. Palmer; insomuch that though he has a promise, and is sure of being made her chyrurgeon, he is at a loss what to do in it, whether to take it or no, since the King's mind is so altered and favour to all her dependents, whom she is fain to let go back into Portugall (though she brought them from their friends against their wills with promise of preferment), without doing any thing for them. That her owne physician did tell him within these three days that the Queene do know how the King orders things, and how he carries himself to my Lady Castlemaine and others, as well as any body; but though she hath spirit enough, yet seeing that she do no good by taking notice of it, for the present she forbears it in policy; of which I am very glad. But I pray God keep us in peace; for this, with other things, do give great discontent to all people.

25th. Up and to the office, and there with Mr. Coventry sat all the morning, only we two, the rest being absent or sick. Dined at home with my wife upon a good dish of neats' feet and mustard, of which I made a good meal.

26th (Lord's day). Put on my new Scallop, which is very fine. To church, and there saw the first time

Mr. Mills in a surplice; but it seemed absurd for him to pull it over his eares in the reading-pew, after he had done, before all the church, to go up to the pulpitt, to preach without it.   Home and dined, and Mr. Sympson, my joyner that do my dining-room, and my brother Tom with me to a delicate fat pig. Tom takes his disappointment of his mistress to heart; but all will be well again in a little time.   Then to church again, and heard a simple Scot preach most tediously. Then to my uncle Wight's to show my fine band and to see Mrs. Margaret Wight, but she was not there. All this day soldiers going up and down the towne, there being an alarme, and many Quakers and others clapped up; but I believe without any reason: only they say in Dorsetshire there hath been some rising discovered. So after supper home, and then to my study, and making up my monthly account to myself. I find myself, by my expense in bands and clothes this month, abated a little of my last, and that I am worth 679*l.* still; for which God be praised. So home and to bed with quiett mind, blessed be God, but afeard of my candle's going out, which makes me write thus slubberingly.

27th. Up and by water to wait upon the Duke, and walking in the matted Gallery, by and by comes Mr. Coventry and Sir John Minnes, and then to the Duke, and after he was ready, to his closet, where I did give him my usual account of matters.   Thence to my Lord Sandwich, who now-a-days calls me into his chamber, and alone did discourse with me about the jealousy that the Court have of people's rising; wherein he do much dislike my Lord Monk's being so eager against a company of poor wretches, dragging them up and down the streete; but would have him rather to take some of the greatest ringleaders of them, and punish them; whereas this do but tell the world the King's fears and doubts. For Dunkirke, he wonders any wise people should be so troubled thereat, and scorns all their talk against it, for that he says it was not Dunkirke, but the other places, that did and would annoy us, though we had that, as much as if we had it not. He also took notice of the new Ministers of State, Sir H. Bennet and Sir Charles Barkeley, their bringing in, and the high game that my Lady Castlemaine plays at Court (which I took occasion to mention as that the people do take notice of), all which he confessed. Afterwards he told me of poor Mr. Spong, that being with other people examined before the King and Council (they being laid up as suspected persons; and it seems Spong is so far thought guilty as that they intend to pitch upon him to put to the wracke or some other torture), he do take knowledge of my Lord Sandwich, and said that he was well known to Mr. Pepys. But my Lord knows, and I told him, that it was only in matter of musique and pipes, but that I thought him to be a very innocent fellow; and indeed I am very sorry for him. After my Lord and I had done in private, we went out, and with Captain Cuttance and Bunn did look over their draught of a bridge for Tangier, which will be brought by my desire to our office by them to-morrow. Thence to Westminster Hall, and there walked long with Mr. Creed, and then to the great half-a-crowne ordinary, at the King's Head, near Charing Crosse, where we had a most excellent neat dinner and very high company, and in a noble manner. After dinner he and I into another room over a pot of ale and talked. He showed me our commission, wherein the Duke of York, Prince Rupert, Duke of Albemarle, Lord Peterborough, Lord Sandwich, Sir G. Carteret, Sir William Compton, Mr. Coventry, Sir R. Ford, Sir William Rider, Mr. Cholmley, Mr. Povy, myself, and Captain Cuttance, in this order are joyned for the carrying on the service of Tangier, which I take for a great honour to me. He told me what great faction there is at Court; and above all, what is whispered, that young Crofts is lawful son to the King, the King being married to his mother.[1] How true this is, God knows; but I believe the Duke of York will not be fooled in this of three crowns. Thence to White Hall, and walked long in the galleries till (as they are commanded to all strange persons), one came to tell us, we not being known, and being observed to walk there four or five houres (which was not true, unless they count my walking there in the morning), he was commanded to ask who we were; which being told, he excused his question, and was satisfied. These things speake great

---

fear and jealousys. So to the Exchange; among other things, observing one very pretty Exchange lass, with her face full of black patches, which was a strange sight. At Sir W. Batten's I met with Mr. Mills, who tells me that he could get nothing out of the mayde hard by (that did poyson herself) before she died, but that she did it because she did not like herself, nor anything she did a great while. It seems she was well-favoured enough, but crooked, and this was all she could be got to say, which is very strange.

29th (Lord Mayor's day).[1] Intended to have made me fine, and by invitacion to have dined with the Lord Mayor to-day, but going to see Sir W. Batten this morning, I found Sir G. Carteret and Sir J. Minnes going with Sir W. Batten and myself to examine Sir G. Carteret's accounts for the last year, whereupon I settled to it with them all the day long. I received a letter this day from my father, speaking more trouble about my uncle Thomas his business, and of proceeding to lay claim to Brampton and all my uncle left, because it is given conditional that we should pay legacys, which to him we have not yet done, but I hope that will do us no hurt; God help us if it should, but it disquiets my mind. I have also a letter from my Lord Sandwich desiring me upon matters of concernment to be with him early to-morrow morning. Sir G. Carteret, who had been at the examining most of the late people that are clapped up, do say that he do

---

[1] Sir John Robinson, Lieutenant of the Tower, Mayor.

not think that there hath been any great plotting among them, though they have a good will to it; but their condition is so poor, and silly, and low, that they do not fear them at all.

30th. To my Lord Sandwich, who was up in his chamber and all alone, and did acquaint me with his business; which was, that our old acquaintance Mr. Wade (in Axe Yard) hath discovered to him 7,000*l.* hid in the Tower, of which he was to have two for discovery; my Lord himself two, and the King the other three, when it was found; and that the King's warrant runs for me on my Lord's part, and one Mr. Lee for Sir Harry Bennet, to demand leave of the Lieutenant of the Tower for to make search. After he had told me the whole business, I took leave; and at noon, comes Mr. Wade with my Lord's letter. So we consulted for me to go first to Sir H. Bennet, who is now with many of the Privy Counsellors at the Tower, examining of their late prisoners, to advise with him when to begin. So I went; and the guard at the Tower gate, making me leave my sword at the gate, I was forced to stay so long in the ale-house hard by, till my boy run home for my cloake, that my Lord Mayor that now is, Sir John Robinson, Lieutenant of the Tower, with all his company, was gone with their coaches to his house in Minchen Lane. So my cloake being come, I walked thither; and there, by Sir G. Carteret's means, did presently speak with Sir H. Bennet, who did give me the King's warrant, for the paying of 2,000*l.* to my Lord, and other two to the discoverers. After a little discourse, dinner came in; and I dined with them. There was my Lord Mayor, my Lord Lauderdale, Mr. Secretary Morris, to whom Sir H. Bennet would give the upper hand; Sir Wm. Compton, Sir G. Carteret, and myself, and some other company, and a brave dinner. After dinner, Sir H. Bennet did call aside the Lord Mayor and me, and did break the business to him, who did not, nor durst appear the least averse to it, but did promise all assistance forthwith to set upon it. So Mr. Lee and I to our office, and there walked till Mr. Wade and one Evett his guide did come, and W. Griffin, and a porter with his picke-axes, &c.; and so they walked along with us to the Tower, and Sir H. Bennet and my Lord Mayor did give us full power to fall to work. So our guide demands a candle, and down into the cellars he goes, inquiring whether they were the same that Baxter [1] alway had. We went into several little cellars, and then went out a-doors to view, and to the Cole Harbour; [2] but none did answer so well to the marks which was given him to find it by, as one arched vault. Where, after a great deal of council whether to set upon it now, or delay for better and more full advice, to digging we went till almost eight o'clock at night, but could find nothing. But, however, our guides did not at all seem discouraged; for that they

---

[1] For Barkestead, one of the regicides. For his committal to the Tower see 17th March, 1661–62. (M. B.)

[2] The meaning of this word, though applied to a great many localities, has never been satisfactorily explained.

being confident that the money is there they look for, but having never been in the cellars, they could not be positive to the place, and therefore will inform themselves more fully now they have been there, of the party that do advise them. So locking the door after us, we left work to-night, and up to the Deputy Governor (my Lord Mayor, and Sir H. Bennet, with the rest of the company being gone an houre before) ; and he do undertake to keep the key of the cellars, that none shall go down without his privity. But, Lord ! to see what a young simple fantastique coxcombe is made Deputy Governor, would make one mad ; and how he called out for his night-gowne of silk, only to make a show to us ; and yet for half an houre I did not think he was the Deputy Governor, and so spoke not to him about the business, but waited for another man ; at last I broke our business to him ; and he promising his care, we parted. And Mr. Lee and I by coach to White Hall, where I did give my Lord Sandwich an account of our proceedings, and some encouragement to hope for something hereafter. This morning, walking with Mr. Coventry in the garden, he did tell me how Sir G. Carteret had carried the business of the Victuallers' money to be paid by himself, contrary to old practice ; at which he is angry I perceive, but I believe means no hurt, but that things may be done as they ought. He expects Sir George should bespatter him privately, in revenge, not openly. Against which he prepares to bedaube him, and swears he will do it from the beginning, from Jersey to this day. And as to his own taking of too large fees or rewards for places that he had sold, he will prove that he was directed to it by Sir George himself among others. And yet he did not deny Sir G. Carteret his due, in saying that he is a man that do take the most pains, and gives himself the most to do business of any man about the Court, without any desire of pleasure or divertisements ; which is very true. But which pleased me mightily, he said in these words, that he was resolved, whatever it cost him, to make an experiment, and see whether it was possible for a man to keep himself up in Court by dealing plainly and walking uprightly. In the doing whereof, if his ground do slip from under him, he will be contented ; but he is resolved to try, and never to baulke taking notice of any thing that is to the King's prejudice, let it fall where it will ; which is a most brave resolucion. He was very free with me ; and by my troth, I do see more reall worth in him than in most men that I do know. I would not forget two passages of Sir J. Minnes's at yesterday's dinner. The one, that to the question how it comes to pass that there are no boars seen in London, but many sowes and pigs ; it was answered, that the constable gets them a-nights. The other, Thos. Killigrew's way of getting to see plays when he was a boy. He would go to the Red Bull, and when the man cried to the boys, "Who will go and be a devil, and he shall see the play for nothing?" then would he go in, and be a devil upon the stage, and so get to see plays.

31st. Thus ends this month, I and my family in good health, but weary heartily of dirt, but now in hopes within two or three weeks to be out of it. My head troubled with much business, but especially my fear of Sir J. Minnes claiming my bed-chamber of me, but I hope now that it is almost over, for I perceive he is fitting his house to go into it the next week. Then my law businesses for Brampton makes me mad almost, for that I want time to follow them, but I must by no means neglect them. I thank God I have no crosses, but only much business to trouble my mind with. In all other things as happy a man as any in the world, for the whole world seems to smile upon me, and if my house were done that I could diligently follow my business, I would not doubt to do God, and the King, and myself good service. And all I do impute almost wholly to my late temperance, since my making of my vowes against wine and plays, which keeps me most happily and contentfully to my business; which God continue! Public matters are full of discontent, what with the sale of Dunkirke, and my Lady Castle-maine, and her faction at Court; though I know not what they would have more than to debauch the king, whom God preserve from it! And then great plots are talked to be discovered, and all the prisons in towne full of ordinary people, taken from their meeting-places last Sunday. But for certain some plots there hath been, though not brought to a head.

November 1st. With Mr. Creed to the Trinity House, to a great dinner there, by invitacion, and much company. It seems one Captain Evans makes his Elder Brother's dinner to-day. Among other discourses one Mr. Oudant, secretary to the late Princesse of Orange, did discourse of the convenience as to keeping the highways from being deep, by their horses, in Holland (and Flanders where the ground is as miry as ours is), going in their carts and waggons as ours in coaches, wishing the same here as an expedient to make the ways better, and I think there is something in it, where there is breadth enough. Thence to my office, sent for to meet Mr. Lee again, from Sir H. Bennet. And he and I, with Wade and his intelligencer and labourers, to the Tower cellars, to make one tryall more; where we staid two or three hours digging, and dug a great deal all under the arches, as it was now most confidently directed, and so seriously, and upon pretended good grounds, that I myself did truly expect to speed; but we missed of all: and so we went away the second time like fools. And to our office; and I by appointment to the Dolphin Taverne, to meet Wade and the other, Captn. Evett, who now do tell me plainly, that he that do put him upon this is one that had it from Barkestead's own mouth, and was advised with by him, just before the King's coming in, how to get it out, and had all the signs told him how and where it lay, and had always been the great confidant of Barkestead even to the trusting him with his life and all he had. So that he did much convince me that there is good ground for what we go about. But I fear it may be that he did find some conveyance of it away, without the helpe of this man, before he died.   But he is resolved to go to the party once more, and then to determine what we shall do further.

2nd (Lord's day). Lay long with pleasure talking with my wife, in whom I never had greater content, blessed be God ! than now, she continuing with the same care and thrift and innocence, so long as I keep her from occasions of being otherwise, as ever she was in her life, and keeps the house as well.   To church, where Mr. Mills preached a very ordinary sermon, after he had read the service, and shifted himself, as he did the last day.   So home to dinner, and then to church, and there being a lazy preacher I slept out the sermon. My wife and I spent a good deal of this evening in reading Du Barta's [1] Imposture and other parts which my wife of late has taken up to read, and is very fine as anything I meet with.

3d. To White Hall, to the Duke's ; but found him gone a-hunting.   Thence to my Lord Sandwich, from whom I receive every day more and more signs of his confidence and esteem of me.   Here I met with Pierce the chyrurgeon, who tells me that my Lady Castlemaine is with child ; but though it being the King's, yet her Lord being still in towne, and sometimes seeing of her, though never to eat together or cohabit, it will be laid to him.   He tells me also how the Duke of York is smitten in love with my Lady

---

[1] A French poet. De Thou speaks of him in the most flattering terms. He died 1590, at the age of 46. (M. B.)

Chesterfield [1] (a virtuous lady, daughter to my Lord of Ormond); and so much, that the duchesse of York hath complained to the King and her father about it, and my Lady Chesterfield is gone into the country for it. At all which I am sorry: but it is the effect of idlenesse, and having nothing else to employ their great spirits upon. Thence with Mr. Creed and Mr. Moore to Wilkinson's, and there I did give them and Mr. Howe their dinner of roast beef, cost me 5*s*. At night to my office, and did business; and there came to me Mr. Wade and Evett, who have been again with their prime intelligencer, a woman, I perceive: and though we have missed twice, yet they bring such an account of the probability of the truth of the thing, though we are not certain of the place, that we shall set upon it once more; and I am willing and hopefull in it. So we resolved to set upon it again on Wednesday morning; and the woman herself will be there in a disguise, and confirm us in the place.

4th. This morning we had news by letters that Sir Richard Stayner is dead at sea in the Mary, which is now come into Portsmouth from Lisbon; which we are sorry for, he being a very stout seaman.

5th. My Lady Batten did send to speak with me, and told me very civilly that she did not desire, nor hoped I did, that anything should pass between us but what was civill, though there was not the neigh-

---

[1] Lady Elizabeth Butler, daughter of James, Duke of Ormond, married Philip, second Earl of Chesterfield. Ob. 1665. Vide "Mémoires de Grammont."

bourliness between her and my wife that was fit to be, and so complained of my mayde's mocking of her; when she called "Nan" to her mayde within her own house, my mayde Jane in the garden overheard her, and mocked her, and of my wife's speaking unhandsomely of her; to all which I did give her a very respectfull answer, such as did please her, and am sorry indeed that this should be, though I do not desire there should be any acquaintance between my wife and her. But I promised to avoyde such words and passages for the future. So home, and by and by Sir W. Pen did send for me to his bedside, and tell me how really Sir J. Minnes did resolve to have one of my rooms, and that he was very angry and hot, and said he would speak to the Duke. To which, knowing that all this was but to scare me, I did tell him plainly how I did not value his anger more than he did mine, and that I should be willing to do what the Duke commanded, and I was sure to have justice of him, and that was all I did say to him about it, though I was much vexed, and after a little stay went home; and then telling my wife she did put me into heart, and resolve to offer him to change lodgings, and I believe that that will one way or other bring us to some end in this dispute. At night I called up my mayds, and schooled Jane, who did answer me so humbly and drolly about it, that though I seemed angry, I was much pleased with her and my wife also.

7th. Up and being by appointment called upon by Mr. Lee, he and I to the Tower, to make our third attempt upon the cellar. And now privately the woman, Barkestead's great confidant, is brought, who do positively say that this is the place which he did say the money was hid in, and where he and she did put up the 50,000*l.*[1] in butter firkins; and the very day that he went out of England did say that neither he nor his would be the better for that money, and therefore wishing that she and hers might. And so left us, and we full of hope did resolve to dig all over the cellar, which by seven o'clock at night we performed. At noon we sent for a dinner, and upon the head of a barrel dined very merrily, and to work again. But at last we saw we were mistaken; and after digging the cellar quite through, and removing the barrels from one side to the other, we were forced to pay our porters, and give over our expectacions, though I do believe there must be money hid somewhere by him, or else he did delude this woman in hopes to oblige her to further serving him, which I am apt to believe. Thence by coach to White Hall, and at my Lord's lodgings, hearing that Mrs. Sarah is married, I did joy her and kiss her, she owning of it; and it seems it is to a cooke. I am glad she is disposed of, for she grows old, and is very painfull,[2] and one I have reason to wish well for her old service to me. Then to my brother's, where my wife, by my order, is to stay a night or two while my house is made clean.

9th (Lord's day). Walked to my brother's, where

---

[1] Sic in MS. (M. B.)   [2] Painstaking. (M. B.)

my wife is, calling at many churches, and then to the Temple, hearing a bit there too, and observing that in the streets and churches the Sunday is kept in appearance as well as I have known it at any time. Then to dinner to my brother's, and after dinner to see Mr. Moore, who is pretty well, and he and I to St. Gregory's, where I escaped a great fall down the staires of the gallery : so into a pew there and heard Dr. Ball [1] make a very good sermon, though short of what I expected, as for the most part it do fall out.

10th. A little to the office, and so with Sir J. Minnes, Sir W. Batten, and myself by coach to White Hall, to the Duke, who, after he was ready, did take us into his closett. Thither came my Lord General Monk, and did privately talk with the Duke about having the life-guards pass through the City to-day only for show and to fright people, for I perceive there are great fears abroad ; for all which I am troubled and full of doubt that things will not go well. He being gone, we fell to business of the Navy. Among other things, how to pay off this fleete that is now come from Portugall ; the King of Portugall sending them home, he having no more use for them, which we wonder at, that his condition should be so soon altered. And our landmen also are coming back, being almost starved in that poor country. Having done here I went by my Lord Sandwich's, who was not at home, and so to Westminster Hall, where full of terme, and

---

[1] Dr. Ball was then rector of St. Mary Woolchurch, and in 1665 Master of the Temple.

here met with many about business, among others my cozen Roger Pepys, who is all for a composition with my uncle Thomas. Thence to my Lord Crew's, and dined with him and his brother, I know not his name. Where very good discourse. Among others, of France's intention to make a patriarch of his own, independent from the Pope, by which he will be able to cope with the Spaniard in all councils, which hitherto he has never done. My Lord Crew told us how he heard my Lord of Holland [1] say that, being Embassador about the match with the Queene-Mother that now is, the King of France [2] insisted upon a dispensation from the Pope, which my Lord Holland making a question of, and that he was commanded to yield to nothing to the prejudice of our religion, says the King of France, "You need not fear that, for if the Pope will not dispense with the match, my Bishopp of Paris shall." By and by come in great Mr. Swinfen, [3] the Parliament-man, who, among other discourse of the rise and fall of familys, told us of Bishopp Bridgeman [4] (brother [5] of

---

[1] Henry Rich, second son of Robert, first Earl of Warwick. He had been created Lord Kensington before the embassy here alluded to, and was afterwards advanced to the Earldom of Holland, September 24, 1624. He was beheaded by the Parliament in 1649.

[2] Louis XIII., in 1624.

[3] John Swinfen, M.P. for Tamworth.

[4] John Bridgeman, Bishop of Chester, ancestor of the present Earl of Bradford. Great Levers, the seat alluded to, must probably have been bought by Sir Orlando Bridgeman, or some other member of the family, not by the Bishop, as he died in 1652. Pepys seems to speak of a person then living. See *ante*, Oct. 10, 1660.

[5] Sic in MS. Had Sir Orlando Bridgeman, son of the Bishop of Chester, who died 1642, a brother also a Bishop? (M. B.)

Sir Orlando) who lately hath bought a seat anciently of the Levers, and then the Ashtons ;[1] and so he hath in his great hall window (having repaired and beautified the house) caused four great places to be left for coates of armes.   In one he hath put the Levers, with this motto, "Olim."   In another the Ashtons, with this, "Heri."   In the next his own, with this, "Hodie."   In the fourth nothing but this motto, "Cras nescio cujus."   Thence towards my brother's ; met with Jack Cole in Fleete Street.   I found him a little conceited, but he had good things in him, and a man may know the temper of the City by him, he being of a general conversation, and can tell how matters go ; and upon that score I will encourage his acquaintance. To my brother's, and taking my wife up, carried her to Charing Crosse, and there showed her the Italian motion, much after the nature of what I showed her a while since in Covent Garden.   Their puppets here are somewhat better, but their motions not at all. Thence by coach to my Lady's, and, hiding my wife with Sarah below, I went up and heard some musique with my Lord, and afterwards discoursed with him alone, and so good night to him and home.   The towne, I hear, is full of discontents, and all know of the King's new bastard by Mrs. Haslerigge,[2] and as far as I can hear will never be contented with Episcopacy, they are so cruelly set for Presbytery, and the Bishopps carry themselves so high, that they are never likely to gain anything upon them.

---

[1] Ashton Hall, in Lancashire.   [2] See Oct. 17th, 1662.   (M. B.)

11th. All the morning sitting at the office, and then to dinner with my wife, and so to the office again (where a good while Mr. Bland was with me, telling me very fine things in merchandize, which, but that the trouble of my office do cruelly hinder me, I would take some pains in) till late at night. Towards the evening I, as I have done for three or four nights, studying something of Arithmetique, which do please me well to see myself come forward.

12th. By my wife's appointment came two young ladies,[1] sisters, acquaintances of my wife's brother's, who are desirous to wait upon some ladies, and proffer their service to my wife. The youngest, indeed, hath a good voice, and sings very well, besides other good qualitys; but I fear hath been bred up with too great liberty for my family, and I fear greater inconveniences of expenses, and my wife's liberty will follow, which I must study to avoid till I have a better purse; though, I confess, the gentlewoman, being pretty handsome, and singing, makes me have a good mind to her. Anon I took them by coach and carried them to a friend's of theirs. I walked home, calling a little in Paul's Churchyard, and, I thank God, can read and never buy a book, though I have a great mind to it. So to the Dolphin Taverne near home, by appointment, and there met with Wade and Evett, and have resolved to make a new attempt upon another discovery, in which God give us better fortune

---

[1] The two Gosnells.

than in the other, but I have great confidence that there is no cheat in these people, but that they go upon good grounds, though they have been mistaken in the place of the first. From thence to my office and there made an end, though late, of my collection of the prices of masts for these twelve years to this day, in order to the buying of some of Wood, and I bound it up in painted paper to lie by as a book for future use. So home and to supper and to bed, and a little before and after we were in bed we had much talke and difference between us about my wife's having a woman, which I seemed much angry at, that she should go so far in it without consideration or my being consulted.

13th. Up and began our discontent again and sorely angered my wife, who indeed do live very lonely, but I do perceive that it is want of worke that do make her and all other people think of ways of spending their time worse, and this I owe to my building, that do not admit of her undertaking any thing of worke, because the house has been and is still so dirty. I to my office all the morning and dined with discontent with my wife at noon, and so to my office, and there this afternoon we had our first meeting upon our commission of inspecting the Chest,[1] and there met Sir J. Minnes, Sir Francis

---

[1] The Chest at Chatham was originally planned by Sir Francis Drake and Sir John Hawkins in 1588, after the defeat of the Armada; the seamen voluntarily agreed to have "defalked" out of their wages certain sums to form a fund for relief. The property became considerable, as well as the abuses, and

Clerke,[1] Mr. Heath, Atturney of the Dutchy, Mr. Prinn, Sir W. Rider, Captn. Cocke, and myself. Our first work was to read over the Institution, which is a decree in Chancery in the year 1617, upon an inquisition made at Rochester about that time into the revenues of the Chest, which had then, from the year 1588 or 1590, by the advice of the Lord High Admiral and principal officers then being, by consent of the seamen, been settled, paying sixpence per month, according to their wages then, which was then but 10*s.* which is now 24*s.* We adjourned to a fortnight hence. So broke up, and I to see Sir W. Pen, who is now pretty well, but lies in bed still; he cannot rise to stand. Then to my office late, and this afternoon my wife in her discontent sent me a letter, which I am in a quandary what to do, whether to read it or not, but I purpose not, but to burn it before her face, that I may put a stop to more of this nature. But I must think of some way, either to find her somebody to keep her company, or to set her to worke, and by employment to take up her thoughts and time. After doing what I had to do I went home to supper, and there was very sullen to my wife, and so went to bed and to sleep (though with much ado, my mind being troubled) without speaking one word to her.

---

in 1802 the Chest was removed to Greenwich. In 1817 the stock amounted to £300,000 Consols. — *Hist. of Rochester,* p. 346. See also "Diary," June 2, 1662.

[1] M. P. for Rochester, and knighted there by Charles II., May 28, 1660.

14th. She begun to talk in the morning and to be friends, believing all this while that I had read her letter, which I perceive by her discourse was full of good counsel, and relating the reason of her desiring a woman, and how little charge she did intend it to be to me, so I begun and argued it as full and plain to her, and she to reason it highly to me, to put her away, and take one of the Bowyers if I did dislike her, that I did resolve when the house is ready she shall try her for a while; the truth is, I having a mind to have her come for her musique and dancing. So to my office, where we met this afternoon about answering a great letter of my Lord Treasurer.

15th. All the morning at the office, dined with my wife pleasantly, then among my painters, and by and by went to my Civil Lawyers about my uncle's suit, and so home again and saw my painters make an end of my house this night, which is my great joy, and so to my office and did business till ten at night, and so home and to supper, and after reading part of Bussy d'Ambois, a good play I bought to-day, to bed.

16th (Lord's day). After long talking pleasantly with my wife, up and to church. So home and to dinner. By and by comes Tom, and after a little talke I with him towards his end, but seeing many strangers and coaches coming to our church, and finding that it was a sermon to be preached by a probationer for the Turkey Company, to be sent to Smyrna, I returned thither. And several Turkey merchants filled all the best pews (and some in ours) in the Church, but a most pitiful sermon it was upon a text in Zachariah, and a great time he spent to show whose son Zachary was, and to prove Malachi to be the last prophet before John the Baptist.

17th. To the Duke's to-day, but he is gone a-hunting. At home I found my wife dressing by appointment by her woman that I think is to be, and her other sister being here to-day with her, I took Mr. Creed, that came to dine, to an ordinary, and after dinner home and spent an hour or two till almost dark, talking with my wife, and making Mrs. Gosnell sing; and then, there being no coach to be got, by water to White Hall; but Gosnell not being willing to go through bridge, we were forced to land and take water again, and put her and her sister ashore at the Temple. I am mightily pleased with her humour and singing. At White Hall by appointment, Mr. Creed carried my wife and I to the Cockpitt, and we had excellent places, and saw the King, Queene, Duke of Monmouth,[1] his son, and my Lady Castlemaine, and all the fine ladies; and "The Scornfull Lady," well performed. They had done by eleven o'clock, and it being fine moonshine, we took coach and home, but could wake nobody at my house, and so were fain to have my boy get through one of the windows, and so opened the door and called up the mayds, and went to supper and to bed.

---

[1] This entry seems to have been corrected by Pepys at a later time, for Monmouth was not created a Duke till 14th Feb., 1662-3.

18th. Up and to the office, and at noon I dined at Sir W. Batten's, Sir John Minnes being here, and he and I very kind, but I every day expect to pull a crow with him about our lodgings. Meeting my uncle Thomas, he and I to my cozen Roger's chamber, and there I did give my uncle him and Mr. Philips to be my two arbiters against Mr. Cole and Punt, but I expect no great good of the matter. Thence walked home, and my wife came home, having been abroad to-day, laying out above 12*l.* in linen, and a copper, and a pot, and bedstead, and other household stuff, which troubles me also, so that my mind to-night is very heavy and divided. Late at my office, drawing up a letter to my Lord Treasurer, which we have been long about.

20th. All the morning sitting at the office, at noon with Mr. Coventry to the Temple to advise about Field's, but our lawyers not being in the way we went to St. James's, and there at his chamber dined, and I am still in love more and more with him for his real worth. After dinner to the Temple, to Mr. Thurland;[1] and thence to my Lord Chief Baron, Sir Edward Hale's,[2] and take Mr. Thurland to his chamber, where he told us that Field will have the better of us; and that we must study to make up the business as well as we can, which do much vex and

---

[1] Edward Thurland, M.P. for Ryegate, afterwards knighted.

[2] Sir Matthew Hale succeeded Sir Orlando Bridgeman as Chief Baron of the Exchequer (according to Beatson), in 1666: there is consequently some mistake.

trouble us : but I am glad the Duke is concerned in it.

21st. Within all day long, helping to put up my hangings in my house in my wife's chamber, to my great content. In the afternoon I went to speak to Sir J. Minnes at his lodgings, where I found many great ladies, and his lodgings made very fine indeed. To supper and to bed : this night having first put up a spitting sheet, which I find very convenient. This day come the King's pleasure-boats from Calais, with the Dunkirke money, being 400,000 pistolles.

22nd. This morning, from some difference between my wife and Sarah, her mayde, my wife and I fell out cruelly, to my great discontent. But I do see her so set against the wench,[1] whom I take to be a most extraordinary good servant, that I was forced for the wench's sake to bid her get her another place, which shall cost some trouble to my wife, however, before I suffer to be. After doing much business at my office I went home and caused a new fashion knocker to be put on my doore, and did other things to the putting my house in order. This day I bought the book of country dances against my wife's woman Gosnell comes, who dances finely ; and there meeting Mr. Playford[2] he did give me his Latin songs of Mr. Deering's,[3]

---

[1] "Wench" originally meant young woman only, without the contemptuous familiarity now annexed to it. (M. B.)

[2] John Playford, a seller of musical instruments and books, near the Temple church. His portrait is in Burney's "Hist. of Music."

[3] There is a copy of Dering's Latin songs in the British Museum, entitled "Cantica Sacra ad duas et tres voces composita." London, 1662, folio.

which he lately printed.   This day Mr. Moore told me that for certain the Queene-Mother is married to my Lord St. Albans, and he is like to be made Lord Treasurer.   Newes that Sir J. Lawson hath made up a peace now with Tunis and Tripoli, as well as Argiers, by which he will come home very highly honoured.

23rd (Lord's day). To church to hear Mr. Mills. In the afternoon to church again, and heard drowsy Mr. Graves.   To Sir W. Batten's, and heard how Sir R. Ford's daughter is married to a fellow without friends' consent, and the match carried on and made up at Will Griffin's, our doorkeeper.   I talked to my brother to-day, who desires me to give him leave to look after his mistress still; and he will not have me put to any trouble or obligation in it, which I did give him leave to do.   I hear to-day how old rich Audley[1] is lately dead, and left a very great estate, and made a great many poor familys rich, not all to one.   Among others, one Davis,[2] my old schoolfellow at Paul's, and since a bookseller in Paul's Church Yarde: and it seems do forgive one man 60,000*l.* which he had wronged him of, but names not his name; but it is well known to be the scrivener in Fleete Streete, at whose house he lodged.   There is

---

[1] There is an old Tract called, "The Way to be Rich, according to the Practice of the great Audley, who began with 200*l.* in 1605, and dyed worth 400,000*l.* November, 1662."   London, printed for E. Davis, 1662.

[2] 1652, Dec. 24, "Died John Daves, Old Jewry, broaker, a· prisoner buried in St. Olave's, Old Jewry: his son, Tho. Daves, a bookseller, was afterwards an alderman and Lord Mayor of London, enriched by the legacy of Hugh Audley." — SMITH's *Obituary*, p. 33.

also this week dead a poulterer, in Gracious Streete, which was thought rich, but not so rich, that hath left 800*l.* per annum, taken in other men's names, and 40,000 Jacobs in gold.

24th. Sir J. Minnes, Sir W. Batten, and I, going forth toward White Hall, we hear that the King and Duke are come this morning to the Tower to see the Dunkirke money. So we by coach to them, and there went up and down all the magazines with them; but methought it was but poor discourse and frothy that the King's companions (young Killigrew among the rest), had with him. We saw none of the money, but Mr. Slingsby [1] did show the King, and I did see, the stamps of the new money that is now to be made by Blondeau's [2] fashion, which are very neat, and like the King. Thence the King to Woolwich, though a very cold day; and the Duke to White Hall, commanding us to come after him; and in his closett, my Lord Sandwich being there, did discourse with us about getting some of this money to pay off the Fleets, and other matters; and then away hence and, it being almost dinner time, I to my Lord Crew's, and dined with him, and had very good discourse, and he seemed to be much pleased with my visits. By coach (my cozen, Thomas Pepys, going along with me) homeward, and I set him down by the way; but, Lord! how he did endeavour to find out a ninepence to clubb with me for the coach, and for want

---

[1] Henry Slingsby, Master of the Mint.
[2] See 9th March, 1662–63. (M. B.)

was forced to give me a shilling, and how he still cries "Gad!" and talks of Popery coming on, as all the Fanatiques do, of which I was ashamed.

25th. Up and to the office all the morning, and at noon with the rest, by Mr. Holy, the ironmonger's invitation, to the Dolphin, to a venison pasty, very good, and rare at this time of the year. Great talke among people how some of the Fanatiques do say that the end of the world is at hand, and that next Tuesday is to be the day. Against which, whenever it shall be, good God fit us all.

26th. In the morning to the Temple to my cozen Roger, who now desires that I would excuse him from arbitrating, he not being able to stand for me as he would do, without appearing too high against my uncle Thomas, which will raise his clamour. With this I am very well pleased, for I did desire it, and so I shall choose other counsel. All day long till twelve o'clock at night getting my house in order, my wife putting up the red hangings and bed in her woman's chamber, and I my books and all other matters in my chamber and study, which is now very pretty.

27th. At my waking, I found the tops of the houses covered with snow, which is a rare sight, that I have not seen these three years. To the office, where we sat till noon; when we all went to the next house upon Tower Hill, to see the coming by of the Russia Embassador; for whose reception all the City trained-bands do attend in the streets, and the King's life-guards, and most of the wealthy citizens in their black velvet coats, and gold chains (which remain of their gallantry at the King's coming in), but they staid so long that we went down again to dinner. And after I had dined, I heard they were coming, and so I walked to the Conduit in the Quarrefowr,[1] at the end of Gracious-street and Cornhill; and there (the spouts thereof running very near me upon all the people that were under it) I saw them pretty well go by. I could not see the Embassador in his coach; but his attendants in their habits and fur caps very handsome, comely men, and most of them with hawkes upon their fists to present to the King. But Lord! to see the absurd nature of Englishmen, that cannot forbear lauging and jeering at every thing that looks strange. So back to the office, and there we met and sat till seven o'clock, making a bargain with Mr. Wood for his masts of New England.

28th. A very hard frost; which is newes to us after having none almost these three years. By ten o'clock to Ironmongers' Hall, to the funeral of Sir Richard Stayner.[2]　Here we were, all the officers of the Navy, and my Lord Sandwich, who did discourse with us about the fishery, telling us of his Majesty's resolution to give 200*l.* to every man that will set out a Busse;[3] and advising about the effects of this encouragement,

---

[1] A place where four ways met. Quadrivium.

"*Nonne libet medio ceras implere capaces Quadrivio ?*"

Juv., *Sat.* i. 63.

So Cairfax, or Carfax, Quatre vois, at Oxford. (M. B.)

[2] He was buried at Greenwich, 28th Nov. 1662.

[3] A small sea-vessel used by the Hollanders for the herring-fishery.

which will be a very great matter certainly. Here we had good rings, and by and by were to take coach; and I being got in with Mr. Creed into a four-horse coach, which they came and told us were only for the mourners, I went out, and so took this occasion to go home.

29th. To the office; and this morning came Sir G. Carteret to us (being the first time since his coming from France): he tells us, that the silver which he received for Dunkirke did weigh 120,000 weight. To my Lord's, where my Lord and Mr. Coventry, Sir Wm. Darcy,[1] one Mr. Parham (a very knowing and well-spoken man in this business), with several others, did meet about stating the business of the fishery, and the manner of the King's giving of this 200*l.* to every man that shall set out a new-made English Busse by the middle of June next. In which business we had many fine pretty discourses; and I did here see the great pleasure to be had in discoursing of publique matters with men that are particularly acquainted with this or that business. Having come to some issue, wherein a motion of mine was well received, about sending these invitations from the King to all the fishing-ports in general, with limiting so many Busses to this, and that port, before we know the readiness of subscribers, we parted, and I walked home all the way, in my way calling upon my cozen Turner and Mr. Calthrop at the Temple, for their consent to be

---

[1] Third son of Sir Conyers Darcy, summoned to Parliament as Lord Darcy, 1642.

my arbitrators, which they are willing to. My wife and I pretty pleasant, for that her brother brings word that Gosnell, which my wife and I in discourse do pleasantly call our Marmotte, will certainly come next weeke without fail, which God grant may be for the best.

30th (Lord's day). To church in the morning, and Mr. Mills made a pretty good sermon. Dined alone with my wife to-day with great content, my house being quite clean from top to bottom. In the afternoon I to the French church here in the city, and stood in the aisle all the sermon, with great delight hearing a very admirable sermon, from a very young man, upon the article in our creed, in order of catechisme, upon the Resurrection. Thence home, and to visit Sir W. Pen, who continues still bed-rid. Here was Sir W. Batten and his Lady, and Mrs. Turner, and I very merry, talking of the confidence of Sir R. Ford's new-married daughter, though she married so strangely lately, yet appears at church as briske as can be, and takes place of her elder sister, a mayde. Thence home and to supper, and to make up my monthly accounts, and I do find that, through the fitting of my house this month, I have spent in that and kitchen 50*l.* this month; so that now I am worth but 660*l.*, or thereabouts. This being done and fitted myself for the Duke to-morrow, to prayers and to bed. This day I first did wear a muffe, being my wife's last year's muffe, and now I have bought her a new one, this serves me very well. Thus ends this month; in great frost; myself and family all well, but my mind much disordered about my uncle's law business, being now in an order of being arbitrated between us, which I wish to God it were done. I am also somewhat uncertain what to think of my going about to take a woman-servant into my house, in the quality of a woman for my wife. My wife promises it shall cost me nothing but her meat and wages, and that it shall not be attended with any other expenses, upon which termes I admit of it; for that it will, I hope, save me money in having my wife go abroad on visits and other delights; so that I hope the best, but am resolved to alter it, if matters prove otherwise than I would have them.   Publique matters in an ill condition of discontent against the height and vanity of the Court, and their bad payments : but that which troubles most, is the Clergy, which will never content the City, which is not to be reconciled to Bishopps : the more the pity that differences must still be.   Dunkirke newly sold, and the money brought over; of which we hope to get some to pay the Navy : which by Sir J. Lawson's having dispatched the business in the Straights, by making peace with Argier,[1] Tunis, and Tripoli (and so his fleete will also shortly come home), will now every day grow less, and so the King's charge be abated; which God send!

---

[1] The ancient name for Algiers.

> "*Prosp.* Where was she born? speak; tell me.
> *Ari.* Sir, in *Argier*."
>
> SHAKESPEARE, *Tempest*, act i. sc. 2.   (M. B.)

December 1st. Up and by coach with Sir John Minnes and Sir W. Batten to White Hall to the Duke's chamber, where, as is usual, my Lord Sandwich and all of us, after his being ready, to his closett, and there discoursed of matters of the Navy, and here Mr. Coventry did do me the great kindness to take notice to the Duke of my pains in making a collection of all contracts about masts, which have been of great use to us. Thence I to my Lord Sandwich's, to Mr. Moore; and then over the Parke (where I first in my life, it being a great frost, did see people sliding with their skeates,[1] which is a very pretty art), to Mr. Coventry's chamber to St. James's, where we all met to a venison pasty, and were very merry, Major Norwood being with us, whom they did play upon for his surrendering of Dunkirke. Here we staid till three or four o'clock; and so to the Council Chamber, where there met the Duke of York, Prince Rupert, Duke of Albemarle, my Lord Sandwich, Sir Wm. Compton, Mr. Coventry, Sir J. Minnes, Sir R. Ford, Sir W. Rider, myself, and Captain Cuttance, as Commissioners for Tangier. And after our Commission was read by Mr. Creed, who I perceive is to be our Secretary, we did fall to discourse of matters: as, first, the supplying them forthwith with victualls; then the reducing it to make way for the money, which upon their reduction is to go to the building of the Mole; and so to other matters, ordered as against next meeting. This done

---

[1] Introduced about this time from Holland. The word is derived from the Dutch *schaatzen*. (M. B.)

we broke up, and I to the Cockpitt, with much crowding and waiting, where I saw "The Valiant Cidd"[1] acted, a play I have read with great delight, but is a most dull thing acted, which I never understood before, there being no pleasure in it, though done by Betterton and by Ianthe, and another fine wench that is come in the room of Roxalana;[2] nor did the King or Queene once smile all the whole play, nor any of the company seem to take any pleasure but what was in the greatness and gallantry of the company. Thence to my Lord's, and with a linke walked home by 12 o'clock, knocked up my boy, and put myself to bed.

2nd. Before I went to the office my wife and I had another falling out about Sarah, against whom she has a deadly hate, I know not for what, nor can I see but she is a very good servant. Then to the office, and then to dinner with my wife at home, and after dinner did give Jane a very serious lesson, against we take her to be our chamber-mayde, which I spoke so to her that the poor girle cried and did promise to be very dutifull and carefull. So to the office, where we sat as Commissioners for the Chest, and so examined most of the old accountants to the Chest about it. This night first put on a wastecoate.

3rd. Called up by Commissioner Pett, and with him by water, much against my will, to Deptford, and after

---

[1] Translated from the well-known Cid of Corneille.

[2] Elizabeth Davenport appears to have left the stage, Pepys always afterwards speaking of the *new Roxalana*, whom he once calls Mrs. Norton. See *ante*, Feb. 18, 1661-2.

drinking a warm morning draft, with Mr. Wood and our officers measuring all the morning his New England masts, with which sight I was pleased for my information, though I perceive great neglect and indifference in all the King's officers in what they do for the King. That done, to the Globe, and there dined, and so by water with Mr. Pett home again, all the way reading his Chest accounts, in which I did see things which did not please me ; as his allowing himself 300*l.* for one year's looking to the business of the Chest, and 150*l.* per annum for the rest of the years. But I found no fault to him himself, but shall when they come to be read at the Board. We did also call at Limehouse to view two Busses that are building, that being a thing we are now very hot upon. Our call was to see what dimensions they are of, being 50 feet by the keel and about 60 tons. Home and did a little business, and so taking Mr. Pett by the way, we walked to the Temple, in our way seeing one of the Russia Embassador's coaches go along, with his footmen not in liverys, but their country habits ; one of one colour and another of another, which was very strange.

5th. Up, it being a snow and hard frost, and being up I did call up Sarah, who do go away to-day or to-morrow. I paid her her wages, and gave her 10*s.* myself, and my wife 5*s.* to give her. The wench cried, and I was ready to cry too, but to keep peace I am content she should go. This being done, I walked towards Guildhall, thither being summoned by the Commissioners for the Lieutenancy ; but they sat not this morning.　So meeting in my way W. Swan, I took him to a house thereabouts, and gave him a morning draft of buttered ale; he telling me much of his Fanatique stories, as if he were a great zealot, when I know him to be a very rogue.　But I do it for discourse, and to see how things stand with him and his party; who I perceive have great expectation that God will not bless the Court nor Church, as it is now settled, but they must be purified.　The worst news he tells me, is that Mr. Chetwind is dead, my old and most ingenious acquaintance.　He is dead, worth 3000*l.*, which I did not expect, he living so high as he did always and neatly.　He hath given W. Symons his wife 300*l.*, and made Will one of his executors. Home, and there I find Gosnell come, who, my wife tells me, is likely to prove a pretty companion, of which I am glad, and in the evening do entertain myself with my wife and her, who sings exceeding well, and I shall take great delight in her.

6th. Up and to the office.　Dined at home with my wife and Gosnell, my mind much pleased with her, and after dinner sat with them a good while, till my wife seemed to take notice of my being at home now more than at other times.　I went to the office, and there till late, and after a song by Gosnell we to bed.

7th (Lord's day).　To church this morning with my wife, which is the first time she hath been at church since her going to Brampton, and Gosnell attending her, which was very gracefull.　In the afternoon I thought to go to the French church; but find-

ing the Dutch congregation there, and then finding
the French congregation's sermon begun in the Dutch,
I returned home, and up to our gallery, where I found
my wife and Gosnell, and after a drowsy sermon, we
all three to my aunt Wight's, where great store of her
usuall company, and here we staid a pretty while talking, I differing from my aunt, as I commonly do, in
our opinion of the handsomeness of the Queene, which
I oppose mightily, saying that if my nose be handsome, then is her's, and such like, and so with my
wife only to see Sir W. Pen, who is now got out of his
bed, and sits by the fire-side.

8th. Up, and carrying Gosnell by coach, set her
down at Temple Barr. By the way she was telling
me how Balty did tell her that my wife did go every
day in the weeke to Court and plays, and that she
should have liberty of going abroad as often as she
pleased, and many other lies, which I am vexed at,
and I doubt the wench did come in some expectation
of, which troubles me. Then into the Parke, to see
them slide with their skeates, which is very pretty.
And so to the Duke's, where the Committee for Tangier met: and here we sat down all with him at a
table, and had much good discourse about the business. Home by coach, where I find my wife troubled
about Gosnell, who brings word that her uncle, Justice
Jiggins, requires her to come three times a week to
him, to follow some business that her mother intrusts
her withall, and that, unless she may have that leisure
given her, he will not have her take any place; for

which we are both troubled, but there is no helpe for it, and believing it to be a good providence of God to prevent my running behindhand in the world, I am somewhat contented therewith, and shall make my wife so, who, poor wretch, I know will consider of things, though in good earnest the privacy of her life must needs be irksome to her.

9th. After sitting all the morning in hopes to have Mr. Coventry dine with me, he was forced to go to White Hall. After dinner staid within all the afternoon, being vexed in my mind about the going away of Sarah this afternoon, who cried mightily, and so was I ready to do, and Jane did also, and then anon went Gosnell away, which did trouble me too ; though upon many considerations, it is better that I am rid of the charge. All together makes my house appear to me very lonely. My wife and I melancholy to bed.

10th. This morning rose, receiving a messenger from Sir G. Carteret and a letter from Mr. Coventry, one contrary to another, about our letter to my Lord Treasurer, at which I am troubled, but I went to Sir George, and being desircus to please both, I think I have found out a way to do it. So back to the office with Sir J. Minnes, in his coach, but so great a snow that we could hardly pass the streets. Then to the Dolphin, where Sir J. Minnes, Sir W. Batten, and I, did treat the Auditors of the Exchequer, Auditors Wood and Beale, and hither came Sir G. Carteret to us. We had a good dinner, cost us 5*l.* and 6*s.*, whereof my share 26*s.*, and after dinner did discourse of our salarys and other matters, which I think now they will allow. Thence home, and there I found our new cook-mayde Susan come, who is recommended to us by my wife's brother, for which I like her never the better, but being a good well-looked lass, I am willing to try, and Jane begins to take upon her as a chamber-mayde.

11th. Up, it being a great frost upon the snow, and we sat all the morning upon Mr. Creed's accounts, wherein I did him some service and some disservice. At noon he dined with me, and we sat all the afternoon together, discoursing of ways to get money, which I am now giving myself wholly up to, and in the evening to my office, concluding all matters concerning our great letter so long in doing to my Lord Treasurer, till almost one in the morning, and then home with my mind much eased, and so to bed.

12th. From a very hard frost, when I wake, I find a very great thaw, and my house overflown with it, which vexed me.

13th. We sat, Mr. Coventry and I (Sir G. Carteret being gone), and among other things, Field and Stint did come, and received the 41*l.* given him by the judgement against me and Harry Kem;[1] and we did also sign bonds in 500*l.* to stand to the award of Mr. Porter and Smith for the rest: which, however, I did not sign to till I got Mr. Coventry to go up with me to Sir W. Pen; and he did promise me be-

---

[1] In the matter of the false imprisonment: see *ante*, 4th Feb. 1661-2, and 21st Oct. 1662.

fore him to bear his share in what should be awarded, and both concluded that Sir W. Batten would do no less.

14th (Lord's day). To church and then home, and had a neat dinner by ourselves, and after dinner walked to White Hall and my Lord's, and up and down till chappell time, and then to the King's chappell, where I heard the service, and so to my Lord's, and there Mr. Howe and Pagett, the counsellor, an old lover of musique. We sang some Psalms of Mr. Lawes, and played some symphonys between till night, that I was sent for to Mr. Creed's lodging, and there was Captain Ferrers and his lady and W. Howe and I; we supped very well and good sport in discourse. After supper I was sent for to my Lord, with whom I staid talking about his, and my owne, and the publique affairs, with great content, he advising me as to my owne choosing of Sir R. Bernard for umpire in the businesses between my uncle and us, that I would not trust to him upon his direction, for he did not think him a man to be trusted at all; and so bid him good night, and to Mr. Creed's again; Mr. Moore, with whom I intended to have lain, lying physically without sheets; and there, after some discourse, to bed, and lay ill, though the bed good, my stomach being sicke all night with my too heavy supper.

15th. Up and to my Lord's and thence to the Duke, and followed him into the Parke, where, though the ice was broken and dangerous, yet he would go slide upon his scates, which I did not like, but he slides very well. So back and to his closett, whither my Lord Sandwich comes, and there Mr. Coventry and we three had long discourse together about the matters of the Navy; and, indeed, I find myself more and more obliged to Mr. Coventry, who studies to do me all the right he can in every thing to the Duke. Thence walked a good while up and down the gallerys; and among others, met with Dr. Clerke, who in discourse tells me, that Sir Charles Barkeley's greatness is only his being pimp to the King, and to my Lady Castlemaine. And yet for all this, that the King is very kind to the Queene; who, he says, is one of the best women in the world. Strange how the King is bewitched to this pretty Castlemaine. I walked up and down the gallerys, spending my time upon the pictures, till the Duke and the Committee for Tangier met (the Duke not staying with us), where the only matter was to discourse with my Lord Rutherford,[1] who is this day made Governor of Tangier, for I know not what reasons; and my Lord of Peterborough to be called home; which, though it is said it is done with kindness, yet all the world may see it is done

---

[1] Andrew Rutherford, son of William Rutherford, of Quarry-holes, went young into the French service, and became a lieutenant-general of that kingdom. At the Restoration he brought over an honourable testimony from the King of France, and was created a Baron of Scotland, and in 1663 advanced to the Earldom of Teviot for his management of the sale of Dunkirk, of which he was Governor. He was afterwards appointed Governor of Tangier, and was killed by the Moors in 1664: dying without issue, his earldom became extinct; but the barony of Rutherford descended, according to the patent, to Sir Thomas Rutherford, of Hunthill.

otherwise, and I am sorry to see a Catholicke Governor sent to command there, where all the rest of the officers almost are such already. But God knows what the reason is! and all may see how slippery places all courtiers stand in. Thence home, in my way calling upon Sir John Berkenheade,[1] to speak about my assessment of 42*l.* to the Loyal Sufferers; which, I perceive, I cannot helpe; but he tells me I have been abused by Sir R. Ford, which I shall hereafter make use of when it shall be fit. Thence called at the Major-General's, Sir R. Browne, about my being assessed armes to the militia; but he was abroad; and so driving through the backside of the Shambles in Newgate Market, my coach plucked down two pieces of beef into the dirt, upon which the butchers stopped the horses, and a great rout of people in the street, crying that he had done him 40*s.* and 5*l.* worth of hurt; but going down, I saw that he had done little or none; and so I give them a shilling for it and they were well contented, and so home, and there to my Lady Batten's, who tells me she hath just now a letter from Sir William, how that he and Sir J. Minnes did very narrowly escape drowning on the roade, the waters are so high; but is well. But, Lord! what a hypocrite-like face she made to tell it me. Thence to Sir W. Pen and sat long with him in discourse, I making myself appear one of

---

[1] Sir John Berkenhead, F.R.S., a political author held in some esteem M. P. for Wilton, 1661, and knighted the following year. Master of the Faculty Office, and Court of Requests. Ob. 1679.

greater action and resolution as to publique business than I have hitherto done, at which he listens, but I know is a rogue in his heart and likes not, but I perceive I may hold up my head, and the more the better, I minding of my business as I have done, in which God do and will bless me. So home and with great content to bed, and talk and chat with my wife while I was at supper, to our great pleasure.

16th. Up and to the office, and thither came Mr. Coventry and Sir G. Carteret, and among other business was Strutt's the purser, against Captn. Browne, Sir W. Batten's brother-in-law, but, Lord! though I believe the Captain has played the knave, though I seem to have a good opinion of him and to mean well, what a most troublesome fellow that Strutt is, such as I never did meet with his fellow in my life. His talking and ours to make him hold his peace set my head off akeing all the afternoon with great pain. So to dinner, thinking to have had Mr. Coventry, but he could not go with me; and so I took Captn. Murford. Of whom I do hear what the world says of me; that all do conclude Mr. Coventry, and Pett, and me, to be of a knot; and that we do now carry all things before us; and much more in particular of me, and my studiousnesse, &c. to my great content. To White Hall to Secretary Bennet's, and agreed with Mr. Lee to set upon our new adventure at the Tower to-morrow. Thence to my Lord's, and having sat talking with Mr. Moore bewailing the vanity and disorders of the age, I went by coach to my brother's, where I met Sarah, my late mayde, who told me out of good will to me, for she loves me dearly, that I would beware of my wife's brother, for he is begging or borrowing of her and often, and told me of her Scallop whisk,[1] and borrowing of 50*s.* for Will, which she believes was for him and her father. I do observe so much goodness and seriousness in the mayde, that if she had anything in the world I would commend her for a wife for my brother Tom. After much discourse and her professions of love to me and all my relations, I bade her good night and did kiss her. So by coach home and to my office, did some business, and so home to supper and to bed.

17th. This morning come Mr. Lee, Wade, and Evett, intending to have gone upon our new design to the Tower; but it raining, and the work being to be done in the open garden, we put it off to Friday next.

18th. Up to the office, Mr. Coventry and I alone sat till two o'clock, and then he inviting himself to my house to dinner, of which I was proud; but my dinner being a legg of mutton and two capons, they were not done enough, which did vex me; but we made shift to please him, I think; but I was, when he was gone, very angry with my wife and people. This afternoon came my wife's brother and his wife. She is a most little and yet, I believe, pretty old girle, not handsome, nor has any thing in the world pleasing, but, they say, she plays mighty well on the Base Violl.

---

[1] See note, 22nd Nov. 1660. (M. B.)

19th. Up and by appointment with Mr. Lee, Wade, Evett, and workmen to the Tower, and with the Lieutenant's leave set them to work in the garden, in the corner against the mayne-guard, a most unlikely place. It being cold, Mr. Lee and I did sit all the day till three o'clock by the fire in the Governor's house; I reading a play of Fletcher's, being " A Wife for a Month," wherein no great wit or language. Having done we went to them at work, and having wrought below the bottom of the foundation of the wall, I bid them give over, and so all our hopes ended; and so went home and to my office, there reading in Sir W. Petty's book, and so home and to bed, a little displeased with my wife, who, poor wretch, is troubled with her lonely life, which I know not how without great charge to help as yet, but I will study how to do it.

20th. Up and had 100*l.* brought me by Prior of Brampton in full of his purchase money for Barton's house and some land. So to the office, and thence with Mr. Coventry in his coach to St. James's, with great content and pride to see him treat me so friendly; and dined with him, and so to White Hall together; where we met upon the Tangier Commission, and discoursed many things thereon; but little will be done before my Lord Rutherford comes there, as to the fortification or Mole. That done, my Lord Sandwich and I walked together a good while in the matted gallery, he acquainting me with his late enquiries into the Wardrobe business to his content;

and tells me how things stand.[1] And that the first year was worth about 3,000*l.* to him, and the next about as much; so that at this day, if he were paid, it will be worth about 7,000*l.* to him. But it contents me above all things to see him trust me as his confidant: so I bid him good night, he being to go into the country, to keep his Christmas, on Monday next.

21st (Lord's day). To Church, and so home to dinner alone with my wife very pleasant. After dinner to White Hall, and there to chappell, and from thence up stairs, and up and down the house and gallerys on the King's and Queene's side, and so through the garden to my Lord's lodgings, where there was Mr. Gibbons, Madge, Mallard, and Pagett; and by and by comes in my Lord Sandwich, and so we had great store of good musique. By and by comes in my simple Lord Chandois,[2] who (my Lord Sandwich being gone out to Court) began to sing psalms, but so dully that I was weary of it. At last we broke up; and

---

1 " The Royal Wardrobe occupied the site of the present Wardrobe Court, immediately to the north of the church of St. Andrew's, and gave to the parish the name of St. Andrew by the Wardrobe, by which it is still known. This building was erected about the middle of the fourteenth century by Sir John Beauchamp, Knight of the Garter, a son of Guido, Earl of Warwick, by whose heirs it was sold to Edward III. Mr. Malcolm has printed some extracts from the manuscript Account-book, since preserved in the Harleian Collection, of a Keeper of this Wardrobe, from the middle of April to Michaelmas, 1481. The keeper's salary appears to have been £100 per annum, that of his clerk 1*s.* a day, and the wages of the tailors 6*d.* a day each."— *The Town*, by Leigh Hunt. (M. B.)

2 William, seventh Lord Chandos. Ob. 1676.

by and by comes in my Lord Sandwich again, and he and I to talk together about his businesses, and so he to bed and I and Mr. Creed and Captain Ferrers fell to a cold goose pye of Mrs. Sarah's, heartily, and so spent our time till past twelve o'clock, and then with Creed to his lodgings, and so with him to bed, and slept till

22nd. Six or seven o'clock and so up, and by the fireside read a good part of "The advice to a daughter," which a simple coxcomb has wrote against Osborne, but in all my life I never did nor can expect to see so much nonsense in print. Thence to my Lord's, who is getting himself ready for his journey to Hinchingbroke. My Lord and his people being gone, I walked to Mr. Coventry's chamber, where I found him gone out into the Parke with the Duke, so the boy being there ready with my things, I shifted myself into a riding-habitt, and followed him through White Hall, and in the Parke Mr. Coventry's people having a horse ready for me (so fine a one that I was almost afeard to get upon him, but I did, and found myself more feared than hurt) [1] and followed the Duke, who, with some of his people (among others Mr. Coventry) was riding out. And with them to Hide Parke. Where Mr. Coventry asking leave of the Duke, he bid us go to Woolwich. So he and I to the waterside, and our horses coming by the ferry, we by oars over to Lambeth, and from thence, with brave dis-

---

[1] The vulgarism is still common.

course by the way, rode to Woolwich, where we put
in practice my new way of the Call-booke, which will
be of great use. Here, having staid a good while,
we got up again and brought night home with us and
foule weather. Home and presently shifted myself,
and so had the barber come; and my wife and I to
read "Ovid's Metamorphoses," which I brought her
home from Paul's Churchyard to-night.

23rd. Sat all the morning, and after dinner to make
up my accounts with her, and find that my ordinary
housekeeping comes to 7*l.* a month, which is a great
deal. By and by comes Dr. Pierce, who tells me that
my Lady Castlemaine's interest at Court increases, and
is more and greater than the Queene's; that she hath
brought in Sir H. Bennet, and Sir Charles Barkeley;
but that the Queene is a most good lady, and takes all
with the greatest meekness that may be. He tells me
too that Mr. Edward Montagu is quite broke at Court
with his repute and purse; and that he lately was
engaged in a quarrell against my Lord Chesterfield:
but that the King did cause it to be taken up. He
tells me, too, that the King is much concerned in the
Chancellor's sicknesse, and that the Chancellor is as
great, he thinks, as ever he was with the King. He
also tells me what the world says of me, "that Mr.
Coventry and I do all the business of the office
almost:" at which I am highly proud.

24th. Took money in my pocket to pay many reckonings to-day in the towne, as my bookseller's, and
paid at another shop 4*l.* 10*s.* for "Stephens's Thesau-

rus Græcæ Linguæ," given to Paul's Schoole.[1] So to
my brother's and shoemaker, and so to my Lord
Crew's, and dined alone with him. I understand there
are great factions at Court, and something he said that
did imply a difference like to be between the King
and the Duke, in case the Queene should not be with
child. I understand, about this bastard.[2] He says,
also, that some great man will be aimed at when Parliament comes to sit again; I understand, the Chancellor: and that there is a bill will be brought in, that
none that have been in armes for the Parliament shall
be capable of office. And that the Court are weary
of my Lord Albemarle and Chamberlin.[3] He wishes
that my Lord Sandwich had some good occasion to
be abroad this summer which is coming on, and that
my Lord Hinchingbroke were well married, and Sydney[4] had some place at Court. He pities the poor
ministers that are put out, to whom, he says, the King
is beholden for his coming in, and that if any such
thing had been foreseen he had never come in. After
this, and much other discourse of the sea, and breed-
ing young gentlemen to the sea, I went away, and

---

[1] See December 27, 1661, *ante*.

[2] James Crofts, son of Charles II. by Lucy Waters, soon made Duke of
Monmouth. (M. B.)

[3] Edward, Earl of Manchester.

[4] Lord Sandwich's second son, who married afterwards Anne, daughter
and heir of Sir Francis Wortley of Wortley, by whom he was father of Edward
Wortley Montagu, the husband of the celebrated Lady Mary Wortley Montagu. Their daughter married John Stuart, third Earl of Bute, whose second
son took the name and estates of Wortley, and was father of the first Lord
Wharncliffe.

homeward met Mr. Creed at my bookseller's in Paul's
Church-yard, who takes it ill my letter last night to
Mr. Povy, wherein I accuse him of the neglect of the
Tangier boats, in which I must confess I did not do
altogether like a friend; but however it was truth, and
I must owne it to be so, though I fall wholly out with
him for it. Thence home and to my office alone to
do business, and read over half of Mr. Bland's discourse concerning trade, which (he being no scholler
and so knows not the rules of writing) is very good.
This evening Mr. Gauden sent me, against Christmas,
a great chine of beef and three dozen tongues. I did
give 5*s.* to the man that brought it, and half-a-crowne
to the porters.   This day also the parish-clerke brought
the general bill of mortality, which cost me half-a-
crowne more.

25th. Christmas Day. With my boy walked, it
being a most brave cold and dry frosty morning, and
had a pleasant walk to White Hall, where I intended
to have received the Communion with the family, but
I came a little too late. So I walked up into the
house and spent my time looking over pictures, particularly the ships in King Henry the VIIIth's Voyage
to Bullen;[1] marking the great difference between
their build then and now. By and by down to the

---

[1] Boulogne. These pictures were given by George III. to the Society of
Antiquaries, who in return presented to the King a set of Hearne's works, on
large paper. The pictures were reclaimed by George IV., and are now at
Hampton Court. They have been engraved in the " Vetusta Monumenta,"
published by the Society. The set of Hearne's works is now in the King's
Library, in the British Museum.

chappell again, where Bishopp Morley[1] preached upon the song of the Angels, "Glory to God on high, on earth peace, and good will towards men." Methought he made but a poor sermon, but long, and reprehending the mistaken jollity of the Court for the true joy that shall and ought to be on these days, particularized concerning their excess in playes and gaming, saying that he whose office it is to keep the gamesters in order and within bounds, serves but for a second rather in a duelle, meaning the groome-porter. Upon which it was worth observing how far they are come from taking the reprehensions of a bishopp seriously, that they all laugh in the chappell when he reflected on their ill actions and courses. He did much press us to joy in these publique days of joy, and to hospitality. But one that stood by whispered in my eare that the Bishopp do not spend one groate to the poor himself. The sermon done, a good anthem followed, with vialls, and then the King came down to receive the Sacrament. But I staid not, but calling my boy from my Lord's lodgings, and giving Sarah some good advice, by my Lord's order, to be sober and look after the house, I walked home again with great pleasure, and there dined by my wife's bed-side with great content, having a mess of brave plum-porridge and a roasted pullet for dinner, and I sent for a mince-pie abroad, my wife not being well to make any herself yet.

26th. Up, my wife to the making of Christmas pies

---

[1] George Morley, Bishop of Winchester, to which see he was translated from Worcester in 1662. Ob. 1684.

all day, being now pretty well again, and I abroad to several places about businesses, among others bought a bake-pan in Newgate Market, and sent it home, it cost me 16*s*. To the Wardrobe. Hither come Mr. Battersby; and we falling into a discourse of a new book of drollery in verse called Hudebras, I would needs go find it out, and met with it at the Temple: cost me 2*s*. 6*d*. But when I came to read it, it is so silly an abuse of the Presbyter Knight going to the warrs, that I am ashamed of it; and by and by meeting at Mr. Townsend's at dinner, I sold it to him for 18*d*. Here we dined with many tradesmen that belong to the Wardrobe, but I was weary soon of their company, and broke up dinner as soon as I could, and away, with the greatest reluctancy and dispute (two or three times my reason stopping my sense and I would go back again) within myself, to the Duke's house and saw " The Villaine," which I ought not to do without my wife, but that my time is now out that I did undertake it for. But, Lord! to consider how my natural desire is to pleasure, which God be praised that he has given me the power by my late oathes to curbe so well as I have done, and will do again after two or three plays more. Here I was better pleased with the play than I was at first,[1] understanding the design better than I did. Here I saw Gosnell and her sister at a distance, and could have found it in my heart to have accosted them, but thought it not prudent.

---

[1] See 20th October, 1662.

Home and found my wife busy among her pies, but angry for some saucy words that her mayde Jane has given her, which I will not allow of, and therefore will give her warning to be gone. As also we are both displeased for some slight words that Sarah, now at Sir W. Pen's, hath spoke of us, but it is no matter. We shall endeavour to joyne the lion's skin to the fox's tail. So to my office, and then to my study and supper and bed. Being also vexed at my boy for his staying playing abroad when sent of errands.

27th. Up, and while I am dressing I sent for my boy's brother, William, that lives in towne here as a groome, to whom and their sister Jane I told my resolution to keep the boy no longer. So to the office, and there Mr. Coventry and I sat till noon, and then I stept to the Exchange, and after dinner with my wife to the Duke's Theatre, and saw the second part of "Rhodes,"[1] done with the new Roxalana;[2] which do it rather better in all respects for person, voice, and judgment, than the first Roxalana. Not so well pleased with the company at the house to-day, which was full of citizens, there hardly being a gentleman or woman in the house; a couple of pretty ladies by us that made great sport in it, being jostled and crowded by prentices. So home, and I to my study making

---

[1] "The Siege of Rhodes," a tragi-comedy, in two parts, by Sir Wm. Davenant.

[2] An actress whose name is unknown, but she had been seduced by the Earl of Oxford, and had recently quitted the stage. For her history, *vide* "Mémoires de Grammont."

up my monthly accounts, which is now fallen again to 630*l.* or thereabouts, which not long since was 680*l.*, at which I am sorry, but I trust in God I shall get it up again, and in the meantime will live sparingly.

28th (Lord's day). Up and with my wife to church, and coming out, went out both before my Lady Batten, he not being there, which I believe will vex her. After dinner my wife to church again, and I to the French church, where I heard an old man make a tedious, long sermon, till they were fain to light candles to baptize the children by. Home, and there fell to the renewing my last year's oathes, whereby it has pleased God so much to better myself and practise, and so down to supper, and then prayers and bed.

29th. To Westminster Hall, where I staid reading at Mrs. Mitchell's shop, and sent for half a pint of sack for her. She told me what I heard not of before, the strange burning of Mr. De Laun, a merchant's house in Loathbury, and his lady (Sir Thomas Allen's [1] daughter) and her whole family; not one thing, dog nor cat, escaping; [2] nor any of the neighbours almost hearing of it till the house was quite down and burnt. How this should come to passe, God knows, but a most strange thing it is! Hither came Jack Spicer to me, and I took him to the Swan, where Mr. Herbert did give me my breakfast of cold chine of pork; and here Spicer and I talked of Ex-

---

[1] Sir Thomas Alleyne, Lord Mayor of London, 1660.
[2] The seven inmates all perished. — RUGGE's *Diurnal.*

chequer matters, and how the Lord Treasurer [1] hath now ordered all monies to be brought into the Exchequer, and hath settled the King's revenue, and given to every general expence proper assignments; to the Navy 200,000*l.* and odde. He also told me of the great vast trade of the goldsmiths in supplying the King with money at dear rates. Thence to White Hall, and got up to the top gallerys in the Banquetting House, to see the audience of the Russia Embassadors; [2] which [took place] after long waiting and fear of the falling of the gallery (it being so full, and part of it being parted from the rest, for nobody to come up merely from the weaknesse thereof) : and very handsome it was. After they were come in, I went down and got through the croude almost as high as the King and the Embassadors, where I saw all the presents, being rich furs, hawkes, carpets, cloths of tissue, and sea-horse teeth. The King took two or three hawkes upon his fist, having a glove on, wrought with gold, given him for the purpose. The son of one of the Embassadors was in the richest suit for pearl and tissue, that ever I did see, or shall, I believe. After they and all the company had kissed the King's

---

[1] The Earl of Southampton. (M. B.)

[2] " On Monday last, betwixt two and three in the afternoon, His Majesty gave audience to the great Lord Ambassador, the great Duke and Governor of Toulsky, Peeter, the son of Simon, surnamed Prozorofskee, to the Lord Governor of Coarmeski, John, the son of Offonassey, surnamed Zelebousky, and Juan Stephano, Chancellor, &c., Ambassadors from the Emperor of Russia. They passed along from York House to White Hall through His Majesties guards who stood on both sides of the street, and made a lane for their more orderly procession."—*Mercurius Publicus*, Jan. 1, 1662–3.

hand, then the three Embassadors and the son, and no more, did kiss the Queene's. One thing more I did observe, that the chief Embassador did carry up his master's letters in state before him on high; and as soon as he had delivered them, he did fall down to the ground and lay there a great while. After all was done, the company broke up; and I spent a little while walking up and down the gallery seeing the ladies, the two Queenes, and the Duke of Monmouth [1] with his little mistress,[2] which is very little, and like my brother-in-law's wife. Thence I went away, and getting a coach went home and sat late talking with my wife about our entertaining Dr. Clerke's lady and Mrs. Pierce shortly, being in great pain that my wife hath never a winter gowne, being almost ashamed of it, that she should be seen in a taffeta one, when all the world wears moyre;[3] but we could not come to any resolution what to do therein, other than to appear as she is.

30th. Up and to the office, whither Sir W. Pen came, the first time that he has come downstairs since his late great sicknesse of the goute. We with Mr. Coventry sat till noon, then I to the Change ward, to see what play was there, but I liked none of them, and so homeward, and calling in at Mr. Rawlinson's,

---

[1] The Duke of Monmouth is here spoken of by anticipation, or else Pepys has corrected the entry at a later time. He was not created Duke until 14th Feb., 1662-3.

[2] Lady Anne Scot.

[3] By *moyre* is meant *mohair*. See the note on ferrandin, Jan. 28, 1662-3.

where he stopped me to dine with him and two East India officers of ships and Howell our turner. With the officers I had good discourse, particularly of the people at the Cape of Good Hope, of whom they of their own knowledge do tell me these one or two things : viz. that they never sleep lying, but always sitting upon the ground, that their speech is not so articulate as ours, but yet they understand one another well, that they paint themselves all over with the grease the Dutch sell them (who have a fort there) and soot. After dinner drinking five or six glasses of wine, which liberty I now take till I begin my oathe again, I went home and took my wife into coach, and carried her to Westminster ; there visited Mrs. Ferrers, and staid talking with her a good while, there being a little, proud, ugly, talking lady there, that was much crying up the Queene-Mother's Court at Somerset House above our own Queene's ; there being before her no allowance of laughing and the mirth that is at the other's ; and indeed it is observed that the greatest Court now-a-days is there. Thence to White Hall, where I carried my wife to see the Queene in her presence-chamber ; and the maydes of honour and the young Duke of Monmouth playing at cards. Some of them, and but a few, were very pretty ; though all well dressed in velvet gowns. Thence to my Lord's lodgings, where Mrs. Sarah did make us my Lord's bed, and Mr. Creed being sent for, sat playing at cards till it was late, and so good night, and with great pleasure to bed.

31st. Lay pretty long in bed, and then I up and to Westminster Hall, and so to the Swan, sending for Mr. W. Bowyer, and there drank my morning draft, and had some of his simple discourse. Among other things he tells me how the difference comes between his fair cozen Butler and Collonell Dillon, upon his opening letters of her brother's from Ireland, complaining of his knavery, and forging others to the contrary; and so they are long ago quite broke off. Thence to a barber's and so to my wife, and at noon took her to Mrs. Pierce's by invitacion to dinner, where there came Dr. Clerke and his wife and sister and Mr. Knight, chief chyrurgeon to the King and his wife. We were pretty merry, the two men being excellent company, but I confess I am wedded from the opinion either of Mrs. Pierce's beauty upon discovery of her naked neck to-day, being undrest when we came in, or of Mrs. Clerke's genius, which I so much admired, I finding her to be so conceited and fantastique in her dress this day and carriage, though the truth is, witty enough. After dinner with much ado the doctor and I got away to follow our business for a while, he to his patients and I to the Tangier Committee, where the Duke of York was, and we staid at it a good while, and thence in order to the despatch of the boats and provisions for Tangier away, Mr. Povy,[1] in his coach,

---

[1] Thomas Povy, who had held, under Cromwell, a high situation in the Office of Plantations, was appointed in July, 1660, Treasurer and Receiver-General of the Rents and Revenues of James Duke of York; but his royal master's affairs falling into confusion, he surrendered his patent on the 27th

carried Mr. Gauden and I into London to Mr. Bland's, the merchant, where we staid discoursing upon the reason of the delay of the going away of these things a great while. Then to eat a dish of anchovies, and drink wine and syder, and very merry, but above all things pleased to hear Mrs. Bland talk like a merchant in her husband's business very well, and it seems she do understand it and perform a great deal. Thence merry back, Mr. Povy and I to White Hall; he carrying me thither on purpose to carry me into the ball this night before the King. All the way he talking very ingenuously, and I find him a fine gentleman, and one that loves to live nobly and neatly, as I perceive by his discourse of his house, pictures, and horses. He brought me first to the Duke's chamber, where I saw him and the Duchesse at supper; and thence into the room where the ball was to be, crammed with fine ladies, the greatest of the Court. By and by comes the King and Queene, the Duke and Duchesse, and

July, 1668, for a consideration of £2,000. He was also First Treasurer for Tangier, which office he resigned to Pepys. Povy had apartments at White-hall, besides his lodgings in Lincoln's Inn, and a villa near Hounslow, called the Priory, which he had inherited from Justinian Povy, who purchased it in 1625. He was one of the sons of Justinian Povy, Auditor-General to Queen Anne of Denmark in 1614, whose father was John Povy, citizen and embroiderer of London. Justinian obtained a grant of arms: *sable*, a bend engrailed between six cinque-foils, *or*, with an annulet for difference. Thomas Povy had two brothers — Richard, who was Commissioner-General of Provisions at Jamaica; and William, Provost-Marshal at Barbadoes. Evelyn describes Thomas Povy, then one of the Masters of Requests [" Diary," 29th February, 1675-6], as " a nice contriver of all elegances, and exceedingly formal." By Pepys's report he was " a wretched accountant." His letter-books are in the British Museum.

all the great ones: and after seating themselves, the King takes out the Duchesse of York; and the Duke, the Duchesse of Buckingham; the Duke of Monmouth, my Lady Castlemaine; and so other lords other ladies: and they danced the Bransle.[1]   After that, the King led a lady a single Coranto;[2] and then the rest of the lords, one after another, other ladies: very noble it was, and great pleasure to see.   Then to country dances; the King leading the first, which he called for; which was, says he, "Cuckolds all awry,"[3] the old dance of England.   Of the ladies that danced, the Duke of Monmouth's mistress, and my Lady Castlemaine, and a daughter of Sir Harry de Vicke's,[4] were the best.   The manner was, when the King dances, all the ladies in the room, and the Queene

---

[1] *Branle.* Espèce de danse de plusieurs personnes, qui se tiennent par la main, et qui se menent tour-à-tour. — *Dictionnaire de l'Académie.*

Bransle, or branle, or brawl, a kind of dance, not unlike a country dance.

"Master, will you win your love with a French *brawl ?*"
                    SHAKESPEARE, *Love's Labour's Lost*, act iii. sc. 1.

It seems that several persons united in this dance, and took hands to perform it, and that it contained some kind of representation of a battle.

" My grave Lord Keeper led the *brawls ;*
The seals and maces danced before him."
                              GRAY.   (M. B.)

[2] *Coranto*, from correre, Italian, to run. A swift and lively dance.

" And teach lavoltas high, and swift *corantos*."
              SHAKESPEARE, *Henry V.*, act iii. sc. 5.   (M. B.)

The tune of " Cuckolds all awry " may be seen in Chappell's " Collection."

[4] Sir Henry de Vic of Guernsey, Bart., had been twenty years Resident for Charles II. at Brussels, and was Chancellor of the Order of the Garter. He died 1672, and was buried in Westminster Abbey. His only daughter, Anne Charlotte, married John Lord Fresheville, Baron of Stavely.

herself, stand up : and indeed he dances rarely, and much better than the Duke of York. Having staid here as long as I thought fit, to my infinite content, it being the greatest pleasure I could wish now to see at Court, I went out, leaving them dancing.

Thus ends this year with great mirth to me and my wife. Our condition being thus :—we are at present spending a night or two at my Lord's lodgings at White Hall. Our home at the Navy-office, which is and hath a pretty while been in good condition, finished and made very convenient. My family is myself and wife, William, my clerke; Jane, my wife's upper mayde, but, I think, growing proud and negligent upon it : we must part, which troubles me; Susan, our cook-mayde, a pretty willing wench, but no good cooke; and Wayneman, my boy, who I am now turning away for his naughty tricks. We have had from the beginning our healths to this day very well, blessed be God! Our late mayde Sarah going from us (though put away by us) to live with Sir W. Pen do trouble me, though I love the wench, so that we do make ourselves a little strange to him and his family for it, and resolved to do so. The same we are for other reasons to my Lady Batten and hers. By my last year's diligence in my office, blessed be God! I am come to a good degree of knowledge therein; and am acknowledged so by all the world, even the Duke himself, to whom I have a good accesse : and by that, and my being Commissioner with him for Tangier, he takes much notice of me; and I doubt not but, by the continuance of the same endeavours, I shall in a little time come to be a man much taken notice of in the world, specially being come to so great an esteem with Mr. Coventry. The only weight that lies heavy upon my mind is the ending the business with my uncle Thomas about my dead uncle's estate, which is very ill on our side, and I fear when all is done I must be forced to maintain my father myself, or spare a good deal towards it out of my own purse, which will be a very great pull back to me in my fortune. But I must be contented and bring it to an issue one way or other. Publique matters stand thus: The King is bringing, as is said, his family, and Navy, and all other his charges, to a less expence. In the mean time, himself following his pleasures more than with good advice he would do; at least, to be seen to all the world to do so. His dalliance with my Lady Castlemaine being publique, every day, to his great reproach; and his favouring of none at Court so much as those that are the confidants of his pleasure, as Sir H. Bennet and Sir Charles Barkeley; which, good God! put it into his heart to mend, before he makes himself too much contemned by his people for it! The Duke of Monmouth is in so great splendour at Court, and so dandled by the King, that some doubt, if the King should have no child by the Queene (which there is yet no appearance of), whether he would not be acknowledged for a lawful son; and that there will be a difference follow upon it between the Duke of York and him; which God prevent! My Lord Chancellor is threatened by people to be questioned, the next sitting of the Parliament, by some spirits that do not love to see him so great: but certainly he is a good servant to the King. The Queene-Mother is said to keep too great a Court now; and her being married to my Lord St. Alban's is commonly talked of; and that they had a daughter between them in France, how true, God knows. The Bishopps are high, and go on without any diffidence in pressing uniformity; and the Presbyters seem silent in it, and either conform or lay down, though without doubt they expect a turn, and would be glad these endeavours of the other Fanatiques would take effect; there having been a plot lately found, for which four have been publickly tried at the Old Bayley and hanged. My Lord Sandwich is still in good esteem, and now keeping his Christmas in the country; and I in good esteem, I think, as any man can be, with him. Mr. Moore is very sickly, and I doubt will hardly get over his late fit of sicknesse, that still hangs on him. In fine, for the good condition of myself, wife, family, and estate, in the great degree that it is, and for the public state of the nation, so quiett as it is, the Lord God be praised!

January 1st, 1662–3. To White Hall, where I spent a little time walking among the courtiers, which I perceive I shall be able to do with great confidence, being now beginning to be pretty well known among them. Among other discourse, Mrs. Sarah tells us

how the King sups at least four times every week
with my Lady Castlemaine; and most often stays till
the morning with her, and goes home through the
garden all alone privately, and that so as the very
centrys take notice of it and speak of it. She tells
me, that about a month ago she [Lady Castlemaine]
quickened at my Lord Gerard's [1] at dinner, and cried
out that she was undone; and all the lords and men
were fain to quit the room, and women called to
helpe her. In fine, I find that there is nothing
almost but bawdry at Court from top to bottom, as,
if it were fit, I could instance, but it is not necessary;
only they say my Lord Chesterfield, groom of the stole
to the Queene, is either gone or put away from the
Court upon the score of his lady's having smitten the
Duke of York, so as that he is watched by the Duchesse of York, and his lady is retired into the country
upon it. How much of this is true, God knows, but
it is common talke. After dinner to the Duke's
house,[2] where we saw "The Villaine" againe; and
the more I see it, the more I am offended at my first
undervaluing the play, it being very good and pleas-

---

[1] Charles Lord Gerard of Brandon, Gentleman of the Bedchamber to
Charles II., and Captain of his Guards; created Earl of Macclesfield 1679,
and died about 1693. His wife, mentioned afterwards, was a French lady,
whose name has not been preserved. Macclesfield House, then Lord Gerard's
residence, was in Soho. The names are preserved in Macclesfield Street and
Gerard Street.

[2] The Duke's Theatre, so called from the Duke of York. The Duke's,
or Sir William Davenant's Company, removed in 1662 from Salisbury Court,
near Fleet Street, to a new theatre in Portugal Row, or Portugal Street, near
Lincoln's Inn Fields. (M. B.)

ant, and yet a true and allowable tragedy. The house was full of citizens, and so the less pleasant, but that I was to make an end of my gaddings, and to set to my business for all the year again to-morrow. Here we saw the old Roxalana [1] in the chief box, in a velvet gowne, as the fashion is, and very handsome, at which I was glad. So to my office to set down these two or three days' journall, and to close the last year therein, and so that being done, home to supper, and to bed, with great pleasure talking and discoursing with my wife of our late observations abroad.

2nd. To the office, dined at home, and in the afternoon to the Treasury office, where Sir W. Batten was paying off tickets, but so simply and arbitrarily, upon a dull pretence of doing right to the King, but to the wrong of poor people, that I was weary of it. At last we broke up, and I to see Sir W. Pen, who is fallen sicke again. I staid a while talking with him, and so to my office, practising some arithmetique.

4th (Lord's day). Up and to church, where a lazy sermon, and so home to dinner to a good piece of powdered beef,[2] but a little too salt. At dinner my wife did propound my having of my sister Pall again to be her woman, since one we must have, hoping that in that quality possibly she may prove better than she did before, which I take very well of her, and will consider of it, it being a very great trouble to me that I should have a sister of so ill a nature, that I

---

[1] Mrs. Davenport.   [2] Salted beef. (M. B.)

must be forced to spend money upon a stranger when it might better be upon her, if she were good for anything. After dinner I and she walked, though it was dirty, to White Hall, being much afeard of being seen by anybody, and was, I think, of Mr. Coventry, which so troubled me that I made her go before, and I ever after loitered behind. She to Mr. Hunt's, and I to White Hall Chappell, and then up to walk up and down the house, which now I am well known there, I shall forbear to do, because I would not be thought a lazy body by Mr. Coventry and others by being seen, as I have lately been, to walk up and down doing nothing. So to Mr. Hunt's, and there was most prettily and kindly entertained by him and her, who are two as good people as I hardly know any, and so neat and kind one to another. Here we staid late, and so to my Lord's to bed.

5th. Up and to the Duke, who himself told me that Sir J. Lawson was come home to Portsmouth from the Streights with great renowne among all men, and, I perceive, mightily esteemed at Court by all. The Duke did not stay long in his chamber; but to the King's chamber, whither by and by the Russia Embassadors come; who, it seems, have a custom that they will not come to have any treaty with our or any King's Commissioners, but they will themselves see at the time the face of the King himself, be it forty days one after another; and so they did to-day only go in and see the King; and so out again to the Council-chamber. The Duke returned to his cham-

ber, and so to his closett, where Sir G. Carteret, Sir
J. Minnes, Sir W. Batten, Mr. Coventry, and myself
attended him about the business of the Navy; and
after much discourse and pleasant talke he went away.
And I took Sir W. Batten and Captain Allen into the
wine cellar to my tenant (as I call him, Serjeant Dal-
ton), and there drank a great deal of variety of wines,
more than I have drunk at one time, or shall again
a great while, when I come to return to my oathes,
which I intend in a day or two. Thence to my Lord's
lodging, where Mr. Hunt and Mr. Creed dined with
us, and were very merry. And after dinner he and I
to White Hall, where the Duke and the Commissioners
for Tangier met, but did not do much: my Lord
Sandwich not being in towne, nobody making it their
business. So up, and Creed and I to my wife again,
and after a game or two at cards, to the Cockpitt,
where we saw " Claracilla," [1] a poor play, done by the
King's house; (but neither the King nor Queene were
there, but only the Duke and Duchesse, who did show
some impertinent and, methought, unnaturall dalli-
ances there, before the whole world, such as kissing,
and leaning upon one another); but to my very little
content, they not acting in any degree like the Duke's
people. So home (there being here this night Mrs.
Turner and Mrs. Martha Batten of our office) to my
Lord's lodgings again, and to a game at cards, we
three and Sarah, and so to supper and apples and ale,
and to bed with great pleasure, blessed be God !

---

[1] A tragi-comedy by Thomas Killigrew.

6th (Twelfth Day). Up and Mr. Creed brought a pot of chocolate ready made for our morning draft, and then he and I to the Duke's, but I was not very willing to be seen at this end of the towne, and so returned to our lodgings, and Creed and I to St. Paul's Church-yard, to my bookseller's, and then into St. Paul's Church, and there finding Elborough, my old schoolfellow at Paul's, now a parson, whom I know to be a silly fellow, I took him out and walked with him, making Mr. Creed and myself sport with talking with him, and so sent him away, and thence to the Exchange, where we met with Major Thomson, formerly of our office, who do talk very highly of liberty of conscience, which now he hopes for by the King's declaration, and that he doubts not that if he will give it, he will find more and better friends than the Bishopps can be to him, and that if he do not, there will many thousands in a little time go out of England, where they may have it. But he says that they are well contented that if the King thinks it good, the Papists may have the same liberty with them. He tells me, and so do others, that Dr. Calamy is this day sent to Newgate for preaching, Sunday was se'nnight, without leave, though he did it only to supply the place ; when otherwise the people must have gone away without ever a sermon, they being disappointed of a minister : but the Bishop of London will not take that as an excuse. Thence into Wood Street, and there bought a fine table for my dining-room, cost me 50*s.* ; and while we were buying it, there was a scare-fire[1] in an ally over against us, but they quenched it. After dinner to the Duke's house, and there saw "Twelfth Night" acted well, though it be but a silly play, and not related at all to the name or day. Home and found all well, only myself somewhat vexed at my wife's neglect in leaving of her scarfe, waistcoate, and night-dressings in the coach to-day that brought us from Westminster, though, I confess, she did give them to me to look after. I believe it might be as good as 25*s.* loss or thereabouts. So to my office to set down my last three days' journall, and writing to my father about my sending him some wine and things this week, for his making an entertainment of some friends in the country, and so home. This night making an end wholly of Christmas, with a mind fully satisfied with the great pleasures we have had by being abroad from home, and I do find my mind so apt to run to its old want of pleasures, that it is high time to betake myself to my late vowes, which I will to-morrow, God willing, perfect and bind myself to, that so I may, for a great while, do my duty, as I have well begun, and increase my good name and esteem in the world, and get money, which sweetens all things, and whereof I have much need. So home to supper and to bed, blessing God for his mercy to bring me home, after much pleasure, to my house and business with health and resolution to fall hard to worke again.

---

[1] *Scar-fire* or *scarefire*. An alarm of fire; the cry, *Fire, fire;* or sometimes, as here, the fire itself. (M. B.)

7th. Up pretty early, that is by seven o'clock, it not being yet light before or then. So to my office all the morning, signing the Treasurer's ledger, part of it where I have not put my hand, and then eat a mouthful of pye at home to stay my stomach, and so with Mr. Waith by water to Deptford, and there among other things viewed old pay-books, and found that the Commanders did never heretofore receive pay for the rigging time, but only for seatime, contrary to what Sir J. Minnes and Sir W. Batten told the Duke the other day. I also searched all the ships in the Wett Docke for fire, and found all in good order, it being very dangerous for the King that so many of his ships lie together there. I was among the canvass in stores also, with Mr. Harris, the saylemaker, and learnt the difference between one sort and another, to my great content, and so by water home again, where my wife tells me stories how she hears that by Sarah's going to live at Sir W. Pen's, all our affairs of my family are made known and discoursed of there and theirs by my people, which do trouble me much, and I shall take a time to let Sir W. Pen know how he has dealt in taking her without our full consent. So to the office, and by and by home to supper, and so to prayers and to bed.

8th. Up pretty early, and sent my boy to the carrier's with some wine for my father, for to make his feast among his Brampton friends this Christmas, and my muffe to my mother, sent as from my wife. But before I sent my boy out, I beat him for a lie he told me. Dined at home; and there being the famous new play acted the first time to-day, which is called "The Adventures of Five Hours," at the Duke's house, being, they say, made or translated by Colonel Tuke,[1] I did long to see it; and so we went; and though early, were forced to sit almost out of sight, at the end of one of the lower formes, so full was the house. And the play, in one word, is the best, for the variety and the most excellent continuance of the plot to the very end, that ever I saw, or think ever shall, and all possible, not only to be done in the time, but in most other respects very admittable, and without one word of ribaldry; and the house, by its frequent plaudits, did show their sufficient approbation. So home; with much ado in an houre getting a coach home, and now resolving to set up my rest as to plays till Easter, if not Whitsuntide next, excepting plays at Court.

9th. Waking in the morning, my wife begun to speak again of the necessity of her keeping somebody to bear her company; for her familiarity with her other servants is it that spoils them all, and other company she hath none, which is too true, and called for Jane to reach her out of her trunk, giving her the keys to that purpose, a bundle of papers, and pulls out a paper, a copy of what, a pretty while since, she had wrote in a discontent to me, which I would not read, but burnt. She now read it, and it was so

---

[1] Sir George Tuke of Cressing Temple, in Essex, Mr. Evelyn's cousin. The play was taken from the original of the Spanish poet Calderon.

piquant, and wrote in English, and most of it true, of the retiredness of her life, and how unpleasant it was; that being wrote in English, and so in danger of being met with and read by others, I was vexed at it, and desired her and then commanded her to tear it. When she desired to be excused it, I forced it from her, and tore it, and withal took her other bundle of papers from her, and leapt out of the bed and clapped them into the pocket of my breeches, that she might not get them from me, and having got on my stockings and breeches and gowne, I pulled them out one by one and tore them all before her face, though it went against my heart to do it, she crying and desiring me not to do it, but such was my passion and trouble to see the letters of my love to her, and my Will wherein I had given her all I have in the world, when I went to sea with my Lord Sandwich, to be joyned with a paper of so much disgrace to me and dishonour, if it should have been found by any body. Having torn them all, saving a bond of my uncle Robert's, which she hath long had in her hands, and our marriage license, and the first letter that ever I sent her when I was her servant,[1] I took up the pieces and carried them into my chamber, and there, after many disputes with myself whether I should burn them or no, and having picked up the pieces of the paper she read to-day, and of my Will which I tore, I burnt all the rest, and so went out to my office troubled in

---

[1] Lover. (M. B.)

mind.   Hither comes Major Tolhurst, one of my old acquaintance in Cromwell's time, and sometimes of our clubb, to see me, and I could do no less than carry him to the Mitre, Tolhurst telling me the manner of their collierys in the north.   We broke up, and I home to dinner.   And to see my folly, as discontented as I am, when my wife came I could not forbear smiling all dinner till she began to speak bad words again, and then I began to be angry, and so to my office. Mr. Bland came in the evening to me hither, and sat talking to me about many things of merchandise, and I should be very happy in his discourse, durst I confess my ignorance to him, which is not so fit for me to do.   There coming a letter to me from Mr. Pierce, the surgeon, by my desire appointing his and Dr. Clerke's coming to dine with me next Monday, I went to my wife and agreed upon matters, and at last for my honour am forced to make her presently [1] a new Moyre gowne to be seen by Mrs. Clerke, which troubles me to part with so much money, but, however, it sets my wife and I to friends again, though I and she never were so heartily angry in our lives as to-day almost, and I doubt the heartburning will not be soon over, and the truth is I am sorry for the tearing of so many poor loving letters of mine from sea and elsewhere to her.   So to my office again, and there the Scrivener brought me the end of the manuscript which I am going to get together of things of

---

[1] forthwith.   (M. B.)

the Navy, which pleases me much. So home, and mighty friends with my wife again, and so to bed.

10th. To the office, and sat till noon, then rose and to dinner, and then to the office again, where Mr. Creed sat with me till late talking very good discourse, as he is full of it, though a cunning knave in his heart, at least not to be too much trusted.

11th (Lord's day). Lay long talking pleasant with my wife, then up and to church, and after a pitifull sermon of the young Scott, home to dinner. So to my office all the afternoon writing orders myself to have ready against to-morrow, that I might not appear negligent to Mr. Coventry.

12th. To Sir W. Pen's to see Sir J. Lawson, who I heard was there, where I found him the same plain man that he was, after all his success in the Straights, with which he is come loaded home. Thence to Sir G. Carteret, and with him in his coach to White Hall, and first I to see my Lord Sandwich, and after talking a little with him, he and I to the Duke's chamber, where Mr. Coventry and he and I in the Duke's closett and Sir J. Lawson discoursing upon business of the Navy, and particularly got his consent to the ending some difficulties in Mr. Creed's accounts. Thence with Mr. Creed to the King's Head ordinary, but people being set down, we went to two or three places; at last found some meat at a Welch cook's at Charing Crosse, and here dined and our boys. After dinner to the 'Change to buy some linen for my wife, and going back met our two boys. Mine had struck down

Creed's boy in the dirt, with his new suit on, and the boy taken by a gentlewoman into a house to make clean, but the poor boy was in a pitifull taking and pickle; but I basted my rogue soundly. Thence to my Lord's lodgings. I found my Lord within, and he and I went out through the garden towards the Duke's chamber, to sit upon the Tangier matters; but a lady called to my Lord out of my Lady Castlemaine's lodging, telling him that the King was there and would speak with him. My Lord could not tell what to bid me say at the Committee to excuse his absence, but that he was with the King; nor would suffer me to go into the Privy Garden (which is now a through-passage, and common), but bid me to go through some other way, which I did; so that I see he is a servant of the King's pleasures too, as well as business. So I went to the Committee, where we spent all this night attending to Sir J. Lawson's description of Tangier and the place for the Mole, of which he brought a very pretty draught. So to my Lady Batten's, and sat with her awhile; but I did it out of design to get some oranges for my feast to-morrow of her, which I did. So home, and found my wife's new gowne come home, and she mightily pleased with it. But I appeared very angry that there were no more things got ready against to-morrow's feast, and in that passion sat up long, and went discontented to bed.

13th. So my poor wife rose by five o'clock in the morning, before day, and went to market and bought fowles and many other things for dinner, with which

I was highly pleased, and the chine of beef was down also before six o'clock, and my own jacke, of which I was doubtfull, do carry it very well. Things being put in order, and the cooke come, I went to the office, where we sat till noon and then broke up, and I home, whither by and by comes Dr. Clerke and his lady, his sister, and a she-cozen, and Mr. Pierce and his wife, which was all my guests. I had for them, after oysters, at first course, a hash of rabbits, a lamb, and a rare chine of beef. Next a great dish of roasted fowle, cost me about 30*s.*, and a tarte, and then fruit and cheese. My dinner was noble and enough. I had my house mighty clean and neat; my room below with a good fire in it; my dining-room above, and my chamber being made a withdrawing-chamber; and my wife's a good fire also. I find my new table very proper, and will hold nine or ten people well, but eight with great room. After dinner the women to cards in my wife's chamber. At night to supper, had a good sacke posset and cold meat, and sent my guests away about ten o'clock at night, both them and myself highly pleased with our management of this day; and indeed their company was very fine, and Mrs. Clerke a very witty, fine lady, though a little conceited and proud. I believe this day's feast will cost me near 5*l.*

14th. To the office till 10 at night upon business, and numbering and examining part of my sea-manuscript with great pleasure, my wife sitting working by me.

15th. I took Mr. Coventry to dine with me, I having

a wild goose roasted, and a cold chine of beef and a barrel of oysters ; and then he and I to fit ourselves for horseback, he having brought me a horse ; and so to Deptford, the ways being very dirty. There we walked up and down the Yarde and Wett Docke, and did our main business, which was to examine the proof of our new way of the call-bookes, which we think will be of great use. And so I home with his horse, leaving him to go over the fields to Lambeth.

16th. Mr. Battersby, the apothecary, coming to see me, I called for the cold chine of beef and made him eat, and drink wine, and talked, there being with us Captain Brewer, the paynter, who tells me how highly the Presbyters do talk in the coffee-houses still, which I wonder at.

17th. Sat till two o'clock and then home to dinner, and Creed with me, and after dinner I took Creed by coach and to the Duke's playhouse, where we did see "The Five Hours" entertainment again, which indeed is a very fine play, though, through my being out of order, it did not seem so good as at first ; but I could discern it was not any fault in the play. Thence with him to the China alehouse, and there drank a bottle or two, and so home.

18th (Lord's day). Up, and after the barber had done I went to church, and thence home to dinner alone with my wife, very pleasant, and after dinner to church again, and heard a dull, drowsy sermon, and so home and to my office, perfecting my vowes again for the next year, which I have now done, and sworn to in the presence of Almighty God to observe upon the respective penalties thereto annexed, and then to Sir W. Pen's, to see how he do, and find him pretty well, and ready to go abroad again.

19th. Up and to White Hall, and while the Duke is dressing himself I went to wait on my Lord Sandwich, whom I found not very well, and Dr. Clerke with him. He is feverish, and hath sent for Mr. Pierce to let him blood. Then to the Duke, and in his closett discoursed as we use to do, and then broke up. That done, I singled out Mr. Coventry into the matted gallery, and there I told him the complaints I meet every day about our Treasurer's or his people's paying no money, but at the goldsmith's shops, where they are forced to pay fifteen or twenty sometimes per cent. for their money, which is a most horrid shame, and that which must not be suffered. Nor is it likely that the Treasurer (at least his people) will suffer Maynell the Goldsmith to go away with 10,000*l*. per annum, as he do now get, by making people pay after this manner for their money. To Mr. Povy's, where really he made a most excellent and large dinner, of their variety, even to admiration, he bidding us, in a frolique, to call for what we had a mind, and he would undertake to give it us: and we did for prawns, swan, venison, after I had thought the dinner was quite done, and he did immediately produce it, which I thought great plenty, and he seems to set off his rest in this plenty and the neatness of his house, which he after dinner showed me, from room to room, so beset with delicate pictures,

and above all, a piece of perspective in his closett in
the low parler; his stable, where was some most delicate horses, and the very racks painted, and mangers,
with a neat leaden painted cistern, and the walls done
with Dutch tiles, like my chimnies. But still, above
all things, he bid me go down into his wine-cellar,
where upon several shelves there stood bottles of all
sorts of wine, new and old, with labells pasted upon
each bottle, and in the order and plenty as I never
saw books in a bookseller's shop; and herein, I observe, he puts his highest content, and will accordingly
commend all that he hath, but still they deserve to be
so. Here dined with me Dr. Whore and Mr. Scawen.
To my Lord Chancellor's, where the King was to meet
my Lord Treasurer, &c., many great men, to settle
the revenue of Tangier. I staid talking awhile there,
but the King not coming I walked to my brother's.
This day, by Dr. Clerke, I was told the occasion of
my Lord Chesterfield's going and taking his lady (my
Lord Ormond's daughter) from Court. It seems he
not only hath been long jealous of the Duke of York,
but did find them two talking together, though there
were others in the room, and the lady by all opinions
a most good, virtuous woman. He, the next day, (of
which the Duke was warned by somebody that saw
the passion my Lord Chesterfield was in the night
before,) went and told the Duke how much he did
apprehend himself wronged, in his picking out his lady
of the whole Court to be the subject of his dishonour;
which the Duke did answer with great calmnesse, not

seeming to understand the reason of complaint, and that was all that passed : but my Lord did presently pack his lady into the country in Derbyshire, near the Peake,[1] which is become a proverb at Court, to send a man's wife to the Devil's **** a' Peake, when she vexes him.

21st. Commissioner Pett and I by agreement went to Deptford, and after a turne or two in the yarde, to Greenwich, and thence walked to Woolwich. Here we did business, and on board the Tangier-merchant, a ship freighted by us, that has long lain on hand in her despatch to Tangier, but is now ready for sailing. Back, and dined at Mr. Ackworth's,[2] where a pretty dinner, and she a pretty, modest woman ; but above all things we saw her Rocke, which is one of the finest things done by a woman that ever I saw. I must have my wife to see it. After dinner on board the Elias, and found the timber brought by her from the forest of Deane to be exceeding good. The Captain gave each of us two barrels of pickled oysters put up for the Queene mother. So to the Docke again, and took in Mrs. Ackworth and another gentlewoman, and carried them to London, and at the Globe taverne, in Eastcheap, did give them a glass of wine, and so parted. I home.

22nd. To the office, where Sir W. Batten and Sir J. Minnes are come from Portsmouth. We sat till

---

[1] Bretby Hall, the country-seat of the Earls of Chesterfield, is no longer standing. There is a good view of it by Knyff and Kip.

[2] Who held some office in Deptford Yard.

dinner time. Then home, and Mr. Dixon by agreement came to dine, to give me an account of his
success with Mr. Wheatly for his daughter for my
brother; and in short it is, that his daughter cannot
fancy my brother because of his imperfection in his
speech, which I am sorry for, but there the business
must die, and we must look out for another. There
came in also Mrs. Lodum, with an answer from her
brother Ashwell's daughter, who is likely to come to
me, and with her my wife's brother, and I carried
Commissioner Pett in with me, so I feared want of
victuals, but I had a good dinner, and mirth, and so
rose and broke up, and with the rest of the officers
to Mr. Russell's buriall, where we had wine and rings,
and a great and good company of aldermen and the
livery of the Skinners' Company. We went to St.
Dunstan's in the East church, where a sermon, but
I staid not. So to my Lord's, and there find him
not sicke, but expecting his fit to-night of an ague.
Here we were very busy about getting provisions sent
forthwith to Tangier.

23rd. Up and hastened Mr. Creed in despatching
some business relating to Tangier, and I away, hearing
that my Lord had a bad fit. Thence to Mr. Grant,
and he and I to a coffee-house, where Sir J. Cutler [1]

---

[1] Citizen and grocer of London; most severely handled by Pope. Two
statues were erected to his memory — one in the College of Physicians, and
the other in the Grocers' Hall. They were erected and one removed (that in
the College of Physicians) before Pope stigmatized "sage Cutler." Pope
says that Sir John Cutler had an only daughter; in fact, he had two: one

was; and he did finally make it out that the trade of England is as great as ever it was, only in more hands; and that of all trades there is a greater number than ever there was, by reason of men taking more 'prentices, because of their having more money than heretofore. His discourse was well worth hearing. Coming by Temple Bar I bought "Audley's Way to be Rich,"[1] a serious pamphlett, and some good things worth my minding. Thence homewards, and meeting Sir W. Batten, turned back again to a coffee-house, and there drunk more and hear much discourse, but little to be learned, but of a design in the north of a rising, which is discovered, among some men of condition, and they sent for up. Thence to the 'Change, and so to dinner to Sir W. Batten's to a cod's head, and so to my office, and after stopping to see Sir W. Pen where was Sir J. Lawson and his lady and daughter, which is pretty enough, I came back, and there set to business pretty late, finishing the margenting my Navy-Manuscript. So home and to bed.

24th. To the office all the morning, then to the Exchange to look out for a ship for Tangier. So to dinner at home, and then down to Redriffe, to see a ship hired for Tangier, and found her ready to sail.

25th (Lord's day). Lay till 9 a-bed, then up, and

---

married to Lord Radnor; the other, mentioned afterwards by Pepys, the wife of Sir William Portman.

[1] Vide note, 23rd November, 1662.

being trimmed by the barber, I walked towards White Hall, calling upon Mr. Moore, whom I found still very ill of his ague. I discoursed with him about my Lord's estate against I speak with my Lord this day. Thence to the King's Head ordinary at Charing Crosse, and sent for Mr. Creed, where we dined very finely and good company, good discourse. I understand the King of France is upon consulting his divines upon the old question, what the power of the Pope is? and do intend to make war against him, unless he do right him for the wrong his Embassador [1] received; and banish the Cardinall Imperiall, by which I understand this day is not meant the Cardinall belonging or chosen by the Emperor, but the name of his family is Imperiali.[2] Thence to walk in the Parke, which we did two hours. Our discourse upon the rise of most men that we know, and observing them to be the results of chance, not policy, in

---

[1] On the 20th of August the Duc de Créqui, then French ambassador at Rome, was insulted by the Corsican armed police, a force whose ignoble duty it was to assist the Sbirri, and the Pope Alexander VII. at first refused reparation for the affront offered to the French. Louis, as in the case of D'Estrades, took prompt measures. He ordered the Papal Nuncio forthwith to quit France; he seized upon Avignon, and his army prepared to enter Italy. Alexander found it necessary to submit. In fulfilment of a treaty signed at Pisa in 1664, Cardinal Chigi, the Pope's nephew, came to Paris, to tender the Pope's apology to Louis. The guilty individuals were punished; the Corsicans banished for ever from the Roman States; and in front of the guard-house which they had occupied a pyramid was erected, bearing an inscription, which embodied the Pope's apology. This pyramid Louis permitted Clement IX. to destroy on his accession.

[2] Lorenzo Imperiali, of Genoa. He had been appointed Governor of Rome by Innocent X., in 1654, and he had acted in that capacity at the time of the tumult.

any of them, particularly Sir J. Lawson's, from his
declaring against Charles Stuart in the river of
Thames, and for the Rump.   Thence to my Lord,
who had his ague fit last night, but is now pretty
well, and I staid talking with him an houre alone in
his chamber, about sundry publique and private matters.   Among others, he wonders what the project
should be of the Duke's going down to Portsmouth
again now with his Lady, at this time of the year : it
being no way, we think, to increase his popularity,
which is not great ; nor yet safe to do it, for that
reason, if it would have any such effect.   Captn.
Ferrers tells me of my Lady Castlemaine's and Sir
Charles Barkeley being the great favourites at Court,
and growing every day more and more so ; and that
upon a late dispute between my Lord Chesterfield,
that is the Queene's Lord Chamberlain, and Mr.
Edward Montagu, her Master of the Horse, who
should have the precedence in taking the Queene's
upperhand abroad out of the house, which Mr. Montagu challenges, it was given to my Lord Chesterfield.
So that I perceive he goes down the wind in honour
as well as every thing else, every day.   So walk to
my brother's and talked with him, who tells me that
this day a messenger is come, that tells us how
Collonel Honiwood,[1] who was well yesterday at Can-

---

[1] Colonel Henry Honywood, of Little Archer's Court River, Kent, who
had taken up arms against Charles I. He was the son of Arthur Honywood,
of Lincoln's Inn and Maidstone, and had sepulture at Christ Church, Canterbury. — HASTED'S *Kent*, vol. iv. p. 40.

terbury, was flung by his horse in getting up, and broke his scull, and so is dead.

26th. Up and by water with Sir W. Batten to White Hall, drinking a glasse of wormewood wine at the Stillyard, and so up to the Duke, and with the rest of the officers did our common service; thence to my Lord Sandwich's, but he was in bed, and had a bad fit last night, and so I went to Westminster Hall, it being Terme time, it troubling me to think that I should have any business there to trouble myself and thoughts with. Here I met with Monsieur Raby, who is lately come from France. He tells me that my Lord Hinchingbroke and his brother do little improve there, and are much neglected in their habits and other things; but I do believe he hath a mind to go over as their tutour, and so I am not apt to believe what he says therein. But I had a great deal of very good discourse with him, concerning the difference between the French and the Pope, and the occasion, which he told me very particularly, and to my great content; and of most of the chief affairs of France, which I did enquire: and that the King is a most excellent Prince, doing all business himself; and that it is true he hath a mistresse, Madamoiselle La Valiere, one of the Princess Henriette's women, that he courts for his pleasure every other day, but not so as to make him neglect his publique affairs. He tells me how the King do carry himself nobly to the relations of the dead Cardinall,[1] and will not suffer one pasquill

---

[1] Cardinal Mazarine.

to come forth against him ; and that he acts by what directions he received from him before his death. Having discoursed long with him, I went and dined at Mr. Povy's, and had just such another dinner as I had the other day there. But above all things I do the most admire his piece of perspective especially, he opening me the closett door, and there I saw that there is nothing but only a plain picture hung upon the wall. After dinner Mr. Gauden and I to settle the business of the Tangier victualling, which I perceive none of them yet have hitherto understood but myself. Thence by coach to White Hall, and met upon the Tangier Commission, our greatest business the discoursing of getting things ready for my Lord Rutherford to go about the middle of March next. So by coach home, being melancholy, overcharged with business, and methinks I fear that I have some ill offices done to Mr. Coventry. I believe that Sir W. Batten has made him believe that I do too much crow upon having his kindness.

27th. I have news this day from Cambridge that my brother hath had his bachelor's cap put on ; but that which troubles me is, that he hath the pain of the stone, it beginning just as mine did.

28th. To my Lord Sandwich's, whom I find missing his ague fit to-day, and is pretty well, playing at dice, and by this means I see how time and example may alter a man ; he being now acquainted with all sorts of pleasures and vanities, which heretofore he never thought of nor loved, nor, it may be, hath allowed, with Ned Pickering and his page Loud. Thence to the Temple to my cozen Roger Pepys, and thence to Serjt. Bernard to advise with him and retain him against my uncle, my heart and head being very heavy with the business. Thence to Wotton's, the shoemaker, and there bought another pair of new boots, and here I drank with him and his wife, a pretty woman, they broaching a vessel of syder a-purpose for me. So home, and there found my wife come home, and seeming to cry; for bringing home in a coach her new ferrandin ¹ waistecoate, in Cheapside, a man asked her whether that was the way to the Tower; and while she was answering him, another, on the other side, snatched away her bundle out of her lap, and could not be recovered, but ran away with it, which vexes me cruelly, but it cannot be helped. So to my office, and there till almost 12 at night with Mr. Lewes, learning to understand the manner of a purser's account, which is very hard and little understood by my fellow officers, and yet mighty necessary. So at last with great content broke up and home to supper and bed.

---

¹ Farrendine or Ferrandine. There is uncertainty as to the precise nature of this material. Mr. Wright, in his " Dictionary of Obsolete Words," describes it as a coarse sort of stuff. From resemblance to the French word *ferrandine*, a silk stuff, some have thought it to be a kind of silk; others think it was cloth, and so named from Farringdon, in Berkshire, a county formerly celebrated for its woollen manufactures. In the list of Lord Shaftesbury's wardrobe, there is mentioned:

"A new farwendine suit and coat, with garters, knots, and waist-belt.

"*Item.* An old farwendine suit, laced with garters and knots."

See " Life of first Earl of Shaftesbury," by Christie, vol. ii. p. 103. (M. B.'

29th. Lay chiding, and then pleased with my wife and did consent to her having a new waistcoate made her for that which she lost yesterday. So to the office. At noon dined with Mr. Coventry at Sir J. Minnes his lodgings, the first time that ever I did yet, and am sorry for doing it now, because of obliging me to do the like to him again.

30th. A solemn fast for the King's murther, and we were forced to keep it more than we would have done, having forgot to take any victuals into the house. I to church in the forenoon, and Mr. Mills made a good sermon upon David's heart smiting him for cutting off the garment of Saul. So to my office, and all alone making up my month's accounts, which to my great trouble I find that I am got no further than 640*l.* But I have had great expenses this month, I pray God the next may be a little better. My manuscript is brought home handsomely bound, to my full content; and now I think I have a better collection in reference to the Navy, and shall have by the time I have filled it, than any of my predecessors.

31st. Up and to my office, and there we sat till noon. So home to dinner late, and not very good, only a rabbit not half roasted, which made me angry with my wife. In the evening examining my wife's letter intended to my Lady, and another to Mademoiselle; they were so false spelt that I was ashamed of them, and took occasion to fall out about them with my wife, and so she wrote none, at which, however, I was sorry, because it was in answer to a letter of Madam about business. Late home to supper, and to bed.

February 1st (Lord's day). Up and to church, a good sermon. So home and had a good dinner with my wife, which I was pleased to see it neatly done. After dinner walked to my Lord Sandwich. Many discourses we had; but, among others, how Sir R. Bernard is turned out of his Recordership of Huntingdon by the Commissioners for Regulation, &c., at which I am troubled, because he, thinking it is done by my Lord Sandwich, will act some of his revenge, it is likely, upon me in my business, so that I must cast about me to get some other counsel to rely upon. It being a fine frost, my boy lighting me I walked home, and after supper up to prayers, and then alone with my wife and Jane did fall to tell her what I did expect would become of her since, after so long being my servant, she had carried herself so as to make us be willing to put her away, and desired God to bless her, but bid her never to let me hear what became of her, for that I could never pardon ingratitude. This day Creed and I walking in White Hall garden did see the King coming privately from my Lady Castlemaine's; which is a poor thing for a Prince to do; and I expressed my sense of it to Creed in terms which I should not have done, but that I believe he is trusty in that point.

2nd. Up, and after paying Jane her wages, I went away, because I could hardly forbear weeping, and she cried, saying it was not her fault that she went away, and indeed it is hard to say what it is, but only her not desiring to stay that she go now. By coach with Sir J. Minnes and Sir W. Batten to the Duke; and after discourse as usual with him in his closett, I went to my Lord's: the King and Duke being gone to chappell, it being a collar-day, it being Candlemas-day; where I staid with him until towards noon, there being Jonas Moore [1] talking about some mathematical businesses, and thence I walked at noon to Mr. Povy's, where Mr. Gauden met me, and after a neat and plenteous dinner as usual, we fell to our victualling business, till Mr. Gauden and I did almost fall out, he defending himself in the readiness of his provision, when I know that the ships everywhere stay for them. Thence Mr. Povy and I, after a turn in the Parke seeing them slide, met at the Committee for Tangier. Thence with Mr. Coventry down to his chamber, where he did tell me how he did make it not only his desire, but as his greatest pleasure, to make himself an interest by doing business truly and justly, though he thwarts others greater than himself, not striving to make himself friends by addresses; and by this he thinks and observes he do live as contentedly (now he finds himself secured from fear of want), and, take one time with another, as void of fear or cares, or more, than they that (as his own termes were) have quicker pleasures and sharper agonies than he. At my cozen Roger's chamber I met Madam

---

[1] Jonas Moore, a most celebrated mathematician, knighted by Charles II., and made Surveyor of the Ordnance. Ob. 1679.

Turner, she and her daughter having been at the play to-day at the Temple, it being a revelling time with them. Thence called at my brother's, who is at church, at the buriall of young Cumberland, a lusty young man.

3rd. To the office, at noon to dinner, where Mr. Creed dined with me, and Mr. Ashwell, with whom after dinner I discoursed concerning his daughter coming to live with us.

4th. To Paul's Schoole, it being Apposition-day there. I heard some of their speeches, and they were just as schoolboys' used to be, of the seven liberal sciences; but I think not so good as ours were in our time. Thence to Bow Church, to the Court of Arches, where a judge sits, and his proctors about him in their habits, and their pleadings all in Latin. Here I was sworn to give a true answer to my uncle's libells. And back again to Paul's Schoole, and went up to see the head forms posed in Latin, Greek, and Hebrew, but I think they did not answer in any so well as we did, only in geography they did pretty well. Dr. Wilkins [1] and Outram [2] were examiners. So down to the school, where Dr. Crumlum did me much honour by telling many what a present I had made to the school, shewing my Stephanus, in four volumes, cost me 4*l.* 10*s.* He also shewed us,

---

[1] John Wilkins, D.D., afterwards Bishop of Chester.

[2] William Outram, D.D., Prebendary of Westminster. Ob. 1679; one of the ablest and best of the Conformists, and eminent for his piety and charity, and an excellent preacher.

upon my desire, an old edition of the grammar of Colett's, where his epistle to the children is very pretty; and in rehearsing the creed it is said "borne of the cleane Virgin Mary." Thence with Mr. Elborough to a cook's shop to dinner, but I found him a fool, as he ever was, or worse. Thence to my cozen Roger Pepys and Mr. Phillips about my law business, which stand very bad, and so home, where I found our new mayde Mary.

5th. To dinner, and found it so well done, above what I did expect from my mayde Susan, now Jane is gone, that I did call her in and give her sixpence. Thence walked to the Temple, and there at my cozen Roger Pepys' chamber met by appointment with my uncle Thomas and his son Thomas, and there I shewing them a true state of my uncle's estate as he has left it with the debts, &c., lying upon it, we did come to some quiett talke and fair offers against an agreement on both sides, though I do offer quite to the losing of the profit of the whole estate for 8 or 10 years together, yet if we can gain peace, and set my mind at a little liberty, I shall be glad of it. I did give them a copy of this state, and we are to meet to-morrow with their answer.

6th. Up and to my office about business examining people what they could swear against Field, and the whole is, that he has called us cheating rogues and cheating knaves, for which we hope to be even with him. Thence to Lincoln's Inn Fields; and it being too soon to go to dinner, I walked up and down, and looked upon the outside of the new theatre, now a building in Covent Garden,[1] which will be very fine. And so to a bookseller in the Strand, and there bought Hudibras again, it being certainly some ill humour to be so against that which all the world cries up to be the example of wit; for which I am resolved once again to read him, and see whether I can find it or no. So to Mr. Povy's, and there found them at dinner, and dined there, there being, among others, Mr. Williamson,[2] Latin Secretary, who, I perceive, is a pretty knowing man and a scholler, but, it may be, thinks himself to be too much so. Thence to the Temple, to my cozen Roger Pepys, where met us my uncle Thomas and his son; and, after many high demands, we at last came to a kind of agreement upon very hard terms, which are to be prepared in writing against Tuesday next. So home, and being called by a coachman who had a fare in him, he carried me beyond the Old Exchange, and there set down his fare, who would not pay him what was his due, because he carried a stranger with him, and so after wrangling he was fain to be content with 6*d.*, and being vexed the coachman would not carry me home a great while, but set me down there for the other 6*d.*, but with fair words he was willing to it, and

---

[1] Killigrew's, opened 8th of April, 1663.

[2] Joseph Williamson, Keeper of the State Paper Office at White Hall, and in 1663 made Under-Secretary of State, and soon afterwards knighted. In 1664 he became Secretary of State, which appointment he filled four years. He represented Thetford or Rochester in different parliaments, and was in 1678 President of the Royal Society. Ob. 1701.

so I came home and to my office, setting business in order, and so to supper and to bed, my mind being in disorder as to the greatness of this day's business, but yet glad that my trouble therein is like to be over.

7th. To my office, whither by agreement Mr. Coventry came before the time of sitting to confer about preparing an account of the extraordinary charge of the Navy since the King's coming, more than is properly to be applied and called the Navy charge. So by and by we sat till noon. Then home to dinner, and in the afternoon some of us met again, and thence to my writing of letters late, and making my Alphabet to my new Navy book very pretty. And so after writing to my father by the post about the endeavour to come to a composition with my uncle, though a very bad one, desiring him to be contented therewith, I went home to supper and to bed.

8th (Lord's day). Up, and it being a very great frost, I walked to White Hall to chappell, where there preached little Dr. Duport,[1] of Cambridge, upon Josiah's words, — "But I and my house, we will serve the Lord." But though a great scholler, he made the most flat dead sermon, both for matter and manner of delivering that ever I heard, and very long beyond his hour, which made it worse. Thence with Mr. Creed to the King's Head ordinary. After dinner

---

[1] James Duport, D.D., Dean of Peterborough 1664, and Master of Magdalene College, Cambridge, 1668. Ob. 1679.

Sir Thomas Willis [1] and another stranger, and Creed and I, fell a-talking; they of the errours and corruption of the Navy, and great expence thereof, not knowing who I was, which at last I did undertake to confute, and disabuse them: and they took it very well, and I hope it was to good purpose, they being Parliament-men. Creed and I and Captn. Ferrers to the Parke, and there walked finely, seeing people slide, we talking all the while; and Captn. Ferrers telling me, among other Court passages, how about a month ago, at a ball at Court, a child was dropped by one of the ladies in dancing, but nobody knew who, it being taken up by somebody in their handkercher. The next morning all the Ladies of Honour appeared early at Court for their vindication, so that nobody could tell whose this mischance should be. But it seems Mrs. Wells [2] fell sicke that afternoon, and

---

[1] Sir Thomas Willis, Bart., ob. Nov. 1705, aged 90, and was buried at Ditton, in Cambridgeshire, where he possessed some property. In 1679, he had been put out of the Commission of the Peace for that County, for concurring with the Fanatic party in opposing the Court. — COLES's MSS.

[2] Winifred Wells, who has been considered as one of Charles's mistresses; but the "*petite disgrace*," as Hamilton styles it, here related, occurred to another of the Queen's Maids of Honour, Mary Kirk, sister to the Countess of Oxford. She retired from the Court, and, three years afterwards, having assumed the name of Warmestre, and having passed as a widow, married Sir Thomas Vernon, who was Killigrew's cousin. "The merry Mrs. Kirke," says Warburton, speaking of the Court at Oxford, in 1642, "is said to have fascinated the grave Prince Maurice." This was the mother of Lady Vernon. "The Queen," says Lord Cornbury, in a letter to the Marchioness of Worcester, 10th June, 1662, "is much concerned that the English ladies spend so much time in dressing themselves. She fears they bestow but little on God Almighty and on housewifery. We are a very unsettled family, not one Lady of the Bed-Chamber named, besides my Lady Suffolk, who is

hath disappeared ever since, so that it is concluded that it was her. Another story was how my Lady Castlemaine, a few days since, had Mrs. Stuart [1] to an entertainment, and at night began a frolique that they two must be married, and married they were, with ring and all other ceremonies of church service, and ribbands [2] and a sack posset in bed, and flinging the stocking; but in the close, it is said that my Lady Castlemaine, who was the bridegroom, rose, and the King came and took her place. This is said to be very true. Another story was how Captain Ferrers and W. Howe both have often, through my Lady Castlemaine's window, seen her go to bed and Sir Charles Barkeley in her chamber. The little Duke of Monmouth, it seems, is ordered to take place of all Dukes, and so to follow Prince Rupert now, before the Duke of Buckingham, or any else.

---

waiting; and they say both the number and persons you formerly heard mentioned, will be much altered. The four Dressers are fixed, who are my Lady Scroope, Lady Wood, Mrs. Frazier, and Mrs. La Garde. The Maids of Honour are likewise in waiting — viz., Mrs. Cary, Mrs. Stuart, Mrs. Wells, Mrs. Price, Mrs. Boynton, Mrs. Warmestry. The Maids of the Privy Chamber are but two, my Lady Mary Savage and my Lady Betty Livingstone, my Lord Newborough's daughter."— ELIOT WARBURTON's *Memoirs of Prince Rupert*, vol. iii., pp. 461-4. This seems to be the best account of Queen Catherine's household; but Warmestry, if it is correct, was the Maid of Honour's real name, and not that which she assumed when banished from the Court.

[1] Frances Terese, eldest daughter of Walter Stuart, third son of the first Lord Blantyre, one of the greatest beauties of the Court of Charles II., became the third wife of Charles Lennox, sixth Duke of Lennox, and fourth Duke of Richmond. She died October 15, 1702, without issue, having survived her husband thirty years. Pepys spells her name Stuart, Steward, and Stewart; the first is right.

[2] See *ante*, Jan. 24, 1659-60, note.

9th. Could not rise and go to the Duke, as I should have done with the rest, but keep my bed and by the Apothecary's advice, Mr. Battersby, I am to sweat soundly, it being some disorder given the blood, but by what I know not, unless it be by my late quantitys of Dantzic-girkins that I have eaten. In the evening came Sir J. Minnes and Sir W. Batten to see me, and Sir J. Minnes advises me to the same thing, but would not have me take anything from the apothecary, but from him, his Venice treacle being better than the others, which I did consent to and did anon take and fell into a great sweat and slept pretty well.

10th. In the morning most of my disease, that is, itching and pimples, were gone. In the morning visited by Mr. Coventry and others, and very glad I am to see that I was so much inquired after. This evening Sir W. Warren [1] came himself to the door and left a letter and box for me, and went his way. His letter mentions his giving me and my wife a pair of gloves; but, opening the box, we found a pair of plain white gloves for my hand, and a fair state dish of silver, and cup, with my armes, ready cut upon them, worth, I believe, about 18*l.* which is a very noble present, and the best I ever had yet. So after some contentful talke with my wife, she to bed and I to rest.

11th. My wife and I dined on a pullet and I eat heartily, having eat nothing since Sunday but water gruel and posset drink. At night my wife read Sir

---

[1] Afterwards Sir William Warren.

H. Vane's tryall to me and I find it a very excellent thing, worth reading, and him to have been a very wise man.

12th. Up and find myself pretty well and so to the office and there all the morning. Home to dinner, thither there came my wife's brother and brought Mary Ashwell with him, whom we find a very likely person to please us, both for person, discourse and other qualitys. Then came an old man from Mr. Povy, to give me some advice about his experience in the stone, which I am beholden to him for, and was well pleased with it, his chief remedy being Castle Soap in a posset. Then in the evening to the office, late writing letters and my Journall since Saturday, and so home to supper and to bed.

13th. This morning Mr. Cole, our timber merchant, sent me five couple of ducks. Dined upon one couple to day. To my office, where late upon business; Mr. Bland sitting with me, talking of my Lord Windsor's being come home from Jamaica, unlooked-for; which makes us think that these young Lords are not fit to do any service abroad, though it is said that he could not have his health there, but hath razed a fort of the King of Spain upon Cuba, which is considerable, or said to be so, for his honour. This day I bought the second part of Dr. Bates's Elenchus, which reaches to the fall of Richard, and no further, for which I am sorry. This evening my wife had a great mind to choose Valentines against to-morrow, I Mrs. Clerke, or Pierce, she Mr. Hunt or Captain Ferrers,

but I would not because of getting charge both to me
for mine and to them for her, which did not please
her.

14th. To the Temple, where my uncle Thomas, and
his sons both, and I, did meet at my cozen Roger's
and there signe and seale to an agreement. All being
done I took the father and his son Thos. home
by coach, and did pay them 30*l.*, the arrears of the
father's annuity, and with great seeming love parted,
and I presently to bed, my head akeing mightily with
the hot dispute I did hold with my cozen Roger and
them in the business.

15th (Lord's day). Trimmed by the barber, and so
sending Will to church, myself staid at home, hanging up in my green chamber my picture of the Soveraigne. So to dinner, to three more ducks and two
teals, my wife and I. Then to Church, where a dull
sermon. In the morning read over my vowes, which
through sicknesse I could not do the last Lord's day,
and not through forgetfulness or negligence, so that
I hope it is no breach of my vowe not to pay my
forfeiture. So after prayers to bed, talking long with
my wife and teaching her things in astronomy.

16th. By coach to White Hall and, after we had
done our usual business with the Duke, to my Lord
Sandwich and by his desire to Sir W. Wheeler, who
was brought down in a sedan chair from his chamber,
being lame of the goute, to borrow 1000*l.* of him for
my Lord's occasions, but he gave me a very kind
denial that he could not, but if any body else would,

he would be bond with my Lord for it. So to Westminster Hall, and there find great expectation what the Parliament will do, when they come two days hence to sit again, in matters of religion. The great question is, whether the Presbyters will be contented to let the Papists have the same liberty of conscience with them, or no, or rather be denied it themselves: and the Papists, I hear, are very busy designing how to make the Presbyters consent to take their liberty, and to let them have the same with them, which some are apt to think they will. It seems a priest was taken in his vests officiating somewhere in Holborne the other day, and was committed by Secretary Morris, according to law; and they say the Bishop of London did give him thanks for it. Thence to my Lord Crew's and dined there, there being much company, and the abovesaid matter is now the present publique discourse. So to the Temple, where at the Solicitor General's I found Mr. Cholmely and Creed reading to him the agreement for him to put into form about the contract for the Mole at Tangier, which is done at 13*s*. the Cubical yarde, though upon my conscience not one of the Committee, besides the parties concerned, do understand what they do therein, whether they give too much or too little. So home and to see Sir W. Pen, and sat and played at cards with him, his daughter, and Mrs. Rooth, and so to my office a while, and then home and to bed.

17th. Up and to my office, my wife being gone to Chelsey with her brother and sister and Mrs. Lodum,

to see the wassel [1] at the schoole, where Mary Ashwell is. To my Lord Sandwich, whom I found at
cards with Pickering; but he made an end soon: and
so all alone, he told me he had a great secret to tell
me, such as no flesh knew but himself, nor ought;
which was this: — that yesterday morning Eschar,
Mr. Edward Montagu's man, did come to him from
his master with some of the Clerkes of the Exchequer,
for my Lord to sign to their books for the Embassy
money; [2] which my Lord very civilly desired not to
do till he had spoke with his master himself. In the
afternoon, my Lord and my Lady Wright being at
cards in his chamber, in comes Mr. Montagu; and
desiring to speak with my Lord at the window in his
chamber, he began to charge my Lord with the greatest ingratitude in the world: that he that had received
his earldom, garter, 4,000*l.* per annum, and whatever
he is in the world, from him, should now study him
all the dishonour that he could; and so fell to tell my
Lord, that if he should speak all that he knew of him,
he could do so and so. In a word, he did rip up all
that could be said that was unworthy, and in the
basest terms they could be spoken in. To which my
Lord answered with great temper, justifying himself,
but endeavouring to lessen his heat, which was a
strange temper in him, knowing that he did owe all he
hath in the world to my Lord, and that he is now all
that he is by his means and favour. But my Lord did

---

[1] See note, 26th December, 1661. (M. B.)
[2] That to Portugal, respecting the Royal marriage.

forbear to increase the quarrel, knowing that it would
be to no good purpose for the world to see a difference in the family; but did allay them so as that he
fell to weeping. And after much talke (among other
things Mr. Montagu telling him that there was a fellow
in the towne, naming me, that had done ill offices,
and that if he knew it to be so, he would have him
cudgelled) my Lord did promise him that, if upon
account he saw that there was not many tradesmen
unpaid, he would sign the books; but if there was, he
could not bear with taking too great a debt upon him.
So this day he sent him an account, and a letter assuring him there was not above 200*l.* unpaid; and so my
Lord did sign to the Exchequer books. Upon the
whole, I understand fully what a rogue he is, and how
my Lord do think and will think of him ·for the future;
telling me that thus he has served his father my Lord
Manchester, and his whole family, and now himself: ·
and which is worst, that he hath abused, and in
speeches every day do abuse, my Lord Chancellor,
whose favour he hath lost; and hath no friend but
Sir H. Bennet, and that (I knowing the rise of the
friendship) only from the likeness of their pleasures,
and acquaintance, and concernments, they have in the
same matters of lust and baseness; for which, God
forgive them! But he do flatter himself, from promises of Sir H. Bennet, that he shall have a pension of
2,000*l.* per annum, and be made an Earl. My Lord
told me he expected a challenge from him, but told
me there was no great fear of him, for there was no

man lies under such an imputation as he do in the business of Mr. Cholmely, who, though a simple sorry fellow, do brave him and struts before him with the Queene, to the sport and observation of the whole Court. He did keep my Lord at the window, thus reviling and braving him above an houre, my Lady Wright being by; but my Lord tells me she could not hear every word, but did well know what their discourse was; she could hear enough to know that. So that he commands me to keep it as the greatest secret in the world, and bids me beware of speaking words against Mr. Montagu, for fear I should suffer by his passion thereby. After he had told me this I took coach and home and played on the viall, which I have not done this long time before upon any instrument, and at last I to my office, being fearful of being too much taken with musique, for fear of returning to ·my old dotage thereon, and so neglect my business as I used to do. Mr. Pickering tells me the story is very true of the child being dropped at the ball at Court; and that the King had it in his closett a week after, and did dissect it; and making great sport of it, said that in his opinion it must have been a month and three hours old; and that, whatever others think, he hath the greatest loss (it being a boy, as he says), that hath lost a subject by the business. He tells me, too, that the other story, of my Lady Castlemaine's and Stuart's marriage, is certain, and that it was in order to the King's coming to Stuart, as is believed generally. He tells me that Sir H. Bennet is a Catholique, and how all the Court almost is changed to the worse since his coming in, they being afeard of him. And that the Queene-Mother's Court is now the greatest of all; and that our own Queene hath little or no company come to her, which I know also to be very true, and am sorry to see it.

18th. To my office all the morning, casting up with Captain Cocke their accounts of 500 tons of hempe brought from Riga, and bought by him and partners upon account, wherein are many things worth my knowledge. So at noon to dinner, taking Mr. Hater with me because of losing them, and in the afternoon he and I alone at the office, finishing our account of the extra charge of the Navy, not properly belonging to the Navy, since the King's coming in to Christmas last; and all extra things being abated, I find that the true charge of the Navy to that time hath been after the rate of 374,743*l.* a-year. I made an end by eleven o'clock at night. This day the Parliament met again, after their long prorogation; but I know not any thing what they have done, being within doors all day.

19th. To my office, where abundance of business all the morning. Dined by my wife's bedside, she not being yet well. We fell out almost upon my discourse of delaying the having of Ashwell. To my office till twelve at night, drawing out copies of the overcharge of the Navy. So home and to bed, being weary, sleepy, and my eyes begin to fail me, looking so long by candlelight upon white paper. This day I read the King's speech to the Parliament yesterday;

which is very short, and not very obliging; but only telling them his desire to have a power of indulging tender consciences, not that he will yield to have any mixture in the uniformity of the Church's discipline; and says the same for the Papists, but declares against their ever being admitted to have any offices or places of trust in the kingdom; but, God knows, too many have.

20th. By water with Commissioner Pett to Deptford, and there looked over the yarde, and had a call, wherein I am very highly pleased with our new manner of call-books, being my invention. Thence thinking to have gone down to Woolwich in the Charles pleasure boat, but she run aground, and so by oars to the towne, and there dined, and then to the yarde at Mr. Ackworth's, discoursing with the officers of the yarde about their stores of masts, which was our chief business, and having done something therein, took boat and to the pleasure boat, which was come down to fetch us back. It carried us to Cuckold's Point, and so by oars to the Temple, and so walked home and to my office.

21st. To the office, where Sir J. Minnes (most of the rest being at the Parliament-house), all the morning answering petitions and other business. Towards noon there comes a man in as if upon ordinary business, and shows me a writ from the Exchequer, called a Commission of Rebellion, and tells me that I am his prisoner in Field's business; which methought did strike me to the heart, to think that we could not sit

in the middle of the King's business. I told him how
and where we were employed, and bid him have a
care ; and perceiving that we were busy, he said he
would, and did withdraw for an houre : in which time
Sir J. Minnes took coach and to Court, to see what he
could do from thence ; and our solicitor against Field
came by chance and told me that he would go and
satisfy the fees of the Court, and would end the business. So he went away about that, and I staid in my
closett, till by and by the man and four more of his
fellows came to know what I would do ; I told them
to stay till I heard from the King or my Lord Chief
Baron, to both whom I had now sent. With that they
consulted, and told me that if I would promise to stay
in the house they would go and refresh themselves,
and come again, and know what answer I had : so
they away, and I home to dinner. Before I had dined,
the bayleys come back again with the constable, and
at the office knock for me, but found me not there ;
and I hearing in what manner they were come, did
forbear letting them know where I was ; so they stood
knocking and enquiring for me. By and by at my
parler-window comes Sir W. Batten's Mungo, to tell
me that his master and lady would have me come to
their house through Sir J. Minnes's lodgings, which
I could not do ; but, however, by ladders, did get over
the pale between our yards, and so to their house,
where I found them (as they have reason) to be much
concerned for me, my lady especially. The fellows
staid in the yarde swearing with one or two constables,

and some time we locked them into the yarde, and by and by let them out again, and so kept them all the afternoon, not letting them see me, or know where I was. One time I went up to the top of Sir W. Batten's house, and out of one of their windows spoke to my wife out of one of ours; which methought, though I did it in mirth, yet I was sad to think what a sad thing it would be for me to be really in that condition. By and by comes Sir J. Minnes, who (like himself and all that he do) tells us that he can do no good, but that my Lord Chancellor wonders that we did not cause the seamen to fall about their eares: which we wished we could have done without our being seen in it; and Captain Grove being there, he did give them some affront, and would have got some seamen to have drubbed them, but he had not time, nor did we think it fit to have done it, they having executed their commission; but there was occasion given that he did draw upon one of them and he did complain that Grove had pricked him in the breast, but no hurt done; but I see that Grove would have done our business to them if we had bid him. By and by comes Mr. Clerke, our solicitor, who brings us a release from our adverse atturney, we paying the fees of the commission, which comes to five markes, and the charges of these fellows, which are called the commissioners, but are the most rake-shamed rogues that ever I saw in my life; so he showed them this release, and they seemed satisfied, and went away with him to their atturney to be paid by him. But before they went,

Sir W. Batten and my lady did begin to taunt them, but the rogues answered them as high as themselves, and swore they would come again, and called me rogue and rebel, and they would bring the sheriffe and untile his house, before he should harbour a rebel in his house, and that they would be here again shortly. Well, at last they went away, and I by advice took occasion to go abroad, and walked through the streete to show myself among the neighbours, that they might not think worse than the business is. I home to Sir W. Batten's again, where Sir J. Lawson, Captain Allen, Spragg,[1] and several others, and all our discourse about the disgrace done to our office to be liable to this trouble, which we must get removed. Hither comes Mr. Clerke by and by, and tells me that he hath paid the fees of the Court for the commission; but the men are not contented with under 5*l.* for their charges, which he will not give them, and therefore advises me not to stir abroad till Monday that he comes or sends to me again, whereby I shall not be able to go to White Hall to the Duke of York, as I ought. Here I staid vexing, and yet pleased to see every body, man and woman, my Lady and Mr. Turner especially, for me; and so home, where my people are mightily sur-

---

[1] Edward Spragge, knighted for his gallant conduct as a Captain, in the first sea-fight with the Dutch in 1665. After rendering many important naval services to his country, he was unfortunately drowned, on the 11th of August, 1673, whilst passing in a boat to the " Royal Charles," from his own ship, which had been disabled in the action with Van Tromp. He lies buried in Westminster Abbey, without any memorial; nor have we the slightest record of his early history, or of the family from which he was descended.

prized to see this business, but it troubles me not very much, it being nothing touching my particular person or estate. Sir W. Batten tells me that little is done yet in the Parliament-house, but only this day it was moved and ordered that all the members of the House do subscribe to the renouncing of the Covenant, which, it is thought, will try some of them. There is also a bill brought in for the wearing of nothing but cloth or stuffs of our owne manufacture, and is likely to be passed. Among other talke this evening, my lady did speak concerning Commissioner Pett's calling the present King bastard, and other high words heretofore ; and Sir W. Batten did tell us, that he did give the Duke or Mr. Coventry an account of that and other like matters in writing under oathe, of which I was ashamed, and for which I was sorry, but I see there is an absolute hatred never to be altered there, and Sir J. Minnes, the old coxcomb, has got it by the end, which troubles me for the King's service, though I do truly hate the expressions laid to him. To my office and set down this day's Journall, and so home with my mind out of order, though not very sad with it, but ashamed for myself something, and for the honour of the office much more.

22d (Lord's day). Went not out all the day ; but after dinner to Sir W. Batten's and Sir W. Pen's, where discoursing much of yesterday's trouble and scandal ; but that which troubled me most was Sir J. Minnes coming from Court at night, and instead of bringing great comfort from thence (but I expected no better from him), he tells me that the Duke and Mr. Coventry make no great matter of it. So at night discontented to prayers, and to bed.

23d. Up by times; and not daring to go by land, did (Griffin going along with me for fear), slip to White Hall by water; where to Mr. Coventry, and, as we used to do, to the Duke; the other of my fellows being come. But we said nothing of our business, the Duke being sent for to the King, that he could not stay to speak with us. This morning came my Lord Windsor [1] to kiss the Duke's hand, being returned from Jamaica. He tells the Duke, that from such a degree of latitude going thither he began to be sicke, and was never well till his coming so far back again, and then presently begun to be well. He told the Duke of their taking the fort of St. Jago, upon Cuba, with his men; but upon the whole, I believe, that he did matters like a young lord, and was weary of being upon service out of his own country, where he might have pleasure. For methought it was a shame to see him this very afternoon, being the first day of his coming to towne, to be at a playhouse. To my Lord Sandwich; it was a great trouble to me (and I had great apprehensions of it) that my Lord desired me to go to Westminster Hall, to the Parliament-house doore, about business; and to Sir Wm. Wheeler,[2] which

---

[1] Created Earl of Plymouth, 6th December, 1682.

[2] Sir William Wheler, of Westminster, was created a Baronet, August 11, 1660, with remainder to his cousin, Charles Wheler, who succeeded to the honour, upon his death. He was then M. P. for Queenborough.

I told him I would do, but durst not go for fear of being taken by these rogues; but was forced to go to White Hall and take boat, and so land below the Tower at the Iron-gate; and so the back way over Little Tower Hill; and with my cloake over my face, took one of the watermen along with me, and staid behind a wall in the New-buildings behind our garden, while he went to see whether any body stood within the Merchants' Gate, and there standing but a little dirty boy before the gate, did make me quake and sweat to think he might be a Trepan. But there was nobody, and so I got safe into the garden, and coming to open my office doore, something behind it fell in the opening, which made me start. So that God knows in what a sad condition I should be if I were truly in debt: and therefore ought to bless God that I have no such reall reason, and to endeavour to keep myself, by my good deportment and good husbandry, out of any such condition. At home I find, by a note that Mr. Clerke in my absence hath left here, that I am free; and that he hath stopped all matters in Court; and I was very glad of it, and immediately had a light thought of taking pleasure to rejoice my heart, and so resolved to take my wife to a play at Court to-night, and the rather because it is my birth-day, being this day thirty years old, for which let me praise God. While my wife dressed herself, Creed and I walked out to see what play was acted to-day, and we find it "The Slighted Mayde."[1] But, Lord!

---

[1] A Comedy, by Sir Robert Stapylton, acted at Lincoln's Inn Fields.

to see that though I knew myself to be out of danger, yet I durst not go through the streete, but round by the garden into Tower Streete. By and by took coach, and to the Duke's house, where we saw it well acted, though the play hath little good in it, being most pleased to see the little girle dance in boy's apparel, she having very fine legs, only bends in the hams, as I perceive all women do. The play being done, we took coach and to Court, and there got good places, and saw "The Wilde Gallant," [1] performed by the King's house, but it was ill acted, and the play so poor a thing as I never saw in my life almost, and so little answering the name, that from beginning to end, I could not, nor can at this time, tell certainly which was the Wild Gallant. The King did not seem pleased at all, the whole play, nor any body else. My Lady Castlemaine was all worth seeing to-night, and little Steward.[2] Mrs. Wells do appear at Court again, and looks well ; so that, it may be, the late report of laying the dropped child to her was not true.[3] It being done, we got a coach and got well home about 12 at night. Now as my mind was but very ill satisfied with these two plays themselves, so was I in the midst of them sad to think of the spending so much money and

---

[1] Dryden's first play. Evelyn saw it at Court, 5th February, 1662–3, the night (as appears from the original Prologue) on which it was first acted. Dryden has a copy of verses to the Countess of Castlemaine on her encouraging his first play.

[2] Frances, daughter of Walter Stewart, son of Lord Blantyre, married Charles, fifth Duke of Richmond, and died 1702.

[3] See *ante*, Feb. 8, 1662–3, and note.

venturing upon the breach of my vowe, which I found myself sorry for. But I did make payment of my forfeiture presently, though I hope to save it back again by forbearing two plays at Court for this one at the Theatre, or else to forbear that to the Theatre, which I am to have at Easter. But it being my birthday and my day of liberty regained to me, and lastly, the last play that is likely to be acted at Court before Easter, because of the Lent coming in, I was the easier content to fling away so much money. This day I was told that my Lady Castlemaine hath all the King's Christmas presents, made him by the peers, given to her, which is a most abominable thing; and that at the great ball she was much richer in jewells than the Queene and Duchesse put both together.

24th. Waked by Mr. Clerke's being come to consult me about Field's business, and he says we shall trounce him. Then up, and to the office, and at 11 o'clock by water and to Westminster, and to Sir W. Wheeler's about my Lord's borrowing of money, and then to my Lord, who continues ill. Among other things, he tells me that he hears the Commons will not agree to the King's late declaration, nor will yield that the Papists have any ground given them to raise themselves up again in England, which I perceive by my Lord was expected at Court.

25th. To my office, where with Captain Cocke making an end of his last night's accounts till noon, and so home to dinner, my wife being come in from laying out about 4*l.* in provision of several things against Lent.   The Commons in Parliament, I hear, are very high to stand to the Act of Uniformity, and will not indulge the Papists (which is endeavoured by the Court Party) nor the Presbyters.

26th.   Up and drinking a draft of wormewood wine with Sir W. Batten at the Steelyard, he and I by water to the Parliament-house: he went in, and I walked up and down the Hall.   All the newes is the great oddes yesterday in the votes between them that are for the Indulgence to the Papists and Presbyters, and those that are against it, which did carry it by 200 against 30.   And pretty it is to consider how the King would appear to be a stiff Protestant and son of the Church; and yet would appear willing to give a liberty to these people, because of his promise at Breda.   And yet all the world do believe that the King would not have this liberty given them at all. Thence to my Lord's, who, I hear, has his ague again, for which I am sorry, and Creed and I to the King's Head ordinary, where much good company. Among the rest a young gallant lately come from France, who was full of his French, but methought not very good, but he had enough to make him think himself a wise man a great while.   Thence by water from the New Exchange home to the Tower. Troubled this evening that my wife is not come home from Chelsey, whither she is gone to see the play at the schoole where Ashwell is, but she came at last, it seems, by water, and tells me she is much pleased with Ashwell's acting and carriage.

27th. About 11 o'clock, Commissioner Pett and I walked to Chyrurgeon's Hall (we being all invited thither, and promised to dine there) ; where we were led into the Theatre; and by and by comes the reader, Dr. Tearne,[1] with the Master and Company, in a very handsome manner : and all being settled, he begun his lecture ; and his discourse being ended, we had a fine dinner and good learned company, many Doctors of Phisique, and we used with extraordinary great respect. Among other observables we drank the King's health out of a gilt cup[2] given by King Henry VIII. to this Company, with bells hanging at it, which every man is to ring by shaking after he hath drunk up the whole cup. There is also a very excellent piece of the King, done by Holbein, stands up in the Hall, with the officers of the Company kneeling to him to receive their Charter. After dinner Dr. Scarborough took some of his friends, and I went with them, to see the body of a lusty fellow, a seaman, that was hanged for a robbery. I did touch the dead body with my bare hand : it felt cold, but methought it was a very unpleasant sight. It seems one Dillon, of a great family, was, after much endeavours to have saved him, hanged with a silken halter this Sessions (of his own preparing), not for honour only, but it seems, it being soft and sleek it do slip close and kills, that is, strangles presently : whereas, a stiff one do not

---

[1] Christopher Terne, of Leyden, M.D., originally of Cambridge, and Fellow of the College of Physicians. Ob. 1673.

[2] Still existing, and has been engraved.

come so close together, and so the party may live the longer before killed. But all the Doctors at table conclude, that there is no pain at all in hanging, for that it do stop the circulation of the blood; and so stops all sense and motion in an instant. Thence with great satisfaction to me back to the Company, where I heard good discourse, and so to the afternoon Lecture upon the heart and lungs, &c., and that being done we broke up, and back to the office. Here late, and to Sir W. Batten's to speak upon some business, where I found Sir J. Minnes pretty well fuddled I thought: he took me aside to tell me how being at my Lord Chancellor's to-day, my Lord told him that there was a Great Seale passing for Sir W. Pen, through the impossibility of the Comptroller's duty to be performed by one man; to be as it were joynt-comptroller with him, at which he is stark mad; and swears he will give up his place. For my part, I do hope, when all is done, that my following my business will keep me secure against all their envys. But to see how the old man do strut, and swear that he understands all his duty as easily as crack a nut, and easier, he told my Lord Chancellor, for his teeth are gone; and that he understands it as well as any man in England; and that he will never leave to record that he should be said to be unable to do his duty alone; though, God knows, he cannot do it more than a child. All this I am glad to see fall out between them, and myself safe, and yet I hope the King's service well done for all this, for I would not that should be hindered by any of our private differences.

28th. The House have this noon been with the King to give him their reasons for refusing to grant any indulgence to Presbyters or Papists; which he, with great content and seeming pleasure, took, saying, that he doubted not but he and they should agree in all things, though there may seem a difference in judgement, he having writ and declared for an indulgence: and that he did believe never prince was happier in a House of Commons, than he was in them. To my Lord Sandwich, who continues troubled with his cold. Our discourse most upon the outing of Sir R. Bernard, and my Lord's being made Recorder in his stead, which he seems well contented with, saying, that it may be for his convenience to have the chief officer of the towne dependent upon him, which is very true. Home, and had a good supper of an oxe's cheek, of my wife's dressing and baking, and so to my office till past eleven at night, making up my month's account, and find that I am at a stay with what I was last, that is 640*l.* At the Privy Seale I did see the docquet by which Sir W. Pen is made the Comptroller's assistant, as Sir J. Minnes told me last night, which I must endeavour to prevent.

March 1st (Lord's day). Walked to White Hall, to the Chappell, where preached one Dr. Lewes, said heretofore to have been a great witt; but he read his sermon every word, and that so brokenly and low, that nobody could hear at any distance, nor I anything worth hearing that sat near. But, which was strange, he forgot to make any prayer before sermon, which all wonder at, but they impute it to his forgetfulness. After sermon a very fine anthem; so I up into the house among the courtiers, seeing the fine ladies, and, above all, my Lady Castlemaine, who is above all, that only she I can observe for true beauty. The King and Queene being set to dinner I went to Mr. Fox's, and there dined with him. Much genteel company, and, among other things, I hear for certain that peace is concluded between the King of France and the Pope; and also I heard the reasons given by our Parliament yesterday to the King why they dissent from him in matter of Indulgence, which are very good quite through, and which I was glad to hear. Thence to my Lord Sandwich, who continues with a great cold, locked up; and, being alone, we fell into discourse of my uncle the Captain's death and estate, and I took the opportunity of telling my Lord how matters stand, and read his will, and told him all, what a poor estate he hath left, at all which he wonders strangely, which he may well do. Thence after singing some new tunes with W. Howe I walked home, whither came Will. Joyce, whom I have not seen here a great while, nor desire it a great while again, he is so impertinent a coxcomb, and yet good natured. He gone, we all to bed, without prayers, it being washing day to-morrow.

2nd. Up early and by water with Commissioner Pett to Deptford, and there took the Jemmy yacht, that the King and the Lords virtuosos built the other day, down to Woolwich, where we discoursed of several matters both there and at the Ropeyarde, and so to the yacht again, and went down four or five miles with extraordinary pleasure, it being a fine day, and a brave gale of wind, and had some oysters brought us aboard newly taken, which were excellent, and eat with great pleasure. There also coming into the river two Dutchmen, we sent a couple of men on board and bought three Holland cheeses, cost 4*d.* a piece, excellent cheeses, whereof I had two and Commissioner Pett one. So back again to Woolwich, and going aboard the Hulke to see the manner of the iron bridles, which we are making of for to save cordage to put to the chain, I did fall from the ship-side into the ship (Kent), and had like to have broke my left hand, but I only sprained some of my fingers, which, when I came ashore I sent to Mrs. Ackworth for some balsam, and put to my hand, and was pretty well within a little while after. We dined at the White Hart with several officers, and after dinner went and saw the Royal James brought down to the stern of the Docke (the main business we came for), and then to the Ropeyarde, and saw a trial between Riga hempe and a sort of Indian grasse, which is pretty strong, but no comparison between it and the other for strength, and it is doubtful whether it will take tarre or no. So to the yacht again, and carried us almost to London, so by our oars home to the office, and thence Mr. Pett and I to Mr. Grant's coffee-house, whither he and Sir J. Cutler came to us and had much discourse, mixed discourse, and so broke up, and so home where I found my poor wife all alone at work, and the house foule, it being washing day, which troubled me, because that to-morrow I must be forced to have friends at dinner.

3rd (Shrove Tuesday). At noon, by promise, Mrs. Turner and her daughter, and Mrs. Morrice, came along with Roger Pepys to dinner. We were as merry as I could be, having but a bad dinner for them ; but so much the better, because of the dinner which I must have at the end of this month. And here Mrs. The. shewed me my name upon her breast as her Valentine, which will cost me 20*s*. After dinner I took them down into the wine cellar, and broached my tierce of claret for them. This afternoon Roger Pepys tells me, that for certain the King is for all this very highly incensed at the Parliament's late opposing the Indulgence; which I am sorry for, and fear it will breed great discontent.

5th. To the Lobby, and spoke with my cozen Roger, who is going to Cambridge to-morrow. In the Hall I do hear that the Catholiques are in great hopes for all this, and do set hard upon the King to get Indulgence. Matters, I hear, are all naught in Ireland, and that the Parliament has voted, and the people, that is, the Papists, do cry out against the Commissioners sent by the King; so that they say the English interest will be lost there. Thence I went to see my Lord Sandwich, who I found very ill, and by his cold being several nights hindered from sleep, he is hardly able to open his eyes, and is very weak and sad upon it, which troubled me much. So after talking with Mr. Cooke, whom I found there, about his folly for troubling me and other friends in getting him a place (that is, storekeeper of the Navy at Tangier) before there is any such thing, I returned to the Hall, and thence back with the two knights home, where I found Mr. Moore. Then came in Mr. Hawley and dined with us, and after dinner to the office, and I do find that I shall meet with nothing to oppose my growing great in the office but Sir W. Pen, who is now well again, and comes into the office very briske, and, I think, to get up his time that he has been out of the way by being mighty diligent at the office, which, I pray God, he may be, but I hope by mine to weary him out, for I am resolved to fall to business as hard as I can drive, God giving me health.

6th. Up betimes, and about eight o'clock by coach with four horses, with Sir J. Minnes and Sir W. Batten to Woolwich, a pleasant day, and so into Mr. Falconer's where we had some fish, which we brought with us, dressed; and there dined with us his new wife, which had been his mayde, but seems to be a genteel woman, well enough bred and discreet. This day it seems the House of Commons have been very high against the Papists, being incensed by the stir which they make for their having an Indulgence; which, without doubt, is a great folly in them to be so hot upon at this time, when they see how averse already the House have showed themselves from it. This evening Mr. Povy tells me that my Lord Sandwich is this day so ill that he is much afeard of him, which puts me to great pain, not more for my owne sake than for his poor family's.

7th. Up betimes, and to the office, where some of us sat all the morning. At noon Sir W. Pen began to talk with me like a counterfeit rogue very kindly about his house and getting bills signed for all our works, but he is a cheating fellow, and so I let him talk and answered nothing. So we parted. I to dinner, and there met The. Turner who is come on foot in a frolique to beg me to get a place at sea for John, their man, which is a rogue; but, however, it may be, the sea may do him good in reclaiming him, and therefore I will see what I can do. She dined with me; and after dinner I took coach, and carried her home; in our way, in Cheapside, lighting and giving her a dozen pair of white gloves as my Valentine. Thence to my Lord Sandwich, who is gone to Sir W. Wheeler's for his more quiet being, where he slept well last night, and I took him very merry, playing at cards, and much company with him. So I left him, and Creed and I to Westminster Hall, and there walked a good while. He told me how for some words of my Lady Gerard's,[1] against my Lady Castlemaine to the Queene, the King did the other

---

[1] Vide note, Jan. 1, 1662-63.

day affront her in going out to dance with her at a ball, when she desired it as the ladies do, and is since forbid attending the Queene by the King; which is much talked of, my Lord her husband being a great favourite.

8th (Lord's day). To White Hall to-day: I heard Dr. King, Bishop of Chichester, make a good and eloquent sermon upon these words, "They that sow in tears, shall reap in joy." Thence (the chappell in Lent being hung with black, and no anthem sung after sermon, as at other times,) to my Lord Sandwich at Sir W. Wheeler's. I found him out of order, thinking himself to be in a fit of ague, but in the afternoon he was very cheery. I dined with Sir William, where a good but short dinner, not better than one of mine commonly of a Sunday. After dinner up to my Lord, there being Mr. Rumball. My Lord, among other discourse, did tell us of his great difficultys passed in the business of the Sound, and of his receiving letters from the King there, but his sending them by Whet-stone was a great folly; and the story how my Lord being at dinner with Sydney,[1] one of his fellow pleni-potentiarys and his mortal enemy, did see Whetstone, and put off his hat three times to him, but the fellow would not be known, which my Lord imputed to his coxcombly humour (of which he was full), and bid Sydney take notice of him too, when at the very time

---

[1] The famous Algernon Sydney, one of the Ambassadors sent to Sweden and Denmark by Richard Cromwell.

he had letters[1] in his pocket from the King, as it proved afterwards. And Sydney afterwards did find it out at Copenhagen, the Dutch Commissioners telling him how my Lord Sandwich had hired one of their ships to carry back Whetstone to Lubeck, he being come from Flanders from the King. But I cannot but remember my Lord's æquanimity in all these affairs with admiration.

9th. About noon Sir J. Robinson, Lord Mayor, desiring way through the garden from the Tower, called in at the office and there invited me (and Sir W. Pen, who happened to be in the way) to dinner, which we did; and there had a great Lent dinner of fish, little flesh. There dined with us to-day Mr. Slingsby,[2] of the Mint, who showed us all the new pieces both gold and silver (examples of them all), that are made for the King, by Blondeau's[3] way; and compared them with those made for Oliver. The pictures of the latter made by Symons,[4] and of the King by one Rotyr,[5] a German, I think, that dined

---

[1] These letters are in Thurloe's "State Papers," vol. vii. One was from the King, the other from Chancellor Hyde.

[2] Master of the Mint, frequently mentioned by Evelyn.

[3] There is an account of this matter in Hawkins's "English Coins," pp. 213, 214.

[4] Thomas Simon, an engraver of coins and medals. The greatest of English die sinkers. Ob. 1665.

[5] Although modern numismatists may smile at the preference given by Mr. Slingsby to Rotier's coins, Pepys's remark that Oliver's crowns were then selling at 25s. or 30s. is very curious, for it is to this day considered doubtful whether these beautiful pieces by Simons were current coin or pattern pieces. Snelling, in his "Silver Coinage," 1762, calls them "very scarce," and so they

with us also. He extolls those of Rotyr's above the others; and, indeed, I think they are the better, because the sweeter of the two; but, upon my word, those of the Protector are more like in my mind, than the King's, but both very well worth seeing. The crownes of Cromwell are now sold, it seems, for 25*s.* and 30*s.* a-piece.

10th. Up and to my office all the morning, and great pleasure it is to be doing my business betimes. About noon Sir J. Minnes came to me and staid half an houre with me talking about his business with Sir W. Pen, and (though with me an old doter) yet he told me freely how sensible he is of Sir W. Pen's treachery. I am pleased to hear that his knavery is found out. Dined upon a poor Lenten dinner at home, my wife being vexed at a fray this morning with my Lady Batten about my boy's going thither to turn the water-cock with their mayds' leave, but my Lady was mighty high upon it and she would teach his mistress better manners, which my wife answered

---

remain, as the prices which they still bring at sales seem to show, varying from 2*l.* 10*s.* to 11*l.*, according to condition.

Mr. Joseph Gibbs, of the Inner Temple, who kindly furnished the above remarks, has one of the crowns *without any flaw*, for which he paid 4*l.* 18*s.*; and Mr. Cureton, the coin collector, had six sets of the semoneys at the time he was robbed and nearly murdered, in the winter of 1850. Pepys's evidence of the high value of the crowns in 1663 strengthens the idea that they were pattern pieces only. There is a tradition that the die became cracked across the neck after a few impressions were struck, which having been considered ominous, the issue was stopped, but the truth of the story must still remain matter of conjecture.

There were three brothers named Rotier, all Medallists; Philip introduced the likeness of Mrs. Stewart in the figure of Britannia.

aloud that she might hear, that she could learn little manners of her.

11th. Up betimes, and to my office, walked a little in the garden with Sir W. Batten, talking about the difference between his Lady and my wife yesterday, and I doubt my wife is to blame. Newes by Mr. Wood that Butler, our chief witness against Field, was sent by him to New England contrary to our desire, which made me mad almost; and so Sir J. Minnes, Sir W. Pen, and I dined together at Trinity House. However, in the afternoon Wood sends us word that he has appointed another to go, who shall overtake the ship in the Downes. So I was late at the office, among other things, writing to the Downes, to the Commander-in-Chief, and putting things into the surest course I could to helpe the business.

12th. After dinner comes my uncle Thomas with a letter to my father, wherein, as we desire, he and his son do order their tenants to pay their rents to us, which pleases me well. He being gone, I to the office, where at the choice of maisters and chyrurgeons for the fleete now going out, I did my business as I could wish, both for the persons I had a mind to serve, and in getting the warrants signed drawn by my clerks, which I was afeard of. Sat late, and having done I went home, where I found Mary Ashwell come to live with us, of whom I hope well, and pray God she may please us, and find by her discourse and carriage to-night that she is not proud, but will do what she is bid, but for want of being abroad knows not how to give the respect to her mistress, as she will do when she is told it, she having been used only to little children, and there was a kind of mistress over them.

13th. To Mrs. Hunt's, and there found my wife, and so took them up by coach, and carried them to Hide Park, where store of coaches and good faces.

14th. To my office, and a great rant I did give to Mr. Davis, of Deptford, and others about their usage of Michell, in his Bewpers,[1] which he serves in for flaggs, which did trouble me, but yet it was in defence of what was truth. So home to dinner, where Creed dined with me, and walked a good while in the garden with me after dinner, talking, among other things, of the poor service which Sir J. Lawson did really do in the Streights, for which all this great fame and honour done him is risen. So to my office, where all the afternoon giving maisters their warrants for this voyage, for which I hope hereafter to get something at their coming home. In the evening my wife and I and Ashwell walked in the garden, and I find she is a pretty ingenuous[2] girle at all sorts of fine work, which pleases me very well, and I hope will be very good entertainment for my wife without much cost.

15th (Lord's day). Up and with my wife and her

---

[1] A kind of cloth or material for flags. (M. B.)

[2] *Ingenuous* and *ingenious*. There was a time when the uttermost confusion reigned in the use of these words, and also in the words "ingenuity" and "ingenuousness." In respect of "ingenious" and "ingenuous," the first now indicates mental, the second moral qualities; "ingenious" being from "ingenium," and "ingenuous" from "ingenuus." See Trench's "Select Glossary." (M. B.)

woman Ashwell the first time to church, where our pew was so full with Sir J. Minnes's sister and her daughter, that I perceive, when we come all together, some of us must be shut out, but I suppose we shall come to some order what to do therein. Dined at home, and to church again in the afternoon.

16th. To my office, where, with several Maisters of the King's ships, Sir J. Minnes and I advising upon the business of Slopps, wherein the seaman is so much abused by the Pursers. After dinner to the Duke where we met of course, and talked of our Navy matters. Then to the Commission of Tangier, and there had my Lord Peterborough's Commission read over; and Mr. Secretary Bennet did make his querys upon it, in order to the drawing one for my Lord Rutherford more regularly, that being a very extravagant thing. Here long discoursing upon my Lord Rutherford's despatch, and so broke up, and going out of the Court I met with Mr. Coventry, and so he and I walked half a houre in the long stone gallery, where we discoursed of many things, among others how the Treasurer doth intend to come to pay in course, which is the thing of the world that will do the King the greatest service in the Navy, and which joys my heart to hear of. He tells me of the busines of Sir J. Minnes, and Sir W. Pen; which, he said, was chiefly to make Mr. Pett's being joyned with Sir W. Batten to go down the better. And how he well sees that neither one nor the other can do their duties without helpe. To my wife at my Lord's lodgings, where I heard Ashwell play first upon the harpsicon, and I find she do play pretty well, which pleaseth me very well. Thence home by coach, buying at the Temple the printed virginall-book for her.

17th. To St. Margaret's Hill [1] in Southwark, where the Judge of the Admiralty came, and the rest of the Doctors of the Civill law, and some other Commissioners, whose Commission of Oyer and Terminer was read, and then the charge, given by Dr. Exton,[2] which methought was somewhat dull, though he would seem to intend it to be very rhetoricall, saying that Justice had two wings, one of which spread itself over the land, and the other over the water, which was this Admiralty Court. That being done, and the jury called, they broke up, and to dinner to a taverne hard by, where a great dinner, and I with them; but I perceive that this Court is yet but in its infancy (as to its rising again), and their design and consultation was, I could overhear them, how to proceed with the most solemnity, and spend time, there being only two businesses to do, which of themselves could not spend much time. In the afternoon to the court again, where, first, Abraham, the boatswain of the King's pleasure-boat, was tried for drowning a man; and next, Turpin, accused by our wicked rogue Field, for stealing the King's timber; but after full examination, they were both acquitted, and as I was glad of the

---

[1] The old Admiralty Court, then held at the Marshalsea, and finally abolished 31st December, 1849.

[2] Sir Thomas Exton, Dean of the Arches and Judge of the Admiralty Court.

first, for the saving the man's life, so I did take the other as a very good fortune to us; for if Turpin had been found guilty, it would have sounded very ill in the eares of all the world, in the business between Field and us. Sir W. Batten and I to my Lord Mayor's,[1] where we found my Lord with Colonel Strangways[2] and Sir Richard Floyd,[3] Parliament-men, in the cellar drinking, where we sat with them, and then up; and by and by comes in Sir Richard Ford. In our drinking which was always going, we had many discourses, but from all of them I do find Sir R. Ford a very able man of his brains and tongue, and a scholler. But my Lord Mayor I find to be a talking, bragging Bufflehead,[4] a fellow that would be thought to have led all the City in the great business of bringing in the King, and that nobody understood his plots, and the dark lanthorne he walked by; but led them and plowed with them as oxen and asses (his own words) to do what he had a mind: when in every discourse I observe him to be as very a cox-combe as I could have thought had been in the City. But he is resolved to do great matters in pulling down the shops quite through the City, as he hath done in many places, and will make a thorough passage quite through the City, through Canning-street, which in-

---

[1] Sir John Robinson. (M. B.)

[2] Giles Strangways, M.P. for Dorsetshire.

[3] Probably Sir Richard Lloyd, M.P. for Radnorshire.

[4] *Bufflehead.* From the German "Büffel," a wild ox. "Du bist ein büffels-topf." Thou art a buffle-head — a blockhead. (M. B.)

deed will be very fine. And then his precept, which he, in vain-glory, said he had drawn up himself, and hath printed it, against coachmen and carrmen affronting of the gentry in the streete ; it is drawn so like a fool, and some faults were openly found in it, that I believe he will have so much wit as not to proceed upon it though it be printed. Here we staid talking till eleven at night, Sir R. Ford breaking to my Lord our business of our patent to be Justices of the Peace in the City, which he stuck at mightily ; but, however, Sir R. Ford knows him to be a fool, and so in his discourse he made him appear, and cajoled him into a consent to it : but so as I believe when he comes to his right mind to-morrow he will be of another opinion ; and though Sir R. Ford moved it very weightily and neatly, yet I had rather it had been spared now. But to see how he do rant, and pretend to sway all the City in the Court of Aldermen, and says plainly that they cannot do, nor will he suffer them to do, any thing but what he pleases ; nor is there any officer of the City but of his putting in ; nor any man that could have kept the City for the King thus well and long but him. And if the country can be preserved, he will undertake that the City shall not dare to stir again. When I am confident there is no man almost in the City cares for him, nor hath he brains to outwit any ordinary tradesman.

18th. To my office, where all the morning. After dinner by water to Redriffe, my wife and Ashwell with me, and so walked and left them at Halfway house ;

I to Deptford, where up and down the storehouses, and on board two or three ships now getting ready to go to sea, and so back home again, merry with our Ashwell, who is a merry jade, and so awhile to my office, and then home to supper, and to bed. This day my tryangle which was put in tune yesterday, did please me very well, Ashwell playing upon it pretty well.

19th. To Woolwich all alone by water, where took the officers most abed. I walked and enquired how all matters and businesses go, and by and by to the Clerke of the Cheque's house, and there eat some of his good Jamaica brawne, and so walked to Greenwich. Part of the way Deane walking with me; talking of the pride and corruption of most of his fellow officers of the yarde, and which I believe to be true. So to Deptford, where I did the same to great content, and see the people begin to value me as they do the rest. At noon Mr. Wayth took me to his house, where I dined, and saw his wife, a pretty woman, and had a good fish dinner, and after dinner he and I walked to Redriffe talking of several errors in the Navy, by which I learned a great deal, and was glad of his company. So after doing my owne business in my office, writing letters, &c., home to supper, and to bed, being weary and vexed that I do not find other people so willing to do business as myself, when I have taken pains to find out what in the yards is wanting and fitting to be done.

20th. Over the water, and walked to Deptford,

where up and down the yarde, and met the two clerks of the Cheques to conclude by our method their call-books, which we have done to great perfection, and so walked home again. In Fleete Streete bought me a little sword, with gilt handle, cost 23*s.*, and silk stockings to the colour of my riding cloth suit, cost 15*s.*, and bought me a belt there too, cost 15*s.* Thence homewards, and meeting with Mr. Kirton's kinsman in Paul's Church Yarde, he and I to a coffee-house; where I hear how there had like to have been a surprizall of Dublin by some discontented protest-ants, and other things of like nature; and it seems the Commissioners have carried themselves so high for the Papists that the others will not endure it. Hewlett and some others are taken and clapped up; and they say the King hath sent over to dissolve the Parliament there, who went very high against the Commissioners. Pray God send all well!

21st. By appointment our full board met, and Sir Philip Warwick and Sir Robert Long [1] came from my Lord Treasurer to speak with us about the state of the debts of the Navy; and how to settle it, so as to begin upon the new foundation of 200,000*l.* per annum, which the King is now resolved not to exceed.

22d (Lord's day). Wrote out our bill for the Parliament about our being made Justices of Peace in the

---

[1] Sir Robert Long, who came of an ancient family in Wiltshire, had been Secretary to Charles II. during his exile, and was subsequently made Auditor of the Exchequer and a Privy Councillor, and created a Baronet in 1662, with remainder to his nephew James. He died unmarried in 1673.

City. So to church, where a dull formall fellow that prayed for the Right Hon. John Lord Barkeley, Lord President of Connaught, &c. To my Lord Sandwich, and with him talking a good while; I find the Court would have this Indulgence go on, but the Parliament are against it. Matters in Ireland are full of discontent. Thence with Mr. Creed to Captain Ferrers, where many fine ladies; the house well and prettily furnished. She (Mrs. Ferrers) lies in, in great state, Mr. G. Montagu, Collonel Williams, Cromwell that was,[1] and Mrs. Wright as proxy for my Lady Jemimah, were witnesses. Very pretty and plentiful entertainment, could not get away till nine at night. My coach cost me 7s. So to prayers, and to bed. This day though I was merry enough yet I could not get yesterday's quarrel with Captain Holmes out of my mind, and a natural fear of being challenged by him for the words I did give him, though nothing but what did become me as a principal officer.

23rd. To Whitehall, being fearful almost, so poor a spirit I have, of meeting Major Holmes. By and by the Duke comes, and we with him about our usual

---

1 "*Cromwell that was,*" appears to have been Henry Cromwell, grandson of Sir Oliver Cromwell, and first cousin, once removed, to the Protector. He was seated at Bodsey House, in the Parish of Ramsey, which had been his father's residence, and held the commission of a Colonel. He served in several Parliaments for Huntingdonshire, voting, in 1660, for the restoration of the monarchy; and as he knew the name of Cromwell would not be grateful to the Court, he disused it, and assumed that of Williams, which had belonged to his ancestors, and he is so styled in a list of Knights of the proposed Order of the Royal Oak. He died at Huntingdon, 3rd August, 1673. — Abridged from NOBLE's *Memoirs of the Cromwells*, vol. i. p. 70.

business, and then the Committee for Tangier, where, after reading my Lord Rutherford's commission and consented to, Sir R. Ford, Sir W. Rider, and I were chosen to bring in some laws for the Civill government of it, which I am little able to do, but am glad to be joyned with them, for I shall learn something of them. Thence to see my Lord Sandwich, and who should I meet at the door but Major Holmes. He would have gone away, but I told him I would not spoil his visitt, and would have gone, but however we fell to discourse and he did as good as desire excuse for the high words that did pass in his heat the other day, which I was willing enough to close with, and after telling him my mind we parted, and I left him to speak with my Lord, and I by coach home, where I found Will. Howe come home to-day with my wife, and staid with us all night, staying late up singing songs. This day Greatorex brought me a very pretty weather-glasse for heat and cold.

24th. Lay pretty long, that is, till past six o'clock, and then up and W. Howe and I very merry together, till having eat our breakfast, he went away, and I to my office. By and by Sir J. Minnes and I to the Victualling Office by appointment to meet several persons upon stating the demands of some people of money from the King. Here we went into their Bake-house, and saw all the ovens at work, and good bread too, as ever I would desire to eat. Thence Sir J. Minnes and I homewards calling at Browne's, the mathematician in the Minnerys, with a design of buying White's ruler to measure timber with, but could not agree on the price. So home, and to dinner, and so to my office, where we sat anon, and among other things had Cooper's [1] business tried against Captain Holmes, but I find Cooper a fuddling, troublesome fellow, though a good artist, and so am contented to have him turned out of his place, nor did I see reason to say one word against it, though I know what they did against him was with great envy and pride.

25th (Lady-day). To the Sun Taverne, to my Lord Rutherford, and dined with him, and some others, his officers, and Scotch gentlemen, of fine discourse and education. My Lord used me with great respect, and discoursed upon his business as with one that he did esteem, and indeed I do believe that this garrison is likely to come to something under him. By and by he went away, forgetting to take leave of me, my back being turned, looking upon the aviary, which is there very pretty, and the birds begin to sing well this spring. This evening came Captain Grove about hiring ships for Tangier. I did hint to him my desire that I could make some lawfull profit thereof, which he promises.

26th. This day is five years since it pleased God to preserve me at my being cut of the stone, of which I bless God I am in all respects well. But I could not get my feast to be kept to-day as it used to be,

---

[1] Cooper taught Pepys arithmetic, and Pepys got him appointed Master of the Reserve (see Diary, Aug. 7, 1662), from which office Captain Holmes wanted him to be summarily dismissed. Pepys opposed his discharge without hearing his defence. (M. B.)

because of my wife's being ill and other disorders by my servants being out of order. This morning came a new cooke-mayde at 4*l.* per annum, the first time I ever did give so much. She did live last at my Lord Monk's house, and indeed at dinner did get what there was very prettily ready and neate for me, which did please me much. This morning my uncle Thomas was with me according to our agreement, and I paid him the 50*l.* which was against my heart to part with, and yet I must be contented; I used him very kindly, and I desire to continue so voyd of any discontent as to my estate, that I may follow my business the better.

27th. At my office all the morning. Thence to the Exchequer, and thence with Creed into Fleete Streete, and calling at several places about business; in passing at the Hercules pillars he and I dined though late, and thence with one that we found there, a friend of Captain Ferrer's I used to meet at the playhouse, they would have gone to some gameing house, but I would not but parted, and staying a little in Paul's Church-yard, at the foreign Bookseller's looking over some Spanish books, and with much ado keeping myself from laying out money there, as also with them, being willing enough to have gone to some idle house with them, I got home, and after a while at my office, to supper, and to bed.

28th. To Deptford. So home, and after a little while hearing Ashwell play on the tryangle, to my office, and there, late writing a chiding letter to my poor father about his being so unwilling to come to an account with me, which I desire he might do, that I may know what he spends, and how to order the estate so as to pay debts and legacys as far as may be.

29th. To church, home to dinner. After dinner in comes Mr. Moore, and sat and talked with us a good while ; among other things telling me, that neither my Lord nor he are under apprehensions of the late discourse in the House of Commons, concerning resumption of Crowne lands, which I am very glad of. He being gone, up to my chamber, reading over some papers which I found in my man William's chest of drawers, among others some old precedents concerning the practice of this office heretofore, which I am glad to find and shall make use of, among others an oathe, which the Principal Officers were bound to swear at their entrance into their offices, which I would be glad were in use still. Then fell hard to make up my monthly accounts, letting my family go to bed after prayers. I staid up long, and find myself, as I think, fully worth 670*l.* So with good comfort to bed, finding that though it be but little, yet I do get ground every month. I pray God it may continue so with me.

30th. To the Duke, where we did our usual business, and afterwards to the Tangier Committee, where among other things we all of us sealed and signed the Contract for building the Mole with my Lord Tiviott, Sir J. Lawson, and Mr. Cholmeley. A thing I did with a very ill will, because a thing which I did not at all understand, nor any or few of the whole board.

We did also read over the propositions for the Civill government and Law Merchant of the towne, as they were agreed on this morning at the Glassehouse by Sir R. Ford and Sir W. Rider, who drew them, Mr. Povy and myself as a Committee appointed to prepare them.

April 1st. I went to the Temple to my Cozen Roger Pepys, to see and talk with him a little; who tells me that, with much ado, the Parliament do agree to throw down Popery; but he says it is with so much spite and passion, and an endeavour of bringing all Non-conformists into the same condition, that he is afeard matters will not yet go so well as he could wish. Calling at my brother's they tell me that my father is not yet up. At which I wondered, not thinking that he was come. So I up to his bedside and staid an houre or two talking with him. Among other things he tells me how unquiett my mother is grown, that he is not able to live almost with her, if it were not for Pall. Home, calling on the virginall maker, buying a rest for myself to tune my tryangle, and taking one of his people along with me to put it in tune once more, by which I learned how to·go about it myself for the time to come. To my office all the afternoon; Lord! how Sir J. Minnes, like a mad coxcomb, did swear and stamp, swearing that Commissioner Pett hath still the old heart against the King that ever he had, and that this was his envy against his brother that was to build the ship, and all the damnable reproaches in the world, at which I was ashamed, but said little; but, upon the whole, I find him still a foole, led by the nose with stories told by Sir W. Batten, whether with or without reason. So, vexed in my mind to see things ordered so unlike gentlemen, or men of reason, I went home and to bed.

2nd. By coach to Westminster Hall with Sir W. Pen. By and by the House rises and I home again with him, all the way talking about the business of Holmes; I did on purpose tell him my mind freely, and let him see that it must be a wiser man than Holmes (in these very words) that shall do me any hurt while I do my duty. I to remember him of Holmes' words against Sir J. Minnes, that he was a knave, rogue, coward, and that he will kick him and pull him by the eares, which he remembered all of them and may have occasion to do it hereafter to his owne shame to suffer them to be spoke in his presence without any reply but what I did give him, which has caused all this feud. But I am glad of it, for I would now and then take occasion to let the world know that I will not be made a novice. Sir W. Pen took occasion to speak about my wife's strangenesse to him and his daughter, and that believing at last that it was from his taking of Sarah to be his mayde, he hath now put her away, at which I am glad. He told me, that this day the King hath sent to the House his concurrence wholly with them against the Popish priests, Jesuits, &c., which gives great content, and I am glad of it.

3rd. To White Hall and to Chappell, which being

most monstrous full, I could not go into my pew, but sat among the quire. Dr. Creeton, the Scotchman, preached a most admirable, good, learned, honest and most severe sermon, yet comicall, upon the words of the woman concerning the Virgin, "Blessed is the womb that bare thee and the paps that gave thee suck; and he answered, Nay; rather is he blessed that heareth the word of God, and keepeth it." He railed bitterly ever and anon against John Calvin, and his brood, the Presbyterians, and against the present terme, now in use, of "tender consciences." He ripped up Hugh Peters [1] (calling him the execrable skellum [2]), his preaching and stirring up the mayds of the city to bring in their bodkins and thimbles. Thence going out of White Hall, I met Captain Grove, who did give me a letter directed to myself from himself. I discerned money to be in it, and took it, knowing, as I found it to be, the proceed of the place I have got him to be, the taking up of vessels for Tangier. But I did not open it till I came home to my office, and there I broke it open, not looking into it till all the money was out, that I might say I saw no money in the paper, if ever I should be questioned about it. There was a piece in gold and 4*l.* in silver. So home to dinner with my

---

[1] Hugh Peters, a native of Fowey, in Cornwall, expelled from St. John's College, Cambridge, for irregularity. He was then an actor, and afterwards took orders, and was celebrated for his buffoonery in the pulpit. He was so bitter against Charles the First, that at the Restoration he was excepted from the act of pardon, and was hanged and quartered, 1660. (M. B.)

[2] *Skellum.* Rogue, rascal. (M. B.)

father and wife, and after dinner up to my tryangle, where I found that above my expectation Ashwell has very good principles of musique and can take out a lesson herself with very little pains. Thence to the Tangier Committee, where we find ourselves at a great stand; the establishment being but 70,000*l.* per annum, and the forces to be kept in the towne at the least estimate that my Lord Rutherford can be got to bring it is 53,000*l.* The charge of this year's work of the Mole will be 13,000*l.*; besides 1,000*l.* a-year to my Lord Peterborough as a pension, and the fortifications and contingencys, which puts us to a great stand. I find at Court that there is some bad newes from Ireland of an insurrection of the Catholiques there, which puts them into an alarme. I hear also in the City that for certain there is an embargo upon all our ships in Spayne, upon this action of my Lord Windsor's at Cuba, which signifies little or nothing, but only he hath a mind to say that he hath done something before he comes back again.

4th. To my office. Home to dinner, whither by and by comes Roger Pepys, Mrs. Turner and her daughter, Joyce Norton, and a young lady, a daughter of Coll. Cockes, my uncle Wight, his wife and Mrs. Anne Wight. This being my feast, in lieu of what I should have had a few days ago for my cutting of the stone, for which the Lord make me truly thankful. Very merry at, before, and after dinner, and the more for that my dinner was great, and most neatly dressed by our owne only mayde. We had a fricasee of rabbits and chickens, a leg of mutton boiled, three carps in a dish, a great dish of a side of lambe, a dish of roasted pigeons, a dish of four lobsters, three tarts, a lamprey pie (a most rare pie), a dish of anchovies, good wine of several sorts, and all things mighty noble and to my great content. After dinner to Hide Parke; my aunt, Mrs. Wight and I in one coach, and all the rest of the women in Mr. Turner's; Roger being gone in haste to the Parliament about the carrying this business of the Papists, in which it seems there is great contest on both sides, and my uncle and father staying together behind. At the Parke was the King, and in another coach my Lady Castlemaine, they greeting one another at every tour. Here about an houre and home, and I found the house as clear as if nothing had been done there to-day from top to bottom, which made us give the cooke 12*d.* a piece, each of us.

5th (Lord's day). Up and spent the morning, till the Barber came, in reading in my chamber part of Osborne's advice to his Son, which I shall not never enough admire for sense and language, and being by and by trimmed, to Church, myself, wife, Ashwell &c. Home and while dinner was prepared to my office to read over my vows with great affection and to very good purpose. Then to church again, where a simple bawling young Scot preached.

6th. To my office and there made an end of reading my book that I have of Mr. Barlow's of the Journall of the Commissioners of the Navy, who begun to act in the year 1628 and continued six years, wherein is fine observations and precedents out of which I do purpose to make a good collection. To the Committee of Tangier, where I found, to my great joy, my Lord Sandwich, the first time I have seen him abroad these some months, and by and by he rose and took leave, being, it seems, this night to go to Kensington or Chelsey, where he hath taken a lodging for a while to take the ayre.

7th. To my office. At noon to the Exchange, and after dinner to the office, where Sir J. Minnes did make a great complaint to me alone, how my clerke Mr. Hater had entered in one of the Sea books a ticket to have been signed by him before it had been examined, which makes the old foole mad almost, though there was upon enquiry the greatest reason in the world for it. Which though it vexes me, yet it is most to see from day to day what a coxcomb he is, and that so great a trust should lie in the hands of such a foole.

8th. By water to White Hall, to chappell; where preached Dr. Pierce, the famous man that preached the sermon so much cried up, before the King against the Papists. His matter was the Devil tempting our Saviour, being carried into the Wilderness by the spirit. And he hath as much of natural eloquence as most men that ever I heard in my life, mixed with so much learning. After sermon I went up and saw the ceremony of the Bishop of Peterborough's paying homage upon the knee to the King, while Sir H. Bennet,

Secretary, read the King's grant of the Bishopric of Lincolne, to which he is translated. His name is Dr. Lany.[1] Here I also saw the Duke of Monmouth, with his Order of the Garter, the first time I ever saw it. I hear that the University of Cambridge did treat him a little while since with all the honour possible, with a comedy at Trinity College, and banquet; and made him Master of Arts there. All which, they say, the King took very well. Dr. Raynbow,[2] Master of Magdalen, being now Vice-Chancellor.

9th. To my office, and anon we met upon finishing the Treasurer's accounts. At noon dined at home and am vexed to hear my wife tell me how our mayde Mary do endeavour to corrupt our cook mayde, which did please me very well, but I am resolved to rid the house of her as soon as I can.

10th. After great expectation from Ireland, and long stop of letters, there is good newes come, that all is quiett after our great noise of troubles there, though some stir hath been as was reported. To the Royall Oake Taverne, in Lumbarde Streete, where Alexander Broome[3] the poet was, a merry and witty man, I believe, if he be not a little conceited, and

---

[1] Benjamin Lany, S.T.P., made Bishop of Peterborough 1660, translated to Lincoln 1662-63, and to Ely, 1667.

[2] Edward Rainbow, chaplain to the King, and Dean of Peterborough, and in 1664 Bishop of Carlisle. Ob. 1684.

[3] Alexander Brome, an attorney in the Lord Mayor's Court, author of "Loyal Songs and Madrigals," much sung by the Cavaliers, and of a translation of portions of Horace. His death is recorded in the "Diary" on the 3rd July, 1666. He was regretted as an agreeable companion.

here drank a sort of French wine, called Ho Bryan,[1] that hath a good and most particular taste that I never met with.   Then to my Lord's lodgings, met my wife, and walked to the New Exchange.   There laid out 10*s.* upon pendents and painted leather gloves, very pretty and all the mode.

12th (Lord's day).   To church, where I found our pew altered by taking some of the hind pew to make ours bigger.   After dinner got a coach and to Graye's Inn walks, where some handsome faces.   Coming home to-night, a drunken boy was carrying by our constable to our new pair of stocks to handsel them, being a new pair and very handsome.

13th.   Up by five o'clock and to my office, where hard at work till towards noon, and home and eat a bit, and so with Sir W. Batten to the Stillyard, and there eat a lobster together, and anon to the Tangier Committee, where we had very fine discourse from Dr. Walker and Wiseman,[2] civilians, against our erecting a court-merchant at Tangier, and well answered by my Lord Sandwich (whose speaking I never till now observed so much to be very good) and Sir R. Ford.   By and by the discourse being ended, we fell to my Lord Rutherford's dispatch, which do not please him, he being a Scott, and one resolved to scrape every penny that he can get by any way, which the Committee will not agree to.   He took offence at something and rose away, without taking leave of the

---

[1] Haut Brion.   (M. B.)

[2] Afterwards Sir William Walker and Sir Robert Wiseman.

board, which all took ill, though nothing said but only by the Duke of Albemarle, who said that we ought to settle things as they ought to be, and if he will not go upon these terms another man will, no doubt.

14th. By barge to Woolwich, to see "The Royal James" launched, where she has been under repair a great while. Then to Mr. Falconer's to a dinner of fish of our own sending, and when it was just ready to come upon the table, word is brought that the King and Duke are come, so they all went away to shew themselves, while I staid and had a little dish or two by myself, resolving to go home, and by the time I had dined they came again, having gone to little purpose, the King, I believe, taking little notice of them. So they to dinner, and I staid a little with them, and so good bye. I walked to Greenwich, studying the slide rule for measuring of timber, which is very fine, and so home pretty weary. Anon they all came home, the ship well launched. Sir G. Carteret tells me to-night that he perceives the Parliament is likely to make a great bustle before they will give the King any money; will call all things into question; and, above all, the expences of the Navy; and do enquire into the King's expences everywhere, and into the truth of the report of people being forced to sell their bills at 15 per cent. losse in the Navy; and, lastly, that they are in a very angry pettish mood at present, and not likely to be better.

15th. After talking with my father awhile, I to my office, and there hard at it till almost noon, and then went down the river with Maynes, the purveyor, to show a ship's lading of Norway goods. So home, and after dinner up with my wife and Ashwell a little to the Tryangle, and so I down to Deptford by land about looking out a couple of catches fitted to be speedily set forth in answer to a letter of Mr. Coventry's to me. Which done, I walked back again, all the way reading of my book of Timber measure, comparing it with my new Sliding Rule brought home this morning with great pleasure. Taking boat again I went to Shishe's yard, and with him pitched upon a couple, and so home a little weary.

16th. Met to pass Mr. Pitts' (Sir J. Lawson's Secretary and Deputy Treasurer) accounts for the voyage last to the Streights, wherein the demands are strangely irregular, and I dare not oppose it alone for making an enemy and do no good, but only bring a review upon my Lord Sandwich, but God knows it troubles my heart to see it, and to see the Comptroller, whose duty it is, to make no more matter of it.

17th. It being Good Friday, our dinner was only sugar-sopps and fish; the only time that we have had a Lenten dinner all this Lent. This morning Mr. Hunt, the instrument maker, brought me home a Basse Viall to see whether I like it, which I do not very well, besides I am under a doubt whether I had best buy one, because of spoiling my present mind and love to business. To Paul's Church Yarde, to cause the title of my English "Mare Clausum" to be changed, and the new title, dedicated to the King, to be put to it, because I am ashamed to have the other seen dedicated to the Commonwealth.

18th. At dinner was Mr. Creed, all dinner, and walking in the garden the afternoon, he and I talking of the ill management of our office, which God knows is very ill for the King's advantage. I would I could make it better.

19th (Easter day). Up and this day put on my close-kneed coloured suit, which, with new stockings of the colour, with belt, and new gilt-handled sword, is very handsome. To church alone, and after dinner to church again, where the young Scotchman preaching I slept all the while. After supper, fell in discourse of dancing, and I find that Ashwell hath a very fine carriage, which makes my wife almost ashamed of herself to see herself so outdone, but to-morrow she begins to learn to dance for a month or two. So to prayers and to bed. Will being gone, with my leave, to his father's this day for a day or two, to take physique these holydays.

20th. Begun to look over my father's accounts, which he brought out of the country with him by my desire, whereby I may see what he has received and spent, and I find that he is not anything extravagant, and yet it do so far outdo his estate that he must either think of lessening his charge, or I must be forced to spare money out of my purse to helpe him through, which I would willing do as far as 20*l.* goes. To Mr. Grant's. There saw his prints, which he shewed me, and indeed are the best collection of

any things almost that ever I saw, there being the
prints of most of the greatest houses, churches, and
antiquitys in Italy and France and brave cutts. I had
not time to look them over as I ought. With Sir G.
Carteret and Sir John Minnes to my Lord Treasurer's,
thinking to have spoken about getting money for paying the Yards ; but we found him with some ladies at
cards : and so, it being a bad time to speak, we parted.
This day the little Duke of Monmouth was marryed
at White Hall, in the King's chamber ; and to-night
is a great supper and dancing at his lodgings, near
Charing-Cross. I observed his coate at the tail of his
coach : he gives the arms of England, Scotland, and
France, quartered upon some other fields,[1] but what it
is that speaks his being a bastard I know not.

21st. I ruled with red ink my English " Mare
Clausum," which, with the new orthodox title, makes
it now very handsome. So to business and home to
supper to play a game at cards with my wife ; Ashwell plays well at cards, and will teach us to play ;
I wish it do not lose too much of my time, and put
my wife too much upon it.

22nd. To the Change, and so to my uncle Wight's,
by invitation, whither my father, wife, and Ashwell

---

[1] The arms granted to the Duke of Monmouth, 8th April, 1665, were,
Quarterly, i. and iv.; Ermine, on a pile *gu.*, three lions passant gardant *or ;*
ii. and iii., *or*, an inescutcheon of France, within a double tressure flory
counter flory, *gu.* On the 22nd of April, 1667, another grant was made to
the Duke of the arms of Charles II., with a baton sinister *arg.;* over all, an
inescutcheon of Scott. The present Duke of Buccleuch bears these arms
quarterly. It is quite clear that Pepys knew nothing of heraldry.

came, where we had but a poor dinner, and not well dressed; besides, the very sight of my aunt's hands and greasy manner of carving, did almost turn my stomach. After dinner by coach to the King's Playhouse, where we saw but part of " Witt without mony," [1] which I do not like much, but coming late put me out of tune, and it costing me four half-crownes for myself and company.

23rd. St. George's day and Coronacion, the King and Court being at Windsor, at the installing of the King of Denmarke by proxy and the Duke of Monmouth. I, with my father, sat all the morning looking over his country accounts. I find his spending hitherto has been (without extraordinary charges) at full 100*l.* per annum, which troubles me, and I did let him apprehend it, so as that the poor man wept, though he did make it well appear to me that he could not have saved a farthing of it. I did tell him how things stand with us, and did shew my distrust of Pall, both for her good nature and housewifery, which he was sorry for, telling me that indeed she carries herself very well and carefully, which I am glad to hear, though I doubt it was but his doting and not being able to find her miscarriages so well nowadays as he could heretofore have done. Spend the evening with my father. At cards till late, and being at supper, my boy being sent for some mustard, staid half an houre in the streets, it seems at a bonfire, at

---

[1] Probably by Fletcher alone. (M. B.)

which I was very angry, and resolve to beat him to-morrow.

24th. Up betimes, and with my salt eele went down in the parler and there got my boy and did beat him till I was fain to take breath two or three times, yet for all I am afeard it will make the boy never the better, he is grown so hardened in his tricks, which I am sorry for, he being capable of making a brave man, and is a boy that I and my wife love very well. So made me ready, and to my office, where all the morning, and at noon home, whither came Captain Holland, who is lately come home from sea, and has been much harassed in law about the ship which he has bought, so that it seems in a despair he endeavoured to cut his own throat, but is recovered it; and it seems — whether by that or any other persuasion (his wife's mother being a great zealot) he is turned almost a Quaker, his discourse being nothing but holy, and that impertinent, that I was weary of him.

25th. Up betimes and to my vyall and song book a pretty while, and so to my office, and there we sat all the morning. Among other things Sir W. Batten had a mind to cause Butler (our chief witnesse in the business of Field, whom we did force back from an employment going to sea to come back to attend our law sute) to be borne as a mate on the Rainbow in the Downes in compensation for his loss for our sakes. This he orders an order to be drawn by Mr. Turner for, and after Sir J. Minnes, Sir W. Batten, and Sir W. Pen had signed it, it came to me and I was going to put it up into my book, thinking to consider of it and give them my opinion upon it before I parted with it, but Sir W. Pen told me I must sign or give it him again, for it should not go without my hand. I told him what I meant to do, whereupon Sir W. Batten was very angry, and in a great heat told me that I should not think as I have heretofore done, make them sign orders and not sign them myself. Which what ignorance or worse it implies is easy to judge, when he shall sign to things (and the rest of the board too as appears in this business) for company and not out of their judgment. After some discourse I did convince them that it was not fit to have it go, and Sir W. Batten first, and then the rest, did willingly cancel all their hands and tear the order, for I told them, Butler being such a rogue as I know him, and we have all signed him to be to the Duke, it will be in his power to publish this to our great reproach, that we should take such a course as this to serve ourselves in wronging the King by putting him into a place he is no wise capable of, and that in an Admiral ship. In the evening merrily practising to dance, which my wife hath begun to learn this day of Mr. Pembleton, but I fear will hardly do any great good at it, because she is conceited that she do well already, though I think no such thing. At Westminster Hall, this day, I buy a book lately printed and licensed by Dr. Stradling,[1] the Bishop of London's chaplin, being a book

---

[1] George Stradling, D.D., in 1672 made Dean of Chichester. Ob. 1688.

discovering the practices and designs of the papists, and the fears of some of our own fathers of the Protestant church heretofore of the return to Popery as it were prefacing it. The book is a very good book; but forasmuch as it touches one of the Queene-mother's father confessors, the Bishop, which troubles many good men and members of Parliament, hath called it in, which I am sorry for. Another book I bought, being a collection of many expressions of the great Presbyterian Preachers upon publique occasions, in the late times, against the King and his party, as some of Mr. Marshall, Case, Calamy, Baxter, &c.,[1] which is good reading now, to see what they then did teach, and the people believe, and what they would seem to believe now. Lastly, I did hear that the Queene is much grieved of late at the King's neglecting her, he having not supped once with her this quarter of a yeare, and almost every night with my Lady Castlemaine; who hath been with him this St. George's feast at Windsor, and came home with him last night; and, which is more, they say is removed as to her bed from her owne home to a chamber in White Hall, next to the King's owne; which I am sorry to hear, though I love her much.

26th (Lord's-day). Tom coming, with whom I was

---

[1] "Evangelium Armatum. A Specimen, or Short Collection of several Doctrines and Positions destructive to our Government, both Civil and Ecclesiastical, preached and vented by the known leaders and abettors of the pretended Reformation, such as Mr. Calamy, Mr. Jenkins, Mr. Case, Mr. Baxter, Mr. Caryll, Mr. Marshall, and others." London: Printed for William Garret, 1663, 4to.

angry for botching my camlott coat, to tell me that my father and he would dine with me, and that my father was at our church, I got me ready and had a very good sermon of a country minister upon "How blessed a thing it is for brethren to live together in unity!" All the afternoon upon my accounts, and find myself worth full 700*l*., for which I bless God, it being the most I was ever worth in money. In the evening my wife, Ashwell, and the boy and I, and the dogg, over the water and walked to Half-way house, and beyond into the fields, gathering of cow-slipps, and so to Half-way house, with some cold lamb we carried with us, and there supped, and had a most pleasant walke back again, Ashwell all along teilling us some parts of their maske at Chelsey Schoole, which was very pretty, and I find she hath a most prodigious memory, remembering so much of things acted six or seven years ago. So home, and after reading my vows, being sleepy, without prayers to bed, for which God forgive me!

27th. Will Griffin tells me this morning that Captain Browne, Sir W. Batten's brother-in-law, is dead of a blow given him two days ago by a seaman, a servant of his, being drunk, with a stone striking him on the forehead, for which I am sorry, he having a good woman and several small children. By water to White Hall; but found the Duke of York gone to St. James's for this summer; and thence with Mr. Coventry and Sir W. Pen up to the Duke's closett. And a good while with him about our Navy business; and so

I to White Hall, and there alone a while with my Lord Sandwich discoursing about his debt to the Navy, wherein he hath given me some things to resolve him in.   Thence to my Lord's lodgings, and thither came Creed to me, and he and I walked a great while in the garden, and thence to an alehouse in the market place to drink fine Lambeth ale, and so home, where I found Mary gone from my wife, she being too high for her, though a very good servant, and my boy too will be going in a few days, for he is not for my family, he is grown so out of order and not to be ruled, and do himself desire to be gone, which I am sorry for, because I love the boy and would be glad to bring him to good.   The Queene (which I did not know) it seems was at Windsor, at the late St. George's feast there ; and the Duke of Monmouth dancing with her with his hat in his hand, the King came in and kissed him, and made him put on his hat, which every body took notice of.

28th. Up betimes and to my office, only stepped up to see my wife and her dancing master at it, and I think after all she will do pretty well. So to dinner and then I to my office casting up my Lord's sea accounts over again, and putting them in order for payment.

29th. To Chelsey, where we found my Lord all alone at a little table with one joynt of meat at dinner ; we sat down and very merry talking, and mightily extolling the manner of his retirement, and the goodness of his diet : the mistress of the house,

Mrs. Becke, having been a woman of good condition heretofore, a merchant's wife, and hath all things most excellently dressed; among others, her cakes admirable, and so good that my Lord's words were, they were fit to present to my Lady Castlemaine. From ordinary discourse my Lord fell to talk of other matters to me, of which chiefly the second part of the fray, which he told me a little while since of, between Mr. Edward Montagu and himself; that he hath forborn coming to him almost two months, and do speak not only slightly of my Lord every where, but hath complained to my Lord Chancellor of him, and arrogated all that ever my Lord hath done to be only by his direction and persuasion. Whether he hath done the like to the King or no, my Lord knows not; but my Lord hath been with the King since, and finds all things fair; and my Lord Chancellor hath told him of it, but with so much contempt of Mr. Montagu, as my Lord knows himself very secure against any thing the foole can do; and notwithstanding all this, so noble is his nature, that he professes himself ready to show kindness and pity to Mr. Montagu on any occasion. My Lord told me of his presenting Sir H. Bennet with a gold cupp of 100*l.*, which he refuses, with a compliment; but my Lord would have been glad he had taken it, that he might have had some obligations upon him which he thinks possible the other may refuse to prevent it; not that he hath any reason to doubt his kindnesse. But I perceive great differences there are at Court; and Sir H. Bennet and my Lord Bristol, and their faction, are likely to carry all things before them (which my Lord's judgment is, will not be for the best), and particularly against the Chancellor, who, he tells me, is irrecoverably lost: but, however, that he will not actually joyne in any thing against the Chancellor, whom he do owne to be his most sure friend, and to have been his greatest; and therefore will not openly act in either, but passively carry himself even. The Queene, my Lord tells me, he thinks he hath incurred some displeasure with, for his kindness to his neighbour, my Lady Castlemaine. My Lord tells me he hath no reason to fall for her sake, whose wit, management, nor interest, is not likely to hold up any man, and therefore he thinks it not his obligation to stand for her against his owne interest. The Duke and Mr. Coventry my Lord says he is very well with, and fears not but they will show themselves his very good friends, specially at this time, he being able to serve them, and they needing him, which he did not tell me wherein. Talking of the business of Tangier, he tells me that my Lord Teviott[1] is gone away without the least respect paid to him, nor indeed to any man, but without his commission; and (if it be true what he says) having laid out seven or eight thousand pounds in commodities for the place; and besides having not only disobliged all the Commissioners for Tangier, but also Sir Charles Barkeley the other day, who spoke in behalf of Colonel Fitz-Gerald,

---

[1] See *ante*, Dec. 15, 1662, note.

that having been deputy-governor there already, he ought to have expected and had the governorship upon the death or removal of the former governor. And whereas it is said that he and his men are Irish, which is indeed the main thing that hath moved the King and Council to put in Teviott to prevent the Irish having too great and the whole command there under Fitz-Gerald; he further said that there was never an Englishman fit to command Tangier; my Lord Teviott answered yes, that there were many more fit than himself or Fitz-Gerald either. So that Fitz-Gerald being so great with the Duke of York, and being already made deputy-governor, independent of my Lord Teviott, and he being also left here behind him for a while, my Lord Sandwich do think that, putting all these things together, the few friends he hath left, and the ill posture of his affairs, my Lord Teviott is not a man of the conduct and management that either people take him to be, or is fit for the command of the place. And here, speaking of the Duke of York and Sir Charles Barkeley, my Lord tells me that he do very much admire the good management, and discretion, and nobleness of the Duke, that whatever he may be led by him or Mr. Coventry singly in private, yet he did not observe that in publique matters, but he did give as ready hearing and as good acceptance to any reasons offered by any other man against the opinions of them, as he did to them, and would concur in the prosecution of it. Then we came to discourse upon his own sea accompts, and

came to a resolution what and how to proceed in
them; wherein, though I offered him a way of evad-
ing the greatest part of his debt honestly, by making
himself debtor to the Parliament, before the King's
time, which he might justly do, yet he resolved to go
openly and nakedly in it, and put himself to the kindness of the King and Duke, which humour, I must
confess, and so did tell him (with which he was not a
little pleased) had thriven very well with him, being
known to be a man of candid and open dealing, without any private tricks or hidden designs as other men
commonly have in what they do. From that we had
discourse of Sir G. Carteret, and of many others; and
upon the whole I do find that it is a troublesome thing
for a man of any condition at Court to carry himself
even, and without contracting enemys or envyers;
and that much discretion and dissimulation is necessary to do it. Anon I took leave, and coming down
found my father unexpectedly in great pain and desiring for God's sake to get him a bed to lie upon, which
I did, and W. Howe and I staid by him, in so great
pain as I never saw, poor wretch, and with that patience, crying only: terrible, terrible pain, God helpe
me, God helpe me, with the mournful voice, that made
my heart ake. He desired to rest a little alone to see
whether it would abate, and W. Howe and I went
down and walked in the gardens, which are very fine,
and a pretty fountayne, with which I was finely wetted,
and up to a banquetting house, with a very fine pros-
pect, and so back to my father, who I found in such

pain that I could not bear the sight of it without weeping. At last I got him to go to the coach, and driving hard, meeting in the way with Captain Ferrers going to my Lord, to tell him that my Lady Jemimah is come to towne, and that Will Stankes is come with my father's horses, we got home and all helping we got him to bed presently, and after half an hour's lying in his naked bed, he was at good ease and so fell to sleep, and we went down whither W. Stankes was come with his horses. But it is very pleasant to hear how he rails at the rumbling and ado that is in London over it is in the country, that he cannot endure it.

30th. Up, and after drinking my morning draft with my father, who is very well again, and W. Stankes, I went forth to Sir W. Batten, who is going (to no purpose as he uses to do) to Chatham upon a survey. So to my office and then to the Exchange, and back home to dinner, where Mrs. Hunt, my father, and W. Stankes; but, Lord! what a stir Stankes makes with his being crowded in the streets and wearied in walking in London, and would not be wooed by my wife and Ashwell to go to a play, nor to White Hall, or to see the lyons,[1] though he was carried in a coach. I never could have thought there had been upon earth a man so little curious in the world as he is.

May 1st. Up betimes and my father with me, and he and I all the morning and Will Stankes settling our

---

[1] See 7th May, 1662. (M.B.)

The lions were in the Tower; whence the word lionize, which may puzzle the etymologists of the next century, the menagerie no longer existing.

matters concerning our Brampton estate, &c., and I find that there will be, after all debts paid within 100*l.*, 50*l.* per annum clear coming towards my father's maintenance, besides 25*l.* per annum annuities to my Uncle Thomas and Aunt Perkins. After dinner I got my father, brother Tom, and myself together, and I advised my father to good husbandry and to living within the compass of 50*l.* a year, and all in such kind words, as not only made them but myself to weep, and I hope it will have a good effect. That being done, we all took horse, and I, upon a horse hired of Mr. Game, saw him out of London, at the end of Bishopsgate Streete, and so I turned and rode, with some trouble, through the fields, and then Holborne, &c., towards Hide Parke, whither all the world, I think, are going; and in my going, almost thither, met W. Howe coming galloping upon a little crop black nag; it seems one that was taken in some ground of my Lord's, by some mischance being left by his master, a thiefe; this horse being found with black cloth eares on, and a false mayne, having none of his owne; and I back again with him to the Chequer, at Charing Crosse, and there put up my owne dull jade, and by his advice saddled a delicate stone horse of Captain Ferrers's, and with that rid in state to the Parke, where none better mounted than I almost, but being in a throng of horses, seeing the King's riders showing tricks with their managed horses, which were very strange, my stone-horse was very troublesome, and begun to fight with other horses, to the dangering him and myself, and with much ado I got out, and kept myself out of harm's way. Here I saw nothing good, neither the King, nor my Lady Castlemaine, nor any great ladies or beauties being there, there being more pleasure a great deal at an ordinary day; or else those few good faces that there were choked up with the many bad ones, there being people of all sorts to some thousands, I think. Going thither in the highway, just by the Parke gate, I met a boy in a sculler boat, carried by a dozen people at least, rowing as hard as he could drive, it seems upon some wager. By and by, about seven or eight o'clock, homeward; and changing my horse again, I rode home, coaches going in great crowds to the further end of the towne almost. In my way, in Leadenhall Streete, there was morris-dancing, which I have not seen a great while. So set my horse up at Game's, paying 5*s.* for him, and went to hear Mrs. Turner's daughter play on the harpsicon; but, Lord! it was enough to make any man sicke to hear her; yet I was forced to commend her highly. So home to supper. This day Captain Grove sent me a side of pork, which was the oddest present, sure, that was ever made any man; and the next, I remember I told my wife, I believe would be a pound of candles, or a shoulder of mutton; but the fellow do it in kindness, and is one I am beholden to. So to bed very weary, and a little galled for lack of riding, praying to God for a good journey to my father, of whom I am afeard, he being so lately ill.

22nd. Being weary last night, I slept till almost seven o'clock, a thing I have not done many a day. So up and to my office, being come to some angry words with my wife about neglecting the keeping of the house clean, I calling her beggar, and she me pricklouse, which vexed me. So to the Exchange and then home to dinner, and very merry and well pleased with my wife, and so to the office again, where we met extraordinary upon drawing up the debts of the Navy to my Lord Treasurer.

3rd (Lord's day). To church, where Sir W. Pen showed me the young lady which young Dawes,[1] that sits in the new corner-pew in the church, hath stole away from Sir Andrew Rickard,[2] her guardian, worth 1,000*l.* per annum present, good land, and some money, and a very well-bred and handsome lady: he, I doubt, but a simple fellow. However, he got this good luck to get her, which methinks I could envy him with all my heart. To church in the afternoon and so home again, and up to teach Ashwell the grounds of time and other things on the tryangle, and made her take out a Psalm very well, she having a good eare and hand.

---

[1] John, son of Sir Thomas Dawes, of Putney. He married Christian, daughter and heir of William Lyons, Esq., of Barking, Essex, and was created a Baronet in June, 1663. His third son, Sir William Dawes, became Archbishop of York.

[2] Sir Andrew Rickard, an eminent London merchant, chairman of the East India and Turkey companies; knighted 10th July, 1662. He was one of the principal inhabitants of St. Olave's, Hart Street, in the church of which parish he lies buried, and there his statue is still to be seen. He died 6th

4th. The dancing-master came, whom standing by, seeing him instructing my wife, when he had done with her, he would needs have me try the steps of a coranto;[1] and what with his desire and my wife's importunity, I did begin, and then was obliged to give him entry-money 10*s.*, and am become his scholler. The truth is, I think it a thing very useful for a gentleman, and sometimes I may have occasion of using it, and though it cost me what I am heartily sorry it should, besides that I must by my oathe give half as much more to the poor, yet I am resolved to get it up some other way, and then it will not be above a month or two in the year. So though it be against my stomach yet I will try it a little while; if I see it comes to any great inconvenience or charge I will fling it off. After I had begun with the steps of half a coranto, which I think I shall learn well enough, he went away, and we to dinner, and by and by out by coach, and set my wife down at my Lord Crew's, and I to St. James's; where Mr. Coventry, Sir W. Pen and I staid a good while for the Duke's coming in, but not coming, we walked to White Hall; and meeting the King, we followed him into the Parke, where Mr. Coventry and he talking of building a new yacht, which the King is resolved to have built out of his privy purse, he having some contrivance of his own. The talke being done, we fell off to White Hall, leav-

---

September, 1672, æt. suæ 68. He was father-in-law to John, Lord Berkeley, of Stratton, frequently mentioned by Pepys.

[1] *Coranto.* See note, 31st Dec. 1662. (M. B.)

ing the King in the Parke, and going back, met the Duke going towards St. James's to meet us. So he turned back again, and to his closett at White Hall; and there, my Lord Sandwich present, we did our weekly errand, and so broke up; and I down into the garden with my Lord Sandwich (after we had sat an houre at the Tangier Committee); and after talking largely of his own businesses, we began to talk how matters are at Court: and though he did not flatly tell me any such thing, yet I do suspect that all is not kind between the King and the Duke, and that the King's fondness to the little Duke do occasion it; and it may be that there is some fear of his being made heire to the Crown. But this my Lord did not tell me, but is my guess only; and that my Lord Chancellor is without doubt falling past hopes.

5th. Walked a good while up and down with Sir J. Minnes, he telling many old stories of the Navy, and of the state of the Navy at the beginning of the late troubles, and I am troubled at my heart to think, and shall hereafter cease to wonder, at the bad success of the King's cause, when such a knave as he (if it be true what he says) had the whole management of the fleete, and the design of putting out of my Lord Warwicke,[1] and carrying the fleete to the King, wherein he failed most fatally to the King's ruine. In the evening Deane of Woolwich went home with me and showed me the use of a little sliding

---

[1] Henry Rich, Earl of Warwick and Holland; beheaded for putting himself in arms to aid Charles I.

ruler, less than that I bought the other day, which is the same with that, but more portable. I find him an ingenious fellow, and a good servant in his place to the King. Then came Sir W. Warren, and he and I talked about merchandise, trade, and getting of money. I made it my business to enquire what way there is for a man bred like me to come to understand anything of trade. He did most discretely answer me in all things, shewing me the danger for me to meddle either in ships or merchandise of any sort or common stocks, but what I have to keep at interest, which is a good, quiett, and easy profit, and once in a little while something offers that with ready money you may make use of money to good profit. Wherein I concur much with him, and parted late with great pleasure and content in his discourse.

6th. Towards noon to the Exchange with Creed, where we met Sir J. Minnes coming in his coach from Westminster, who tells us, in great heat, that the Parliament will make mad work; that they will render all men incapable of any military or civil employment that have borne arms in the late troubles against the King, excepting some persons; which, if it be so, as I hope it is not, will give great cause of discontent, and I doubt will have but bad effects. To the Trinity House, and there dined, where, among other discourse worth hearing among the old seamen, they tell us that they have catched often in Greenland in fishing whales with the iron grapnells that had formerly been struck into their bodies covered over with fat; that they have had eleven hogsheads of oyle out of the tongue of a whale.

7th. To Westminster, and there up and down from the Hall to the Lobby, the Parliament sitting. Sir Thomas Crew this day tells me that the Queene, hearing that there was 40,000*l.* per annum brought into her account among the other expences of the Crown to the Committee of Parliament, she took order to let them know that she hath yet for the payment of her whole family received but 4,000*l.*, which is a notable act of spirit, and I believe is true. So by coach to my Lord Crew's, and there dined with him. He tells me of the order the House of Commons have made for the drawing an Act for the rendering none capable of preferment or employment in the State, but who have been loyall and constant to the King and Church; which will be fatal to a great many, and makes me doubt lest I myself, with all my innocence during the late times, should be brought in, being employed in the Exchequer; but, I hope, God will provide for me.

8th. To my office, there preparing letters to my father of great import in the settling of our affairs, and putting him upon a way of good husbandry, I promising to make out of my own purse him up to 50*l.* per annum, till either by my uncle Thomas's death or the fall of the Wardrobe place he be otherwise provided. That done I by water to the Strand, and there viewed the Queene-Mother's works at

Somersett House,[1] and thence to the new playhouse, but could not get in to see it. So to visit my Lady Jemimah, who is grown much since I saw her; but lacks mightily to be brought into the fashion of the court to set her off. Thence to the Temple, and there sat till one o'clock reading at Playford's in Dr. Usher's body of Divinity his discourse of the Scripture, which is as much, I believe, as is anywhere said by any man, but yet there is room to cavill, if a man would use no faith to the tradition of the Church in which he was born, which I think to be as good an argument as most is brought for many things, and it may be for that among others. Thence to my brother's, and there took up my wife and Ashwell to the Theatre Royall,[2] being the second day of its being opened. The house is made with extraordinary good contrivance, and yet hath some faults, as the narrowness of the passages in and out of the pitt, and the distance from the stage to the boxes, which I am confident cannot hear; but for all other things it is well, only, above all, the musique being below, and most of it sounding under the very stage, there is no hearing of the bases at all, nor very well of the trebles, which sure must be mended. The play was "The Humerous Lieutenant,"[3] a play that hath little

---

[1] Somerset House was greatly improved for Henrietta-Maria. The river front was built by Inigo Jones, and the County Fire Office in Regent Street, is a copy of it.

[2] Near Drury Lane. See note, 19th March, 1666. (M. B.)

[3] By Beaumont and Fletcher. (M. B.)

good in it, nor much in the very part which, by the King's command, Lacy now acts instead of Clun. In the dance, the tall devil's actions was very pretty. The play being done, we home by water, having been a little shamed that my wife and woman were in such a pickle, all the ladies being finer and better dressed in the pitt than they used, I think, to be. To my office to set down this day's passage, and, though my oathe against going to plays do not oblige me against this house, because it was not then in being, yet believing that at the time my meaning was against all publique houses, I am resolved to deny myself the liberty of two plays at Court, which are in arreare to me for the months of March and April, which will more than countervail the excess, so that this month of May is the first that I must claim a liberty of going to a Court play according to my oathe. So to supper, and at supper comes Pembleton, and afterwards we all up to dancing till late, and they say that I am like to make a dancer.

9th. Up betimes and to my office, whither sooner than ordinary comes Mr. Hater desiring to speak a word to me alone, which I was from the disorder of his countenance amused at, and so the poor man began telling me that by Providence being the last Lord's day at a meeting of some Friends upon doing of their duties, they were surprised, and he carried to the Counter, but afterwards released; however, hearing that Sir W. Batten do hear of it, he thought it good to give me an account of it, lest it might tend to any prejudice to me. I was extraordinary surprised with it, and troubled for him, knowing that now it is out it is impossible for me to conceal it, or keep him in employment under me without danger to myself. I cast about all I could, and did give him the best advice I could, desiring to know if I should promise that he would not for the time to come commit the same, he told me he desired that I would rather forbear to promise that, for he durst not do it, whatever God in His providence shall do with him, and that for my part he did bless God and thank me for all the love and kindness I have shewed him hitherto. I could not without tears in my eyes discourse with him further, but at last did pitch upon telling the truth of the whole to Mr. Coventry as soon as I could, and to that end did use means to prevent Sir W. Batten from going to that end to-day, lest he might doe it to Sir G. Carteret or Mr. Coventry before me; which I did prevail and kept him at the office all the morning. At noon dined at home with a heavy heart for the poor man, and after dinner went to Westminster, where at Mr. Jervas's, my old barber, I did try two or three borders and perriwiggs, meaning to wear one; and yet I have no stomach for it, but that the pains of keeping my hair clean is so great. He trimmed me, and at last I parted, but my mind was almost altered from my first purpose, from the trouble that I foresee will be in wearing them also.

10th (Lord's day). Up betimes, and put on a black cloth suit, with white lynings under all, as the fashion is to wear, to appear under the breeches. So being ready walked to St. James's, where I sat talking with Mr. Coventry about several businesses of the Navy, and afterwards, the Duke being gone out, he and I walked to White Hall together over the Parke, I telling him what had happened to Tom Hater, at which he seems very sorry, but tells me that if it is not made very publique, it will not be necessary to put him away at present, but give him good caution for the time to come. However, he will speak to the Duke about it and know his pleasure. Parted with him there, and I walked back to St. James's, and was there at masse, and was forced in the crowd to kneel down; and masse being done, to the King's Head ordinary, whither I sent for Mr. Creed and there we dined, where many Parliament-men; and most of their talk was about the news from Scotland, that the Bishop of Galloway was besieged in his house by some woman, and had like to have been outraged, but I know not how he was secured; which is bad news, and looks just as it did in the beginning of the late troubles. From thence they talked of rebellion; and I perceive they make it their great maxime to be sure to master the City of London, whatever comes of it or from it. After that to some other discourse, and, among other things, talking of the way of ordinaries, that it is very convenient, because a man knows what he hath to pay: one did wish that, among many bad, we could learn two good things of France, which were that we would not think it below the gentleman, or

person of honour at a taverne, to bargain for his meat
before he eats it ; and next, to take no servant without certificate from some friend or gentleman of his
good behaviour and abilities.   Hence with Creed into
St. James's Parke, and there walked all the afternoon,
and thence on foot home, and after a little while at
my office walked in the garden with my wife, and so
to supper, and after prayers to bed.

11th. Up betimes, and by water to Woolwich on
board the Royall James, to see in what dispatch she
is to be carried about to Chatham.   So to the yarde
a little, and thence on foot to Greenwich, where going
I was set upon by a great dogg, who got hold of my
garters, and might have done me hurt ; but, Lord, to
see in what a maze I was, that, having a sword about
me, I never thought of it, or had the heart to make
use of it, but might, for want of that courage, have
been worried.   Took water there and home, and after
dinner by coach with Sir W. Pen to St. James's, where
we attended the Duke of York : and, among other
things, Sir G. Carteret and I had a great dispute about
the different value of the pieces of eight rated by Mr.
Creed at 4*s.* and 5*d.*, and by Pitts at 4*s.* and 9*d.*, which
was the greatest husbandry to the King? he persisting
that the greatest sum was ; which is as ridiculous a
piece of ignorance as could be imagined.   However,
it is to be argued at the Board, and reported to the
Duke next week ; which I shall do with advantage, I
hope.   I went homeward, after a little discourse with
Mr. Pierce the surgeon, who tells me that my Lady

Castlemaine hath now got lodgings near the King's chamber at Court; and that the other day Dr. Clerke and he did dissect two bodies, a man and a woman, before the King, with which the King was highly pleased. I called upon Mr. Crumlum, and did give him the 10*s.* remaining, not laid out of the 5*l.* I promised him for the schoole, with which he will buy strings, and golden letters upon the books I did give them. So home, and finding Pembleton there we did dance till it was late, and so to supper and to bed.

12th. A little angry with my wife for minding nothing now but the dancing-master, having him come twice a day which is a folly. To my office, where we sat late, our chief business being the reconciling the business of the pieces of eight mentioned yesterday before the Duke of York, wherein I have got the day, and they are all brought over to what I said, of which I am proud.

13th. Busy all the morning, and at noon home to dinner, and after dinner Pembleton came and I practised. But, Lord! to see how my wife will not be thought to need telling by me or Ashwell, and yet will plead that she has learnt but a month, which causes many short fallings out between us. Mr. Barrow, storekeeper of Chatham, came, who tells me many things, how basely Sir W. Batten has carried himself to him, and in all things else like a passionate dotard, to the King's great wrong. God mend all, for I am sure we are but in an ill condition in the Navy, however the King is served in other places. Home to supper, to cards, and to bed.

14th. Met Mr. Moore; and with him to an ale-house in Holborne; where in discourse he told me that he fears the King will be tempted to endeavour the setting the Crown upon the little Duke, which may cause troubles; which God forbid, unless it be his due! He told me my Lord do begin to settle to business again, which I am glad of, for he must not sit out, now he has done his owne business by getting his estate settled, and that the King did send for him the other day to my Lady Castlemaine's, to play at cards, where he lost 50*l.*; for which I am sorry, though he says my Lord was pleased at it, and said he would be glad at any time to lose 50*l.* for the King to send for him to play, which I do not so well like. This day we received a baskett from my sister Pall, made by her of paper, which hath a great deale of labour in it for country innocent work.

15th. I walked in the Parke, discoursing with the keeper of the Pell Mell, who was sweeping of it; who told me of what the earth is mixed that do floor the Mall, and that over all there is cockle-shells powdered, and spread to keep it fast; which, however, in dry weather, turns to dust and deads the ball. Thence to Mr. Coventry; and sitting by his bedside, he did tell me that he sent for me to discourse upon my Lord Sandwich's allowances for his several pays, and what his thoughts are concerning his demands; which he could not take the freedom to do face to face, it being not so proper as by me: and did give me a most friendly and ingenuous account of all; telling me how

unsafe, at this juncture, while every man's, and his
actions particularly, are descanted upon, it is either
for him to put the Duke upon doing, or my Lord
himself to desire anything extraordinary, 'specially the
King having been so bountifull already; which the
world takes notice of even to some repinings. All
which he did desire me to discourse to my Lord of;
which I have undertaken to do. We talked also of
our office in general, with which he told me that he
was now-a-days nothing so satisfied as he was wont to
be. I confess I told him things are ordered in that
way that we must of necessity break in a little time a
pieces. After done with him about these things, he
told me that for Mr. Hater the Duke's word was in
short that he found he had a good servant, an Ana-
baptist, and unless he did carry himself more to the
scandal of the office, he would bear with his opinion
till he heard further, which do please me very much.
Thence walked to Westminster, and there up and
down in the Hall and the Parliament House all the
morning; and at noon by coach to my Lord Crew's,
hearing that my Lord Sandwich dined there; where I
told him what had passed between Mr. Coventry and
myself; with which he was contented, though I could
perceive not very well pleased. And I do believe that
my Lord do find some other things go against his
mind in the house; for in the motion made the other
day in the House by my Lord Bruce,[1] that none be

---

[1] Robert Bruce, second Earl of Elgin, created, in 1663–4, Baron and
Viscount Bruce and Earl of Ailesbury (English honours). He was also a

capable of employment but such as have been loyal
and constant to the King and Church, that the General [Monk] and my Lord were mentioned to be
excepted ; and my Lord Bruce did come since to my
Lord, to clear himself that he meant nothing to his
prejudice, nor could it have any such effect if he did
mean it. After discourse with my Lord, to dinner
with him ; there dining there my Lord Montagu[1] of
Boughton, Mr. William Montagu[2] his brother, the
Queene's Sollicitor, &c., and a fine dinner. Their talk
about a ridiculous falling-out two days ago at my Lord
of Oxford's house, at an entertainment of his, there
being there my Lord of Albemarle, Lynsey,[3] two of
the Porters,[4] my Lord Bellasses, and others, where
there were high words and some blows, and pulling
off perriwiggs ; till my Lord Monk took away some of
their swords, and sent for some soldiers to guard the
house till the fray was ended. To such a degree of
madness the nobility of this age is come ! After dinner I went up to Sir Thomas Crew, who lies there not
very well in his head, being troubled with vapours and
fits of dizzinesse : and there I sat talking with him all

Privy Councillor, and one of the Lords of the King's Bedchamber. He died
in 1685, just after his appointment as Lord Chamberlain to James II.

[1] Edward, second Lord Montagu of Boughton, in 1664 succeeded his
father, who had been created a Baron by James I., and died 1683, leaving a
son, afterwards Duke of Montagu.

[2] Afterwards Lord Chief Baron of the Exchequer. Ob. 1707, æt. 89.

[3] Montagu Bertie, second Earl of Lindsey, whose mother was Elizabeth,
daughter of Edward, first Lord Montagu of Boughton.

[4] Charles and Thomas Porter. The latter was engaged in a fatal duel
with Sir H. Bellassis. See 29th July, and 8th and 12th Aug., 1667.

the afternoon from one discourse to another, the most
was upon the unhappy posture of things at this time;
that the King do mind nothing but pleasures, and
hates the very sight or thoughts of business; that my
Lady Castlemaine rules him, who, he says, hath all
the tricks of Aretin [1] that are to be practised. If any
of the sober counsellors give him good advice, and
move him in anything that is to his good and honour,
the other part, which are his counsellors of pleasure,
take him when he is with my Lady Castlemaine, and
in a humour of delight, and then persuade him that
he ought not to hear nor listen to the advice of those
old dotards or counsellors that were heretofore his
enemies: when, God knows! it is they that now-a-
days do most study his honour. It seems the present
favourites now are my Lord Bristol, Duke of Buckingham, Sir H. Bennet, my Lord Ashley, and Sir Charles
Barkeley; who, among them, have cast my Lord
Chancellor upon his back, past ever getting up again;
there being now little for him to do, and he waits at
Court attending to speak to the King as others do:
which I pray God may prove of good effects, for it is
feared it will be the same with my Lord Treasurer
shortly. But strange to hear how my Lord Ashley, by
my Lord Bristol's means (he being brought over to
the Catholique party against the Bishopps, whom he
hates to the death, and publicly rails against them;

---

[1] " The name of Aretin will be execrated by the modest and virtuous for
the obscenities, the profane and immoral writings with which he has insulted
the world. He died 1556." — LEMPRIERE'S *Universal Biography.* (M. B.)

not that he is become a Catholique, but merely opposes the Bishopps; and yet, for aught I hear, the Bishopp of London keeps as great with the King as ever) is got into favour, so much that, being a man of great business and yet of pleasure, and drolling too, he, it is thought, will be made Lord Treasurer upon the death or removal of the good old man.[1] My Lord Albemarle, I hear, do bear through and bustle among them, and will not be removed from the King's good opinion and favour, though none of the Cabinett; but yet he is envied enough. It is made very doubtful whether the King do not intend the making of the Duke of Monmouth legitimate; but surely the Commons of England will never do it, nor the Duke of York suffer it, whose lady, I am told, is very troublesome to him by her jealousy. But it is wonderful that Sir Charles Barkeley should be so great still, not [only] with the King, but Duke also; who did so stiffly swear that he had lain with her. No care is observed to be taken of the main chance, either for maintaining of trade or opposing of factions, which, God knows, are ready to break out, if any of them (which God forbid!) should dare to begin; the King and every man about him minding so much their pleasures or profits. My Lord Hinchingbroke, I am told, hath had a mischance to kill his boy by his birding-piece going off as he was a-fowling. The gun was charged with small shot, and hit the boy in the face and about the tem-

---

[1] The Earl of Southampton.

ples, and he lived four days. In Scotland, it seems, for all the newes-books tell us every week that they are all so quiett, and everything in the Church settled, the old woman had like to have killed, the other day, the Bishop of Galloway, and not half the Churches of the whole kingdom conform. Strange were the effects of the late thunder and lightning about a week since at Northampton, coming with great rain, which caused extraordinary floods in a few houres, bearing away bridges, drowning horses, men, and cattle. Two men passing over a bridge on horseback, the arches before and behind them were borne away, and that left which they were upon : but, however, one of the horses fell over, and was drowned. Stacks of faggots carried as high as a steeple, and other dreadful things ; which Sir Thomas Crew showed me letters to him about from Mr. Freemantle and others, that it is very true. The Portugalls have choused [1] us, it seems, in the Island of Bombay, in the East Indys ; for after a great charge of our fleets being sent thither with full

---

[1] A *chiaus* was a Turkish word signifying "interpreter." In 1609 Sir Robert Shirley sent a messenger, or *chiaus*, to this country as his agent. Sir Robert followed him as Ambassador from the Grand Signior and the Sophy; but before he reached England his agent had *chiaused* the Turkish and Persian merchants here of 4,000*l.* and taken his flight. This is alluded to by Ben Jonson in the *Alchemist*, which appeared in 1610:

> " *D.*   What do you think of me,
> That I am a *chiaus* ?
>   *F.* What's that?
>   *D.*   The Turk was here.
> As one would say, Do you think I am a Turk ?"
>
>   *Alchemist*, act i. sc. 1. (M. B.)

commission from the King of Portugall to receive it, the Governour by some pretence or other will not deliver it to Sir Abraham Shipman, sent from the King, nor to my Lord of Marlborough; [1] which the King takes highly ill, and I fear our Queene will fare the worse for it. The Dutch decay there exceedingly, it being believed that their people will revolt from them there, and they forced to give over their trade. Sir Thomas showed me his picture and Sir Anthony Vandike's, in crayon in little, done exceedingly well. Having thus freely talked with him, and of many more things, I took leave, and by coach to St. James's, and there told Mr. Coventry what I had done with my Lord with great satisfaction, and so well pleased home.

16th. After dinner comes Pembleton, and I being out of humour would not see him, pretending business, but, Lord! with what jealousy did I walk up and down my chamber listening to hear whether they danced or no. So to my office awhile, and, my jealousy still reigning, I went in and did go up to them to practise, and did make an end of "La Duchesse," [2] which I think I should, with a little pains, do very well.

17th (Lord's day). Up and in my chamber all the morning, preparing my great letters to my father, stating to him the perfect condition of our estate.

18th. I walked to White Hall, and into the Parke,

---

[1] James Ley, third Earl of Marlborough, killed in the great sea-fight with the Dutch, 1665.

[2] The name of a dance.

seeing the Queene and Mayds of Honour passing through the house going to the Parke. But above all, Mrs. Stuart is a fine woman, and they say now a common mistress to the King, as my Lady Castlemaine is; which is a great pity. Thence taking a coach to Mrs. Clerke's, took her, and my wife, and Ashwell, and a Frenchman, a kinsman of hers, to the Parke, where we saw many fine faces, and one exceeding handsome, in a white dress over her head, with many others very beautiful. Staying there till past eight at night, I carried Mrs. Clerke and her Frenchman home, and thence home ourselves, talking much of what we had observed to-day of the poor household stuff of Mrs. Clerke and mere show and flutter that she makes in the world; and pleasing myself in my owne house and manner of living more than ever I did by seeing how much better and more substantially I live than others do.

19th. With Sir John Minnes to the Tower; and by Mr. Slingsby, and Mr. Howard, Controller of the Mint, we were shown the method of making this new money. That being done, the Controller would have us dine with him and his company, the King giving them a dinner every day. And very merry and good discourse about the business we have been upon, and after dinner went to the Assay Office and there saw the manner of assaying of gold and silver, and how silver melted down with gold do part, just being put into aqua-fortis, the silver turning into water, which they can bring again into itself out of the water. And here I was made thoroughly to understand the business of the fineness and coarseness of metals, and have put down my lessons with my other observations therein. At table they told us of two cheats, the best I ever heard. One, of a labourer discovered to convey away the bits of silver by swallowing them, and so they could not find him out, though, of course, they searched all the labourers; but, having reason to doubt him, they did, by threats and promises, get him to confess, and did find 7*l.* of it in his house at one time. The other that got a way of coyning as good and passable and large as the true money is, and yet saved fifty per cent. to himself, which was by getting moulds made to stamp groats like old groats, which is done so well, and I did beg two of them which I keep for rarities, that there is not better in the world, and is as good, nay, better than those that commonly go, which was the only thing that they could find out to doubt them by, besides the number that the party do go to put off, and then coming to the Comptroller of the Mint, he could not, I say, find out any other thing to raise any doubt upon, but only their being so truly round or near it. He was neither hanged nor burned, the cheat was thought so ingenious, and being the first time they could ever trap him in it, and so little hurt to any man in it, the money being as good as commonly goes. Thence to the office till the evening, and then over the water to the Half-way House, where we played at nine-pins. Then home to supper and bed, being late. The most observables in the making of money which I observed to-day, is the steps of their doing it.

1. Before they do anything they assay the bullion, which is done, if it be gold, by taking an equal weight of that and of silver, of each a small weight, which they reckon to be six ounces or half a pound troy; this they wrap up in within leade. If it be silver, they put such a quantity of that alone and wrap it up in leade, and then putting them into little earthen cupps made of stuffe like tobacco pipes, and put them into a burning hot furnace, where, after a while, the whole body is melted, and at last the leade in both is sunk into the body of the cupp, which carries away all the copper or dross with it, and left the pure gold and silver embodyed together, of that which hath both been put into the cupp together, and the silver alone in these where it was put alone in the leaden case. And to part the silver and the gold in the first experiment, they put the mixed body into a glass of aquafortis, which separates them by spitting out the silver into such small parts that you cannot tell what it becomes, but turns into the very water and leaves the gold at the bottom clear of itself, with the silver wholly spit out, and yet the gold in the form that it was double together in when it was a mixed body of gold and silver, which is a great mystery; and after all this is done to get the silver together out of the water is as strange. But the nature of the assay is thus : the piece of gold that goes into the furnace twelve ounces, if it comes out again eleven ounces, and the piece of silver which goes in twelve and comes out again eleven and two pennyweights, are just of the alloy of the standard

of England. If it comes out, either of them, either the gold above eleven, as very fine will sometimes within very little of what it went in, or the silver above eleven and two pennyweight, as that also will sometimes come out eleven and ten penny weight or more, they are so much above the goodness of the standard, and so they know what proportion of worse gold and silver to put to such a quantity of the bullion to bring it to the exact standard. And on the contrary, if it comes out lighter, then such a weight is beneath the standard, and so requires such a proportion of fine metal to be put to the bullion to bring it to the standard, and this is the difference of good and bad, better and worse than the standard, and also the difference of standards, that of Seville being the best and that of Mexico worst, and I think they said none but Seville is better than ours.

2. They melt it into long plates, which, if the mould do take ayre, then the plate is not of an equal heavinesse in every part of it, as it often falls out.

3. They draw these plates between rollers to bring them to an even thicknesse all along and every plate of the same thicknesse, and it is very strange how the drawing it twice easily between the rollers will make it as hot as fire, yet cannot touch it.

4. They bring it to another pair of rollers, which they call adjusting it, which bring it to a greater exactnesse in its thicknesse than the first could be.

5. They cut them into round pieces, which they do with the greatest ease, speed, and exactnesse in the world.

6. They weigh these, and where they find any to be too heavy they file them, which they call sizeing them, or light, they lay them by, which is very seldom, but they are of a most exact weight, but however, in the melting, all parts by some accident not being close alike, now and then a difference will be, and, this filing being done, there shall not be any imaginable difference almost between the weight of forty of these against another forty chosen by chance out of all their heapes.

7. These round pieces having been cut out of the plates, which in passing the rollers are bent, they are sometimes a little crooked or swelling out or sinking in, and therefore they have a way of clapping 100 or 2 together into an engine, which with a screw presses them so hard that they come out as flat as is possible.

8. They bleach them.

9. They mark the letters on the edges, which is kept as the great secret by Blondeau, who was not in the way, and so I did not speak with him to-day.

10. They mill them, that is, put on the marks on both sides at once with great exactnesse and speede, and then the money is perfect. The mill is after this manner : one of the dyes, which has one side of the piece cut, is fastened to a thing fixed below, and the other dye (and they tell me a payre of dyes will last the marking of £10,000 before it be worne out, they and all other their tools being made of hardened steel, and the Dutchman who makes them is an admirable artist, and has so much by the pound for

every pound that is coyned to find a constant supply of dyes) to an engine above, which is moveable by a screw, which is pulled by men ; and then a piece being clapped by one sitting below between the two dyes, when they meet the impression is set, and then the man with his finger strikes off the piece and claps another in, and then the other men they pull again and that is marked, and then another and another with great speede. They say that this way is more charge to the King than the old way, but it is neater, freer from clipping or counterfeiting, the putting of the words upon the edges being not to be done (though counterfeited) without an engine of the charge and noise that no counterfeit will be at or venture upon, and it employs as many men as the old and speedier. They now coyne between 16 and 24,000 pounds in a week. At dinner they did discourse very finely to us of the probability that there is a vast deal of money hid in the land, from this : — that in King Charles's time there was near ten millions of money coyned, besides what was then in being of King James's and Queene Elizabeth's, of which there is a good deale at this day in being. Next, that there was but 750,000*l.* coyned of the Harp and Crosse money,[1] and of this there was

---

[1] "This was the money coined by the Commonwealth, having on one side a shield bearing the Cross of St. George," and on the other a shield bearing a harp. — HAWKINS's *English Silver Coins*, p. 208. See also May 13, 1660, *ante*, where the harp was taken out of all the naval flags, no doubt because Charles II. objected to the arms used during the Protectorate.

500,000*l.* brought in upon its being called in. And from very good arguments they find that there cannot be less of it in Ireland and Scotland than 100,000*l.*; so that there is but 150,000*l.* missing; and of that, suppose that there should be not above 50,000*l.* still remaining, either melted down, hid, or lost, or hoarded up in England, there will then be but 100,000*l.* left to be thought to have been transported. Now, if 750,000*l.* in twelve years' time lost but a 100,000*l.* in danger of being transported, then 10,000,000*l.* in thirty-five years' time will have lost but 3,888,880*l.* and odd pounds; and as there is 650,000*l.* remaining after twelve years' time in England, so after thirty-five years' time, which was within this two years, there ought in proportion to have been resting 6,111,120*l.* or thereabouts, beside King James's and Queene Elizabeth's money. Now that most of this must be hid is evident, as they reckon, because of the dearth of money immediately upon the calling-in of the State's money, which was 500,000*l.* that came in; and yet there was not any money to be had in this City, which they say to their own observation and knowledge was so. And therefore, though I can say nothing in it myself, I do not dispute it.

20th. Going down by water to Woolwich took my wife and Ashwell, and going out met Mr. Howe come to see me, and took him with us. The tide against us, so I went ashore at Greenwich before, and did my business at the yarde about putting things in order as to their proceeding to build the new yacht ordered to be built by Christopher Pett, and so to Woolwich towne, where at an alehouse I found them ready to attend my coming, and so took boat again, my walke being very pleasant along the green corne and pease, and most of the way sang, he and I, and eat some cold meat we had, and with great pleasure home, and so he took horse again, and Pembleton coming, we danced a country dance or two and so broke up and to bed, my mind restless and like to be so while she learns to dance. God forgive my folly.

21st. To dinner, my wife and I having high words about her dancing to that degree that I did retire and make a vowe to myself not to oppose her or say anything to dispraise or correct her therein as long as her month lasts, in pain of *2s. 6d.* for every time, which, if God pleases, I will observe, for this roguish business has brought us more disquiett than anything that has happened a great while. After dinner to my office, where late, and then home; and Pembleton being there again, we fell to dance a country dance or two, and so to supper and to bed. But being at supper my wife did say something that caused me to oppose her in, she used the word devil, which vexed me, and among other things I said I would not have her to use that word, she took me up most scornfully, which, before Ashwell and the rest of the world, I know not now-a-days how to checke. So that I fear without great discretion I shall go near to lose too my command over her, and nothing do it more than giving her this occasion of dancing and other pleasures, whereby her mind is taken up from her business and finds other sweets besides pleasing of me. But if this month of her dancing were but out I shall hope with a little pains to bring her to her old wont.

22nd. Up pretty betimes, and shall, I hope, come to myself and business again, after a small playing the truant, for I find that my interest and profit do grow daily, for which God be praised and keep me to my duty. To my office, and anon one tells me that Rundall, the house-carpenter of Deptford, hath sent me a fine blackbird, which I went to see. He tells me he was offered 20*s.* for him as he came along, he do so whistle. Busy all the morning learning to understand the course of the tides, and I think I do now do it. At noon Mr. Creed comes to me, and he and I walked pleasantly to Woolwich, in our way hearing the nightingales sing. Took boat at Greenwich and to Deptford, and found Davis, the storekeeper, a knave and shuffling in the business of Bewpers with Young and Whistler to abuse the King, but I hope I shall be even with them. So home by water and to bed.

23rd. Waked this morning between four and five by my blackbird, which whistles as well as ever I heard any; only it is the beginning of many tunes very well, but there leaves them, and goes no further. To White Hall; where, in the Matted Gallery, Mr. Coventry was, who told us how the Parliament have required of Sir G. Carteret and him an account what money shall be necessary to be settled upon the Navy for the ordinary charge, which they intend to report 200,000*l.* per annum. And how to allott this we met this afternoon, and took their papers for our perusal, and so we parted. Only there was walking in the gallery some of the Barbary company, and there we saw a draught of the armes of the company, which the King is of, and so is called the Royall Company,[1] which is, in a field argent an elephant proper, with a Canton on which England and France is quartered, supported by two Moores. The crest an anchor winged, I think it is, and the motto too tedious: " Regio floret patrocinio commercium, commercioque Regnum." Thence back by water to Greatorex's, and there he showed me his varnish which he had invented, which appears every whit as good, upon a stick which he hath done, as the Indian, though it did not do very well upon my paper ruled with musique lines, for it sunk and did not shine.

24th (Lord's day). Forebore going to church this morning. At noon, dinner, and my wife telling me that there was a pretty lady come to church with Peg Pen to-day, I against my intention had a mind to go to church to see her, and did so, and she is pretty handsome. After sermon to Sir W. Pen's. So home, and read to my wife a fable or two in Ogleby's Æsop, and so to supper, and then to prayers and to bed. My wife this evening discoursing of making clothes

---

[1] The Royal African or Guinea Company of Merchants. (See Strype's " Stow," edit. 1720, b. v., p. 268.) Their house was called the African House (see Pepys, 13th Feb., 1663-4), and stood in Leadenhall Street.

for the country, which I seem against, pleading lacke of money, but I am glad of it in some respects because of getting her out of the way from this fellow Pembleton, and my own liberty to look after my owne business more than of late I have done.

25th. Ashwell came to me with an errand from her mistress to desire money to buy a country suit for her against she goes as we talked last night, and so I did give her 4*l*., and believe it will cost me the best part of 4 more to fit her out, but with peace and honour I am willing to spare anything so as to be able to keep all ends together, and my power over her undisturbed.   To St. James's, and staid there to speak with my Lord Sandwich, and in my staying, meeting Mr. Lewis Phillips of Brampton, he and afterwards others tell me that newes came last night to Court, that the King of France is sicke of the spotted fever, and that they are struck in again ; and this afternoon my Lord Mandeville is gone from the King to make him a visit ; which will be great newes, and of great import through Europe.   By and by, out comes my Lord Sandwich : he told me this day a vote hath passed that the King's grants of land to my Lord Monk and him should be made good ; which pleases him very well.   He also tells me that things do not go right in the House with Mr. Coventry ; I suppose he means in the business of selling of places ; but I am sorry for it.   Thence by coach home, where I found Pembleton, and so I up to dance with them till the evening, when there came Mr. Alsopp, the King's brewer, and Lanyon of Plymouth to see me. Mr. Alsopp tells me of a horse of his that lately, after four days' pain, voided four stones, bigger than that I was cut of, very heavy, and in the middle of each of them either a piece of iron or wood. The King has two of them in his closett, and a third the College of Physicians to keep for rarity.

27th. With Pett to my Lord Ashley, Chancellor of the Exchequer; where we met the auditors about settling the business of the accounts of persons to whom money is due before the King's time in the Navy, and the clearing of their imprests for what little of their debts they have received. I find my Lord, as he is reported, a very ready, quick, and diligent person. Thence I to Westminster Hall, where Terme and Parliament make the Hall full of people; no further newes yet of the King of France, whether he be dead or not. Here I met with my cozen Roger Pepys, and he tells me that his sister Claxton now resolving to give over the keeping of his house at Impington, he thinks it fit to marry again, and would have me, by the helpe of my uncle Wight or others, to look him out a widow between thirty and forty years old, without children, and with a fortune, which he will answer in any degree with a joynture fit for her fortune. A woman sober, and no high-flyer, as he calls it. I demanded his estate. He tells me, which he says also he hath not' done to any, that his estate is not full 800*l.* per annum, but it is 780*l.* per annum, of which 200*l.* is by the death of his last wife, which he will allot for a joynture for a wife, but the rest, which lies in Cambridgeshire, he is resolved to leave entire for his eldest son. I undertook to do what I can in it, and so I shall. He tells me that the King hath sent to the Parliament to hasten to make an end by midsummer, because of his going into the country; so they have set upon four bills to dispatch: the first of which is, he says, too devilish a severe act against conventicles: so beyond all moderation, that he is afeard it will ruin all: telling me that it is matter of the greatest grief to him in the world, that he should be put upon this trust of being a Parliament-man, because he says nothing is done, that he can see, out of any truth and sincerity, but mere envy and design. Thence by water to Chelsey, all the way reading a little book I bought of " Improvement of Trade," a pretty book and many things useful in it. So walked to Little Chelsey, where I found my Lord Sandwich with Mr. Becke, the master of the House, and Mr. Creed at dinner, and I sat down with them, and very merry. After dinner (Mr. Gibbons being come in also before dinner done) to musique, they played a good Fancy,[1] to which my Lord is fallen again, and says he cannot endure a merry tune, which is a strange turn of his humour, after he has for two or three years flung off the practice of Fancies [1] and played only fidlers' tunes.

---

[1] *Fancies.* A name for a sort of light ballads, or airs. " And sung those tunes to the over-scutched huswives that he heard the carmen whistle, and sware they were his *fancies* or his good-nights."—SHAKESPEARE, 2 *Henry IV.*, act iii. sc. 2. Nares' " Glossary." (M. B.)

Then into the Great Garden up to the Banqueting House : and there by my Lord's glass we drew in the species [1] very pretty. Afterwards to ninepins, where I won a shilling, Creed and I playing against my Lord and Cooke. This day there was great thronging to Banstead Downes, upon a great horse-race and foot-race. I am sorry I could not go thither. So home, where I find my wife in a musty humour, and tells me before Ashwell that Pembleton had been there, and she would not have him come in unless I was there, which I was ashamed of; but however, I had rather it should be so than the other way. So to my office, and by and by comes Pembleton, and word is brought me from my wife thereof that I might come home. So I sent word that I would have her go dance, and I would come presently. So being at a great loss whether I should appear to Pembleton or no, I at last resolved to go home, and took Tom Hater with me, and staid a good while in my chamber, and there took occasion to tell him how I hear that Parliament is putting an act out against all sorts of conventicles, and did give him good counsel, not only in his owne behalfe, but my owne, that if he did hear or know anything that could be said to my prejudice, that he would tell me, for in this wicked age (specially Sir W. Batten being so open to my reproaches, and Sir J. Minnes, for the neglect of their duty, and so will think

---

[1] This word is here used as an optical term, and signifies the image painted on the retina of the eye, and the rays of light reflected from the several points of the surface of objects.

themselves obliged to scandalize me all they can to right themselves if there shall be any inquiry into the matters of the Navy, as I doubt there will) a man ought to be prepared to answer for himself in all things that can be inquired concerning. After much discourse of this nature to him I sent him away, and then went up, and there we danced country dances, and single, my wife and I; and my wife paid him off for this month also, and so he is cleared. After dancing we took him down to supper, and were very merry, and I made myself so, and kind to him as much as I could.

28th. To Dr. Williams, to reckon with him for physique that my wife has had for a year or two, coming to almost 4*l.* Then to the Exchange, where I hear that the King had letters yesterday from France that the King there is in a way of living again, which I am glad to hear. At the coffee-house in Exchange Alley I bought a little book, "Counsell to Builders," by Sir Balth. Gerbier.[1] It is dedicated almost to all the men of any condition in England, so that the Epistles are more than the book itself, and both it and them not worth a farthing, that I am ashamed that I bought it. By water, and Creed with us, to the Royall

---

[1] A painter of Antwerp, recommended by Buckingham to Charles I., who knighted him and sent him to Brussels as Resident for the King. He died 1667. (M. B.) He published many works connected with architecture, and was as much a painter as an architect. In the "Parliamentary Intelligencer" are several advertisements of lectures given by him at his academy in Whitefriars, in 1649–50, on all sorts of subjects, in all sorts of languages, with an entertainment of music, "so there be time for the same."

Theatre; but that was so full they told us we could have no room. And so to the Duke's House; and there saw "Hamlett" done, giving us fresh reason never to think enough of Betterton. Who should we see come upon the stage but Gosnell, my wife's maid? but neither spoke, danced, nor sung; which I was sorry for. But she becomes the stage very well. Thence by water home, after we had walked to and fro, backwards and forwards, 6 or 7 times in the Temple walkes, disputing whether to go by land or water. By land home, and thence by water to Half-way House, and there eat some supper we carried with us, and so walked home again, it being late, and by and by to bed, Creed lying with me in the red chamber all night.

29th. This day is kept strictly as a holy-day, being the King's Coronation. Creed and I abroad, and called at several churches; and it is a wonder to see, and by that to guess the ill temper of the City at this time, either to religion in general, or to the King, that in some churches there was hardly ten people, and those poor people. To the Royall Theatre, but they not acting to-day, then to the Duke's house, and there saw "The Slighted Mayde,"[1] wherein Gosnell acted Pyramena, a great part, and did it very well, and I believe will do it better and better, and prove a good actor. The play is not very excellent, but is well acted, and in general the actors, in all particulars, are

---

[1] A Comedy, by Sir Robert Stapylton.

better than at the other house. Thence to the Cocke alehouse, and there having drunk, I sent them with Creed to see the German Princesse,[1] at the Gatehouse, at Westminster, and I to my brother's, to speak with him, and so home and to my office to put down these two days' journalls, and to supper, and then Creed and I to bed with good discourse, only my mind troubled about my spending my time so badly for these seven or eight days; but I must impute it to the disquiet that my mind has been in of late about my wife, and for my going these two days to plays, for which I have paid the due forfeit by money and abating the times of going to plays at Court, which I am now to remember that I have cleared all my times that I am to go to Court plays to the end of this month, and so June is the first time that I am to begin to reckon.

30th. Up betimes, and Creed and I by water to Fleet Streete, and my brother not being ready, he and I walked to the New Exchange, and there drank our morning draught of whay, the first I have done this year; but I perceive the lawyers come all in as they go to the Hall, and I believe it is very good. So to my brother, and there I found my aunt James, a poor, religious, well-meaning, good soul, talking of nothing but God Almighty, and that with so much innocence that mightily pleased me. Here was a fellow that said grace so long like a prayer; I believe the fellow is a

---

[1] Mary Carleton, of whom see more June 7 following, and April 15, 1664.

cunning fellow, and yet I by my brother's desire did give him a crowne, he being in great want, and, it seems, a parson among the fanatiques, and a cozen of my poor aunt's, whose prayers she told me did do me good among the many good souls that did by my father's desires pray for me when I was cut of the stone, and which God did hear, which I also in complaisance did owne; but, God forgive me, my mind was otherwise. I had a couple of lobsters and some wine for her.

31st (Lord's day). Lay long in bed talking with my wife, and do plainly see that her distaste (which is beginning now in her again) against Ashwell arises from her jealousy of me and her, and my neglect of herself, which indeed is true, and I to blame; but for the time to come I will take care to remedy all. So up and to church. Home to dinner, and after dinner up and read part of the new play of "The Five Houres' Adventures,"[1] which though I have seen it twice, yet I never did admire or understand it enough, it being a play of the greatest plot that ever I expect to see, and of great vigour quite through the whole play, from beginning to the end. To church again after dinner, and there the Scot preaching I slept most of the sermon. Being come from church, I to make up my month's accounts, and find myself clear worth 726*l.*, for which God be praised. This month the greatest newes is, the height and heat that the

---

[1] Said to be adapted by Lord Bristol and Sir Samuel Tuke from Calderon's "Los Empeños de Seis Horas." (M. B.)

Parliament is in, in enquiring into the revenue, which displeases the Court, and their backwardness to give the King any money. Their enquiring into the selling of places do trouble a great many; among the chief, my Lord Chancellor (against whom particularly it is carried), and Mr. Coventry; for which I am sorry. The King of France was given out to be poisoned and dead; but it proves to be the measles: and he is well, or likely to be soon well again. I find myself growing in the esteem and credit that I have in the office, and I hope falling to my business again will confirm me in it, and the saving of money, which God grant. So to supper and to bed. Will having neglected to brush my clothes, as he ought to do, till I was ready to go to church, and not then till I bade him, I was very angry, and seeing him make little matter of it, but seeming to make it a matter indifferent whether he did it or no, I did give him a box on the eare, and had it been another day should have done more. This is the second time I ever struck him.

June 1st. Begun again to rise betimes by 4 o'clock, and made an end of "The Adventures of Five Houres," and it is a most excellent play. So to my office and then to my brother's, where I dined (being invited) with Mr. Peter and Deane Honiwood,[1] where Tom did give us a very pretty dinner, and we very pleasant, but not very merry, the Deane being but a weak

---

[1] Dean of Lincoln. (M. B.)

man, though very good. I was forced to rise, being in haste to attend the Duke ; but the Duke having been a-hunting to-day, and so lately come home and gone to bed, we could not see him, and we walked away. And I with Sir J. Minnes to the Strand May-pole ;[1] and there 'light out of his coach, and walked to the New Theatre,[2] which, since the King's players are gone to the Royal one, is this day begun to be employed by the fencers to play prizes at. And here I came and saw the first prize I ever saw in my life : and it was between one Mathews, who did beat at all weapons, and one Westwicke, who was soundly cut several times both in the head and legs, that he was all over blood : and other deadly blows they did give and take in very good earnest, till Westwicke was in a most sad pickle. They fought at eight weapons, three boutes at each weapon. It was very well worth seeing, because I did till this day think that it has only been a cheate ; but this being upon a private quarrel, they

---

[1] The May-pole in the Strand was set up by John Clarges, a blacksmith, whose daughter Ann became the wife of Monk, Duke of Albemarle. It was taken down in 1713 and a new one erected where now is the new church, opposite Somerset House.

> " Amid that area wide they took their stand,
> Where the tall *May-pole* once o'erlooked the Strand;
> But now (so Anne and Piety ordain)
> A church collects the saints of Drury Lane."
>
> POPE, *The Dunciad.*

The pole was taken down in 1717. Its height above ground was originally above one hundred feet. Sit Isaac Newton begged it of the parish and sent it to the Rector of Wanstead, who set it up in Wanstead Park to sustain the largest telescope then in Europe. (M. B.)

[2] Opened 8th April, 1663.

did it in good earnest; and I felt one of their swords, and found it to be very little, if at all blunter on the edge, than the common swords are. Strange to see what a deale of money is flung to them both upon the stage between every boute. But a woeful rude rabble there was, and such noises, made my head ake all this evening. So, well pleased for once with this sight, I walked home. This day I hear at Court of the great plot which was lately discovered in Ireland, made among the Presbyters and others, designing to cry up the Covenant, and to secure Dublin Castle and other places; and they have debauched a good part of the army there, promising them ready money. Some of the Parliament there, they say, are guilty, and some withdrawn upon it; several persons taken, and among others a son of Scott's, that was executed here for the King's murder. What reason the King hath, I know not; but it seems he is doubtfull of Scotland: and this afternoon, when I was there, the Council was called extraordinary; and they were opening the letters this last post's coming and going between Scotland and us and other places. Blessed be God, my head and hands are clear, and therefore my sleep safe. The King of France is well again.

2d. To St. James's, to Mr. Coventry; where I had an hour's private talke with him. Most of it was discourse concerning his own condition, at present being under the censure of the House, being concerned with others in the Bill for selling of offices. He tells me, that though he thinks himself to suffer much in his fame hereby, yet he values nothing more of evil to hang over him; for that it is against no statute, as is pretended, nor more than what his predecessors time out of mind have taken; and that so soon as he found himself to be in an errour, he did desire to have his fees set, which was done; and since that time he hath not taken a token more. He undertakes to prove, that he did never take a token of any captain to get him employed in his life beforehand, or demanded any thing: and for the other accusation, that the Cavaliers are not employed, he looked over the list of them now in the service, and of the twenty-seven that are employed, thirteen have been heretofore always under the King; two neutralls, and the other twelve men of great courage, and such as had either the King's particular commands, or great recommendation to put them in, and none by himself. Besides that, he says it is not the King's nor Duke's opinion that the whole party of the late officers should be rendered desperate. And lastly, he confesses that the more of the Cavaliers are put in, the less of discipline hath followed in the fleete; and that, whenever there comes occasion, it must be the old ones that must do any good, there being only, he says, but Captain Allen good for anything of them all. He tells me, that he cannot guess whom all this should come from; but he suspects Sir G. Carteret, as I also do, at least that he is pleased with it. But he tells me that he will bring Sir G. Carteret to be the first adviser and instructor of him what is to make his place of benefit to him; telling him that Smith did make his place worth 5,000*l.* and he believed 7,000*l.* to him the first year; besides something else greater than all this, which he forbore to tell me. It seems one Sir Thomas Tomkins [1] of the House, that makes many mad motions, did bring it into the House, saying that a letter was left at his lodgings, subscribed by one Benson (which is a feigned name, for there is no such man in the Navy), telling him how many places in the Navy have been sold. And by another letter, left in the same manner since, nobody appearing, he writes him that there is one Hughes and another Butler (both rogues, that have for their roguery been turned out of their places), that will swear that Mr. Coventry did sell their places and other things. I offered him my service, and will with all my heart serve him; but he tells me he do not think it convenient to meddle, or to any purpose, but is sensible of my love therein. So away to Westminster Hall, where I hear more of the plot from Ireland; which it seems hath been hatching, and known to the Lord Lieutenant a great while, and kept close till within three days that it should have taken effect. The terme ended yesterday, and it seems the Courts rose sooner, for want of causes, than it is remembered to have done in the memory of man. To Mr. Beacham, the goldsmith, he being one of the jury to-morrow in Sir W. Batten's case against Field. I have been telling him our case, and I believe he will do us good service there. So

---

[1] M. P. for Weobly, and one of the proposed Knights of the Royal Oak, for Herefordshire.

home, and dined with Sir W. Batten, Sir J. Minnes, and others, at Sir W. Batten's, Captain Allen giving them a Foy[1] dinner, he being to go down to lie Admiral in the Downes this summer. To-night I took occasion with the vintner's man, who came by my direction to taste again my tierce of claret, to go down to the cellar with him to consult about the drawing of it; and there, to my great vexation, I find that the cellar door hath long been kept unlocked, and above half the wine drunk. I was deadly mad at it, and examined my people round, but nobody would confess it. My wife did also this evening tell me a story of Ashwell stealing some new ribbon from her, a yarde or two, which I am sorry to hear, and I fear my wife do take a displeasure against her, that they will hardly stay together, which I should be sorry for, because I know not where to pick such another out anywhere.

3rd. Up betimes, and studying of my double horizontal diall against Deane Honiwood comes to me, who dotes mightily upon it, and I think I must give it him. So after talking with Sir W. Batten, who is this morning gone to Guildhall to his trial with Field, I to my office, and there read all the morning in my statute-book, consulting among others the statute against selling of offices, wherein Mr. Coventry is so much concerned; and though he tells me that the statute do not reach him, yet I much fear that it will. At

---

[1] See note 20th March, 1660. (M. B.)

noon, hearing that the trial is done, and Sir W. Batten come to the Sun behind the Exchange I went thither, where he tells me that he had much ado to carry it on his side, but that at last he did, but the jury, by the Judge's favour, did give us but 10*l.* damages and the charges of the suit, which troubles me ; but it is well it went not against us, which would have been much worse. So to the Exchange, and thence home to dinner, taking Deane of Woolwich along with me, and he and I spent all the afternoon finely, learning of him the method of drawing the lines of a ship, to my great satisfaction, and which is well worth my spending some time in, as I shall do when my wife is gone into the country.

4th. To Westminster Hall, and after I had staid in the Hall a good while, where I heard that this day the Archbishop of Canterbury, Juxon,[1] a man well spoken of by all for a good man, is dead; and the Bishop of London[2] is to have his seat. Home by water, where by and by comes Deane Honiwood, and I showed him my double horizontal diall, and promise to give him one, and that shall be it. So, without eating or drinking, he went away to Mr. Turner's, where Sir J. Minnes do treat my Lord Chancellor and a great deale of guests to-day with a great dinner, which I thank God I do not pay for ; and besides, I doubt it is too late for any man to expect any great service

---

[1] William Juxon, made Bishop of London 1633, translated to Canterbury 1660.

[2] Gilbert Sheldon, who did succeed him.

from my Lord Chancellor, for which I am sorry, and pray God a worse do not come in his room. By and by comes Will Howe to see us, and walked with me an houre in the garden, talking of my Lord's falling to business again, which I am glad of, and his coming to lie at his lodgings at White Hall again. The match between Sir J. Cutts[1] and my Lady Jemimah,[2] he says, is likely to go on; for which I am glad. In the Hall to-day Dr. Pierce tells me that the Queene begins to be briske, and play like other ladies, and is quite another woman from what she was. It may be, it may make the King like her the better, and forsake his two mistresses, my Lady Castlemaine and Stewart.[3]

5th. Up, and by and by the carver coming, I directed him how to make me a neat head for my viall that is making. About 10 o'clock my wife and I, not without some discontent, abroad by coach, and I set her at her father's; but their condition is such that she will not let me see where they live, but goes by herself when I am out of sight. Thence to my brother's, taking care for a passage for my wife the next week in a coach to my father's, and thence to Paul's Churchyarde, where I found several books ready bound for me; among others, the new Concordance of the Bible, which pleases me much, and is a book I hope to make good use of. Thence, taking the little His-

---

[1] Of Childerley, near Cambridge.

[2] Lady Jemima Montagu, daughter to the Earl of Sandwich. It went off, and she married Philip Carteret.

[3] Spelt indiscriminately in the MS. Stuart, Steward, and Stewart.

tory of England with me, I went by water to Deptford, where Sir J. Minnes and Sir W. Batten attending the pay; I dined with them, and there Dr. Britton,[1] parson of the towne, a fine man and good company, dined with us, and good discourse.   I left them and to Mr. Turner's, and there saw Mr. Edward Pepys's lady,[2] who my wife concurs with me to be very pretty, as most women we ever saw.

6th. Walked, drinking my morning draft of whay by the way, to York House, where the Russia Embassador do lie; and there I saw his people go up and down louseing themselves: they are all in a great hurry, being to be gone the beginning of next week. But that that pleased me best, was the remains of the noble soul of the late Duke of Buckingham appearing in his house, in every place, in the door-cases and the windows.   By and by comes Sir John Hebden,[3] the Russia Resident, to me, and he and I in his coach to White Hall, to Secretary Morrice's, to see the orders about the Russia hempe that is to be fetched from Archangel for our King, and that being done, to coach again, and he brought me into the City and so I home; and after dinner abroad by water, and met by appointment Mr. Deane in the Temple Church, and he and

---

[1] Robert Bretton, D.D., vicar of St. Nicholas, Deptford. He was also rector of St. Martin's, Ludgate, and prebendary of Cadington Minor, in the church of St. Paul's. See Evelyn's " Diary," Feb. 20, 1672.

[2] Elizabeth, daughter and co-heir of John Walpole of Bransthorpe, Norfolk. Ob. s. p. s., 1668.

[3] Sir John Hebden, who had made a fortune in Russia by trade. On the 30th May, 1663, he was knighted by Charles, at Whitehall.

I over to Mr. Blackbury's yarde, and thence to other
places, and after that to a drinking house, in all which
places I did so practise and improve my measuring of
timber, that I can now do it with great ease and perfection, which do please me mightily. This fellow
Deane is a conceited fellow, and one that means the
King a great deale of service, more of disservice to
other people that go away with the profits which he
cannot make ; but, however, I learn much of him, and
he is, I perceive, of great use to the King in his place,
and so I shall give him all the encouragement I can.
Home by water, and having wrote a letter for my wife
to my Lady Sandwich to copy out to send this night's
post, I to the office, and wrote there myself several
things, and so home to supper and bed. My mind
being troubled to think into what a temper of neglect
I have myself flung my wife into by my letting her
learn to dance, that it will require time to cure her of,
and I fear her going into the country will but make
her worse ; but only I do hope in the meantime to
spend my time well in my office, with more leisure
than while she is here. Hebden, to-day in the coach,
did tell me how he is vexed to see things at Court
ordered as they are by nobody that attends to business, but every man himself or his pleasures. He
cries up my Lord Ashley to be almost the only man
that he sees to look after business ; and with that ease
and mastery, that he wonders at him. He cries out
against the King's dealing so much with goldsmiths,
and suffering himself to have his purse kept and com-

manded by them.   He tells me also with what exact care and order the States of Holland's stores [1] are kept in their Yards, and every thing managed there by their builders with such husbandry as is not imaginable ; which I will endeavour to understand further, if I can by any means learn.

7th (Lord's day).   Whit Sunday.   Lay long talking with my wife, sometimes angry and ended pleased and hope to bring our matters to a better posture in a little time, which God send.   So up and to church, where Mr. Mills preached, but, I know not how, I slept most of the sermon.   Thence home, and dined with my wife and Ashwell and after dinner discoursed very pleasantly and so I to church again in the afternoon and, the Scot preaching, again slept all the afternoon, and by and by to Sir W. Batten's, to talk about business, where my Lady Batten inveighed mightily against the German Princesse,[2] and I as high in the defence of her wit and spirit, and glad that she is cleared at the sessions.   Thence to Sir W. Pen, who I found ill again of the goute, he tells me that now Mr. Castle and Mrs. Martha Batten do owne themselves to be married, and have been this fortnight. Much good may it do him, for I do not envy him his wife.   So home, and there my wife and I had an

---

[1] Hebden had been resident with the States General in 1660.

[2] This impostor, called the German princess, was tried for bigamy at the Old Bailey and acquitted; she had inveigled a young citizen into marriage under pretence of being a German princess, the citizen pretending, at the same time, to be a nobleman.   For her appearance on the stage see Diary, 15th April, 1664.   (M. B.)

angry word or two upon discourse of our boy, compared with Sir W. Pen's boy, whom I say is much
prettier than ours and she the contrary. It troubles
me to see that every small thing is enough now-a-days
to bring a difference between us. Mrs. Turner, who
is often at Court, do tell me to-day that for certain
the Queene hath much changed her humour, and is
become very pleasant and sociable as any; and they
say is with child, or believed to be so.

8th. To my office, and thence by coach with Sir
J. Minnes to St. James's to the Duke, where Mr. Coventry and us two did discourse with the Duke a little
about our office business, and so to rights home again.
After dinner my wife and I had a little jangling, in
which she did give me the lie, which vexed me, so
that finding my talking did but make her worse, and
that her spirit is lately come to be other than it used
to be, and now depends upon her having Ashwell by
her, before whom she thinks I shall not say nor do
anything of force to her, which vexes me and makes
me wish that I had better considered all that I have
of late done concerning my bringing my wife to this
condition of heat, I went up vexed to my chamber
and there fell examining my new concordance, that I
have bought, with Newman's, the best that ever was
out before, and I find mine altogether as copious as
that and something larger, though the order in some
respects not so good, that a man may think a place
is missing, when it is only put in another place. Up
by and by my wife comes and good friends again, and

to walk in the garden and so anon to supper and to bed.

9th. After ordering some things towards my wife's going into the country, to the office, where I spent the morning upon my measuring rules very pleasantly till noon, and then comes Creed and he and I talked about mathematiques, and he tells me of a way found out by Mr. Jonas Moore [1] which he calls duodecimal arithmetique, which is properly applied to measuring, where all is ordered by inches, which are 12 in a foot, which I have a mind to learn.

10th. All the morning helping my wife to put up her things towards her going into the country and drawing the wine out of my vessel to send. To dinner, and thence to the Royal Theatre by water, and landing, met with Captain Ferrers his friend, the little man that used to be with him, and he with us, and sat by us while we saw " Love in a Maze." [2]   The play is pretty good, but the life of the play is Lacy's part, the clowne, which is most admirable ; but for the rest, which are counted such old and excellent actors, in my life I never heard both men and women so ill pronounce their parts, even to my making myself sicke therewith.   Thence, Creed happening to be with us, we four to the Half-Moone Taverne, I buying some

---

[1] Sir Jonas Moore, an able mathematician, born at Whitby, 1620. At the Restoration Charles II. made him Surveyor-General of the Ordnance. He obtained the foundation of a mathematical school at Christ's Hospital. See Diary, 23rd May, 1661. (M. B.)

[2] By Shirley, licensed 1631. (M. B.)

sugar and carrying it with me, which we drank with wine and thence to the whay-house, and drank a great deal of whay, and so by water home, and thence to see Sir W. Pen who is not in much pain, but his legs swell and so immoveable that he cannot stir them, but as they are lifted by other people and I doubt will have another fit of his late pain. Played a little at cards with him and his daughter who is grown every day a finer and finer lady, and so home to supper and to bed. When my wife and I came first home we took Ashwell and all the rest below in the cellar with the vintner drawing out my wine, which I blamed Ashwell much for and told her my mind that I would not endure it, nor was it fit for her to make herself equal with the ordinary servants of the house.

11th. Spent most of the morning upon my measuring Ruler and with great pleasure I have found out some things myself of great dispatch, more than my book teaches me, which pleases me mightily. Sent my wife's things and the wine to-day by the carrier to my father, but staid my boy from a letter of my father's, wherein he desires that he may not come to trouble his family as he did the last year. Dined at home and then to the office, where we sat all the afternoon, and at night home and spent the evening with my wife and she and I did jangle mightily about her cushions that she wrought with worsteds the last year, which are too little for any use, but were good friends by and by again. But one thing I must confess I do observe, which I did not before, which is, that I cannot blame my wife to be now in a worse humour than she used to be, for I am taken up in my talke with Ashwell, who is a very witty girle, that I am not so fond of her as I used and ought to be, which now I do perceive I will remedy, but I would to the Lord I had never taken any, though I cannot have a better than her. The consideration that this is the longest day in the year is unpleasant to me.

12th. At noon to the Exchange and so home to dinner, and abroad with my wife by water to the Royall Theatre; and there saw "The Committee," [1] a merry but indifferent play, only Lacey's part, an Irish footman, is beyond imagination. Here I saw my Lord Falconbridge,[2] and his Lady, my Lady Mary Cromwell, who looks as well as I have known her, and well clad; but when the House began to fill she put on her vizard,[3] and so kept it on all the play; which

---

[1] "The Committee," a comedy, by Sir Robert Howard.

[2] Thos. Bellasses Viscount Falconberg, frequently called Falconbridge, married Mary, third daughter of Oliver Cromwell. She died 1712.

[3] Black masks were frequently worn by ladies in public in the time of Shakespeare, particularly, and perhaps universally, at the theatres. See Nares' "Glossary." (M. B.)

On the 1st of June, 1704, a song was sung at the theatre in Lincoln's Inn Fields called "The Misses' Lamentation for want of their Vizard Masques at the Theatre." Notwithstanding the gross licentiousness of the drama after the Restoration, numbers of females of all denominations frequented the theatres, though many of them wore masks to disguise their features, and this bad habit had a still worse effect by the facilities which it afforded to intrigue and assignation. The custom is pointedly referred to in Pope's well-known lines:—

> "The fair sat panting at a courtier's play,
> And not a Mask went unimproved away;
> The modest fan was lifted up no more,
> And virgins smiled at what they blushed before."

of late is become a great fashion among the ladies, which hides their whole face. So to the Exchange, to buy things with my wife; among others, a vizard for herself.

13th. Up and betimes to Thames Streete among the tarr men, to look the price of tarr and so to the office and there had a difference with Sir W. Batten about Mr. Bowyer's tarr, which I am resolved to cross, though he sent me last night, as a bribe, a barrel of sturgeon, which, it may be, I shall send back, for I will not have the King abused so abominably in the price of what we buy, by Sir W. Batten's corruption and underhand dealing. So from the office, Mr. Wayth with me, to the Parliament House and there I told Sir G. Carteret all with which he is well pleased, and do recall his willingness yesterday, it seems, to Sir W. Batten, that we should buy a great quantity of tarr, being abused by him. Thence with Mr. Wayth after drinking a cupp of ale at the Swan, talking of the corruption of the Navy and so home, and after dinner by water to the Royall Theatre, where I resolved to bid farewell, as shall appear by my oathes to-morrow against all plays either at publique houses or Court till Christmas be over. Here we saw "The Faithfull Sheepheardesse," [1] a most simple thing, and yet much thronged after, and often shown, but it is only for the scenes' sake, which is very fine indeed and worth seeing; but I am quite out of opinion with any of their

---

[1] By John Fletcher, published 1610. (M. B.)

actings, but Lacy's, compared with the other house. Thence to see Mrs. Hunt, which we did and were much made of; and in our way saw my Lady Castlemaine, who, I fear, is not so handsome as I have taken her for, and now she begins to decay something. This is my wife's opinion also, for which I am sorry. Thence by coach, with a mad coachman, that drove like mad, and down byeways, through Bucklersbury home, everybody through the streete cursing him, being ready to run over them. Yesterday, upon conference with the King in the Banqueting House, the Parliament did agree with much ado, it being carried but by forty-two voices, that they would supply him with a sum of money; but what and how is not yet known, but expected to be done with great disputes the next week. But if done at all, it is well.

14th (Lord's day). To church. Then to dinner, and Tom dined with me, who I think grows a very thriving man, as he himself tells me. He being gone, and sending my people to church, my wife and I did even our reckonings, and had a great deale of serious talke, wherein I took occasion to give her hints of the necessity of our saving all we can. I do see great cause every day to curse the time that ever I did give way to the taking of a woman for her, though I could never have had a better, and also the letting of her learne to dance, by both which her mind is so devilishly taken off her business and minding her occasions, and besides has got such an opinion in her of my being jealous, that it is never to be removed, I fear, nor hardly my trouble that attends it; but I must have patience. I did give her 40*s.* to carry into the country to-morrow with her, whereof 15*s.* is to go for the coach-hire for her and Ashwell, there being 20*s.* paid here already in earnest. In the evening our discourse turned to great content and love, and I hope that after a little forgetting our late differences, and being a while absent one from another, we shall come to agree as well as ever. So to Sir W. Pen's to visit him, and finding him alone, sent for my wife, who is in her riding-suit, to see him, which she hath not done these many months I think. By and by in comes Sir J. Minnes and Sir W. Batten, and so we sat talking. Among other things, Sir J. Minnes brought many fine expressions of Chaucer, which he doats on mightily, and without doubt he is a very fine poet.

15th. Up betimes, and anon my wife did rise and did give me her keys, and put other things in order and herself against going this morning into the country. I was forced to go to Thames Street and strike up a bargain for some tarr, to prevent being abused therein by Hill, who is mightily surprised that I should tell him what I can have the same tarr with his for. Thence home, but finding my wife gone, I took coach and after her to her inne, where I am troubled to see her forced to sit in the back of the coach, though pleased to see her company none but women and one parson; and so, kissing her often, and Ashwell once, I bid them adieu. So home by coach, and thence by water to Deptford to the Trinity House, where I came a little late; but I found them reading their charter, which they did like fools, only reading here and there a bit, whereas they ought to do it all, every word, and then proceeded to the election of a maister, which was Sir W. Batten. Then to the choice of their assistants and wardens, and so rose. I might have received 2*s*. 6*d*. as a younger Brother, but I directed one of the servants of the House to receive it and keep it. Thence to church, where Dr. Britton preached a sermon full of words against the Non-conformists, but no great matter in it, nor proper for the day at all. His text was, "With one mind and one mouth give glory to God, the Father of our Lord Jesus Christ." That done, by water, I in the barge with the Maister, to the Trinity House at London; where, among others, I found my Lord Sandwich and Craven, and my cousin Roger Pepys, and Sir Wm. Wheeler. Anon we sat down to dinner, which was very great, as they always have. Great variety of talke. Mr. Prin, among many, had a pretty tale of one that brought in a bill in parliament for the im-powering him to dispose his land to such children as he should have that should bear the name of his wife. It was in Queen Elizabeth's time. One replied that there are many species of creatures where the male gives the denomination to both sexes, as swan and woodcocke, but not above one where the female do, and that is a goose. Both at and after dinner we had great discourses of the nature and power of spirits, and whether they can animate dead bodies; in all

which, as of the general appearance of spirits, my
Lord Sandwich is very scepticall. He says the greatest warrants that ever he had to believe any, is the
present appearing of the Devil [1] in Wiltshire, much
of late talked of, who beats a drum up and down.
There are books of it, and, they say, very true; but
my Lord observes, that though he do answer to any
tune that you will play to him upon another drum, yet
one tune he tried to play and could not; which makes
him suspect the whole; and I think it is a good argument. Sometimes they talked of handsome women,
and Sir J. Minnes saying that there was no beauty like
what he sees in the country-markets, and specially at
Bury, in which I will agree with him that there is the
prettiest women I ever saw. My Lord replied thus:
"Sir John, what do you think of your neighbour's
wife?" looking upon me. "Do you not think that
he hath a great beauty to his wife? Upon my word
he hath." Which I was not a little proud of.
Thence by barge with my Lord to Blackfriars, and
thence walked home, my head akeing with the healths
I was forced to drink to-day, and up to my wife's
closett, and there played on my viallin a good while,
and without supper anon to bed, sad for want of my

---

[1] Joseph Glanville published a Relation of the famed disturbance at the
house of Mr. Mompesson, at Tedworth, Wilts, occasioned by the beating of
an invisible drum every night for a year. This story, which was believed at
the time, furnished the plot for Addison's play of "The Drummer, or the
Haunted House." In the "Mercurius Publicus," April 16–23, 1663, there is
a curious examination on this subject, by which it appears that one William
Drury, of Uscut, Wilts, was the invisible drummer.

wife, whom I love with all my heart, though of late she has given me some troubled thoughts.

16th. Dined with Sir W. Batten; who tells me that the House have voted the supply, intended for the King, shall be by subsidy.

17th. Up before 4 o'clock, which is the houre I intend now to rise at, and to my office a while, and with great pleasure I fell to my business again. Thence to White Hall, and in the garden spoke to my Lord Sandwich, who is in his gold-buttoned suit, as the mode is, and looks nobly. Captain Ferrers, I see, is come home from France. He tells me the young gentlemen are well there; so my Lord went to my Lord Albemarle's to dinner, and I by water home. I sent my cozen Edward Pepys his Lady, at my cozen Turner's, a piece of venison given me yesterday, and Madam Turner I sent for a dozen bottles of her's, to fill with wine for her. This day I met with Pierce the surgeon, who tells me that the King has made peace between Mr. Edward Montagu and his father Lord Montagu, and that all is well again; at which, for the family's sake, I am very glad, but do not think it will hold long.

18th. Up by four o'clock and to my office, where all the morning writing out in my Navy collections the ordinary estimate of the Navy, and did it neatly. Then dined at home alone, my mind pleased with business, but sad for the absence of my wife. After dinner half an houre at my viallin, and then all the afternoon sitting at the office late, and so home and to bed.

19th. To Lambeth, expecting to have seen the Archbishop lie in state; but it seems he is not laid out yet. And so over to White Hall, and at the Privy Seale Office examined the books, and found the grant of increase of salary to the principall officers in the year 1639, 300*l.* among the Controller, Surveyor, and Clerk of the Shippes. Met Captain Ferrers; who tells us that the King of France is well again, and that he saw him train his Guards, all brave men, at Paris; and that when he goes to his mistresse, Madame La Valiere, a pretty little woman, now with child by him, he goes with his guards with him publiquely, and his trumpets and kettle-drums with him; and yet he says that, for all this, the Queene do not know of it, for that nobody dares to tell her; but that I dare not believe. Thence I to Wilkinson's, where we had bespoke a dish of pease, where we eat them very merrily, and there being with us the little gentleman, a friend of Captain Ferrers, that was with my wife and I at a play a little while ago, we went thence to the Rhenish wine-house, where we called for a red Rhenish wine called Bleahard, a pretty wine, and not mixed, as they say. Here Mr. Moore showed us the French manner, when a health is drunk, to bow to him that drunk to you, and then apply yourself to him, whose lady's health is drunk, and then to the person that you drink to, which I never knew before; but it seems it is now the fashion. Thence by water home and to bed, having played out of my chamber window on my pipe, and making Will read a part of a Latin chapter, in which I perceive in a little while he will be pretty ready, if he spends but a little pains in it.

20th. Mr. Deane, of Woolwich, with me, and he and I all the afternoon down by water, and in a timber yarde, measuring of timber, which I now understand thoroughly, and shall be able in a little time to do the King great service. Home in the evening, and after Will's reading a little in the Latin Testament to bed.

21st (Lord's day). Up betimes, and fell to reading my Latin grammar, which I perceive I have great need of, having lately found it by my calling Will to the reading of a chapter in Latin, and I am resolved to go through it. After being trimmed, I by water to White Hall, and so over the Parke to Mr. Coventry's chamber, where I spent two hours with him about business of the Navy, and how by his absence things are like to go with us. He shewed me a list, which he hath prepared for the Parliament's viewe, if the business of his selling of offices should be brought to further hearing, wherein he reckons up, as I remember, 236 offices of ships which have been disposed of without his taking one farthing. This, of his own accord, he opened his cabinet on purpose to shew me, meaning, I suppose, that I should discourse abroad of it, and vindicate him therein, which I shall with all my power do. At home, being wet, shifted my band and things, and after dinner went up and tried a little upon my tryangle, which I understand fully, and with a little use I believe could bring myself to do something. So to church, and slept all the sermon, the Scot, to whose voice I am not to be reconciled, preaching. So to my office, and read my vows seriously and with content, and so home to supper, prayers, and bed.

22nd. To my office, reading over all our letters of the office that we have wrote since I came into the Navy, whereby to bring the whole series of matters into my memory, and to enter in my manuscript some of them that are needful and of great influence. By and by with Sir W. Batten by coach to Westminster, where all along I find the shops evening with the sides of the houses, even in the broadest streets; which will make the City very much better than it was. I walked in the Hall from one man to another, and hear that the House is still divided about the manner of levying the subsidys which they intend to give the King, both as to the manner, the time, and the number. It seems the House do consent to send to the King to desire that he would be graciously pleased to let them know who it was that did inform him of what words Sir Richard Temple [1] should say, which were to this purpose: "That if the King would side with him, or be guided by him and his party, that he should not lacke money:" but without knowing who told it, they do not think fit to call him to any account for it. Thence with Creed and bought a lobster, and then to an ale-house. Here we eat it, and thence to walk in the Parke a good while. The Duke being gone a-hunting, and by and by came in and shifted himself; he having

---

[1] Sir Richard Temple, of Stowe, Bart., M. P. for Buckingham, and K. B. Ob. 1694.

in his hunting, rather than go about, 'light and led
his horse through a river up to his breast, and came
so home : and being ready, we had a long discourse
with him. But Creed's accounts stick still through the
perverse ignorance of Sir G. Carteret, which I cannot
safely control as I would. Thence to the Parke again
with Creed, talking, who is so knowing, and a man
of that reason, that I cannot but love his company,
though I do not love the man, because he is too wise
to be made a friend of, and acts all by interest and
policy, but is a man fit to learn of. So to White Hall,
and meeting Strutt, the purser, he tells me for a secret
that he was told by Field that he had a judgment
against me in the Exchequer for 400*l*. So I went to
Sir W. Batten, and taking Mr. Batten, his son the
counsellor, with me, by coach, I went to Clerke, our
Solicitor, who tells me there can be no such thing.
I returned home and to my office, setting down this
day's passages, and went to supper, and then a Latin
chapter of Will and to bed.

23rd. Up by four o'clock, and so to my office ; but
before I went out, calling, as I have of late done, for
my boy's copy-book, I found that he had not done
his taske ; so I beat him, and then went up to fetch
my rope's end, but before I got down the boy was
gone. I searched the ceilar with a candle, and from
top to bottom could not find him high nor low. So
to the office ; and after an houre or two, by water to
the Temple, to my cozen Roger ; who, I perceive,
is a deadly high man in the Parliament business, and

against the Court, showing me how they have computed that the King hath spent, at least hath received, about four millions of money since he came in : and in Sir J. Winter's case, in which I spoke to him, he is so high that he says he deserves to be hanged, and all the high words he could give, which I was sorry to see, though I am confident he means well. To the 'Change ; and by and by comes the King and the Queene by in great state, and the streets full of people. I stood in Mr. ———'s balcone. They dine all at my Lord Mayor's ; but what he do for victuals, or room for them, I know not. So home to dinner alone, and there I found that my boy had got out of doors, and came in for his hat and band, and so is gone away to his brother ; but I do resolve even to let him go away for good and all. So I by and by to the office, and there had a great fray with Sir W. Batten and Sir J. Minnes, who, like an old dotard, is led by the nose by him. It was in Captain Cocke's business of hempe, wherein the King is absolutely abused ; but I was for peace sake contented to be quiett and to sign to his bill, but in my manner so as to justify myself, and so all was well : but to see what a knave Sir W. Batten is makes my heart ake.

24th. Up before 4 o'clock, and so to my lute an hour or more, and then by water, drinking my morning draft alone at an alehouse, to St. James's, and there an houre's private discourse with Mr. Coventry, where he told me one thing to my great joy, that in the business of Captain Cocke's hempe, disputed be-

fore him the other day, Mr. Coventry absent, the
Duke did himself tell him since, that Mr. Pepys and
he did stand up and carry it against the rest that were
there, Sir G. Carteret and Sir W. Batten, which do
please me much to see that the Duke do take notice
of me. Speaking of Sir G. Carteret slightly, and
diminishing of his services for the King in Jersey;
that he was well rewarded, and had good lands and
rents, and other profits from the King, all the time
he was there; and that it was always his humour
to have things done his way. He brought an example how he would not let the Castle there be
victualled for more than a month, that so he might
keep it at his beck, though the people of the towne
did offer to supply it more often themselves, which,
when one did propose to the King, Sir George Carteret being by, says Sir George, " Let me know who
they are that would do it, I would with all my heart
pay them." " Ah, by God," says the Commander
that spoke of it, " that is it that they are afeard
of, that you would hug them," meaning that he
would not endure them. Another thing he told me,
how the Duke of York did give Sir G. Carteret and
the Island his profits as Admirall, and other things,
towards the building of a pier there. But it was
never laid out, nor like to be. So it falling out that
a lady being brought to bed, the Duke was to be
desired to be one of the godfathers; and it being
objected that that would not be proper, there being
no peer of the land to be joyned with him, the lady

replied, "Why, let him choose ; and if he will not be a godfather without a peer, then let him even stay till he hath made a pier of his owne."[1]   He tells me, too, that he hath lately been observed to tack about at Court, and to endeavour to strike in with the persons that are against the Chancellor ; but this he says of him, that he do not say nor do any thing to the prejudice of the Chancellor.   But he told me that the Chancellor was rising again, and that of late Sir G. Carteret's business and employment hath not been so full as it used to be while the Chancellor stood up. From that we discoursed of the evil of putting out men of experience in business as the Chancellor, and from that to speak of the condition of the King's party at present, who, as the Papists, though otherwise fine persons, yet being by law kept for these fourscore years out of employment, they are now wholly uncapable of business ; and so the Cavaliers for twenty years, who, says he, for the most part have either given themselves over to look after country and family business, and those the best of them, and the rest to debauchery, &c. ; and that was it that hath made him high against the late Bill brought into the House for the making all men incapable of employment that had served against the King.   Why, says he, in the sea-service, it is impossible to do any thing without them,

---

[1] In the same spirit, long after this, some question arising as to the best material to be used in building Westminster Bridge, Lord Chesterfield remarked that there were too many wooden piers (peers) at Westminster already.

there being not more than three men of the whole
King's side that are fit to command almost; and
these were Captn. Allen, Smith,[1] and Beech;[2] and it
may be Holmes, and Utber, and Batts might do
something. After a good deale of good and fine discourse, I took leave, and so to my Lord Sandwich's
house, where I met my Lord, and there did discourse
of our office businesses, and how the Duke do show
me kindness though I have endeavoured to displease
more or less of my fellow officers, all but Mr. Coventry and Pett; but it matters not. Yes, says my
Lord, Sir J. Minnes, who is great with the Chancellor;
I told him the Chancellor I have thought was declin-
ing, and however that the esteem he has among them
is nothing but for a jester or a ballad maker; at which
my Lord laughs, and asks me whether I believe he
ever could do that well. Thence with Mr. Creed up
and down to an ordinary, and, the King's Head being
full, we went to the other over against it, a pretty man
that keeps it, and good and much meat, better than
the other, but the company and room so small that
he must breake, and there wants the pleasure that the
other house has in its company. Here however dined
an old courtier that is now so, who did bring many
examples and arguments to prove that seldom any
man that brings any thing to Court gets any thing,
but rather the contrary; for knowing that they have

---

[1] Afterwards Sir Thomas Allen, and Sir Jeremy Smith.

[2] Probably Richard Beach, afterwards knighted, and in 1668 Commissioner at Portsmouth.

wherewith to live, they will not enslave themselves to the attendance, and flattery, and fawning condition of a courtier, whereas another that brings nothing, and will be contented to coy, and lie, and flatter every man and woman that has any interest with the persons that are great in favour, and can cheat the King, as nothing is to be got without offending God and the King, there he for the most part, and he alone, saves any thing. This day I observed the house, which I took to be the new tennis-court, newly built next my Lord's lodgings, to be fallen down by the badness of the foundation or slight working, which my cozen Roger and his discontented party cry out upon, as an example how the King's worke is done. It hath beaten down a good deal of my Lord's lodgings, and had like to have killed Mrs. Sarah, she having but newly gone out of it.

25th. Creed and I did draw up a letter to Sir G. Carteret in excuse and preparation for Creed against we meet before the Duke upon his accounts, but I am pleased to see with what secret cunning and variety of artifice this Creed has carried on his business even unknown to me. About this all the morning, only Mr. Bland came to me and told me the newes, which holds to be true, that the Portuguese did let in the Spaniard by a plot, and they being in the midst of the country and we believing that they would have taken the whole country, they did all rise and kill the whole body, near 8,000 men, and Don John of Austria having two horses killed under him, was forced with one man to flee away. Sir G. Carteret at the office did tell us that upon Tuesday last, being with my Lord Treasurer, he showed him a letter from Portugall speaking of the advance of the Spaniards into their country, and yet that the Portuguese were never more courageous than now; for by an old prophecy sent thither some years though not many since from the French King, it is foretold that the Spaniards should come into their country, and in such a valley they should be all killed, and then their country should be wholly delivered from the Spaniards. This was on Tuesday last, and yesterday came the very first newes that in this very valley they had thus routed and killed the Spaniards, which is very strange but true. This noon I received a letter from the country from my wife, wherein she seems much pleased with the country; God continue that she may have pleasure while she is there. She, by my Lady's advice, desires a new petticoat of the new silke striped stuff, very pretty. So I went to Paternoster Row presently, and bought her a very fine rich one, the best I did see there, and much better than she desires or expects.

26th. Mr. Moore coming to see me, he and I discoursed of going to Oxford this commencement, Mr. Nathaniel Crew[1] being Proctor and Mr. Childe commencing Doctor of Musique this year, which I have a great mind to do, and, if I can, will order my matters, so that I may do it. A sad season, that it

---

[1] Nathaniel, third Lord Crewe of Stene, successively Bishop of Oxford and Durham. He died in 1701, s. p., when the title became extinct.

is said there hath not been one fair day these three
months, and I think it is true. At the Parliament
House I spoke with Roger Pepys. The House is
upon the King's answer to their message about Temple,[1] which is, that my Lord of Bristoll did tell him
that Temple did say those words; so the House are
resolved upon sending some of their members to him
to know the truth, and to demand satisfaction if it be
not true. Sir W. Batten, Sir J. Minnes, my Lady
Batten, and I by coach to Bednall Green, to Sir W.
Rider's to dinner, where a fine place, good lady
mother, and their daughter, Mrs. Middleton, a fine
woman. A noble dinner, and a fine merry walke with
the ladies alone after dinner in the garden; the greatest quantity of strawberrys I ever saw, and good.
This very house[2] was built by the blind beggar[3] of
Bednall Green, so much talked of and sang in ballads;
but they say it was only some of the outhouses of it.
At table, discoursing of thunder and lightning, they
told many stories of their own knowledge at table of
their masts being shivered from top to bottom, and
sometimes only within and the outside whole, but Sir
W. Rider did tell a story of his own knowledge, that
a Genoese gally in Legorne Roads was struck by

---

[1] See 1st July, *postea*.

[2] "Called Kirby Castle, the property of Sir William Ryder, Knight, who
died therein 1669." — LYSONS's *Environs*.

[3] The house in which Sir William Ryder resided was built by John Thorpe,
in 1570, for "John Kirby," of whom nothing is known, except that it was
called after him. Pepys was evidently misinformed in supposing that it could
ever have been inhabited by the blind beggar.

thunder, so as the mast was broke a-pieces, and the shackle upon one of the slaves was melted clear off of his leg without hurting his leg. Sir William went on board the vessel, and would have contributed towards the release of the slave whom Heaven had thus set free, but he could not compass it, and so he was brought to his fetters again.

27th. Up by 4 o'clock and a little to my office. Then comes by agreement Sir W. Warren, and he and I from ship to ship to see deales of all sorts, whereby I have encreased my knowledge and with great pleasure. Then to his yarde and house, where I staid discoursing of the expense of the navy and the corruption of Sir W. Batten and his man Wood that he brings or would bring to sell all that is to be sold by the Navy. To the Temple, and so to Lincoln's Inn, and there walked up and down to see the new garden which they are making, and will be very pretty, and so to walke under the Chappell by agreement, whither Mr. Clerke our Solicitor came to me and he fetched Mr. Long, our Attorney in the Exchequer in the business against Field, and I directed him to come to the best and speediest composition he could, which he will do.

28th (Lord's day). Spent most of the afternoon reading in Cicero and other books. Cast up my monthly accounts and to my great trouble I find myself 7*l*. worse than I was the last month, but I confess it is by my reckoning beforehand a great many things, yet however I am troubled to see that I can hardly promise myself to lay up much from month's end to month's end, about 4*l.* or 5*l.* at most, one month with another, without some extraordinary gettings, but I must and I hope I shall continue to have a care of my own expenses. So to the reading my vows seriously and then to supper.

29th. Up and down the streets is cried mightily the great victory got by the Portugalls against the Spaniards, where 10,000 slain, 3 or 4,000 taken prisoners, with all the artillery, baggage, money, &c., and Don John [1] of Austria forced to flee with a man or two with him. With my cozen Roger and Mr. Goldsborough to Gray's Inne to his counsel, one Mr. Rawworth, a very fine man, where it being the question whether I as executor should give a warrant to Goldsborough in my reconveying her estate back again, the mortgage being performed against all acts of the testator, but only my owne, my cozen said he never heard it asked before; and the other that it was always asked, and he never heard it denied, or scrupled before, so great a distance was there in their opinions, enough to make a man forswear ever having to do with the law; so they agreed to refer it to Serjeant Maynard. So home and I up to my lute long and then to bed.

30th. Yesterday and to-day the sun rising very bright and glorious; and yet yesterday, as it hath

---

[1] He was natural son of Philip IV., King of Spain, who after his father's death in 1665 exerted his whole influence to overthrow the Regency appointed during the young king's minority.

been these two months and more, was a foul day the most part of the day. Creed and I to the Parke, whither by and by comes my Lord Sandwich, and he and we walked two hours and more in the Parke and then in Whitehall Gallery discoursing of Mr. Creed's accounts, and how to answer the Treasurer's objections. I find that the business is 500*l.* deep, the advantage of Creed, and why my Lord and I should be concerned to promote his profit with so much dishonour and trouble to us I know not, but however we shall do what we can, though he deserves it not, for there is nothing even to his own advantage that can be got out of him, but by mere force. So full of policy he is in the smallest matters, that I perceive him to be made up of nothing but design. I left him here, being in my mind vexed at the trouble that this business gets me and the distance that it makes between Sir G. Carteret and myself, which I ought to avoyde. This day the only fair day we have had these two or three months. Thus, by God's blessing, ends this book of two years;[1] I being in all points in good health and a good way to thrive and do well. Some money I do and can lay up, but not much, being worth now above 700*l.* besides goods of all sorts. My wife in the country with Ashwell, her woman, with my father; myself at home with W. Hewer and my cooke-mayde Hannah, my boy Wayneman being lately run away from me. In my office, my repute and

---

[1] The end of the Second Volume of Pepys's MS. (M. B.)

understanding good, specially with the Duke and Mr.
Coventry; only the rest of the officers do rather envy
than love me, I standing in most of their lights, specially Sir W. Batten, whose cheats I do daily oppose
to his great trouble, though he appears mighty kind
and willing to keep friendship with me, while Sir J.
Minnes, like a dotard, is led by the nose by him. My
wife and I by my late jealousy, for which I am truly to
be blamed, have not the kindnesse between us which
we used and ought to have and I fear will be lost hereafter if I do not take course to oblige her and yet
preserve my authority. Publique matters are in an ill
condition; Parliament sitting and raising four subsidys
for the King, which is but a little, considering his
wants; and yet that parted withal with great hard-
nesse. They being offended to see so much money
go, and no debts of the publique's paid, but all swal-
lowed by a luxurious Court; which the King it is
believed and hoped will retrench in a little time, when
he comes to see the utmost of the revenue which
shall be settled on him: he expecting to have his
1,200,000*l.* made good to him, which is not yet done
by above 150,000*l.* as he himself reports to the House.
My differences with my uncle Thomas at a good
quiett, blessed be God! and other matters. The
towne full of the great overthrow lately given to the
Spaniards by the Portugall, they being advanced into
the very middle of Portugall. The weather wet for
two or three months together beyond belief, almost
not one fair day coming between till this day. The

charge of the Navy intended to be limited to 200,000*l.* per annum, the ordinary charge of it, and that to be settled upon the Customes. The King yet greatly taken up with Madam Castlemaine and Mrs. Stewart, which God of heaven put an end to! Myself very studious to learne what I can of all things necessary for my place, as an officer of the Navy, reading lately what concerns measuring of timber and knowledge of the tides. I have of late spent much time with Creed, but I find him a fellow of those designs and tricks, that I must cast him off, though he be a very understanding man, and one that much may be learned of as to cunning and judging of other men. Besides too I do perceive more and more that my time of pleasure and idlenesse of any sort must be flung off to attend to getting of some money and the keeping of my family in order, which I fear by my wife's liberty may be otherwise lost.

July 1st. This morning it rained so hard (though it was fair yesterday, and we thereupon in hopes of having some fair weather, which we have wanted these three months) that it wakened Creed, who lay with me last night, and me. I hope we have this morning lighted on an expedient which will right all and yet save Creed the 500*l.* which he did propose to make of the exchange abroad of the pieces of eight which he disbursed. To Westminster Hall, and being in the Parliament lobby, I there saw my Lord of Bristoll come to the Commons House to give his answer to their question, about some words he should tell the King that were spoke by Sir Richard Temple a member of their House. A chair was set at the bar of the House for him, which he used but little, but made an harangue of half an houre bareheaded, the House covered. His speech being done, he came out and withdrew into a little room till the House had concluded of an answer to his speech; which they staying long upon, I went away. And by and by out comes Sir W. Batten; and he told me that his Lordship had made a long and a comedian-like speech, and delivered with such action as was not becoming his Lordship. He confesses he did tell the King such a thing of Sir Richard Temple, but that upon his honour the words were not spoke by Sir Richard, he having taken a liberty of enlarging to the King upon the discourse which had been between Sir Richard and himself lately; and so took upon himself the whole blame, and desired their pardon, it being not to do any wrong to their fellow-member, but out of zeal to the King. He told them, among many other things, that as to his religion he was a Roman Catholique, but such a one as thought no man to have right to the Crown of England but the Prince that hath it; and such a one as, if the King should desire his counsel as to his owne, he would not advise him to another religion than the old true reformed religion of this country, it being the properest of this kingdom as it now stands; and concluded with a submission to what the House shall do with him, saying, that whatever they shall do, says he, — "thanks be to God, this head, this heart, and this sword (pointing to them all), will find me a being in any place in Europe." The House hath hereupon voted clearly Sir Richard Temple to be free from the imputation of saying those words; but when Sir William Batten came out, had not concluded what to say to my Lord, it being argued that to owne any satisfaction as to my Lord from his speech, would be to lay some fault upon the King for the message he should upon no better accounts send to the impeaching of one of their members. Walking out, I hear that the House of Lords are offended that my Lord Digby [1] should come to this House and make a speech there without leave first asked of the House of Lords. I hear also of another difficulty now upon him; that my Lord of Sunderland [2] (whom I do not know) was so near to the marriage of his daughter, [3] as that the wedding-clothes were made, and portion and every thing agreed on and ready; and the other day he goes away nobody yet knows whither, sending her the next morning a release of his right or claim to her, and advice to his friends not to enquire into the reason of this doing, for he hath enough for it; but that he gives them liberty to say and think what they will of him, so they do not demand the reason of his

---

[1] Digby, Earl of Bristol.

[2] Henry, fourth Lord Spence, and second Earl of Sunderland, Ambassador to Spain, 1671. Ob. 1702.

[3] For a similar rumour, see in the Appendix a letter from M. de Lionne, July, 1663. The marriage, nevertheless, took place, and the youthful bride, Lady Ann Digby, second daughter, and eventually sole heir of George Digby, Earl of Bristol, became, by the alliance, the ancestress of the Dukes of Marlborough and Earls of Spencer.

leaving her, being resolved never to have her, but the reason desires and resolves not to give. To Sir W. Batten, to the Trinity House; and after dinner we fell a-talking, Mr. Batten telling us of a late triall of Sir Charles Sedley [1] the other day, before my Lord Chief Justice Foster [2] and the whole bench, for his debauchery a little while since at Oxford Kate's. [3] It seems my Lord and the rest of the Judges did all of them round give him a most high reproofe; my Lord Chief Justice saying, that it was for him, and such wicked wretches as he was, that God's anger and judgments hung over us, calling him sirrah many times. It's said they have bound him to his good behaviour (there being no law against him for it) in 5,000*l.* It being

---

[1] Sir Charles Sedley, Bart., celebrated for his wit and profligacy, and author of several plays. He is said to have been fined 500*l.* for this outrage. He was father to James II.'s mistress, created Countess of Dorchester, and died 1701.

[2] Sir Robert Foster, Knt. Chief Justice of the King's Bench. Ob. 1663.

[3] The details in the original are too gross to print. What can be mentioned is told by Dr. Johnson in the Lives of the Poets, in his life of Sackville, Lord Dorset: "Sackville, who was then Lord Buckhurst, with Sir Charles Sedley and Sir Thomas Ogle, got drunk at the Cock, in Bow Street, by Covent Garden, and going into the balcony exposed themselves to the populace in very indecent postures. At last, as they grew warmer, Sedley stood forth naked, and harangued the populace in such profane language, that the publick indignation was awakened; the crowd attempted to force the door, and being repulsed, drove in the performers with stones, and broke the windows of the house. For this misdemeanour they were indicted, and Sedley was fined five hundred pounds; what was the sentence of the others is not known. Sedley employed Killigrew and another to procure a remission of the King, but (mark the friendship of the dissolute!) they begged the fine for themselves, and exacted it to the last groat. (M. B.)

See Shadwell's "Works," vol. i. p. 45; and art. "Bow Street," in Cunningham's "Handbook of London," edit. 1850.

told that my Lord Buckhurst was there, my Lord
asked whether it was that Buckhurst that was lately
tried for robbery; [1] and when answered Yes, he asked
whether he had so soon forgot his deliverance at that
time, and that it would have more become him to
have been at his prayers begging God's forgiveness,
than now running into such courses again. This day
I hear at dinner that Don John of Austria, since his
flight out of Portugall, is dead of his wounds: [2] so
there is a great man gone, and a great dispute like to
be ended for the crown of Spayne, if the King should
have died before him. I received this morning a
letter from my wife, wherein I find a sad falling out
between my wife and my father and sister and Ashwell
upon my writing to my father to advise Pall not to
keep Ashwell from her mistresse, or making any difference between them. Which Pall telling to Ashwell,
and she speaking some words that her mistresse heard
caused great difference among them; all which I am
sorry from my heart to hear of, and I fear will breed
ill blood not to be laid again. So that I fear my wife
and I may have some falling out about it, or at least
my father and I, but I shall endeavour to salve up all
as well as I can, or send for her out of the country
before the time intended, which I would be loth to do.
My cozen Roger told us the whole passage of my Lord
Digby to-day, much as I have said here above; only
that he did say that he would draw his sword against

---

[1] See an account of this, February 22d, 1661-62.   [2] It was not true.

the Pope himself, if he should offer any thing against his Majesty, and the good of these nations; and that he never was the man that did either look for a Cardinal's cap for himself, or any body else, meaning Abbot Montagu;[1] and the House upon the whole did vote Sir Richard Temple innocent; and that my Lord Digby hath cleared the honour of his Majesty, and Sir Richard Temple's, and given perfect satisfaction of his own respects to the House.

2d. Walking in the garden this evening with Sir G. Carteret and Sir J. Minnes, Sir G. Carteret told us with great contempt how like a stage-player my Lord Digby spoke yesterday, pointing to his head as my Lord did, and saying, " First, for his head," says Sir G. Carteret, " I know what a calfe's head would have done better by half: for his heart and his sword, I have nothing to say to them." He told us that for certain his head cost the late King his, for it was he that broke off the treaty at Uxbridge. He told us also how great a man he was raised from a private gentleman[2] in France by Monsieur Grandmont,[3] and afterwards by the Cardinal,[4] who raised him to be a Lieutenant-generall, and then higher; and entrusted

---

[1] Walter, second son to the first Earl of Manchester, embracing the Catholic religion while on his travels, was made Abbot of Ponthoise through the influence of Mary de' Medici: he afterwards became Almoner to the Queen Dowager of England, and died 1670.

[2] He had, however, in June, 1641, been summoned to the House of Peers in his father's barony of Digby.

[3] Antoine de Grammont, marshal of France, known as a warrior and as a writer. (M. B.)

[4] Cardinal Mazarin.

by the Cardinal, when he was banished out of France, with great matters, and recommended by him to the Queene [1] as a man to be trusted and ruled by: yet when he came to have some power over the Queene, he begun to dissuade her from her opinion of the Cardinal; which she said nothing to till the Cardinal was returned, and then she told him of it; who told my Lord Digby, "Eh bien, Monsieur, vous estes un fort bon amy donc:" but presently put him out of all; and then, from a certainty of coming in two or three years' time to be Mareschall of France (to which all strangers, even Protestants,[2] and those as often as French themselves, are capable of coming, though it be one of the greatest places in France), he was driven to go out of France into Flanders; but there was not trusted, nor received any kindness from the Prince of Condé, as one to whom also he had been false, as he had been to the Cardinal and Grandmont. In fine, he told us how he is a man of excellent parts, but of no great faith nor judgment, and one very easy to get up to great height of preferment, but never able to hold it.

3d. To Westminster, and there Mr. Moore tells me great newes that my Lady Castlemaine is fallen from Court, and this morning retired. He gives me no account of the reason of it, but that it is so: for which I am sorry; and yet if the King do it to leave off not

---

[1] Anne of Austria, Queen of France.

[2] Amongst others, Schomberg, who had commanded the Portuguese in the late fight, obtained this dignity.

only her but all other mistresses, I should be heartily glad of it, that he may fall to look after business. I hear my Lord Digby is condemned at Court for his speech, and that my Lord Chancellor grows great again. With Mr. Creed over the water to Lambeth; but could not, it being morning, get to see the Archbishop's hearse : so over the fields to Southwarke, and there parted, and I spent half an hour in St. Mary Overy's Church, where are fine monuments of great antiquity, I believe, and has been a fine church. Thence to the Change, and meeting Sir J. Minnes there, he and I walked to look upon Backwell's design of making another alley from his shop through over against the Exchange door which will be very noble and quite put down the other two. So home to dinner and then to the office, and entered in my manuscript book the Victualler's contract, and then over the water and walked to see Sir W. Pen, and sat with him a while, and so home late, and to my viall.

4th. To St. James's by water with Sir J. Minnes and Sir W. Batten. We staid while the Duke made himself ready. Among other things Sir Allen Apsley [1] showed the Duke the Lisbon Gazette in Spanish, where the late victory is set down particularly, and to the great honour of the English beyond measure. They have since taken back Evora, which was lost

---

[1] Sir Allen Apsley, a faithful adherent to Charles I., after the Restoration was made Falconer to the King, and Almoner to the Duke of York, in whose regiment he bore a commission. He was in 1661 M.P. for Thetford, and died 1683.

to the Spaniards, the English making the assault, and lost not more than three men. Here I learnt that the English foot are highly esteemed all over the world, but the horse not so much, which yet we count among ourselves the best; but they abroad have had no great knowledge of our horse, it seems. The Duke being ready, we retired with him, and there fell upon Mr. Creed's business, where the Treasurer did, like a mad coxcomb, without reason or method run over a great many things against the account, and so did Sir J. Minnes and Sir W. Batten, which the Duke himself and Mr. Coventry and my Lord Barkely and myself did remove, and Creed being called in did answer all with great method and excellently to the purpose, till the Duke himself did declare that he was satisfied, and my Lord Barkely offered to lay 100*l.* that the King would receive no wrong in the account, and the two last knights held their tongues, or at least by not understanding it did say what made for Mr. Creed, and so Sir G. Carteret was left alone, but yet persisted to say that the account was not good, but full of corruption and foul dealing. And so we broke up to his shame, but I do fear to the loss of his friendship to me a good while, which I am heartily troubled for. Thence with Creed to the King's Head ordinary; but, coming late, dined at the second table very well for 12*d.*; and a pretty gentleman in our company, who confirms my Lady Castlemaine's being gone from Court, but knows not the reason; he told us of one wipe the Queene a little while ago did give her, when she came in and found the Queene under the dresser's hands, and had been so long: "I wonder your Majesty," says she, "can have the patience to sit so long a-dressing?"—"I have so much reason to use patience," says the Queene, "that I can very well bear with it." He thinks that it may be the Queene hath commanded her to retire, though that is not likely. Thence with Creed to hire a coach to carry us to Hide Parke, to-day there being a general muster of the King's Guards, horse and foot: but they demand so high, that I, spying Mr. Cutler the merchant, did take notice of him, and he going into his coach, and telling me that he was going to shew a couple of Swedish strangers the muster, I asked and went along with him; where a goodly sight to see so many fine horses and officers, and the King, Duke, and others come by a-horseback, and the two Queenes in the Queene-Mother's coach, my Lady Castlemaine not being there. And after long being there, I light, and walked to the place where the King, Duke, &c., did stand to see the horse and foot march by and discharge their guns, to show a French Marquisse (for whom this muster was caused) the goodness of our firemen; which indeed was very good, though not without a slip now and then: and one broadside close to our coach we had going out of the Parke, even to the nearnesse as to be ready to burn our hairs. Yet methought all these gay men are not the soldiers that must do the King's business, it being such as these that lost the old King all he had, and were beat by the most ordinary fellows that could be. Thence with much ado out of the Parke, and I lighted and through St. James's down the waterside over to Lambeth, to see the Archbishop's corps (who is to be carried away to Oxford on Monday), but came too late, and so walked over the fields and bridge home. This day in the Duke's chamber there being a Roman story in the hangings, and upon the standards written these four letters — S. P. Q. R., Sir G. Carteret came to me to know what the meaning of those four letters were; which ignorance is not to be borne in a Privy Counsellor, methinks, what a schoolboy should be whipt for not knowing.

5th (Lord's day). Lady Batten had sent twice to invite me to go with them to Walthamstow to-day, Mrs. Martha being married already this morning to Mr. Castle, at this parish church. I could not rise soon enough to go with them, but got myself ready, and so to Games's, where I got a horse and rode thither very pleasantly. Being come thither, I was well received, and had two pair of gloves, as the rest, and walked up and down with my Lady in the garden, she mighty kind to me, and I have the way to please her. A good dinner and merry, but methinks none of the kindness nor bridall respect between the bridegroom and bride, that was between my wife and I, but as persons that marry purely for convenience. After dinner to church by coach, and there my Lady, Mrs. Turner, Mrs. Lemon,[1] and I only, we, in spite to one

---

[1] Both daughters of Sir William Batten.

another, kept one another awake; and sometimes I read in my book of Latin plays, which I took in my pocket, thinking to have walked it. An old doting parson preached. So home. Sir J. Minnes and I in his coach together, talking all the way of chymistry, wherein he do know something, at least, seems so to me, that cannot correct him, Mr. Batten's man riding my horse, and so home and to my office a while to read my vows, then home to prayers and to bed.

6th. At my office all the morning, writing out a list of the King's ships in my Navy collections with great pleasure. At noon Creed comes to me, who tells me how well he has sped with Sir G. Carteret after all our trouble, that he had his tallys up and all the kind words possible from him, which I believe is out of an apprehension what a foole he has made of himself hitherto in making so great a stop therein.

7th. At noon down by barge with Sir J. Minnes to Woolwich, in our way eating of some venison pasty in the barge, I having neither eat nor drank to-day. Here also in Mr. Pett's garden I eat some and the first cherries I have eat this year, off the tree where the King himself had been gathering some this morning. Thence walked alone, only part of the way Deane walked with me, complaining of many abuses in the Yarde, to Greenwich, and so by water to Deptford, where I found Mr. Coventry, and with him up and down all the stores, to the great trouble of the officers, and by his helpe I am resolved to fall hard to work again, as I used to do. So thence he and I by water, and I see he puts his trust most upon me in the Navy, and talks, as there is reason, slightly of the two old knights, and I should be glad by any drudgery to see the King's stores and service looked to as they ought, but I fear I shall never understand half the miscarriages and tricks that the King suffers by. He tells me what Mr. Pett did to-day, that my Lord Bristoll told the King that he will impeach the Chancellor of High Treason: but I find that my Lord Bristoll hath undone himself already in every body's opinion, and now he endeavours to raise dust to put out other men's eyes, as well as his owne; but I hope it will not take, in consideration merely that it is hard for a Prince to spare an experienced old officer, be he never so corrupt; though I hope this man is not so, as some report him to be. He tells me that Don John is yet alive, and not killed, as was said, in the great victory against the Spaniards in Portugall of late. This afternoon, coming from the waterside with Mr. Coventry, I spied my boy on Tower Hill playing with the rest of the boys; so I sent W. Griffin to take him, and he did bring him to me, and so I said nothing to him, but caused him to be stripped (for he was run away with his best suit), and so putting on his other, I sent him going, without saying one word hard to him, though I am troubled for the rogue, though he do not deserve it.

8th. Being weary, and going to bed late last night, I slept till 7 o'clock, it raining mighty hard, and so did every minute of the day after sadly. But I know not what will become of the corn this year, we having had but two fair days these many months. To my office, where all the morning busy, and then at noon home to dinner alone upon a good dish of eeles, given me by Michell, the Bewper's man, and then to my viall a little. In the evening I received letters out of the country, among others from my wife, who me-thinks writes so coldly that I am much troubled at it, and I fear shall have much ado to bring her to her old good temper. So home to supper and musique, which is all the pleasure I have of late given myself, or is fit I should, others spending too much time and money. Going in I stepped to Sir W. Batten, and there staid and talked with him (my Lady being in the country), and sent for some lobsters, and Mrs. Turner came in, and did bring us an umble pie hot out of her oven, extraordinary good, and afterwards some spirits of her making, in which she has great judgment, very good, and so home, merry with this night's refreshment.

9th. To my lawyer's; up and down to the Six Clerks' Office, where I found my bill against Tom Trice dismissed, which troubles me, it being through my neglect, and will put me to charges. So to Mr. Phillips, and discoursed with him about finding me out somebody that will let me have for money an annuity of about 100*l.* per annum for two lives. So home, and there put up my riding things against the evening, in case Mr. Moore should continue his mind to go to Oxford, which I have little mind to do, the weather

continuing so bad and the waters high. Mr. Moore
in the afternoon comes to me and concluded not to
go. By water to Deptford, and there mustered the
Yarde, and went in to Sir W. Pen, who continues ill,
and worse, I think, than before. He tells me my'
Lady Castlemaine was at Court, for all this talke this
weeke ; but it seems the King is stranger than ordinary
to her.

10th. By water to Westminster Hall, where I met
Pierce the chirurgeon, who tells me that for certain
the King is grown colder to my Lady Castlemaine
than ordinary, and that he believes he begins to love
the Queene, and do make much of her, more than he
used to do. Mr. Coventry tells me that my Lord
Bristoll hath this day impeached my Lord Chancellor
in the House of Lords of High Treason. The chief
of the articles are these : 1st. That he should be the
occasion of the peace made with Holland lately upon
such disadvantageous terms, and that he was bribed
to it.   2d. That Dunkirke was also sold by his advice
chiefly, so much to the damage of England. 3d.
That he had 6,000*l.* given him for the drawing-up or
promoting of the Irish declaration lately, concerning
the division of the lands there. 4th. He did carry on
the design of the Portugall match, so much to the
prejudice of the Crown of England, notwithstanding
that he knew the Queene is not capable of bearing
children. 5th. That the Duke's marrying of his
daughter was a practice of his, thereby to raise his
family ; and that it was done by indirect courses.

6th. As to the breaking-off of the match with Parma, in which he was employed at the very time when the match with Portugall was made up here, which he took as a great slur to him, and so it was ; and that, indeed, is the chief occasion of all this fewde. 7th. That he hath endeavoured to bring in Popery, and wrote to the Pope for a cap for a subject of the King of England's (my Lord Aubigny [1]) ; and some say that he lays it to the Chancellor, that a good Protestant Secretary (Sir Edward Nicholas) was laid aside, and a Papist, Sir H. Bennet, put in his room : which is very strange, when the last of these two is his owne creature, and such an enemy accounted to the Chancellor, that they never did nor do agree ; and all the world did judge the Chancellor to be falling from the time that Sir H. Bennet was brought in. Besides my Lord Bristoll being a Catholique himself, all this is very strange. These are the main of the Articles. Upon which my Lord Chancellor desired that the noble Lord that brought in these Articles, would sign to them with his hand ; which my Lord Bristoll did presently. Then the House did order that the Judges should, against Monday next, bring in their opinion, Whether these articles are treason, or no ? and next, they would know, Whether they were brought in regularly or no, without leave of the Lords' House ? After dinner I took boat and down to Gravesend in good time, and thence with a guide post to Chatham, where

---

[1] Brother to the Duke of Lennox, and Almoner to the King.

I found Sir J. Minnes and Mr. Wayth, whom I told all this day's newes, which I left the towne full of, and it is great newes, and will certainly be in the consequence of it.

11th. Up early and to the Docke, and with the Storekeeper and other officers all the morning from one office to another. At noon to the Hill-house, and after seeing the guard-ships, to dinner, and after dinner to the Docke by coach, it raining hard, to see "The Prince" launched, which hath lain in the Docke in repairing these three years. I went into her and was launched in her. Thence by boat ashore to Mr. Barrow's, where Sir J. Minnes and Commissioner Pett; we staid long eating sweetmeats and drinking, and looking over some antiquities of Mr. Barrow's, among others an old manuscript Almanac, that I believe was made for some monastery, in parchment, which I could spend much time upon to understand. Here was a pretty young lady, a niece of Barrow's, which I took much pleasure to look on. Thence by barge to St. Mary's Creeke; where Commissioner Pett (doubtful of the growing greatnesse of Portsmouth by the finding of those creekes there), do design a wett docke at no great charge, and yet no little one; he thinks towards 10,000*l.* And the place, indeed, is likely to be a very fit place, when the King hath money to do it with. To the Hill-house, and anon to supper, and late to bed and slept well. About one or two in the morning the curtains of my bed being drawn waked me, and I saw a man stand there by the inside of my bed calling me French dogg 20 times, one after another, and I starting, as if I would get out of the bed, he fell a-laughing as hard as he could drive, still calling me French dogg, and laid his hand on my shoulder. At last, whether I said anything or no I cannot tell, but I perceived the man, after he had looked wistly upon me, and found that I did not answer him to the name that he called me by, which was Salmon, Sir G. Carteret's clerke, and Robt. Maddox, another of the clerks, he put off his hat on a suddaine, and forebore laughing, and asked who I was, saying, "Are you Mr. Pepys?" I told him yes, and now being come a little better to myself, I found him to be Tom Willson, Sir W. Batten's clerke, and fearing he might be in some melancholy fit, I was at a loss what to do or say. At last I asked him what he meant. He desired my pardon for that he was mistaken, for he thought verily, not knowing of my coming to lie there, that it had been Salmon, the Frenchman, with whom he intended to have made some sport. So I made nothing of it, but bade him good night, and I, after a little pause, to sleep again, being well pleased that it ended no worse, and being a little the better pleased with it, because it was the Surveyor's clerke, which will make sport when I come to tell Sir W. Batten of it, it being a report that old Edgeborough, the former Surveyor, who died here, do now and then walk.

12th (Lord's day). With Sir J. Minnes to church, where an indifferent good sermon. Here I saw Mrs.

Becky Allen, who hath been married, and is this day churched, after her bearing a child. Coming out of the church I kissed her and her sister and mother-in-law. So to dinner and to church again, and after that walked through the Rope-ground to the Docke, and there over and over the Docke and grounds about it, and storehouses, &c., with the officers of the Yarde, and then to Commissioner Pett's and had a good sullybub and other good things, and merry. Thence I walked to the Hillhouse, being myself much dissatisfied, and more than I thought I should have been with Commissioner Pett, being, by what I saw since I came hither, convinced that he is not able to exercise the command in the Yarde over the officers that he ought to do, or somebody else, if ever the service be well looked after there. For I do see he is but a man of words, though indeed he is the ablest man that we have to do service if he would or durst. Sir J. Minnes being gone to bed, I took Mr. Whitfield, one of the clerks, and walked to the Docke about eleven at night, and there got a boat and a crew, and rowed down to the guard-ships, it being a most pleasant moonshine evening that ever I saw almost. The guard-ships were very ready to hail us, being no doubt commanded thereto by their Captain, who remembers how I surprised them the last time I was here. However, I found him ashore, but the ship in pretty good order, and the arms well fixed, charged, and primed. Thence to the Soveraigne, where I found no officers aboard, no arms fixed, nor any powder to prime their few guns, which were charged, without bullet though. So to the London, where neither officers nor anybody awake; I boarded her, and might have done what I would, and at last could find but three little boys; and so spent the whole night in visiting all the ships, in which I found, for the most part, neither an officer aboard, nor any men so much as awake, which I was grieved to find, specially so soon after a great alarum, as Commissioner Pett brought us word that he had provided against, and put all in a posture of defence but a weeke ago, all which I am resolved to represent to the Duke.

13th. So, it being high day, I put in to shore and to bed for two hours just, and so up again, and with the Storekeeper and Clerke of the Rope-yarde up and down the Docke and Rope-house, and by and by mustered the Yarde, and instructed the Clerks of the Cheque in my new way of Call-book, and that and other things done, to the Hill-house, and there we eat something, and so by barge to Rochester, and there took coach hired for our passage to London, and it being a most pleasant and warm day, we got by four o'clock home, and after dressing myself, I walked to the Temple; and there, from my cozen Roger, hear that the Judges have this day brought in their answer to the Lords, That the articles against my Lord Chancellor are not Treason; and to-morrow they are to bring in their arguments to the House for the same. This day also the King did send by my Lord Chamberlain to the Lords, to tell them from him, that the most of the articles against my Lord Chancellor he himself knows to be false. I met the Queene-Mother walking in the Pell Mell, led by my Lord St. Alban's. And finding many coaches at the Gate, I found upon enquiry that the Duchesse is brought to bed of a boy;[1] and hearing that the King and Queene are rode abroad with the Ladies of Honour to the Parke, and seeing a great crowd of gallants staying here to see their return, I also staid walking up and down. By and by the King and Queene, who looked in this dresse (a white laced waistcoate and a crimson short pettycoate, and her hair dressed *à la negligence*) mighty pretty; and the King rode hand in hand with her. Here was also my Lady Castlemaine rode among the rest of the ladies; but the King took, methought, no notice of her; nor when they light did any body press (as she seemed to expect, and staid for it) to take her down, but was taken down by her own gentlemen. She looked mighty out of humour, and had a yellow plume in her hat (which all took notice of), and yet is very handsome, but very melancholy: nor did any body speak to her, or she so much as smile or speak to any body. I followed them up into White Hall, and into the Queene's presence, where all the ladies walked, talking and fiddling with their hats and feathers, and changing and trying one another's by one another's heads, and laughing. But it was the finest sight to me, considering their

---

[1] James, Duke of Cambridge. Ob. 20th June, 1667.

great beautys and dress, that ever I did see in all my life. But, above all, Mrs. Stewart in this dresse, with her hat cocked and a red plume, with her sweet eye, little Roman nose, and excellent taille, is now the greatest beauty I ever saw, I think, in my life; and, if ever woman can, do exceed my Lady Castlemaine, at least in this dress: nor do I wonder if the King changes, which I verily believe is the reason of his coldness to my Lady Castlemaine. Here late, with much ado I left to look upon them, and went away, and by water, and so home and to Sir W. Batten, where I staid telling him and Sir J. Minnes and Mrs. Turner, with great mirth, my being frighted at Chatham by young Edgeborough, and so home to supper and to bed.

14th. This day I hear the Judges, according to order yesterday, did bring into the Lords' House their reasons of their judgments in the business between my Lord Bristoll and the Chancellor; and the Lords do concur with the Judges that the articles are not treason, nor regularly brought into the House, and so voted that a Committee should be chosen to examine them; but nothing to be done therein till the next sitting of this Parliament (which is like to be adjourned in a day or two), and in the mean time the two Lords to remain without prejudice done to either of them.

15th. Captain Grove came and dined with me. He told me of discourse very much to my honour, both as to my care and ability, happening at the Duke of

Albemarle's table the other day, both from the Duke and the Duchesse themselves; and how I paid so much a year to him whose place it was of right, and that Mr. Coventry did report thus of me; which was greatly to my content, knowing how against their minds I was brought into the Navy.

16th. Up and dispatched things into the country and to my father's, and two keggs of Sturgeon and a dozen bottles of wine to Cambridge for my cozen Roger Pepys, which I give him. By and by by water on several deale ships, and stood upon a stage in one place seeing calkers sheathing of a ship. Then at Wapping to my carver's about my Viall head. Thence to the Exchange, and so home to dinner, and then to my office, where a full board, and busy all the afternoon, and among other things made a great contract with Sir W. Warren for 40,000 deales Swinsound. In the morning before I went on the water I was at Thames Streete about some pitch, and there meeting Anthony Joyce, I took him and Mr. Stacy, the Tarr merchant, to the taverne, where Stacy told me many old stories of my Lady Batten's former poor condition, and how her former husband broke, and how she came to her state.

19th. To church, where a sober Doctor made a good sermon. So home to dinner alone, and so to church again, where the Scot made an ordinary sermon, and so to my office, and there read over my vows and increased them by a vowe against all strong drink till November next of any sort or quantity, by which I shall try how I can forbear it. God send it may not prejudice my health, and then I care not. Then I fell to read over a silly play writ by a person of honour (which is, I find, as much as to say a coxcomb), called " Love à la Mode," and that being ended, home, and played on my lute and sung psalms till bedtime, then to prayers and to bed.

20th. Walked to Woolwich, reading Bacon's " Faber fortunæ," which the oftener I read the more I admire. There found Captain Cocke, and to his house, and there dined very finely. With much ado obtained an excuse from drinking of wine, and did only taste a drop of Sacke which he had for his lady, who is, he fears, a little consumptive, and her beauty begins to want its colour. It was Malago Sacke, which, he says, is certainly 30 years old, and I tasted a drop of it, and it was excellent wine, like a spirit rather than wine. Home, and being heartily weary I made haste to bed, and being in bed made Will read and construe three or four Latin verses in the Bible, and chide him for forgetting his grammar.

21st. And so lay long in the morning, till I heard people knock at my door, and so I rose and ranted at Will and the mayde, and swore I could find my heart to kick them down stairs, at which the mayde mumbled at mightily. It was my brother who staid and talked with me, his chief business being about his going about to build his house new at the top, which will be a great charge for him, and above his judgment. By and by comes Mr. Deane, of Wool-

wich, with his draught of a ship, and the bend and
main lines in the body of a ship very finely, and which
do please me mightily, and so am resolved to study
hard, and learne of him to understand a body, and
I find him a very pretty fellow in it, and rational,
but a little conceited, but that's no matter to me.
At noon, by my Lady Batten's desire, I went over the
water to Mr. Castles, who brings his wife home to his
owne house to-day, where I found a great many good
old women, and my Lady, Sir W. Batten, and Sir J.
Minnes. A good, handsome, plain dinner. Home,
and wrote letters to my father and wife about my
desire that they should observe the feast at Brampton,
and have my Lady and the family, and so home to
supper and bed. This day the Parliament kept a fast
for the present unseasonable weather.

22nd. Up, and by and by comes my uncle Thomas,
to whom I paid 10*l.* for his last half year's annuity,
and did get his and his son's hand and seale for
the confirming to us Piggott's mortgage, which was
forgot to be expressed in our late agreement with
him, though intended, and therefore they might have
cavilled at it, if they would. Thence to my Lord
Crew's. My Lord not being come home, I met and
staid below with Captn. Ferrers, who was come to
wait upon my Lady Jemimah to St. James's, she being
one of the four ladies that hold up the mantle at the
christening this afternoon of the Duke's child (a boy).
In discourse of the ladies at Court, Captn. Ferrers
tells me that my Lady Castlemaine is now as great

again as ever she was ; and that her going away was
only a fit of her owne upon some slighting words of
the King, so that she called for her coach at a quarter
of an hour's warning, and went to Richmond ; and
the King the next morning, under pretence of going
a-hunting, went to see her and make friends, and
never was a-hunting at all. After which she came
back to Court, and commands the King as much as
ever, and hath and doth what she will. No longer ago
than last night, there was a private entertainment made
for the King and Queene at the Duke of Buckingham's, and she was not invited : but being at my Lady
Suffolk's,[1] her aunt's (where my Lady Jemimah and
Lord Sandwich dined) yesterday, she was heard to say,
"Well, much good may it do them, and for all that I
will be as merry as they : " and so she went home
and caused a great supper to be prepared. And after
the King had been with the Queene at Wallingford
House,[2] he came to my Lady Castlemaine's, and was
there all night, and my Lord Sandwich with him. He
tells me he believes that, as soon as the King can get
a husband for Mrs. Stewart, however, my Lady Castlemaine's nose will be out of joynt ; for that she comes

---

[1] Barbara Villiers (widow of Philip, son of Viscount Wenman) wife of
James Howard, third Earl of Suffolk. There is a portrait of Lady Suffolk at
Audley End. She died December, 1681, leaving an only child, Elizabeth, who
married Sir Thomas Felton, Bart. From this match are descended the Earls
and Marquis of Bristol, and Charles Ellis, Baron Howard de Walden.

[2] Wallingford House stood on the site of the present Admiralty : it originally belonged to the Knollys family, and during the Protectorate the office
for granting passes to persons going abroad was kept there.

to be in great esteem, and is more handsome than she. I called at Wotton's, the shoemaker, who tells me the reason of Harris's [1] going from Sir Wm. Davenant's house, that he grew very proud and demanded 20*l.* for himself extraordinary, more than Betterton or any body else, upon every new play, and 10*l.* upon every revive; which with other things Sir W. Davenant would not give him, and so he swore he would never act there more, in expectation of being received in the other House; but the King will not suffer it, upon Sir W. Davenant's desire that he would not, for then he might shut up house, and that is true. He tells me that his going is at present a great losse to the House, and that he fears he hath a stipend from the other House privately. He tells me that the fellow grew very proud of late, the King and every body else crying him up so high, and that above Betterton he being a more ayery man, as he is indeed. But yet Betterton, he says, they all say do act some parts that none but himself can do. Thence to my bookseller's, and find my Waggoners done. The very binding cost me 14*s.*, but they are well done, and so with a porter home with them, and so by water to Ratcliffe, and

---

[1] Joseph Harris. That the Christian name of the actor at Davenant's house, and the friend of Pepys, was *Joseph*, rests on the supposition that he was the Joseph Harris author of several plays produced in the reign of William III., and an actor also. If Pepys's Harris and the dramatic poet were identical, he lived into Queen Anne's reign. It seems more probable that they were different persons, and that Pepys's friend was named Henry. There is a mezzotint of Joseph Harris in the character of Cardinal Wolsey, in the Pepysian Library at Cambridge; only one other impression of this print is known to exist, which belongs to Mr. George Daniel, of Canonbury.

there went to speak with Cumberford the platt-maker, and there saw his manner of working, which is very fine and laborious. So down to Deptford, reading Ben Jonson's "Devil is an asse," and so to see Sir W. Pen, who I find walking out of doors a little, but could not stand long, but in doors and I with him, and staid a great while talking, I taking a liberty to tell him my thoughts in things of the office, that when he comes abroad again, he may know what to think of me, and to value me as he ought. Walked home. This day I hear that the Moores have made some attaques upon the outworks of Tangier; but my Lord Teviott,[1] with the loss of about 200 men, did beat them off, and killed many of them. To-morrow the King and Queene for certain go down to Tunbridge. But the King comes back again against Monday to raise the Parliament.

23rd. Up and to my office, and thence by information from Mr. Ackworth I went down to Woolwich, and mustered the three East India ships that lie there, believing that there is great juggling between the Pursers and Clerks of the Cheque in cheating the King of the wages and victuals of men that do not give attendance, and I found very few on board. So to the yarde, and there mustered the yarde, and found many faults, and discharged several fellows that were absent from their business. After dinner with all haste home, and at the office, and by Sir W. Batten's testimony

---

and Sir G. Carteret's concurrence, was forced to consent to a business of Captain Cocke's timber, as bad as anything we have lately disputed about, and all through Sir W. Coventry's not being with us. So up and to supper with Sir W. Batten upon a soused mullett, very good meat, and so home and to bed.

24th. By water to the Temple, and there took leave of my cozen Roger Pepys, who goes out of towne to-day. So to Westminster Hall, and there at Mrs. Michell's shop sent for beer and sugar and drink, and made great cheer with it among her and Mrs. Howlett, her neighbour, and their daughters, especially Mrs. Howlett's daughter, Betty, which is a pretty girle, and one I have long called wife, being, I formerly thought, like my owne wife. After this good neighbourhood, I went to the six clerks' office, and there had a writ for Tom Trice, and paid 20*s.* for it to Wilkinson, and so home, and being sent for presently to Mr. Bland's, where Mr. Povy and Gauden and I were invited to dinner, which we had very finely and great plenty, but for drink, though many and good, I drank nothing but small beer and water. They had a kinswoman, they call daughter, in the house, a short, ugly, red-haired slut, that plays upon the virginalls, and sings, but after such a country manner I was weary of it, but yet could not but commend it. So by and by after dinner comes Monsr. Gotier, who is beginning to teach her, but, Lord ! what a droll fellow it is to make her hold open her mouth, and telling this and that so drolly would make a man burst, but himself I perceive sings very well. Anon we sat down again to a collacon of cheesecakes, tartes, custards, and such like, very handsome, and so up and away home, where I at the office a while, till disturbed by Mr. Hill, of Cambridge, with whom I walked in the garden and then in my dining room, talking of several matters of state till 11 at night. I was not unwilling to hear him talk, though he is full of words, yet a man of large conversation especially among the Presbyters and Independents; he tells me that certainly, let the Bishops alone, and they will ruin themselves, and he is confident that the King's declaration about two years since will be the foundation of the settlement of the Church some time or other, for the King will find it hard to banish all those that will appear Nonconformists upon this Act that is coming out against them. He being gone, I to bed.

25th. Having intended this day to go to Banstead Downes to see a famous race, I sent Will. to get himself ready to go with me; but I hear it is put off, because the Lords do sit in Parliament to-day.[1] However, having appointed Mr. Creed to come to me to Fox Hall, I went over thither, and after some debate, Creed and I resolved to go to Clapham, to Mr. Gaudens.[2] When I came there, the first thing was

---

[1] The tables are turned : the two Houses now seldom sitting on the "Derby" day! In May, 1849, the adjournment of the House of Commons was carried after a division.

[2] Dennis Gauden, Victualler to the Navy; subsequently knighted when Sheriff of London.

to show me his house,[1] which is almost built. I find
it very regular and finely contrived, and the gardens
and offices about it as convenient and as full of good
variety as ever I saw in my life. It is true he hath
been censured for laying out so much money; but he
tells me that he built it for his brother, who is since
dead (the Bishop[2]), who when he should come to
be Bishop of Winchester, which he was promised (to
which bishopricke at present there is no house), he
did intend to dwell here. By and by to dinner, and
in comes Mr. Creed; I saluted his lady, and the
young ladies, and his sister, the Bishop's widow; who
was, it seems, Sir W. Russel's[3] daughter, the Treasurer of the Navy; who I find to be very well-bred,
and a woman of excellent discourse. Towards the
evening we bade them Adieu! and took horse; being
resolved that, instead of the race which fails us, we
would go to Epsum. When we came there we could
hear of no lodging, the town so full; but which was
better, I went towards Ashted, my old place of pleasure, and there we got a lodging in a little hole we
could not stand upright in. While supper was getting ready, I walked up and down behind my cozen
Pepys's house that was, which I find comes little short
of what I took it to be when I was a little boy, as

---

¹ See note to December 19, 1660, *ante.*

² Of Exeter.

³ Sir William Russell, of Strensham, in Worcestershire, Bart. He ad-
vanced 600*l.* to Sir William Davenant, in 1660–1, and had a share in Davenant's theatre.

things use commonly to appear greater than when one comes to be a man and knows more, and so up and down in the closes, which I know so well methinks, and account it good fortune that I lie here that I may have opportunity to renew my old walks. So to our lodging to supper, and among other meats had a brave dish of creame, the best I ever eat in my life, and with which we pleased ourselves much, and by and by to bed, where, with much ado yet good sport, we made shift to lie, but with little ease, and a little spaniel by us, which has followed us all the way, a pretty dogg, and we believe that it follows my horse, and do belong to Mrs. Gauden, which we, therefore, are very careful of.

26th (Lord's-day). Up and to the Wells, where great store of citizens, which was the greatest part of the company, though there were some others of better quality. Thence I walked to Mr. Minnes's house, and thence to Durdan's and walked within the Court Yard and to the Bowling-green, where I have seen so much mirth in my time; but now no family in it (my Lord Barkeley, whose it is, being with his family at London), and so up and down by Minnes wood with great pleasure viewing my old walks, and where Mrs. Hely and I did use to walk and talk, with whom I had the first sentiments of love and pleasure in woman's company, discourse, and taking her by the hand, she being a pretty woman. So I led him to Ashted Church, where we had a dull Doctor, and after sermon home, and staid while our dinner, a couple of large chickens, were dressed, and a good mess of creame, which anon we had with great content, and after dinner he and I to walk, and I led him to the pretty little wood behind my cozen's house, but when we were among the hazel trees and bushes, Lord! what a course we did run for an houre together, losing ourselves, and indeed I despaired I should ever come to any path, I could hardly have believed a man could have been lost so long in so small a room. At last I found out a delicate walk in the middle that goes quite through the wood, and then went out of the wood. Went to our lodging and paid our reckoning, and so mounted, whether to go toward London home or to find a new lodging, and so rode through Epsum, the whole towne over, seeing the various companys that were there walking; which was very pleasant to see how they are there without knowing almost what to do, but only in the morning to drink waters. But Lord! to see how many I met there of citizens, that I could not have thought to have seen there; that they had ever had it in their heads or purses to go down thither. We rode out of the towne through Jowell beyond Nonesuch House a mile, and there our little dogg, as he used to do, fell a running after a flock of sheep, till he was out of sight, and then endeavoured to come back again, the poor thing mistakes our scent, instead of coming forward he hunts us backward. We went back as far as Epsum almost, and hearing nothing of him, we went back to Jowell, and there set up our horses and selves for all night, employing people to look for the dogg in the towne.

We gave order for supper, and while that was dressing walked out through Nonesuch Parke [1] to the house, and there viewed as much as we could of the outside, and looked through the great gates, and found a noble court; and altogether believe it to have been a very noble house, and a delicate parke about it, where just now there was a doe killed for the King to carry up to Court. So walked back again, and by and by our supper being ready, a good leg of mutton, we supped and to bed.

27th. Up in the morning about 7 o'clock, and after a little study, resolved of riding to the Wells to look for our dogg, which we did, but could hear nothing; but it being a much warmer day than yesterday there was great store of gallant company, more than then, to my greater pleasure. There was at a distance, under one of the trees on the common, a company got together that sang. I, at the distance, took them for the Waytes, so I rode up to them, and found them only voices, some citizens met by chance, that sung four or five parts excellently. I have not been more pleased with a snapp of musique, considering the circumstances of the time and place, in all my life anything so pleasant. We drank each of us three cupps, and so, after riding up to the horsemen upon the hill, where they were making of matches to run, we went away and to Jowell, where we found our breakfast, the remains of our supper last night hashed,

---

[1] See 21st Sept., 1665.

and mounted, and with little discourse, I being intent upon getting home in time, we rode hard home, and set up our horses at Fox Hall, and I by water (observing the King's barge attending his going to the House this day) home, it being about one o'clock. So shifting myself, and so by water to Westminster, and there came most luckily to the Lords' House as the House of Commons were going into the Lord's House, and there I crowded in along with the Speaker, and got to stand close behind him, where he made his speech to the King (who sat with his crown on and robes, and so all the Lords in their robes, a fine sight) ; wherein he told his Majesty what they have done this Parliament, and now offered for his royall consent. The greatest matters were a bill for the Lord's day (which it seems the Lords have lost, and so cannot be passed, at which the Commons are displeased) ; the bills against Conventicles and Papists (but it seems the Lords have not passed them), and giving his Majesty four entire subsidys; which last, with about twenty smaller Acts, were passed with this form : The Clerk of the House reads the title of the bill, and then looks at the end and there finds (writ by the King I suppose) " Le Roy le veult," and that he reads. And to others he reads, " Soit fait comme vous desirez." And to the Subsidys, as well that for the Commons, I mean the layety, as for the Clergy, the King writes, " Le Roy remerciant les Seigneurs, &c., Prelats, &c., accepte leur benevolences." The Speaker's speech was far from any oratory, but was as plain (though good matter) as any thing could be, and void of elocution. After the bills passed, the King, sitting on his throne, with his speech writ in a paper which he held in his lap, and scarce looked off of it, I thought, all the time he made his speech to them, giving them thanks for their subsidys, of which, had he not need, he would not have asked or received them ; and that need, not from any extravagancys of his, he was sure, in any thing, but the disorders of the times compelling him to be at greater charge than he hoped for the future, by their care in their country, he should be : and that for his family expenses and others, he would labour however to retrench in many things convenient, and would have all others to do so too. He desired that nothing of old faults should be remembered, or severity for the same used to any in the country, it being his desire to have all forgot as well as forgiven. But, however, to use all care in suppressing any tumults, &c. ; assuring them that the restless spirits of his and their adversaries have great expectations of something to be done this summer. And promised that though the Acts about Conventicles and Papists were not ripe for passing this Sessions, yet he would take care himself that neither of them should in this intervall be encouraged to the endangering of the peace ; and that at their next meeting he would himself prepare two bills for them concerning them. So he concluded, that for the better proceeding of justice he did think fit to make this a Sessions, and to prorogue them to the 16th of March next.   His speech was very plain, nothing at all of spirit in it, nor spoke with any; but rather on the contrary imperfectly, repeating many times his words though he read all : which I was sorry to see, it having not been hard for him to have got all the speech without booke.   So they all went away, the King out of the House at the upper end, he being by and by to go to Tunbridge to the Queene; and I in the Painted Chamber spoke with my Lord Sandwich while he was putting off his robes, who tells me he will now hasten down into the country.   Here meeting Creed, he and I over the water to Fox Hall, and then to the new Spring Garden, walking up and down, but things being dear and little attendance to be had we went away, leaving much brave company there, and so to a less house hard by, where we liked very well their Codlin tarts, having not time, as we intended, to stay the getting ready of a dish of pease.   Thence by water to White Hall, and walked over the Parke to St. James's ; but missed Mr. Coventry ; and so out again, and there the Duke was coming along the Pell-Mell. It being a little darkish, I staid not to take notice of him, but we went directly back again.   And in our walk over the Parke, one of the Duke's footmen came running behind us, and came looking just in our faces to see who we were, and went back again.   What his meaning is I know not, but was fearful that I might not go far enough with my hat off, though methinks that should not be it, besides, there were others covered nearer than myself was, but only it was my fear.

So to White Hall and by water to the Bridge, and so home to bed, weary and well pleased with my journey in all respects. Only it cost me about 20*s.*, but it was for my health, and I hope will prove so.

28th. To my office setting down the Journall of this last three days and so settled to business again, I hope with greater cheerfulness and successe by this refreshment. Late came my Jane and her brother Will to entreat for my taking of the boy again, but I will not hear her, though I would yet be glad to do anything for her sake to the boy, but receive him again I will not, nor give him anything. She would have me send him to sea, which if I could I would do, but there is no ship going out.

29th. To Sir W. Batten and there I dined with my Lady and her daughter and son Castle, and mighty kind she is and I kind to her, but, Lord! how freely and plainly she rails against Commissioner Pett, calling him rogue, and wondering that the King keeps such a fellow in the Navy. Thence by and by walked to see Sir W. Pen at Deptford, reading by the way a most ridiculous play, a new one, called "The Politician Cheated." [1]

30th. To Woolwich, and there came Sir G. Carteret, and then by water back to Deptford, where we dined with him at his house, a very good dinner and mightily tempted with wines of all sorts and brave French Syder, but I drunk none. But that which is

---

[1] A Comedy by Alexander Green.

a great wonder I find his little daughter Betty,[1] that was in hanging sleeves but a month or two ago, and is a very little young child, married, and to whom, but to young Scott,[2] son to Madam Catharine Scott,[3] that was so long in law, and at whose triall I was with her husband; he pleading that it was unlawfully got and would not owne it, but it seems a little before his death he did owne the child, and hath left him his estate, not long since.   So Sir G. Carteret hath struck up of a sudden a match with him for his little daughter.   He hath about 2,000*l.* per annum; and it seems Sir G. C. hath by this means over-reached Sir H. Bennet, who did endeavour to get this gentleman for a sister of his.   By this means Sir G. Carteret hath married two daughters this year both very well.[4]   After dinner parted, and so calling for my five books of the Variorum print bound according to my common binding instead of the other which is more gaudy I went home.   The towne talke this day is of nothing but the great foot-race run this day on Banstead Downes, between Lee, the Duke of Richmond's footman, and a tyler, a famous runner.   And Lee hath beat him; though the King and Duke of York and all men almost did bet three or four to one upon the tyler's head.

31st.   Up early to my accounts and I find myself

---

[1] Her name was Caroline.   Elizabeth died unmarried.

[2] Thomas, eldest son of Sir Thomas Scott, of Scott's Hall, in the parish of Smeeth, Kent.

[3] Prince Rupert was supposed to have intrigued with Mrs. Scott, and was probably the father of the child.

[4] The other daughter was Anne, wife of Sir Nicholas Slaning, K.B.

with clear 730*l.*, the most I ever had yet, which contents me though I encrease but very little. Thence to
my office doing business and so to the Exchange, where
I met Dr. Pierce, who tells me of his good luck to
get to be groom of the Privy-Chamber to the Queene,
and without my Lord Sandwich's helpe, but only by
his good fortune, meeting a man that hath let him have
his right for a small matter, about 60*l.* for which he
can every day have 400*l.* But he tells me my Lord
hath lost much honour in standing so long and so
much for that coxcomb Pickering, and at last not carrying it for him; but hath his name struck out by the
King and Queene themselves after he had been in ever
since the Queene's coming. But he tells me he believes that either Sir H. Bennet, my Lady Castlemaine,
or Sir Charles Barkeley had received some money for
the place, and so the King could not disappoint them,
but was forced to put out this foole rather than a better man. And I am sorry to hear what he tells me
that Sir Charles Barkeley hath still such power over
the King, as to be able to fetch him from the Council-
table to my Lady Castlemaine when he pleases. He
tells me also, as a friend, the great injury that he thinks
I do myself by being so severe in the Yards, and contracting the ill-will of the whole Navy for those offices,
singly upon myself. Now I discharge a good conscience therein, and I tell him that no man can (nor
do he say any say it) charge me with doing wrong;
but rather do as many good offices as any man.
They think, he says, that I have a mind to get a good

name with the King and Duke, who he tells me do not consider any such thing; but I shall have as good thanks to let all alone, and do as the rest. But I believe the contrary; and yet I told him I never go to the Duke alone, as others do, to talk of my owne services. However, I will make use of his council, and take some course to prevent having the single ill-will of the office. Mr. Grant showed me letters of Sir William Petty's, wherein he says, that his vessel which he hath built upon two keeles, (a modell whereof, built for the King, he showed me) hath this month won a wager of 50*l.* in sailing between Dublin and Holyhead with the pacquett-boat, the best ship or vessel the King hath there; and he offers to lay with any vessel in the world.[1] It is about thirty ton in burden, and carries thirty men, with good accommodation, (as much more as any ship of her burden,) and so any vessel of this figure shall carry more men,

---

[1] Amongst the Sloane MSS. in the British Museum there is an English satirical poem on this vessel, the title of which is, "In laudem Navis Geminæ e portu Dublinii ad Regem Carolum II^{dum} missæ." It contains three hundred lines, and is too long and too scurrilous and worthless to print. "Petty," observes Lodge ("Peerage of Ireland," vol. ii. p. 352), "in 1663 raised his reputation still higher by the success of his invention of the double-bottomed ship, against the judgment of all mankind. Thomas Earl of Ossory and other persons of honour embarked on board this ship, which promised to excel all others in sailing, carriage, and security; but she was at last lost in a dreadful tempest, which overwhelmed a great fleet the same night. A model of the vessel was deposited by Petty in Gresham College." Sir W. Petty was born in 1623. At the Restoration he was knighted and created Surveyor-General of Ireland. He died very rich, 1687. The widow of Sir W. Petty was created Baroness Shelburne. He left two sons and a daughter. The eldest son succeeded to the title, but dying without issue, it was revived in Henry, the second son, great-uncle of the first Marquis of Lansdowne. (M. B.)

with better accommodation by half, than any other ship. This carries also ten guns, of about five tons weight. In their coming back from Holyhead they started together, and this vessel came to Dublin by five at night, and the pacquett-boat not before eight the next morning; and when they came they did believe that this vessel had been drowned, or at least behind, not thinking she could have lived in that sea. Strange things are told of this vessel, and he concludes his letter with this position, " I only affirm that the perfection of sayling lies in my principle, finde it out who can."

Aug. 1st. Up betimes and got me ready, and then Mr. Coventry sending for me, he and I by water to Gravesend and there eat a bit and so mounted, I upon one of his horses which met him there, a brave proud horse, all the way talking of businesses of the office and other matters to good purpose. Being come to Chatham, we walked to the yarde looking and inquiring into many businesses, and in the evening went to the Commissioner's and there pressed upon the Commr. to take upon him a power to correct and suspend officers that do not their duty and other things, which he unwillingly answered he would if we would owne him in it. At the Hill house to bed.

2nd (Lord's day). Up and after the barber had done he and I walked to the Docke, and so on board the Mathias, where an excellent sermon of Mr. Hudson's upon " All is yours and you are God's," a most ready, learned, and good sermon, such as I have not heard a good while.   After dinner to the parish church, and there heard a poor sermon with a great deal of false Greek in it, upon these words, "Ye are my friends, if ye do these things which I command you." Thence to the Docke and by water to view St. Mary Creeke, but do not find it so proper for a wett Docke as we would have it, it being uneven ground and hard in the bottom and no great depth of water in places.

3rd. Up both of us very betimes and to the Yarde and see the men called over and choose some to be discharged.   Then to the Ropehouses and viewed them all and made an experiment which was the stronger, English or Riga hempe, the latter proved the stronger, but the other is very good, and much better we believe than any but Riga.   At noon Mr. Pett did give us a very great dinner, too big in all conscience. After dinner we conjured him to look after the yarde and for the time to come that he would take the whole faults and ill management of the yarde upon himself, he having full power and our concurrence to suspend or do anything else that he thinks fit to keep people and officers to their duty.   So walked to the Hill house and mounted and rode to Gravesend, and to bed.

4th. We were called up about four o'clock and took a Gravesend boat, and to London by nine o'clock.   So to the office, where Sir W. Pen met us. My brother John I finde came to towne to my house, as I sent for him, on Saturday last, so at noon home and dined with him, and then by water to Blackbury's, and there talked with him about some masts, and by the way he tells me that Paul's is now going to be repaired in good earnest, and so with him to his garden, where I eat some peaches and apricots ; a very pretty place.   So home, and with my brother eat a bit of bread and cheese, and so to bed, he with me.   This day I received a letter from my wife, which troubles me mightily, wherein she tells me how Ashwell did give her the lie to her teeth, and that thereupon my wife giving her a box on the eare, the other struck her again, and a deal of stir which troubles me, and that my Lady has been told by my father or mother something of my wife's carriage, which altogether vexes me, and I fear I shall find a trouble of my wife when she comes home to get down her head again, but if Ashwell goes I am resolved to have no more, but to live poorly and low again for a good while, and save money and keep my wife within bounds if I can, or else I shall bid adieu to all content in the world. So to bed, my mind somewhat disturbed at this, but yet I shall take care, by prudence, to avoyde the ill consequences which I fear, things not being gone too far yet, and this height that my wife is come to being occasioned by my owne folly in giving her too much head heretofore for the year past.

5th. All the morning at the office, whither Deane of Woolwich came to me and discoursed of the body of ships, which I am now going about to understand, and then I took him to the coffee-house, where he was very earnest against Mr. Grant's report in favour of Sir W. Petty's vessel, even to some passion on both sides almost. So to the Exchange, and thence home to dinner with my brother, and he and I fell upon Des Cartes, and I perceive he has studied him well, and I cannot find but he has minded his book, and do love it. This evening came a letter about business from Mr. Coventry, and with it a silver pen he promised me to carry ink in which is very necessary.

6th. At noon I to the 'Change, and meeting with Sir W. Warren, to a coffee-house, and there finished a contract with him for the office, and so parted, and I to my cozen Mary Joyce's at a gossiping, where much company and good cheer. There was the King's Falconer, that lives by Paul's, and his wife, an ugly pusse, but brought him money. He speaking of the strength of hawkes, which will strike a fowle to the ground with that force that shall make the fowle rebound a great way from the ground, which no force of man or art can do, but it was very pleasant to hear what reasons he and another, one Ballard, a rich man of the same Company of Leather-sellers of which the Joyces are, did give for this. Ballard's wife, a pretty and a well-bred woman, I took occasion to kiss several times, and she to carve, drink, and show me great respect. After dinner to talk and laugh. I drank no wine, but sent for some water, the beer not being good. A fiddler was sent for and there one Mrs. Lurkin, a neighbour, a good, poor woman, did dance and show such tricks that made us all merry, but above all a daughter of Mr. Brumfield's, black, but well-shaped and modest, did dance very well, which pleased me mightily. I begun the Duchesse with her, but could not do it ; but, however, I came off well enough, and made mighty much of her, kissing and leading her home, with her cozen Anthony and Kate Joyce (Kate being very handsome and well, that is, handsomely-dressed to-day, and I grew mighty kind and familiar with her, and kissed her soundly, which she takes very well), and there I left them, having in our way, though nine o'clock at night, carried them into a puppet play, in Lincoln's Inn Fields, where there was the story of Holofernes, and other clockwork, well done. There was at this house to-day Mr. Lawrence, who did give the name, it seems, to my cousin Joyce's child, Samuel, who is a very civil gentleman, and his wife a pretty woman, who, with Kate Joyce, were stewards of the feast to-day, and a double share cost for a man and woman come to 16*s.*, which I also would pay, though they would not by any means have had me do so. I walked home very well contented with this afternoon's work, I thinking it convenient to keep in with the Joyces against a bad day, if I should have occasion to make use of them.

7th. To my office a little, and then to Brown's for my measuring rule, which is made, and is certainly the best and the most commodious for carrying in one's pocket, and myself have the honour of being as it were the inventor of this form of it. Then home, and thither came Sir Fairbrother to me. So by-and-by to dinner. The Dr.'s discourse, which (though he be a very good-natured man) is but simple, was some sport to me. We parted after dinner, and I walked to Deptford and there found Sir W. Pen, and I fell to measuring of some planks that was serving into the yarde, which the people took notice of, and the measurer himself was amused at, for I did it much more ready than he, and I believe Sir W. Pen would be glad I could have done less or he more. So home, and my brother John and I up and I to my musique, and then to discourse with him, and I find him not so thorough a philosopher, at least in Aristotle, as I took him for. So to prayers, and to bed.

8th. I with Mr. Coventry down to the waterside, talking, wherein I see so much goodness and endeavours of doing the King service, that I do more and more admire him. It being the greatest trouble to me, he says, in the world to see not only in the Navy, but in the greatest matters of State, where he can lay his finger upon the sore (meaning this man's faults, and this man's office the fault lies in), and yet dare or can not remedy matters. Thence to the Exchange about several businesses, and so home to dinner, and in the afternoon took my brother John and Will down to Woolwich by water, and after being there a good while, and eating of fruit in Sheldon's garden, we began our walke back again, I asking many things in physics of my brother John, to which he gives me so bad or no answer at all, as in the regions of the ayre he told me that he knew of no such thing, for he never read Aristotle's philosophy and Des Cartes ownes no such thing, which vexed me to hear him say. But

I shall call him to taske, and see what it is that he has studied since his going to the University.

9th. To church, and heard Mr. Mills (who is lately returned out of the country, and it seems was fetched in by many of the parishioners, with great state), preach upon the authority of the ministers, upon these words, "We are therefore embassadors of Christ." Wherein, among other high expressions, he said, that such a learned man used to say, that if a minister of the word and an angell should meet him together, he would salute the minister first; which methought was a little too high. This day I begun to make use of the silver pen (Mr. Coventry did give me,) in writing of this sermon, taking only the heads of it in Latin, which I shall, I think, continue to do. So home and at my office reading my vowes, and so to Sir W. Batten to dinner, being invited. Thence in the afternoon with my Lady Batten, leading her through the streets by the hand to St. Dunstan's Church, hard by us, and heard an excellent sermon of one Mr. Gifford, the parson there, upon "Remember Lot's wife." Home, and staid up a good while examining Will in his Latin below, and my brother along with him in his Greeke, and so to prayers and to bed. This afternoon I was amused at the tune set to the Psalm by the Clerke of the parish, and thought at first that he was out, but I find him to be a good songster, and the parish could sing it very well, and was a very good tune. But I wonder there should be a tune in the Psalms that I never heard of.

10th. By water to White Hall, and so to St. James's, and anon called into the Duke's chamber, and discoursed of our matters, and that being done, he walked, and I in the company with him, to White Hall, and there he took barge for Woolwich, and I up to the Committee of Tangier, where my Lord Sandwich, my Lord Peterborough, (whom I have not seen before since his coming back,) Sir W. Compton, and Mr. Povy. Our discourse about supplying my Lord Teviott with money, wherein I am sorry to see, though they do not care for him, yet they are willing to let him for civility and compliment only have money almost without expecting any account of it; but by this means, he being such a cunning fellow as he is, the King is like to pay dear for our courtiers' ceremony. Thence by coach with my Lords Peterborough and Sandwich to my Lord Peterborough's house; and there, after an hour's looking over some fine books of the Italian buildings, with fine cuts, and also my Lord Peterborough's bowes and arrows, of which he is a great lover, we sat down to dinner, my Lady [1] coming down to dinner also, and there being Mr. Williamson,[2] that belongs to Sir H. Bennet, whom I find a pretty understanding and accomplished man, but a little con-

---

[1] Penelope, daughter of Barnabas, Earl of Thomond, Countess of Peterborough.

[2] Joseph Williamson, Keeper of the Paper Office at White Hall, and in 1665 made Under Secretary of State, and soon afterwards knighted: and in 1674 he became Secretary of State, which situation he retained four years. He represented Thetford and Rochester in several Parliaments, and was in 1678 President of the Royal Society. Ob. 1701.

ceited. After dinner I took leave and went to Great-orex's, and set him to work upon my ruler, to engrave an almanac and other things upon the brasses of it, which a little before night he did, but the latter part he slubbered over, that I must get him to do it over better, or else I shall not fancy my rule, which is such a folly that I am come to now, that whereas before my delight was in multitude of books, and spending money in that and buying alway of other things, now that I am become a better husband, and have left off buying, now my delight is in the neatnesse of everything, and so cannot be pleased with anything unless it be very neat, which is a strange folly. Hither came W. Howe about business, and find by him that my Lord do dote upon one of the daughters of Mrs. [Becke] where he lies, so that he spends his time and money upon her. Here I am told that my Lord Bristoll is either fled or concealed himself, having been sent for to the King, it is believed to be sent to the Tower, but he is gone out of the way. Yesterday, I am told, that Sir J. Lenthall,[1] in Southwarke, did apprehend about one hundred Quakers, and other such people, and hath sent some of them to the gaole at Kingston, it being now the time of the Assizes. Thence home and examined a piece of Will's with my brother, and so to prayers and to bed.

---

[1] Sir John Lenthall was the elder brother of Speaker Lenthall, and uncle of the person of the same name mentioned in the "Diary," May 21, 1660. He had been knighted as early as 1616, and was Marshal of the Marshalsea; and, in 1655, was placed in the Commission of the Peace for Surrey by a

11th. We met and sat at the office all the morning, and at noon I to the 'Change, where I met Dr. Pierce, who tells me that the King comes to towne this day, from Tunbridge, to stay a day or two, and then fetch the Queene from thence, who he says is grown a very debonnaire lady, and now hugs him, and meets him galopping upon the road, and all the actions of a fond and pleasant lady that can be, that he believes he has a chat now and then of Mrs. Stewart, but that there is no great danger of her, she being only an innocent, young, raw girle; but my Lady Castlemaine, who rules the King in matters of state, and do what she list with him, he believes is now falling quite out of favour. After the Queene is come back she goes to the Bath, and so to Oxford, where great entertainments are making for her. This day I am told that my Lord Bristoll hath warrants issued out against him, to have carried him to the Tower; but he is fled away, or hid himself. So much the Chancellor hath got the better of him. Upon the 'Change my brother brings me word that Madam Turner would come and dine with me to-day, so I hasted home and found her and Mrs. Morrice there. After dinner my two ladies and I in Mrs. Turner's coach to Mr. Povy's, and there shewed Mrs. Turner his perspective, and the fine things he is building of now, and so we went through bridge, and I carried them on board the King's pleasure-boat, all the way reading in a book of receipts of

---

special vote of the House of Commons, which explains his crusade against the Quakers. He died in 1668.

making fine meats and sweetmeats, which made us good sport. So I landed them at Greenwich, and there to a garden, and gave them fruit and wine, and so to boat again, and finally, in the cool of the evening, to Lyon Kee, the tide against us, and so landed and walked to the Bridge, and there took a coach by chance passing by, and so I saw them home, and there eat some cold venison with them, and drunk and bade them good night, having been mighty merry with them.

12th. A little to my office, to put down my yesterday's journall, and so abroad to buy a bedstead and do other things. To White Hall, where my Lords Sandwich, Peterborough, and others made a Tangier Committee ; spent the afternoon in reading and ordering with a great deal of alteration, and yet methinks never a whit the better, of a letter drawn by Creed to my Lord Rutherford. The Lords being against anything that looked to be rough, though it was in matter of money and accounts, wherein their courtship may cost the King dear. Only I do see by them, that speaking in matters distasteful to him that we write to, it is best to do it in the plainest way and without ambages or reasoning, but only say matters of fact, and leave the party to collect your meaning. Thence by water to my brother's, and there I hear my wife is come. I home, where methinks I find my wife strange, not knowing, I believe, in what temper she could expect me to be in, but I fell to kind words, and so we were very kind, only she could not forbear telling me how she had been used by them and her mayde, Ashwell, in the country, but I find it will be best not to examine it, for I doubt she's in fault too, and therefore I seek to put it off from my hearing.

13th. Met with Mr. Hoole [1] my old acquaintance of Magdalene, and walked with him an hour in the Parke, discoursing chiefly of Sir Samuel Morland, whose lady [2] is gone into France. It seems he buys ground and a farm in the country, and lays out money upon building, and God knows what ! so that most of the money he sold his pension of 500*l.* per annum for, to Sir Arthur Slingsby,[3] is believed is gone. It seems he hath very great promises from the King, and Hoole hath seen some of the King's letters, under his own hand, to Morland, promising him great things (and among others, the order of the Garter,[4] as Sir Samuel says) ; but his lady thought it below her to ask any thing at the King's first coming, believing the King would do it of himself, when as Hoole do really think if he had asked to be Secretary of State at the King's first coming, he might have had it. And the other day at her going into France, she did speak largely to

---

[1] William, son of Robert Hoole of Walkeringham, admitted of Magdalene College, June, 1648.

[2] Susanne de Milleville, daughter of Daniel de Milleville, Baron of Boessen in France, naturalized 1662. When she died I cannot learn, but Sir Samuel Morland survived a second and a third wife, both buried in Westminster Abbey.

[3] A younger son of Sir Guildford Slingsby, Comptroller of the Navy, knighted by Charles II., and afterwards created a Baronet at Brussels, 1657, which title has long been extinct.

[4] Compare Sir Samuel Morland's own account in his " Autobiography," printed by Halliwell.

the King herself, how her husband hath failed of what his Majesty had promised, and she was sure intended him; and the King did promise still, as he is a King and a gentleman, to be as good as his word in a little time, to a tittle: but I never believe it.

14th. To my brother's, where I found my father very discontented, and would have begun some of the differences between my wife and him, but I desired to hear none of them, and am resolved to make the best of a bad market, and to bring my wife to herself again as soon and as well as I can.

15th. By water down to Deptford, taking into my boat with me Mr. Palmer. He joyed me on my condition, and himself it seems is forced to follow the law in a common ordinary way. He landed with me at Deptford, where he saw by the officers' respect to me a piece of my command, and took notice of it, though God knows I hope I shall not be elated with that, but rather desire to be known for serving the King well, and doing my duty.

16th (Lord's day). With my wife to church. After dinner to church again, and there, looking up and down, I found Pembleton to stand in the aisle against us, he coming too late to get a pew. When, Lord! into what a sweat did it put me! But it makes me mad to see of what a jealous temper I am and cannot helpe it. Here preached a confident young coxcomb. So home, and I staid a while with Sir J. Minnes, at Mrs. Turner's, hearing his parrot talk, laugh, and crow, which it do to admiration.

17th. Up, and then fell into discourse, my wife and I to Ashwell, and much against my will I am fain to express a willingness to Ashwell that she should go from us, and yet in my mind I am glad of it, to ease me of the charge. After dinner comes our old mayde Susan to look for a gorgett that she says she has lost by leaving it here, and by many circumstances it being clear to me that Hannah, our present cook-mayde, not only has it, but had it on upon her necke when Susan came in, and shifted it off presently upon her coming in, I did charge her so home with it, that in a huff she told us she would be gone to-night if I would pay her her wages, which I was glad of, and so fetched her wages, and so she went away in a quarter of an hour's time. Till my house is settled, I do not see that I can mind my business of the office, which grieves me to the heart.

18th. At noon home, and my father came and dined with me, Susan being come and helped my wife to dress dinner. After dinner my father and I talked about our country matters, and in fine I find that he thinks 50*l.* per ann. will go near to keepe them all, which I am glad of.

19th. Up betimes, and my wife up and about the house, Susan beginning to have her drunken tricks. I out and to Mr. Hollyard, and took a note under his hand to drink wine with my beer, without which I was obliged, by my private vowe, to drink none a good while, and have strictly observed it, and by my drinking of small beere and not eating, I am so mightily troubled with wind, that I know not what to do almost. Thence to White Hall, and there met Mr. Moore, and fell a talking about my Lord's folly at Chelsey. So home, and there found my wife almost mad with Susan's tricks, so as she is forced to let her go and leave the house all in dirt, and gets Goody Taylour to do the business for her till another comes.

20th. To my office, and there we sat all the morning, and at noon dined at home, and there found a little girle, which she told my wife her name was Jinny, by which name we shall call her. I think a good likely girle, and a parish child of St. Bride's, of honest parentage, and recommended by the church-warden. In the evening came Commissioner Pett, who fell foule on me for my carriage to him at Chatham, wherein, after protestation of my love and good meaning to him, he was quiett; but I doubt he will not be able to do the service there that any other man of his ability would. This evening the girle that was brought to me to-day for so good a one, being cleansed of lice by my wife, and good, new clothes put on her back, she run away from Goody Taylour that was shewing her the way to the bake-house, and we heard no more of her.

21st. Meeting with Mr. Creed he told me how my Lord Teviott hath received another attaque from Guyland at Tangier with 10,000 men, and at last, as is said, is come, after a personal treaty with him, to a good understanding and peace with him. Thence to my brother's, and there told him how my girle had served us which he sent me, and directed him to get my clothes again, and get the girle whipped. So to Deptford, where I found Sir W. Batten, but he was got to Mr. Waith's to dinner, where I dined with him, a good dinner and good discourse, and his wife, I believe, a good woman. We fell in discourse of Captain Cocke, and how his lady has lost all her fine linen almost, but besides that they say she gives out she had 3,000*l.* worth of linen, which we all laugh at. After dinner to Greenwich to the musique-house, where we had paltry musique, till the master organist came, whom by discourse I afterwards knew, having employed him for my Lord Sandwich, to prick out something, and he did give me a fine voluntary or two, and so home by water, and at home I find my girle that run away brought by a bedel of St. Bride's Parish, and stripped her and sent her away, and a newe one come, which I think will prove a pretty girle. Her name, Susan. This evening I paid Mr. Hunt 3*l.* for my viall, and he tells me that I may, without flattery, say, I have as good a Theorbo viall and viallin as is in England.

22nd. Up by four o'clock to go with Sir W. Batten and Sir J. Minnes to Woolwich. Here we eat and drank at the Clerke of the Cheques, and in taking water at the Tower gate, we drank a cup of strong water, which I did out of pure conscience to my health, and I think is not excepted by my oaths, but it is a thing I shall not do again, hoping to have no such occasion. After breakfast Mr. Castle and I walked to Greenwich, and in our way met some gipsies, who would needs tell me my fortune, and I suffered one of them, who told me many things common as others do, but bade me beware of a John and a Thomas, for they did seek to do me hurt, and that somebody should be with me this day se'nnight to borrow money of me, but I should lend him none. She got ninepence of me. And so I left them and to Greenwich and so to Deptford, where the two knights were come, and so home by water. This day Sir W. Batten tells me that Mr. Newburne is dead of eating cowcumbers,[1] of which, the other day, I heard another, I think Sir Nicholas Crisp's son.

23rd. To church without my wife, she being all dirty as my house is. Home to dinner, and then to walk up and down in my house with my wife, discoursing of our family matters, and I hope, after all my troubles of mind and jealousy, we shall live happily still. To church again, and so home to my wife; and with her read "Iter Boreale,"[2] a poem, made just

---

[1] "Le Grand d'Aussy ('Histoire de la vie privée de Français, edit. Roquefort,' 8vo. tome i. p. 161) cites this passage from Champier, who wrote in the year 1560: 'Le concombre, quoiqu' assez recherché en France, etait cependant un aliment tres malsain, et que les habitants du Forez qui en mangeaient beaucoup etaient sujets à des fievres periodiques.'

"Miss Strickland thinks Mary imported them from Spain. They were grown in England in the time of Tusser (see 'Five Hundred Points of Good Husbandry ')." —BUCKLE, *Common Place Book*, vol. ii. pp. 377-8. (M. B.)

[2] Robert Wild, a Nonconformist Divine, published a poem in 1660, upon Monk's march from Scotland to London, called "Iter Boreale." It is written in a harsh and barbarous style, filled with clenches and earwickets, as the

at the King's coming home ; but I never read it before, and now like it pretty well, but not so as it was cried up.   After supper to prayers and to bed, having been, by a sudden letter coming to me from Mr. Coventry, been with Sir W. Pen, to discourse with him about sending 500 soldiers into Ireland.   I doubt matters do not go very right there.

24th. At my Lord Sandwich's, where I was a good while alone with my Lord ; and I perceive he confides in me and loves me as he uses to do, and tells me his condition, which is now very well : all I fear is that he will not live within compass.   There came to him this morning his prints of the river Tagus and the City of Lisbon, which he measured with his owne hand, and printed by command of the King.   My Lord pleases himself with it, but methinks it ought to have been better done than by Jobing.   Besides I put him upon having some took off upon white sattin, which he ordered presently.   I offered my Lord my accounts, and did give him up his old bond for 500*l.* and took a new one of him for 700*l.*, which I am by lending him more money to make up : and I am glad of it. My Lord would have had me dine with him, but I had a mind to go home to my workmen, and so took a kind good bye of him, and to the New Exchange, and there drank some whey, and so by water home, and found my closett at my office made very neat and

time called them, which having been in the fashion in the reigns of James I. and his unfortunate son, were revived after the Restoration (SCOTT's *Dryden*, vol. xv. p. 296).

clean to my mind mightily, and home to dinner, and then to my office to brush my books, and to supper, then to work in my chamber, making matters of this day's accounts clear in my books, they being a little extraordinary, and so being very late I put myself to bed, the rest being long ago gone.

25th. To the office, where we sat; and being rose, and Mr. Coventry taking his leave, for that he is to go to the Bath with the Duke to-morrow, I to the 'Change. So home at 2 o'clock, and there I found Ashwell gone, and her wages come to 50s., and my wife, by a mistake from me, did give her 20s. more; but I am glad that she is gone and the charge saved. After dinner with my Joyners, and with them till dark night, and they made an end of all; and so having paid them 40s. for their six days' worke, I am glad they have ended and are gone. My wife growing peevish at night, being weary, and I a little vexed to see that she do not retain things in her memory that belong to the house as she ought and I myself do, I went out in a little seeming discontent to the office, and after being there a little while, home to supper and to bed. This noon going to the Exchange, I met a fine fellow with trumpets before him in Leadenhall-street, and upon enquiry I find that he is the clerke of the City Market; and three or four men carried each of them an arrow of a pound weight in their hands. It seems this Lord Mayor[1] begins again an old custome, that

---

[1] Sir John Robinson. See 30th Oct., 1662. (M. B.)

upon the three first days of Bartholomew Fayre, the first, there is a match of wrestling, which was done, and the Lord Mayor there and Aldermen in Moorefields yesterday: to-day shooting: and to-morrow, hunting. And this officer of course is to perform this ceremony of riding through the city, I think to proclaim or challenge any to shoot. It seems that the people of the fayre cry out upon it as a great hindrance to them.

26th. To White Hall, where the Court full of waggons and horses, the King and Court going this day out towards the Bath.[1] Pleased this day to see Captn. Hickes come to me with a list of all the officers of Deptford Yarde, wherein he, being a high old Cavalier, do give me an account of every one of them to their reproach in all respects, and discovers many of their knaverys; and tells me, and so I thank God I hear every where, that my name is up for a good husband for the King, and a good man, for which I bless God; and that he did this by particular direction of Mr. Coventry.

27th. Up, after much pleasant talke with my wife and a little that vexes me, for I see that she is confirmed in it that all that I do is by design, and that my very keeping of the house in dirt, and the doing of this and any thing else in the house, is but to find her employment to keep her within and from minding of her pleasure, which, though I am sorry to see she minds it, is true enough in a great degree. Down to

---

[1] The King lay the first night at Maidenhead, and the second near Newbury.

see some good plank in the river with Sir W. Batten and home again, and after seeing Sir W. Pen, to my office, and there till late doing of business, being mightily encouraged by every body that I meet withal upon the 'Change and every where else, that I am taken notice of for a man that do the King's business wholly and well. For which the Lord be praised, for I know no honour I desire more. I found a feacho (as he calls it) of fine sugar and a case of orange-flower water come from Mr. Cocke, of Lisbon, the fruits of my last year's service to him, which I did in great justice to the man, a perfect stranger.

28th. Cold all night and this morning, and a very great frost they say abroad, which is much, having had no summer at all almost.

29th. Abroad with my wife by water to Westminster, and there left her at my Lord's lodgings, and I to Jervas the barber's, and there was trimmed, and did deliver back a periwigg, which he brought by my desire the other day to show me, having some thoughts, though no great desire or resolution yet to wear one, and so I put it off for a while. Thence to my wife, and calling at both the Exchanges, buying stockings for her and myself, and also at Leadenhall, where she and I, it being candlelight, bought meat for to-morrow, having never a mayde to do it, and I myself bought, while my wife was gone to another shop, a leg of beef, a good one, for six pense,[1] and

---

[1] This must be a mistake in the MS. Query, six shillings? (M. B.)

my wife says is worth my money. So walked home with a woman carrying our things. I am mightily displeased at a letter Tom sent me last night, to borrow 20*l.* more of me, and yet gives me no account, as I have long desired, how matters stand with him in the world. I am troubled also to see how, contrary to my expectation, my brother John neither is the scholler nor minds his studies as I thought he would have done, but loiters away his time, so that I must send him soon to Cambridge again.

31st. Up and at my office all the morning, where Sir W. Batten and Sir J. Minnes did pay the short allowance money to the East India companies, and by the assistance of the City Marshall and his men, did lay hold of two or three of the chief of the companies that were in the mutiny the other day, and sent them to prison. This noon came Jane Gentleman to serve my wife as her chamber mayde. I wish she may prove well. So ends this month, with my mind pretty well in quiett, and in good disposition of health since my drinking at home of a little wine with my beer; but no where else do I drink any wine at all. The King and Queene and the Court at the Bath, my Lord Sandwich in the country newly gone.

Sept. 1st. Up pretty betimes, and after a little at my viall to my office, where we sat all the morning, and I got my bill among others for my carved work (which I expected to have paid for myself) signed at the table, and hope to get the money back again, though if the rest had not got it paid by the king, I never intended nor did desire to have him pay for my vanity. In the evening my brother John coming to me to complain that my wife seems to be discontented at his being here, and shows him great disrespect; so I took and walked with him in the garden, and discoursed long with him about my affairs, and how imprudent it is for my father and mother and him to take exceptions without great cause at my wife, considering how much it concerns them to keep her their friend and for my peace; not that I would ever be led by her to forget or desert them in the main, but yet she deserves to be pleased and complied with a little, considering the manner of life that I keep her to, and how convenient it were for me to have Brampton for her to be sent to when I have a mind or occasion to go abroad to Portsmouth or elsewhere. So directed him how to behave himself to her, and gave him other counsel; and so to my office, where late.

2nd. Up betimes and to my office, and thence with Sir J. Minnes by coach to White Hall, where met us Sir W. Batten, and there staid by the Council Chamber till the Lords called us, being appointed four days ago to attend them with an account of the riott among the seamen the other day, when Sir J. Minnes did as like a coxcomb as ever I saw any man speak in my life, and so we were dismissed, they making nothing almost of the matter. We staid long without, till by and by my Lord Mayor comes, who also was commanded to be there, and he having, we not being within with him, an admonition from the Lords to take better care of preserving the peace, we joyned with him, and the Lords having commanded Sir J. Minnes to prosecute the fellows for the riott, we rode along with my Lord Mayor in his coach to the Sessions House in the Old Bayley, where the Sessions are now sitting. Here I heard two or three ordinary tryalls, among others one (which, they say, is very common now-a-days, and therefore in my now taking of mayds I resolve to look to have somebody to answer for them) a woman that went and was indicted by four names for entering herself a cooke-mayde to a gentleman that prosecuted her there, and after 3 days run away with a silver tankard, a porringer of silver, and a couple of spoons, and being now found is found guilty, and likely will be hanged. By and by up to dinner with my Lord Mayor and the Aldermen, and a very great dinner and most excellent venison, but it almost made me sicke by not daring to drink wine. After dinner into a withdrawing room; and there we talked, among other things, of the Lord Mayor's sword. They tell me this sword, they believe, is at least a hundred or two hundred years old; and another that he hath, which is called the Black Sword, which the Lord Mayor wears when he mournes, but properly is their Lenten sword to wear upon Good Friday and other Lent days, is older than that. Mr. Lewellin, lately come from Ireland, tells me how the English interest falls mightily there, the Irish party being too great, so that most of the old rebells are found innocent, and their lands, which were forfeited and bought or given to the English, are restored to them; which gives great discontent there among the English. Going through the City, my Lord Mayor told me how the piller set up by Exeter House is only to show where the pipes of water run to the City; and observed that this City is as well watered as any city in the world, and that the bringing the water to the City hath cost it first and last above 300,-000*l.*; but by the new building, and the building of St. James's [1] by my Lord St. Albans, which is now about (and which the City stomach I perceive highly, but dare not oppose it), were it now to be done, it would not be done for a million of money.

3rd. To Sir W. Batten, who is going this day for pleasure down to the Downes. I eat a breakfast with them, and at my Lady's desire with them by coach to Greenwich, where I went aboard with them on the Charlotte yacht. The wind very high, and I believe they will be all sicke enough, besides that she is mighty troublesome on the water. I left them under sayle, and I to Deptford, and, after a word or two with Sir J. Minnes, walked to Redriffe and so home. In my way overtaking of a beggar or two that looked like Gypsys, it came into my head what the Gypsys 8 or 9 days ago had foretold, that somebody that day se'n-night should be with me to borrow money, but I should lend none; and looking, when I came to my office,

---

[1] St. Albans Street and Market, on the north side of Pall Mall, removed for the Regent Street improvements. Jermyn Street, St. James's, also takes its name from him.

upon my journall, that my brother John had brought a letter that day from my brother Tom to borrow 20*l.* more of me, which had vexed me so that I had sent the letter to my father into the country, to acquaint him of it, and how little he is beforehand that he is still forced to borrow. But it pleased me mightily to see how, contrary to my expectations, having so lately lent him 20*l.*, and belief that he had money by him to spare, and that after some days not thinking of it, I should look back and find what the Gypsy had told me to be so true.

4th. To Westminster Hall, and there bought the first newes-books of L'Estrange's [1] writing, he beginning this week; and makes, methinks, but a simple beginning. Creed and I to Mr. Povy's, and he not being at home, walked to Lincoln's Inn walks,[2] which they are making very fine, and about one o'clock went back to Povy's; and by and by in comes he, and so we sat down to dinner, and his lady, whom I never saw before (a handsome old woman that brought him

---

[1] Roger L'Estrange, author of numerous pamphlets and periodical papers. He was Licenser of the Press to Charles II. and his successor; and M. P. for Winchester in James II.'s Parliament. Ob. 1704, aged 88. In 1663 L'Estrange set up a paper called " The Public Intelligencer " and " The News." The first of these papers came out on the 1st of August, and continued to be published twice a week till January 19th, 1665, when it was superseded by the scheme of publishing the " London Gazette," the first of which appeared on the 4th of February following. L'Estrange was knighted in the reign of James II. (M. B.)

[2] Lincoln's Inn Fields were first disposed into their present regular appearance by Inigo Jones. He built some of the houses (on the western side), and gave to the ground plot of the square the exact dimensions of the base of one of the pyramids of Egypt. (M. B.)

money that makes him do as he does), and so we had plenty of meat and drink, though I drunk no wine, though mightily urged to it. After dinner done, to see his new cellars, which he has made so fine with so noble an arch and such contrivances for his barrels and bottles, and in a room next to it such a grotto and fountayne, which in summer will be so pleasant as nothing in the world can be almost. But to see how he himself do pride himself too much in it, and command and expect to have all admiration, though indeed everything do highly deserve it, is a little troublesome. Thence Creed and I away, and by his importunity away by coach to Bartholomew Fayre, where I have no mind to go without my wife, and therefore rode through the fayre without lighting, and away home, leaving him there; and at home made my wife get herself presently ready, and so carried her by coach to the fayre, and showed her the monkeys dancing on the ropes, which was strange, but such dirty sport that I was not pleased with it. There was also a horse with hoofs like rams hornes, a goose with four feet, and a cock with three. Thence to another place, and saw some German Clocke works, the Salutation of the Virgin Mary, and several Scriptural stories; but above all there was at last represented the sea, with Neptune, Venus, mermaids, and Ayrid [1] on a dolphin, the sea rocking, so well done, that had it been in a gaudy manner and place, and at a little distance, it had been

---

[1] Arion. (M. B.)

admirable. Thence home by coach with my wife, and I awhile to the office, and so to supper and to bed. This day I read a Proclamation [1] for calling in and commanding every body to apprehend my Lord Bristoll.

5th. After dinner mightily importuned by Captain Hicks, who came to tell my wife the names and story of all the shells, which was a pretty present he made her the other day. He being gone, Creed, my wife, and I to Cornhill, and after many tryalls bought my wife a chintz, that is, a painted Indian callico, for to line her new study, which is very pretty. So home with her, and then I away to Captain Minors upon Tower Hill, and there, abating only some impertinence of his, I did inform myself well in things relating to the East Indys; both of the country and the disappointment the King met with the last voyage, by the knavery of the Portugall Viceroy, and the inconsiderablenesse of the place of Bombaim,[2] if we had had it. But, above all things, it seems strange to me that matters should not be understood before they went out; and also that such a thing as this, which was expected to be one of the best parts of the Queene's portion, should not be better understood; it being, if we had it, but a poor place, and not really so as was described to our King in the draught of it, but a poor little island; whereas they made the King and Lord Chancellor, and other learned men about

---

[1] Dated 25th August, 1663. A copy of it is in the British Museum.
[2] Bombay.

the King, believe that that, and other islands which are near it, were all one piece; and so the draught was drawn and presented to the King, and believed by the King, and expected to prove so when our men came thither; but it is quite otherwise. I hear this day that Sir W. Batten was fain to put ashore at Queenborough with my Lady, who has been so sicke she swears never to go to sea again.

7th. To the Black Spread Eagle in Bride Lane, and there had a chopp of veale and some bread, cheese, and beer, cost me a shilling to my dinner; and so to Bartholomew Fayre, where I met with Mr. Pickering, and he and I to see the monkeys at the Dutch house, which is far beyond the other that my wife and I saw the other day; and thence to see the dancing on the ropes, which was very poor and tedious. But he and I fell in discourse about my Lord Sandwich. He tells me how he is sorry for my Lord at his being at Chelsey, and that his but seeming so to my Lord without speaking one word, had put him clear out of my Lord's favour, so as that he was fain to leave him before he went into the country, for that he was put to eat with his servants; but I could not fish from him, though I knew it, what was the matter; but am very sorry to see that my Lord hath thus much forgot his honour, but am resolved not to meddle with it. The play being done I stole from him and hied home, buying several things at the ironmonger's — dogs, tongs, and shovels — for my wife's closett and the rest of my house. By my letters from Tangier to-day I hear that it grows very strong by land, and the Mole goes on. They have lately killed two hundred of the Moores, and lost about forty or fifty. I am mightily afeard of laying out too much money in goods upon my house, but it is not money flung away, though I reckon nothing money but when it is in the bànk, till I have a good sum beforehand in the world.

8th. Up and to my vyall a while, and then to my office on Phillips having brought me a draught of the Katherine yacht, prettily well done for the common way of doing it. At the office all the morning making up our last half year's account to my Lord Treasurer, which comes to 160,000*l.* or thereabouts, the proper expense of this half year, only with an addition of 13,000*l.* for the 3*d.* due of the last account to the Treasurer for his disbursements, and 1,100*l.* for this half year's; so that in three years and a half his 3*d.* come to 14,100*l.* Dined at home with my wife. It being washing day, we had a good pie baked of a leg of mutton; and then to Moxon's, and there bought a payre of globes cost me 3*l.* 10*s.*, with which I am well pleased, I buying them principally for my wife, who has a mind to understand them, and I shall take pleasure to teach her. But here I saw his great window in his dining room, where there is the two Terrestrial Hemispheres, so painted as I never saw in my life, and nobly done and to good purpose, done by his own hand.

9th. By water to Woolwich, and thence walked to Greenwich; in my way a little boy overtook us with a fine cupp turned out of Lignum Vitæ, which the poor child confessed was made in the King's yarde by his father, a turner there, and that he do often do it, and that I might have one, and God knows what, which I shall examine. So home to dinner, finding my poor wife busy. I met with Ned Pickering, he telling me the whole business of my Lord's folly with this Mrs. Becke, at Chelsey, of all which I am ashamed to see my Lord so grossly play the foole, to the flinging off of all honour, friends, servants, and every thing and person that is good, with his carrying her abroad and playing on his lute under her window, and forty other poor sordid things, which I am grieved to hear; but believe it to no purpose for me to meddle with it, but let him go on till God Almighty and his owne conscience and thoughts of his lady and family do it.

10th. All the morning making a great contract with Sir W. Warren for 3,000*l.* worth of masts; but, good God! to see what a man might do, were I a knave, the whole business from beginning to end being done by me out of the office, and signed to by them upon the once reading of it to them, without the least care or consultation either of quality, price, number, or need of them, only in general that it was good to have a store. But I hope my pains was such, as the King has the best bargaine of masts has been bought these 27 years in this office. Mr. Moore tells me of the good peace that is made at Tangier with the Moores, but to continue but from six months to six months, and that the Mole is laid out and likely to be done with great ease and successe, we to have a quantity of ground for our cattle about the towne to our use.

11th. This morning, about two or three o'clock, knocked up in our back yarde, and rising to the window, being moonshine, I found it was the constable and his watch, who had found our back yarde door open, and so came in to see what the matter was. So I desired them to shut the door, and bid them good night.

12th. Up betimes, and by water to White Hall; and thence to Sir Philip Warwick,[1] and there had half an hour's private discourse with him; and did give him some good satisfaction in our Navy matters, and he also me, as to the money paid and due to the Navy; so as he makes me assured by particulars, that Sir G. Carteret is paid within 80,000*l.* every farthing that we to this day, nay to Michaelmas day next have demanded; and that, I am sure, is above 50,000*l.* more than truly our expenses have been, whatever is become of the money. Home with great content that I have thus begun an acquaintance with him, who is a great man, and a man of as much business as any man in England; which I will endeavour to deserve and keep.

13th (Lord's day). Put my clothes in order against to-morrow's journey to Brampton. At supper saying

---

[1] Sir Philip Warwick was born 1608. In 1646 he was one of the Royal Commissioners empowered to treat with the Parliament. At the Restoration he was returned member for Westminster, and was knighted and replaced in his situation of Clerk to the Signet. (M. B.)

to my wife, in ordinary fondness, "Well! shall you and I never travel together again?" she took me up and offered and desired to go along with me. After some difficulty made I did send about for a horse and other things.

14th. By coach to Bishop's Gate, it being a very promising fair day. There at the Dolphin we met my uncle Thomas and his son-in-law, which seems a very sober man, and Mr. Moore. So Mr. Moore and my wife set out before, and my uncle and I staid for his son Thomas, who, by a sudden resolution, is preparing to go with us, which makes me fear something of mischief which they design to do us. He staying a great while, the old man and I before, and about eight miles off, his son comes after us, and about six miles further we overtake Mr. Moore and my wife, which makes me mightily consider what a great deale of ground is lost in a little time, when it is to be got up again by another, that is to go his owne ground and the other's too; and so after a little bayte (I paying all the reckonings the whole journey) at Ware, to Buntingford, where my wife, by drinking some cold beer, being hot herself, presently after 'lighting, begins to be sicke, and became so pale, and I alone with her in a great chamber there, that I thought she would have died, and so in great horror, and having a great tryall of my true love and passion for her, called the mayds and mistresse of the house, and so with some strong water, she came to be pretty well again; and so to bed, and I having put her to bed with great content, I called in my company, and supped in the chamber by her, and being very merry in talke, supped and then parted. This day my cozen Thomas dropped his hanger, and it was lost.

15th. Up pretty betimes and rode as far as God-manchester, Mr. Moore having two falls, once in water and another in dirt, and there light and eat and drunk, being all of us very weary, but especially my uncle and wife. Thence to Brampton to my father's, and there found all well, and so my father, cozen Thomas, and I up to Hinchingbroke, where I find my Lord and his company gone to Boughton, which vexed me; but there I find my Lady and the young ladies, and there I alone with my Lady two hours, she carrying me through every part of the house and gardens, which are, and will be, mighty noble indeed. Here I saw Mrs. Betty Pickering,[1] who is a very well-bred and comely lady, but very fat. Thence home and to a good supper, after I had had an hour's talke with my father abroad in the fields, wherein he begun to talke very highly of my promises to him of giving him the profits of Sturtlow, as if it were nothing that I give him out of my purse, and that he would have me to give this also from myself to my brothers and sister; I mean Brampton and all, I think. I confess I was angry to hear him talke in that manner, and took him up roundly in it. After supper my uncle and his son to Stankes's to bed, which troubles me, all my father's beds being lent to Hinchingbroke.

---

[1] Afterwards married to Creed.

16th. To the Court, and heard Sir R. Bernard's charges to the Courts Baron and Leete, which took up till noon, and were worth hearing, and after dinner to the Court again, where Sir Robert and his son came by and by, and then to our business, and my father and I having given bond to him for the 21*l.* Piggott owed him, my uncle Thomas did quietly admit himself and surrender to us the lands first mortgaged for our whole debt, and Sir Robert added to it what makes it up 209*l.*, to be paid in six months. So the Court broke up, and so by and by home and to supper, and with my mind in pretty good quiett, to bed.

17th. I was forced to come to a new consideration, whether it was fit for to let my uncle and his son go to Wisbeach about my uncle Day's estate alone or no. and concluded it unfit ; and so, leaving my wife there, I begun a journey with them, and with much ado, through the fenns, along dikes, where sometimes we were ready to have our horses sink to the belly, we got by night, with great deal of stir and hard riding, to Parson's Drove, a heathen place, where I found my uncle and aunt Perkins, and their daughters, poor wretches ! in a sad, poor thatched cottage, like a poor barne, or stable, peeling of hempe, in which I did give myself good content to see their manner of preparing of hempe ; and in a poor condition of habitt took them to our miserable inne, and there, after long stay, and hearing of Frank, their son, the miller, play upon his treble, as he calls it, with which he earnes part of his living, and singing of a country loose song, we sat down to supper; the whole crew, and Frank's wife and child, a sad company, of which I was ashamed, supped with us. By and by newes is brought to us that one of our horses is stole out of the stable, which proves my uncle's, at which I am inwardly glad — I mean, that it was not mine; and at this we were at a great losse; and they doubting a person that lay at next door, a Londoner, some lawyer's clerke, we caused him to be secured in his bed, and other care to be taken to seize the horse; and so about twelve at night or more, to bed in a sad, cold, nasty chamber, only the mayde was indifferent handsome, and so I had a kisse or two of her, and a little after I was asleep they waked me to tell me that the horse was found, which was good newes, and so to sleep till the morning, but was bit cruelly, and nobody else of our company, which I wonder at, by the gnatts.

18th. Up, and got our people together as soon as we could; and after eating a dishe of cold creame, which was my supper last night too, we took leave of our beggarly company, though they seem good people, too; and over most sad Fenns, all the way observing the sad life which the people of the place (which if they be born there, they do call the Breedlings of the place) do live, sometimes rowing from one spot to another, and then wadeing, to Wisbeach, a pretty towne, and a fine church and library,[1] where sundry

---

[1] Watson, in his "History of Wisbeach," p. 239, names some of the printed books in the library there, but does not mention any of the MSS. Secretary Thurloe's gallery had been erected at the expense of the Corpora-

very old abbey manuscripts; and a fine house, built on the church ground by Secretary Thurlow, and a fine gallery built for him in the church, but now all in the Bishop of Ely's hands. After visiting the church, &c., we went out of the towne, by the helpe of a stranger, to find out one Blinkhorne, a miller, of whom we might inquire something of old Day's disposal of his estate, and in whose hands it now is; and by great chance we met him, and brought him to our inne to dinner; and instead of being informed in his estate by this fellow, we find that he is the next heire to the estate, which was matter of great sport to my cozen Thomas and me, to see such a fellow prevent us in our hopes, he being Day's brother's daughter's son, whereas we are but his sister's sons and grandsons; so that, after all, we were fain to propose our matter to him, and to get him to give us leave to look after the business, and so he to have one-third part, and we two to have the other two-third parts, of what should be recovered of the estate, which he consented to; and after some discourse and paying the reckoning, we mounted again, and rode, being very merry at our defeate, to Chatteris, my uncle very weary, and after supper, and my telling of three stories, to their good liking, of spirits, we all three in a chamber went to bed.

19th. Up pretty betimes, and after eating something, we set out and I (being willing thereto) went by a mistake with them to St. Ives, and there, it being

tion, out of gratitude to him for many services rendered to the town. It is now used for the general accommodation of the inhabitants.

known that it was their nearer way to London, I took leave of them, they going straight to London and I to Brampton, where I find my father ill in bed still, and Madam Norbery, whom and her fair daughter and sister I was ashamed to kisse, but did, my lip being sore with riding in the winde and bit with the gnatts: and they being gone, I told my father my successe. And after dinner my wife and I took horse, and rode with marvellous, and the first and only houre of pleasure, that ever I had in this estate since I had to do with it, to Brampton woods; and through the wood rode, and gathered nuts in my way, and then at Graffam to an old woman's house to drink, where my wife used to go; and being in all circumstances highly pleased, and in my wife's riding and good company at this time, I rode, and she showed me the river behind my father's house, which is very pleasant, and so saw her home, and I straight to Huntingdon; and there a barber came and trimmed me, and thence walked to Hinchingbroke, where my Lord and ladies all are just alighted. And so I in among them, and my Lord glad to see me, and the whole company. Here I staid and supped with them, and after a good stay talking, but yet observing my Lord not to be so mightily ingulphed in his pleasure in the country as I expected and hoped, I took leave of them and home.

20th (Lord's day). Up, and finding my father somewhat better, walked to Huntingdon church, where in my Lord's pew, with the young ladies, by my Lord's own showing me the place, I stayed the sermon, and so to Hinchingbroke, walking with Mr. Shepley and Dr. King, whom they account a witty man here, as well as a good physician, and there my Lord took me with the rest of the company, and singly demanded my opinion in the walks in his garden, about the bringing of the crooked wall on the mount to a shape; and so to dinner, there being Collonel Williams and much other company, and a noble dinner. But having before got my Lord's warrant for travelling to-day, there being a proclamation read yesterday against it at Huntingdon, at which I am very glad, I took leave, and after a word or two to my father and mother, my wife and I mounted, and, with my father's boy, upon a horse I borrowed of Captain Ferrers, we rode to Bigglesworth[1] by the helpe of a couple of countrymen, that led us through the very long and dangerous waters, because of the ditches on each side, though it begun to be very dark, and there we had a good breast of mutton roasted, for us.

21st. Up very betimes by breake of day, and got my wife up, whom the thought of this day's long journey do discourage; and after eating something, and changing of a piece of gold to pay the reckoning, we mounted, and through Baldwicke,[2] where a fayre is kept to-day, and a great one for cheese and other such commodities, and so to Hatfield, and here we dined, and my wife being very weary, and believing

---

[1] Biggleswade. (M. B.)　　　　[2] Baldock. (M. B.)

that it would be hard to get her home to-night, and a great charge to keep her longer abroad, I took the opportunity of an empty coach that was to go to London, and left her to come in it to London, for half-a-crowne, and so I and the boy home as fast as we could drive, and it was even night before we got home. To see Sir W. Pen, who is pretty well, and Sir J. Minnes, who is a little lame on one foot, and the rest gone to Chatham, viz. : Sir G. Carteret and Sir W. Batten, who has in my absence inveighed against my contract the other day for Warren's masts, in which he is a knave, and I shall find matter of tryumph, but it vexes me a little. So home, and by and by comes my wife by coach well home, and having got a good fowl ready for supper against her coming, we eat heartily, and so with great content and ease to our owne bed, there nothing appearing so to our content as to be at our owne home, after being abroad awhile.

22nd. This day my wife showed me bills printed, wherein her father, with Sir John Collidon [1] and Sir Edward Ford, [2] have got a patent for curing of smoky

---

[1] Sir John Collidon, or Colliton: see 18th Oct., 1664.

[2] Sir Edward Ford, of Harting, Sussex, Sheriff for that county, and Governor of Arundel Castle in 1642. Ob. 1670. His only daughter married Ralph Grey, Baron Grey of Werke. He was the author of a tract entitled, "Experimental Proposals how the King may have money to pay and maintain his Fleets, with ease to his people: London may be rebuilt, and all proprietors satisfied: money to be at six per cent. on pawns, and the Fishing Trade set up, which alone is able, and sure to enrich us all. And all this without altering, straining, or thwarting, any of our Laws, or Customs, now in use." 4to. 1666.—Repr. *Harl. Miscell.*, iv. 195. Ford was High Sheriff of Sussex,

chimneys. I wish they may do good thereof, but fear it will prove but a poor project. This day the King and Queene are to come to Oxford. I hear my Lady Castlemaine is for certain gone to Oxford to meet him, having lain within here at home this week or two, supposed to have miscarried; [1] but for certain is as great in favour as heretofore; at least Mrs. Sarah at my Lord's, who hears all from their own family, do say so. Every day brings newes of the Turke's advance into Germany, to the awakeing of all the Christian Princes thereabouts, and possessing himself of Hungary. My present care is fitting my wife's closett and my house, and making her a velvet coate, and me a new black cloth suit, and coate and cloake.

23rd. At noon by water to my Lord Crew's, and there dined with him and Sir Thomas, thinking to have them inquire something about my Lord's lodgings at Chelsey, but they did not, nor seem to take the least notice of it, which is their discretion, though it might be better for my Lord and them too if they did, that so we might advise together for the best. To my office, whither by and by came my brother

---

adhered to Charles I., and was knighted in 1643. In 1658 he laid down pipes to supply parts of London with water from the Thames. The second and third Lords Braybrooke descend, in the female line, from his daughter, Catherine Ford, who married Ralph, Lord Grey of Werke, their maternal ancestor.

[1] According to Collins, Henry Fitzroy, Lady Castlemaine's second son by Charles II., was born on the 20th September, 1663. He was the first Duke of Grafton.

John, who is to go to Cambridge to-morrow, and I did give him a most severe reprimand for his bad account he gives me of his studies. This I did with great passion and sharp words, which I was sorry to be forced to say, but that I think it for his good, forswearing doing anything for him, and that which I have yet, and now do give him, is against my heart, and will also be hereafter, till I do see him give me a better account of his studies. I was sorry to see him give me no answer, but, for ought I see, to hear me without great resentment, and such as I should have had in his condition. But I have done my duty, let him do his, for I am resolved to be as good as my word.

24th. I went forth by water to Sir Philip Warwick's, where I was with him a pretty while; and in discourse he tells me, and made it appear to me, that the King cannot be in debt to the Navy at this time 5,000*l.*; and it is my opinion that Sir G. Carteret do owe the King money, and yet the whole Navy debt paid. Thence I parted, being doubtful of myself that I have not spoke with the gravity and weight that I ought to do in so great a business. But I rather hope it is my doubtfulnesse of myself, and the haste which he was in, some very great personages waiting for him without, while he was with me, that made him willing to be gone. To the office by water, where we sat doing little, now Mr. Coventry is not here, but only vex myself to see what a sort of coxcombs we are when he is not here to undertake such a business as we do.

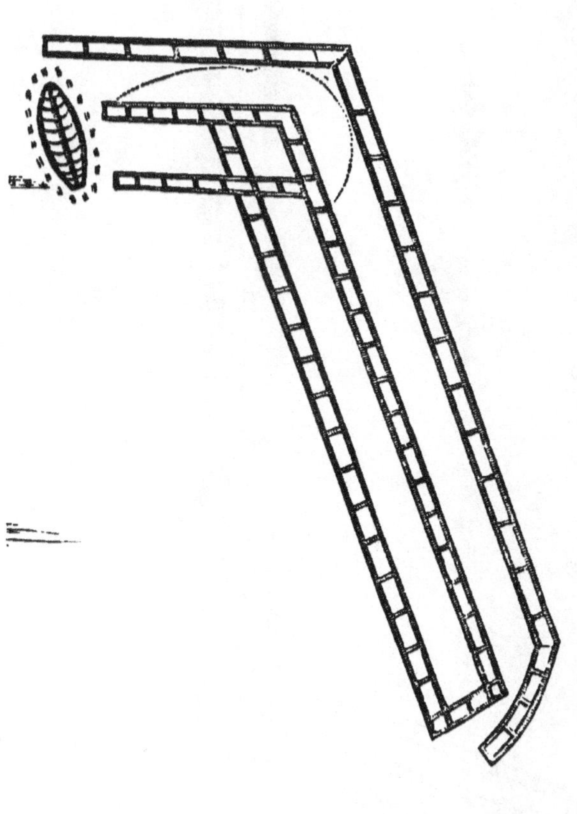

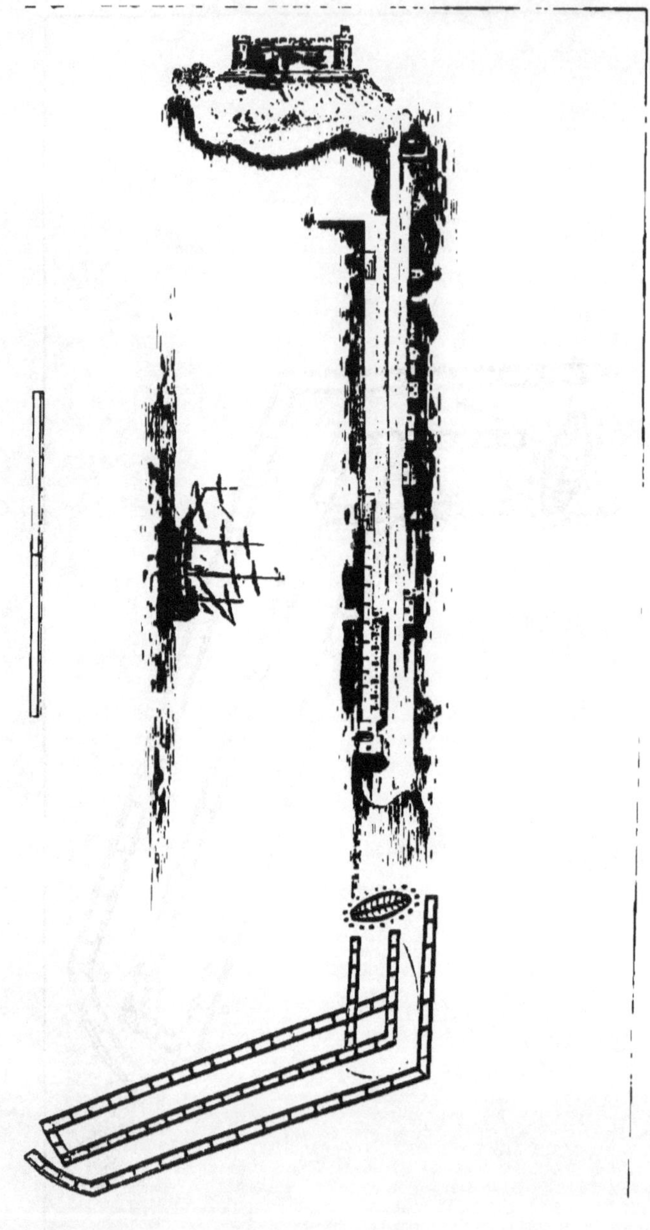

27th (Lord's day). Lay chatting with my wife a good while, then up and got me ready and to church. So home to dinner, and then to church again, where a drowsy sermon, and so home to spend the evening with my poor wife, consulting about her closett, clothes, and other things.

28th. To White Hall, where Sir J. Minnes and I did spend an houre in the Gallery, looking upon the pictures, in which he hath some judgment. And by and by the Commissioners for Tangier met: and there my Lord Teviott, together with Captain Cuttance, Captain Evans, and Jonas Moore, sent to that purpose, did bring us a brave draught of the Mole to be built there; and report that it is likely to be the most considerable place the King of England hath in the world; and so I am apt to think it will. After discourse of this, and of supplying the garrison with some more horse, we rose; and Sir J. Minnes and I home again, finding the streete about our house full, Sir R. Ford [1] beginning his shrievalty to-day: and, what with his and our houses being new painted, the streete begins to look a great deal better than it did, and more gracefull. Newes that the King comes to towne for certain on Thursday next from his progresse.[2]

---

[1] He lived in Hart Street, and the Navy Board had been in treaty for his house.

[2] *Progress.* The travelling of the sovereign to visit different parts of his dominions. These were sometimes very burthensome to the subject, from the right assumed of seizing whatever was wanted for the use of the

29th. Came Mr. Sympson to set up wife's chimney-piece in her closett, which pleases me.

30th. In the afternoon by water to White Hall, to the Tangier Committee; where my Lord Teviott about his accounts; which grieves me to see that his accounts being to be examined by us, there are none of the great men at the Board that in compliment will except against any thing in his accounts, and so none of the little persons dare do it: so the King is abused. To my office, and there I sat late making up my monthly accounts, and, blessed be God, I do find myself 760*l.* creditor, notwithstanding that for clothes for myself and wife, and layings out on her closett, I have spent this month 47*l.* So home, where I found our new cooke-mayde Elizabeth. To-morrow the King, Queene, Duke and his Lady, and the whole Court comes to towne from their progresse. Myself and family well, only my father sicke in the country. All the common talke for newes is the Turke's advance in Hungary, &c.

October 1st. Up and betimes to my office, and then to sit, where Sir G. Carteret, Sir W. B., Sir W. P., Sir J. M., Mr. Coventry and myself, a fuller board than by the King's progresse and the late pays and my absence has been a great while. After dinner I by water to Deptford about a little business, and so back again, buying a couple of good eeles by the way.

2nd. Up betimes and by water to St. James's, and

Court. The privilege was disused in the civil wars, and restrained and abridged by statute under Charles II. (M. B.)

there visited Mr. Coventry as a compliment after his new coming to towne, but had no great talke with him, he being full of business. So back by foot through London, and at the Change met with Mr. Cutler, and he and I to a coffee-house, and there discoursed, and he do assure me that there is great likelyhood of a war with Holland, but I hope we shall be in good condition before it comes to break out. I like his company, and will make much of his acquaintance. So home to dinner with my wife, who is over head and eares in getting her house up. This day I received a letter from Mr. Barlow, with a Terella,[1] which I had hoped he had sent me, but to my trouble I find it is to present from him to my Lord Sandwich, but I will make a little use of it first, and then give it him.

3rd. To the office and home to dinner, and then abroad to buy a bell to hang by our chamber doore to call the mayds. I am troubled to see that my servants and others should be the greatest trouble I have in the world.

4th (Lord's day). Up and to church, my house being miserably overflooded with rayne last night, which makes me almost mad. To church again, and so home, and all the evening most pleasantly passed the time in good discourse of our fortune and family till supper, and so to bed.

---

[1] "*Terella* or *terrella*, a loadstone in the form of a globe, with its poles and equator corresponding with the poles and equator of the earth."— LUDWIG's *German Dictionary*. (M. B.)

5th. Met Creed, and he and I walked two or three hours, talking especially about Tangier, and my Lord Teviot's bringing in of high accounts, and yet if they were higher are like to pass without exception, and then of my Lord Sandwich sending a messenger to know whether the King intends to come to Newmarket, as is talked, that he may be ready to entertain him at Hinchingbroke. Thence home and dined, and my wife all day putting up her hangings in her closett, which she do very prettily herself with her owne hand, to my great content.

6th. My wife waked to ring the bell to call up our mayds to the washing about 4 o'clock, and I was and she angry that our bell did not wake them sooner, but I will get a bigger bell. To the office, where we had a full board, where we examined Cocke's second account, and Sir J. Minnes did boldly assert the truth of it, and that he had examined it, when there is no such thing, but many vouchers, upon examination, missing, and we saw reason to strike off several of his demands, and to bring down his 5 per cent. commission to 3 per cent. So we shall save the King some money, which both the Comptroller and his clerke had absolutely given away. There was also two occasions more of difference at the table; the one being to make out a bill to Captain Smith for his salary abroad as commander-in-chief in the Streights. Sir J. Minnes did demand an increase of salary for his being Vice-Admiral in the Downes, he having received but 40*s.* without an increase, when Sir J. Lawson, in the same voyage, had 3*l.*, and others have also had increase, only he, because he was an officer of the board, was worse used than anybody else, and particularly told Sir W. Batten that he was the opposer formerly of his having an increase. So we hushed up the dispute, and offered, if he would, to examine precedents, and report them, if there was anything to his advantage to be found, to the Duke. The next was, Mr. Chr. Pett and Deane were summoned to give an account of some knees which Pett reported bad, that were to be served in by Sir W. Warren, we having contracted that none should be served but such as were to be approved of by our officers. So that if they were bad they were to be blamed for receiving them. Thence we fell to talk of Warren's other goods, which Pett had said were generally good, and falling to this contract again, I did say it was the most cautious and as good a contract as had been made here. Sir J. Minnes told me angrily that Winter's timber, bought for 33*s.* per loade, was as good, and in the same terms I told him that it was not so, but that he and Sir W. Batten were both abused, and I would prove it was as dear a bargaine as had been made this half yeare, which occasioned high words between them and me, but I am able to prove it and will. At noon Luellin coming to me I took him and Deane, and there met my uncle Thomas, and we dined together, but was vexed that, it being washing-day, we had no meat dressed, but sent to the Cooke's, and my people had so little witt to send in our meat from abroad in that Cooke's dishes, which were marked with the name of the Cooke upon them, by which, if they observed any thing, they might know it was not my owne dinner. After dinner we broke up, and I by coach to White Hall, where at the Committee of Tangier, but, Lord! how I was troubled to see my Lord Teviott's accounts of 10,000*l.* paid in that manner, and I wish 1000 times I had not been there. Thence rose with Sir G. Carteret and to his lodgings, and there discoursed of our frays at the table to-day, and particularly of that of the contract, and the contract of masts the other day, declaring my fair dealing, and so needing not any man's good report of it, and that I would make it so appear to him, if he desired it, which he did, and I will do it.

7th, 8th, 9th, 10th. My great fit of the Collique.[1] I did, however, make shift to go to the office, where we sat, and there Sir J. Minnes and Sir W. Batten did advise me to take some Juniper water, and Sir W. Batten sent to his Lady for some for me, strong water made of Juniper.

12th. At St. James's we attended the Duke all of us. And there, after my discourse, Mr. Coventry of

---

[1] Pepys's prescription for the colic:

"Balsom of Sulphur, 3 or 4 drops in a spoonfull of Syrrup of Coltsfoote, not eating or drinking two hours before or after.

"The making of this Balsom:

"⅔ds of fine Oyle, and ⅓d of fine Brimstone, sett 13 or 14 houres upon ye fire, simpring till a thicke Stuffe lyes at ye Bottome, and ye Balsom at ye topp. Take this off, &c.

"Sir Robt Parkhurst for ye Collique." (M. B.)

his own accord begun to tell the Duke how he found that discourse abroad did run to his prejudice about the fees that he took, and how he sold places and other things; wherein he desired to appeal to his Highness, whether he did any thing more than what his predecessors did, and appealed to us all. So Sir G. Carteret did answer that some fees were heretofore taken, but what he knows not; only that selling of places never was nor ought to be countenanced. So Mr. Coventry very hotly answered to Sir G. Carteret, and appealed to himself whether he was not one of the first that put him upon looking after this taking of fees, and that he told him that Mr. Smith should say that he made 5,000*l.* the first year, and he believed he made 7,000*l.* This Sir G. Carteret denied, and said, that if he did say so he told a lie, for he could not, nor did know, that ever he did make that profit of his place; but that he believes he might say, 2,500*l.* the first year. Mr. Coventry instanced in another thing, particularly wherein Sir G. Carteret did advise with him about the selling of the Auditor's place of the stores, when in the beginning there was an intention of creating such an office. This he confessed, but with some lessening of the tale Mr. Coventry told, it being only for a respect to my Lord FitzHarding.[1] In fine, Mr. Coventry did put into the Duke's hand a

---

[1] Sir Charles Berkeley, mentioned before, created Lord Berkeley of Rathdown and Viscount Fitzharding in Ireland, second son to Sir Charles Berkeley of Bruton, co. Somerset; afterwards made an English peer by the titles of Lord Botetourt and Earl of Falmouth, and killed in the great sea-fight, June, 1665.

list of above 250 places that he did give without receiving one farthing, so much as his ordinary fees for them, upon his life and oathe; and that since the Duke's establishment of fees he had never received one token more of any man; and that in his whole life he never conditioned or discoursed of any consideration from any commanders since he came to the Navy. And afterwards, my Lord Barkeley merrily discoursing that he wished his profit greater than it was, and that he did believe that he had got 50,000*l.* since he came in, Mr. Coventry did openly declare that his Lordship, or any of us, should have not only all he had got, but all that he had in the world (and yet he did not come a beggar into the Navy, nor would yet be thought to speak in any contempt of his Royall Highness's bounty), and should have a year to consider of it too, for 25,000*l.* The Duke's answer was, that he wished we all had made more profit than he had of our places, and that we had all of us got as much as one man below stayres in the Court, which he presently named, and it was Sir George Lane.[1] So home and to dinner, and thence by coach to the Old Exchange, and there cheapened some laces for my wife, and then to the great lace-man in Cheapside, and bought one cost me 4*l.*, more by 20*s.* than I intended, but when I came to see them I was resolved to buy one worth wearing with credit, and so to the New Exchange, and there put it to making.

---

[1] One of the Clerks of the Privy Council, and Secretary to the Marquis of Ormond. He became Viscount Lanesborough.

13th. After dinner John Cole, my old friend, came to see and speak with me about a friend. I find him ingenious, but more and more discern his city pedantry; but however, I will endeavour to have his company now and then, for that he knows much of the temper of the City, and is able to acquaint therein as much as most young men, being of large acquaintance, and himself, I think, somewhat unsatisfied with the present state of things at Court and in the Church. Then to the office, and there busy till late, and so home to my wife, with some ease and pleasure that I hope to be able to follow my business again, which by God's leave I am resolved to return to with more and more eagerness. I find at Court, that either the King is doubtfull of some disturbance, or else would seem so (and I have reason to hope it is no worse), by his commanding all commanders of castles, &c., to repair to their charges; and mustering the Guards the other day himself, where he found reason to dislike their condition to my Lord Gerard, finding so many absent men, or dead pays.[1] My Lady Castlemaine, I hear, is in as great favour as ever, and the King supped with her the very first night he came from Bath : and last night and the night before supped with her; when there being a chine of beef to roast, and the tide rising into their kitchen that it could not be roasted there, and the cooke telling her of it she answered, "Zounds ! she must set the house on fire but it should be roast-

---

[1] This is probably an allusion to the practice of not reporting the deaths of soldiers, that the officers might continue to draw their pay.

ed ! " So it was carried to Mrs. Sarah's husband's,[1] and there it was roasted.

· 14th. After dinner my wife and I, by Mr. Rawlinson's conduct, to the Jewish Synagogue: where the men and boys in their vayles, and the women behind a lattice out of sight; and some things stand up, which I believe is their Law, in a press to which all coming in do bow; and at the putting on their vayles do say something, to which others that hear him do cry Amen, and the party do kiss his vayle. Their service all in a singing way, and in Hebrew. And anon their Laws that they take out of the press are carried by several men, four or five several burthens in all, and they do relieve one another; and whether it is that every one desires to have the carrying of it, I cannot tell, thus they carried it round about the room while such a service is singing. And in the end they had a prayer for the King, in which they pronounced his name in Portugall; but the prayer, like the rest, in Hebrew. But, Lord ! to see the disorder, laughing, sporting, and no attention, but confusion in all their service, more like brutes than people knowing the true God, would make a man forswear ever seeing them more : and indeed I never did see so much, or could have imagined there had been any religion in the whole world so absurdly performed as this. Away thence with my mind strangely disturbed with them, and I to White Hall, and there the Tangier Committee

---

[1] Who was a cook.

met, and so home after I had been a good while with Sir W. Pen, railing and speaking freely our minds against Sir W. Batten and Sir J. Minnes, but no more than the folly of one and the knavery of the other do deserve.

16th. By coach abroad with my wife, leaving her at my Lord's till I went to the Tangier Committee, where very good discourse concerning the Articles of peace to be continued with Guyland, and thence took up my wife, and with her to her tailor's,[1] and then to the Exchange.

17th. To the Dolphin Taverne, and there Mr. Gauden did give us a great dinner. Here we had some discourse of the Queene's being very sicke, if not dead, the Duke and Duchesse of York being sent for betimes this morning to come to White Hall to her.[2]

---

[1] Gowns and other female articles of dress were formerly made by tailors.

> " Come, *taylor*, let us see those ornaments,
>   Lay forth the gown."
>
> SHAKESPEARE, *Taming of the Shrew*, act iv. sc. 3.
>   (M. B.)

[2] The Queen's illness was first noticed in the " Intelligencer " on the 13th October; but Pepys did not hear of it till the 17th. The bulletins of her Majesty's health continued till 15th November Vide in the Appendix some account of the Queen's illness, in the French Ambassador's letters to Louis XIV.

" The condition of the Queen is much worse, and the physicians give us but little hopes of her recovery; by the next you will hear that she is either in a fair way to it or dead. To-morrow is a very critical day with her — God's will be done. The King coming to see her the [this] morning, she told him she willingly left all the world but him, which hath very much afflicted his Majesty and all the Court with him."— *Lord Arlington to the Duke of Buckingham*, Whitehall, 17th Oct., 1663 (BROWN's *Miscellanea Aulica*, p. 306.)

18th (Lord's day). Up, and troubled at a distaste my wife took at a small thing that Jane did, and to see that she should be so vexed, that I took part with Jane, wherein I had reason; but by and by well again, and so my wife in her best gowne and new poynt that I bought her the other day, to church with me, where she has not been these many weeks, and her mayde Jane with her. The parson, Mr. Mills, I perceive, did not know whether to pray for the Queene or no, and so said nothing about her; which makes me fear she is dead. But enquiring of Sir J. Minnes, he told me that he heard she was better last night. To church again, and there a simple coxcombe preached worse than the Scot. After supper to prayers, and read very seriously my vowes, which I am fearful of forgetting by my late great expenses, but I hope in God I do nct, and so to bed.

19th. Waked with a very high wind, and said to my wife, "I pray God I hear not of the death of any great person, this wind is so high!" fearing that the Queene might be dead. So up; and going by coach with Sir W. Batten and Sir J. Minnes to St. James's, they tell me that Sir W. Compton, who it is true had been a little sickly for a week or fortnight, but was very well upon Friday at night last at the Tangier Committee with us, was dead — died yesterday: at which I was most exceedingly surprised, he being, and so all the world saying that he was, one of the worthyest men and best officers of State now in England; and so in my conscience he was: of the best temper, valour, ability of mind, integrity, birth, fine person, and diligence of any one man he hath left behind him in the three kingdoms; and yet not forty years old, or if so, that is all. I find the sober men of the Court troubled for him; and yet not so as to hinder or lessen their mirth, talking, laughing, and eating, drinking, and doing every thing else, just as if there was no such thing, which is as good an instance for me hereafter to judge of death, both as to the unavoidableness, suddenness, and little effect of it upon the spirits of others, let a man be never so high, or rich, or good, but that all die alike, no more matter being made of the death of one than another, and that even to die well, the praise of it is not considerable in the world, compared to the many in the world that know not nor make anything of it, nor perhaps to them (unless to one that is like this poor gentleman, who is one of a thousand, there nobody speaking ill of him) that will speak ill of a man. Coming to St. James's, I hear that the Queene did sleep five hours pretty well to-night, and that she waked and gargled her mouth, and to sleep again; but that her pulse beats fast, beating twenty to the King's or my Lady Suffolk's eleven; but not so strong as it was. It seems she was so ill as to be shaved and pidgeons put to her feet, and to have the extreme unction given her by the priests, who were so long about it that the doctors were angry.[1] The King,

---

[1] "I have heard they put on the Queen's head, when shee was sick, a nightcap of some sort of precious relick to recover her, and gave her extreme

they all say, is most fondly disconsolate for her, and weeps by her, which makes her weep;[1] which one this day told me he reckons a good sign, for that it carries away some rheume from the head. This morning Captain Allen tells me how the famous Ned Mullins, by a slight fall, broke his leg at the ancle, which festered; and he had his leg cut off on Saturday, but so ill done, notwithstanding all the great chyrurgeons about the towne at the doing of it, that they fear he will not live with it, which is very strange, besides the torment he was put to with it. After being a little with the Duke, and being invited to dinner to my Lord Barkeley's, and so, not knowing how to spend our time till noon, Sir W. Batten and I took coach, and to the Coffee-house in Cornhill; where much talke about the Turke's proceedings, and that the plague is got to Amsterdam, brought by a ship from Argier; and it is also carried to Hambrough.

---

unction; and that my Lord Aubignie told her she must impute her recoverie to these. Shee answered not, but rather to the prayers of her husband."— WARD'S *Diary*, p. 98.

[1] "The Queen was given over by her physicians, and the good nature of the king was much affected with the situation in which he saw a princess whom, though he did not love her, yet he greatly esteemed. She loved him tenderly, and thinking that it was the last time she should ever speak to him, she told him 'That the concern he shewed for her death was enough to make her quit life with regret; but that not possessing charms sufficient to merit his tenderness, she had at least the consolation in dying to give place to a consort who might be more worthy of it, and to whom heaven, perhaps, might grant a blessing that had been refused to her.' At these words she bathed his hands with some tears, which he thought would be her last; he mingled his own with hers, and without supposing she would take him at his word, he conjured her to live for his sake."— GRAMMONT, *Memoirs*. (M. B.)

The Duke says the King purposes to forbid any of their ships coming into the river. The Duke also told us of several Christian commanders (French) gone over to the Turkes to serve them; and upon inquiry I find that the King of France do by this aspire to the Empire, and so to get the Crowne of Spayne also upon the death of the King, which is very probable, it seems. Back to St. James's, and there dined with my Lord Barkeley and his lady, where Sir G. Carteret, Sir W. Batten, and myself, with two gentlemen more; my Lady, and one of the ladies of honour to the Duchesse (no handsome woman, but a most excellent hand). A fine French dinner.

20th. Up and to the office, where we sat; and at noon Sir G. Carteret, Sir J. Minnes, and I to dinner to my Lord Mayor's, being invited, where was the Farmers of the Customes, my Lord Chancellor's three sons, and other great and much company, and a very great noble dinner, as this Mayor is good for nothing else. No extraordinary discourse of anything, every man being intent upon his dinner, and myself willing to have drunk some wine to have warmed my belly, but I did for my oathe's sake willingly refrain it, but am so well pleased and satisfied afterwards thereby, for it do keep me always in so good a frame of mind that I hope I shall not ever leave this practice. Thence home, and took my wife by coach to White Hall, and she set down at my Lord's lodgings, I to a Committee of Tangier, and thence with her homeward, calling at several places by the way. Among others at Paul's Churchyarde, and while I was in Kirton's shop, a fellow came to offer kindness or force to my wife in the coach, but she refusing, he went away, after the coachman had struck him, and he the coachman. So I being called, went thither, and the fellow coming out again of a shop, I did give him a good cuff or two on the chops, and seeing him not oppose me, I did give him another; at last found him drunk, of which I was glad, and so left him, and home. This evening at my Lord's lodgings, Mrs. Sarah talking with my wife and I how the Queene do, and how the King tends her being so ill. She tells us that the Queene's sicknesse is the spotted fever; that she was as full of the spots as a leopard: which is very strange that it should be no more known; but perhaps it is not so. And that the King do seem to take it much to heart, for that he hath wept before her;[1] but, for all that, that he hath not missed one night since she was sicke, of supping with my Lady Castlemaine; which I believe is true, for she says that her husband hath dressed the suppers every night; and I confess I saw him myself coming through the street dressing of a great supper to-night, which Sarah says is also for the King and her; which is a very strange thing.

---

[1] The grief of Charles at the Queen's dangerous condition was thus noticed by Waller: —

> "—— when no healing art prevail'd,
> When cordials and elixirs fail'd,
> On your pale cheek he dropt the shower,
> Reviv'd you like a dying flower."

21st. Up, and by and by comes my brother Tom to me, though late, which do vexe me to the blood that I could never get him to come time enough to me, though I have spoke a hundred times; but he is very sluggish, and too negligent ever to do well at his trade I doubt; and having lately considered with my wife very much of the inconvenience of my going in no better plight, we did resolve of putting me into a better garbe, and, among other things, to have a good velvet cloake; that is, of cloth lined with velvet and other things modish, and a perruque, and so I sent him and her out to buy me velvet, and I to the Exchange, and so to Trinity House, and there dined with Sir W. Batten and Sir W. Rider. Thence, having my belly full, away on foot to my brother's, all along Thames Streete, and my belly being full of small beer, I did all alone, for health's sake, drink half a pint of Rhenish wine at the Still-yard, mixed with beer. From my brother's with my wife to the Exchange, to buy things for her and myself, I being in a humour of laying out money, but not prodigally, but only in clothes, which I every day see that I suffer for want of. This evening I begun to enter my wife in arithmetique, in order to her studying of the globes, and she takes it very well, and, I hope, with great pleasure; I shall bring her to understand many fine things.

22nd. This morning, hearing that the Queene grows worse again, I sent to stop the making of my velvet cloake, till I see whether she lives or dies.

23rd. Up, and this morning comes Mr. Clerke, and

tells me that the Injunction against Trice is dismissed again, which troubles me much. So I am to look after it in the afternoon. There comes also by appointment my uncle Thomas, to receive the first payment of his daughter's money. But showing of me the original of the deed by which his daughter gives her right to her legacy to him, and the copy of it attested by the Scrivener for me to keep by me, I did find some difference, and thereupon did look more into it, and at last did find the whole thing a forgery; yet he maintained it again and again, upon oathe, that it had been signed and sealed by my cozen Mary ever since before her marriage. So I told him to his teeth he did like a knave, and so he did, and went with him to the Scrivener at Bedlam, and there found how it came to pass, viz., that he had lost, or pretends to have lost, the true original, and that so he was forced to take this course; but a knave, at least a man that values not what he swears to, I perceive he is. The Queene slept pretty well last night, but her fever continues upon her still. It seems she hath never a Portuguese doctor here. Weary, walked home; in my way bought a large kitchen knife and half a dozen oyster knives. Thence to Mr. Holliard, who tells me that Mullins is dead of his leg cut off the other day, but most basely done. Thence to Mr. Rawlinson's and saw some of my new bottles made, with my crest upon them, filled with wine, about five or six dozen.

24th. Busy all the morning about Mr. Gauden's account, and to dinner with him at the Dolphin, where mighty merry by pleasant stories of Mr. Coventry's and Sir J. Minnes's, which I have put down some of in my book of tales. Just as I was going out my uncle Thomas came to me with a draught of a bond for him and his sons to sign to me about the payment of the 20*l.* legacy, which I agreed to, but he would fain have had from me the copy of the deed, which he had forged and did bring me yesterday, but I would not give him it. Says he, I perceive then you will keep it to defame me with, and desired me not to speak of it, for he did it innocently. Thence by coach with Mr. Coventry to the Temple, and thence I to the Six Clerks' office, and discoursed with my Attorney and Solicitor. Thence called at Wotton's[1] and tried some shoes, but he had none to fit me. He tells me that by the Duke of York's persuasion Harris is come again to Sir W. Davenant upon his terms that he demanded, which will make him very high and proud. The Queene is in a good way of recovery; and Sir Francis Pridgeon[2] hath got great honour by it, it being all imputed to his cordiall, which in her dispaire did give her rest and brought her to some hopes of recovery. It seems that, after the much talke of troubles and a plot, something is found in the North that a party was to rise, and some persons that were

---

[1] His shoemaker.

[2] Vertue (according to Walpole) had seen a portrait of Dr. Prujeon painted by Streater, and a print of " Opinion sitting on a tree," thus inscribed: " Viro clariss. Dᴺᵒ Francisco Prujeano Medico, omnium bonarum artium et elegantiarum fautori et admiratori summo; D. D. D. H. Peacham." He was President of the College of Physicians, 1653.

to command it are found, as I find in a letter that Mr. Coventry read to-day about it from those parts.

25th (Lord's day). Up, and my wife and I to church, where it is strange to see how the use and seeing Pembleton come with his wife thither to church, I begin now to make no great matter of it, which before was so terrible to me. Dined at home, my wife and I alone, a good dinner, and so in the afternoon to church again, where the Scot preached, and I slept most of the afternoon. So home, and after reading my vowes to myself, and my wife with her mayds (who are mighty busy to get it despatched because of their mistress's promise, that when it is done they shall have leave all to go see their friends at Westminster, whither my wife will carry them) preparing for their washing to-morrow, we hastened to supper and to bed.

26th. My wife being waked rung her bell, and the mayds rose and went to washing, we to sleep again till 7 o'clock. To Westminster Hall, and spent the morning walking there, where, it being Terme time, I met several persons, and talked with them, among others Dr. Pierce, who tells me that the Queene is in a way to be pretty well again, but that her delirium in her head continues still; that she talks idle, not by fits, but always, which in some lasts a week after so high a fever, in some more, and in some for ever; that this morning she talked mightily that she was brought to bed, and that she wondered that she should be delivered without pain and without being sicke, and that she was troubled that her boy was but an ugly boy.

But the King being by, said, " No, it is a very pretty boy." — " Nay," says she, " if it be like you it is a fine boy indeed, and I would be very well pleased with it." Seeing of Dr. Pridgeon, she said, " Nay, Doctor, you need not scratch your head, there is hair little enough already in the place." But methinks it was not handsome for the weaknesses of Princes to be talked of thus. Thence Creed and I to the King's Head ordinary, where much and very good company, among others one very talking man, but a scholler, that would needs put in his discourse and philosophy upon every occasion, and though he did well enough, yet his readiness to speak spoilt all. Here they say that the Turkes go on apace, and that my Lord Castlehaven [1] is going to raise 10,000 men here for to go against him ; that the King of France do offer to assist the Empire upon condition that he may be their Generalissimo, and the Dolphin chosen King of the Romans : and it is said that the King of France do occasion this difference among the Christian Princes of the Empire, which gives the Turke such advantages. They say also that the King of Spayne is making all imaginable force against Portugall again. Thence Creed and I to one or two periwigg shops about the Temple, having been very much displeased with one that we saw, a head of greasy and old woman's haire, at Jervas's in the morn-

---

[1] The eldest son of the infamous Earl of Castlehaven had a new creation to his father's forfeited titles, in 1634, and died s. p. 1684. He had served with distinction under the Duke of Ormond, and afterwards joined Charles II. at Paris.

ing ; and there I think I shall fit myself of one very handsomely made. To the Globe in Fleete Streete, and talking of the Emperor [1] at table, one young gentleman, a pretty man, and it seems a Parliament man, did say that he was a sot ; for he minded nothing of the Government, but was led by the Jesuites. Several at table took him up, some for saying that he was a sot in being led by the Jesuites, who are the best counsel he can take. Another commander, a Scottish Collonell, who I believe had several under him, that he was a man that had thus long kept out the Turke till now, and did many other great things, and lastly Mr. Progers,[2] one of our courtiers, who told him that it was not a thing to be said of any Soveraigne Prince, be his weaknesses what they will, to be called a sot, which methinks was very prettily said.

27th. Up, and my uncle Thomas and his scrivener bringing me a bond and affidavit to my mind, I paid him his 20*l.* for his daughter's legacy, and 5*l.* more for a Quarter's annuity. After dinner abroad by coach to Dr. Williams, and with him to the Six Clerks's office, and there I find that my case, through my neglect and the neglect of my lawyers, is come to be very bad, so as that it will be very hard to get my bill retayned again. We parted, and met T. Trice coming into the room, my clerke, and then his began to ask why we could not think, being friends, of re-

---

¹ Leopold: ætatis 24.

² Edward Progers, valet-de-chambre to the King, and confidant of his love affairs. See 22nd February, 1663-4, and Grammont Memoirs. (M. B.)

ferring it; and put it to some good lawyer to judge in it. From one word to more we were resolved to try, and to that end to step to the Pope's Head Taverne, and there he and his Clerke and Attorney and I and my Clerke, and sent for Mr. Smallwood, and by and by comes Mr. Clerke, my Solicitor. I resolved to condescend very low, and after some talke all together Trice and I retired, and he came to 150*l.* the lowest, and I bid him 80*l.* So broke off and then went to our company, and they putting us to a second private discourse, at last I was contented to give him 100*l.* he to spend 40*s.* of it amongst this good company to-morrow come se'nnight at Mr. Rawlinson's. So home. Mr. Coventry tells me to-day that the Queene had a very good night last night; but yet it is strange that still she raves and talks of little more than of her having of children, and fancys now that she hath three children, and that the girle is very like the King. And this morning about five o'clock, the physician feeling her pulse, thinking to be better able to judge, she being still and asleep, waked her, and the first word she said was, " How do the children ? "

28th. This morning Mr. Blackburne came to me, and telling me what complaints Will made of the usage he had from my wife and other discouragements, and I seeing him, instead of advising, rather favouring his kinsman, I told him freely my mind, but friendlily, and so we have concluded to have him have a lodging elsewhere, and that I will spare him

15*l.* of his salary, and if I do not need to keep another 20*l.*

29th. Up, it being my Lord Mayor's day, Sir Anthony Bateman.[1] This morning was brought home my new velvet cloake, that is, lined with velvet, a good cloth the outside, the first that ever I had in my life, and I pray God it may not be too soon now that I begin to wear it. I had it this day brought, thinking to have worn it to dinner, but I thought it would be better to go without it because of the crowde, and so I did not wear it. We met a little at the office, and then home again and got me ready to go forth, my wife being gone forth by my consent before to see her father and mother, and taken her cooke mayde and little girle to Westminster with her for them to see their friends. This morning in dressing myself and wanting a band,[2] I found all my bands that were newly made clean so ill smoothed that I crumpled them, and flung them all on the ground, and was angry with Jane, which made the poor girle mighty sad, so that I was troubled for it afterwards. At noon I went forth, and by coach to Guild Hall; and meet-

---

[1] Second son of Richard Bateman of Hartington, co. Derby, who had been Chamberlain and M. P. for London. Sir A. Bateman married Elizabeth Russell. His elder brother was Sir William Bateman, and his younger Thomas, was created Baronet in 1664.

[2] The *band* succeeded the ruff as the ordinary civil costume. The clergy and lawyers, who now retain bands, formerly wore ruffs. The band was a wide stiff collar, standing out horizontally and squarely, starched, and sometimes edged with lace. Pepys evidently did not possess

" A Chrysostom to *smooth* his band in."   (M. B.)

ing with Mr. Proby (Sir R. Ford's son), and Lieuten-
ant-Colonel Baron, a City commander, we went up and
down to see the tables; where under every salt there
was a bill of fare, and at the end of the table the
persons proper for the table. Many were the tables,
but none in the Hall but the Mayor's and the Lords
of the Privy Council that had napkins [1] or knives,
which was very strange. We went into the Buttry,
and there stayed and talked, and then into the Hall
again : and there wine was offered and they drunk, I
only drinking some hypocras,[2] which do not break my
vowe, it being, to the best of my present judgement,
only a mixed compound drink, and not any wine.
If I am mistaken, God forgive me ! but I hope and
do think I am not.   By and by met with Creed; and

----

[1] As the practice of eating with forks gradually was introduced from
Italy into England, napkins were not so generally used, but considered more
as an ornament than a necessary.

> " The laudable use of forks,
> Brought into custom here, as they are in Italy,
> To the sparing of *napkins*."
>
> BEN JONSON, *The Devil is an Ass*, act v. sc. 3.

The guests probably brought their own knife and fork with them in a case.
(M. B.)

[2] A drink, composed usually of red wine, but sometimes white, with the
addition of sugar and spices.

> " *P.* Stay; what's best to drink a mornings ?
> " *R. Ipocras*, sir, for my mistress if I fetch it, is most dear to her. "
>
> *Old Play.*

Sir Walter Scott (" Quarterly Review," No. lxvi.) says, after quoting
this passage of Pepys, "Assuredly his pieces of bacchanalian casuistry can
only be matched by that of Fielding's chaplain of Newgate, who preferred
punch to wine, because the former was a liquor nowhere spoken against in
Scripture." (M. B.)

we, with the others, went within the several Courts, and there saw the tables prepared for the Ladies and Judges and Bishopps : all great sign of a great dinner to come. By and by about one o'clock, before the Lord Mayor came, come into the Hall, from the room where they were first led into, the Lord Chancellor (Archbishopp before him), with the Lords of the Council, and other Bishopps, and they to dinner. Anon comes the Lord Mayor, who went up to the lords, and then to the other tables to bid wellcome ; and so all to dinner. I sat near Proby, Baron, and Creed at the Merchant Strangers' table ; where ten good dishes to a messe, with plenty of wine of all sorts, of which I drunk none ; but it was very unpleasing that we had no napkins nor change of trenchers, and drunk out of earthen pitchers and wooden dishes.[1] It happened that after the lords had half dined, came the French Embassador, up to the lords' table, where he was to have sat ; but finding the table set, he would not sit down nor dine with the Lord Mayor, who was not yet come, nor have a table to himself, which was offered ; but in a discontent went away again.[2] After I had dined, I and Creed rose and went up and down the house, and up to the ladys' room, and there stayed gazing upon them. But though there were many and fine, both young and old, yet I could not discern one handsome face there ; which was very

---

[1] The city plate was probably melted during the Civil War. (M. B.)

[2] Vide in the Appendix, the Ambassador's account of the affront which he received, and the reparation afterwards made to him.

strange. I expected musique, but there was none but only trumpets and drums, which displeased me. The dinner, it seems, is made by the Mayor and two Sheriffs for the time being, the Lord Mayor paying one half, and they the other. And the whole, Proby says, is reckoned to come to about 7 or 800*l.* at most. Being wearied with looking upon a company of ugly women, Creed and I went away, and took coach and through Cheapside, and there saw the pageants,[1] which were very silly, and thence to the Temple, where meeting Greatorex, he and we to Hercules Pillars, there to show me the manner of his going about of draining of fenns, which I desired much to know, but it did not appear very satisfactory to me, as he discoursed it, and I doubt he will faile in it. To my office a little, to set down my Journall, and so home late to supper and to bed. The Queene mends apace, they say; but yet talks idle still.

30th. To dinner upon a good dish of stewed beef, then by coach with my wife to the New Exchange, and there bought several things, and then back, calling at my periwigg-makers, and there showed my wife the periwigg made for me, and she likes it very well, and so to my brother's, and to buy a pair of boddice for her, and so home. After a little discourse with my wife upon arithmetique, to bed.

31st. Up and to the office, at noon home to dinner, where Creed came and dined with me, and after din-

---

[1] The Lord Mayor's " Show " was then *after* dinner.

ner he and I upstairs, and I showed him my velvet cloake and other things of clothes, that I have lately bought, which he likes very well, and I took his opinion as to some things of clothes, which I purpose to wear, being resolved to go a little handsomer than I have hitherto. Thence to the office, where busy till night, and then to prepare my monthly account and to my great sorrow find myself 43*l.* worse than I was the last month, which was then 760*l.* and now it is but 717*l.* But it hath chiefly arisen from my layings-out in clothes for myself and wife ; viz. for her about 12*l.* and for myself 55*l.*, or thereabouts ; having made myself a velvet cloake, two new cloth suits, black, plain both ; a new shagg gowne, trimmed with gold buttons and twist, with a new hat, and silk tops for my legs, and many other things, being resolved henceforward to go like myself. And also two perriwiggs, one whereof costs me 3*l.* and the other 40*s.* I have worn neither yet, but will begin next week, God willing. So that I hope I shall not need now to lay out more money a great while, I having laid out in clothes for myself and wife, and for her closett and other things without, these two months, this and the last, besides household expenses of victuals, &c., above 110*l.* But I hope I shall with more comfort labour to get more, and with better successe than when, for want of clothes, I was forced to sneake like a beggar.

Thus I end this month. My greatest trouble and my wife's is our family, mighty out of order by this fellow Will's corrupting our mayds by his idle talke and carriage, which we are going to remove by hastening him out of the house, and I am to give him 20*l.* per annum toward his maintenance. The Queene continues light-headed, but in hopes to recover. The plague is much in Amsterdam, and we in fears of it here, which God defend.[1] The Turke goes on mightily in the Emperor's dominions, and the Princes cannot agree among themselves how to go against him. Myself in pretty good health now, after being ill this month for a week together. My father has been very ill in the country, but I hope better again now. I am lately come to a conclusion with Tom Trice to pay him 100*l.*, which is a great deale of money, but I hope it will save a great deale more. But thus everything lessens, which I have and am likely to have, and therefore I must look about me to get something more than just my salary, or else I may resolve to live well and die a beggar.

VOL. III. LIST OF PRINCIPAL MISTAKES IN THE FOURTH EDITION, 1854.

PAGE	LINE			
4	21	For all	. . .	read *kept.*
12	5	" meat	. .	" *neat.*
12	21	" gardens	. .	" *galleries.*
16	6	" here	. .	" *work.*
34	21	" £6,000	. .	" £60,000.
56	5	" fresh	. .	" *foule.*
58	25	" those built	.	" *their build.*

---

[1] Forbid. From the French "defendre." (M. B.)

PAGE	LINE			
59	5	For common	read	*mistaken.*
60	6	" use	"	*verse.*
61	22	" gallant	"	*gentle.*
72	11	" wonder	"	*bawdry.*
113	3	" and	"	*not.*
117	10	" morning	"	*evening.*
117	14	" and	"	*or.*
131	1	" apprehend	"	*affront.*
132	4	" desired	"	*hired.*
137	25	" selling	"	*stealing.*
138	14	" Buffleheaded fellow	"	*Bufflehead, a fellow.*
139	10	" struck at	"	*stuck at.*
151	14	" turn	"	*tour.*
153	21	" Royal Duke	"	*Royal Oake.*
166	16	" sees	"	*says.*
168	16	" envy	"	*enemies.*
177	17	" convenience	"	*contrivance.*
180	29	" her	"	*two.*
181	2	" his	"	*no.*
181	24	" proposing	"	*persisting.*
186	5	" sees	"	*says.*
201	14	" quiet	"	*quick.*
201	23	" wife	"	*widow.*
211	17	" sees	"	*says.*
226	20	" talk	"	*tale.*
227	9	" time	"	*tune.*
233	3	" above	"	*about.*
235	25	" people	"	*why.*
244	3	" gets	"	*yet.*
248	11	" indeed	"	*ended.*
249	12	" content	"	*contempt.*
255	2	" kept	"	*took.*
256	16	" Deane	"	*He (Mr. Coventry).*
258	30	" indiscreet	"	*indirect.*

PAGE		LINE							
301	..	21	For first	.	.	.	read	*just.*
313	..	29	" tongues	.	.		"	*tongs.*
318	..	8	" merry	.	.		"	*weary.*
320	..	1	" Spankes's	.			"	*Frank's.*
320	..	10	" house	.	.		"	*horse.*
320	..	11	" stony	.	.		"	*nasty.*
333	..	12	" business	.	.		"	*taking.*
335	..	17	" little	.	.		"	*all.*
336	..	9	" the Priest	.	.		"	*him.*
339	..	1	" worth	.	.		"	*birth.*
354	..	13	" shirts	.	.	.	"	*suits.*